SUGAR STREET

Naguib Mahfouz

SUGAR STREET

The Cairo Trilogy III

Translated by

William Maynard Hutchins

and

Angele Botros Samaan

DOUBLEDAY

London New York Sydney Auckland Toronto

TRANSWORLD PUBLISHERS LTD
61-63 Uxbridge Road, London W5 5SA

Published 1992 by Doubleday
a division of Transworld Publishers Ltd

Sugar Street was originally published in Arabic in 1957,
under the title *Al-Sukkariyya*.
This translation is published by arrangement with
The American University in Cairo Press.

A catalogue record for this book is available from
the British Library.

ISBN 0385-26937-4

PRINTED IN THE UNITED STATES OF AMERICA

With appreciation to David Morse
—The Editor

SUGAR STREET

Their heads were huddled around the brazier, and their hands were spread over its fire: Amina's thin and gaunt, Aisha's stiff, and Umm Hanafi's like the shell of a turtle. The beautiful pure-white ones were Na'ima's. The January cold was almost severe enough to freeze water at the edges of the sitting room, which had retained its time-honored appearance with its colored mats and the sofas distributed around the sides. The old lantern with its oil lamp had vanished, and hanging in its place was an electric light. The location had changed too, for the coffee hour had returned to the first floor. Indeed the entire upper story had moved downstairs to make life easier for the father, whose heart was no longer strong enough for him to climb to the top.

The family members had changed as well. Amina's body had withered, and her hair had turned white. Although barely sixty, she looked ten years older, and her transformation was nothing compared to Aisha's decline and disintegration. It was ironic or pathetic that the daughter's hair was still golden and her eyes blue, when her listless glance gave no hint of life and her pale complexion seemed the symptom of some disease. With a protruding bone structure and sunken eyes and cheeks, her face hardly appeared that of a thirty-four-year-old woman. Although the years had settled on Umm Hanafi, they did not seem to have marked her in any essential way, hardly diminishing her reserves of flesh and fat. Instead, they had accumulated on her skin and around her neck and mouth like crusts or earthy deposits. But her grave eyes glinted from participation in the family's silent sorrow.

Na'ima stood out in this group like a rose growing in a cemetery, for she had developed into a beautiful young woman of sixteen. Her head enveloped by a halo of golden hair and her face adorned by blue eyes, she was as lovely as her mother, Aisha, had been—or even more captivating—but as insubstantial as a shadow. Her eyes had a gentle, dreamy look suggesting purity, innocence, and otherworldliness. She nestled against her mother's side, as though unwilling to be alone even for a moment.

Rubbing her hands together over the brazier, Umm Hanafi said,

"The builders will finish the project this week after working for a year and a half. . . ."

Na'ima responded sarcastically, "A building for Uncle Bayumi the drinks vendor. . . ."

Aisha raised her eyes from the brazier to look at Umm Hanafi for a moment but made no comment. They had previously learned that the house once belonging to Mr. Muhammad Ridwan would be torn down to allow construction of a four-story building for Uncle Bayumi the drinks vendor. This project had stirred up many old memories about Maryam and her divorce from Yasin—what had become of Maryam?—and about Maryam's mother and her marriage to the drinks vendor Bayumi, who had gained possession of the house half by inheritance and half by purchase. Back then life had been worth living, and hearts had been carefree.

Umm Hanafi continued: "The most beautiful part of it, my lady, is Uncle Bayumi's new place for soft drinks, ice cream, and sweets. It has lots of mirrors and electric lights, with a radio playing day and night. I feel sorry for Hasanayn the barber, Darwish the bean seller, al-Fuli the milkman, and Abu Sari' with his snack shop. They have to look out of their dilapidated premises at the store and apartments of their former comrade."

Pulling her shawl tighter around her shoulders, Amina said, "Glory to God who gives blessings. . . ."

With her arms around her mother's neck, Na'ima commented, "The building blocks off our roof on that side. Once it's inhabited, how can we spend any time up there?"

Amina could not ignore the question raised by her beautiful grand-daughter, if only out of concern for Aisha. She answered, "Pay no attention to the tenants. Do as you like."

She glanced at Aisha to see what impression her gracious reply had made. She was so afraid for her daughter that she was almost frightened of her. But Aisha was busy looking at herself in the mirror above the dresser between her room and her father's. She had not abandoned the custom of examining her reflection, even though it had become a meaningless exercise. With the passing days her face's withered appearance had ceased to alarm her. Whenever a voice inside asked, "Where is the old Aisha?" she would answer indifferently, "And where are her sons, Muhammad and Uthman, and her husband, Khalil?"

Observing this, Amina was saddened, and her gloom quickly affected Umm Hanafi, who was so much a part of the family that their worries were hers.

Na'ima rose and went to the radio, which stood between the doors to the parlor and the dining room. Turning it on, she said, "It's time for the records, Mama."

Aisha lit a cigarette and inhaled deeply. Amina stared at the smoke, which spread out in a thin cloud over the brazier. A voice on the radio sang, "Companions from the good old days, how I wish you would return."

Na'ima resumed her seat, tucking the robe around her. Like her mother, she loved singing. She listened carefully so she could memorize the song and sing it in her pleasing voice. This interest was not dampened by the religious feelings that dominated her entire emotional life. She prayed conscientiously and had fasted during the month of Ramadan since the age of ten. She frequently dreamed of the mysteries of the spiritual realm and welcomed with limitless delight her grandmother's invitations to visit the mosque of al-Husayn. All the same she had never weaned herself from a love of singing. She sang whenever she was alone, in her room or in the bath.

Aisha approved of everything her one remaining child did, for Na'ima was the only bright hope on otherwise gloomy horizons. As pleased by her daughter's piety as by her voice, Aisha even loved and encouraged the girl's excessive attachment to her, not tolerating any comment on it. In fact, she had no patience for any kind of criticism, no matter how trivial or well-intentioned. Her only occupations at home were sitting, drinking coffee, and smoking. Whenever her mother invited her to help with the housework, not from a need for assistance but to distract Aisha from her thoughts, she was annoyed and uttered her famous phrase: "Oh, leave me alone." She would not let Na'ima lift a finger to help with the work either, since she feared the least exertion for her daughter. If she could have performed the prayer ritual for Na'ima, she would have, to spare her the effort.

Amina frequently chided Aisha about this, telling her that Na'ima was almost old enough to marry and needed to learn the duties of a housewife. Aisha always responded angrily, "Don't you see she's like a specter? My daughter can't bear any exertion. Leave her alone. She's my sole hope in the world."

Then, heartbroken, Amina would abandon the conversation. Gazing sadly at Aisha, she saw the personification of shattered hopes.

When she looked at this unhappy face, which seemed to have lost all its vitality, Amina's soul was overcome by sorrow. Apprehensive about distressing her daughter, she had learned to greet Aisha's rude answers and harsh comments with affectionate forbearance.

The voice kept on singing, "Companions from the good old days," while Aisha smoked and listened to the song. She had been fond of singing once, and sorrow and despair had not killed her taste for it. Perhaps they had even enhanced it, since so many of the lyrics were plaintive and melancholy. Of course nothing could ever bring back her companions of the good old days. She wondered at times if that past had been a reality or a dream, a figment of her imagination. Where was that happy home? Where was her fine husband? Where were Uthman and Muhammad? Did only eight years separate her from that past?

Amina rarely liked these songs. The prime attraction of the radio for her was that it allowed her to hear recitations from the holy Qur'an and the news. The sad themes of the songs worried her. She was concerned about their effect on her daughter and remarked to Umm Hanafi one day, "Don't they sound like funeral laments to you?"

She could not stop thinking about Aisha and almost forgot the trouble she was having with high blood pressure. Visits to al-Husayn and to the other saints in their shrines were the only relief she found. Thanks to al-Sayyid Ahmad, who no longer restricted her movements, she was allowed to hurry off to God's sanctuaries whenever she felt the need. Amina herself was no longer the same woman she had once been. Grief and ill health had changed her considerably. With the passing years she had lost her amazing diligence and her extraordinary capacity for tidying up, cleaning, and running her home. Except for services to al-Sayyid Ahmad and Kamal, she paid little attention to the house. Satisfied to supervise, she had turned over the oven room and the pantry to Umm Hanafi and was remiss even in this supervision. Her confidence in their servant was boundless, for Umm Hanafi was part of the household. A lifelong companion, she had shared Amina's good and bad times and had been absorbed into the family, so that she identified with all their joys and sorrows.

They were silent for a time, as though the song had distracted them. Then Na'ima said, "I saw my friend Salma in the street today. She was in grade school with me. Next year she's going to sit for the baccalaureate examination."

Aisha commented with annoyance, "If only your grandfather had let you stay in school, you would have surpassed her. But he refused!"

The protest implied by Aisha's final phrase did not escape her mother, who said, "Her grandfather has his ideas, which he won't abandon. Would you have wanted her to pursue her studies, despite the effort involved, when she's a delicate darling who can't stand fatigue?"

Aisha shook her head without speaking, but Na'ima said with regret, "I wish I had finished my education. All the girls study today, just like boys."

Umm Hanafi observed scornfully, "They study because they can't find a bridegroom. But a beauty like you . . ."

Amina nodded her head in agreement and said, "You're educated, young lady. You have the grade school certificate. Since you won't need to find a job, what more than that would you want? Let's pray that God will strengthen you, clothe your captivating beauty with health, and put some meat and fat on your bones."

Aisha retorted sharply, "I want her to be healthy, not fat. Obesity's a defect, especially in girls. Her mother was the outstanding beauty of her day, and she wasn't fat."

Smiling, Amina said gently, "It's true, Na'ima, your mother was the most beautiful girl of her day."

Aisha sighed and said, "And then she became the cautionary tale of her day."

Umm Hanafi murmured, "May our Lord bring you happiness with Na'ima."

Patting the girl affectionately on the back, Amina said, "Amen, Lord of the universe."

They fell silent again as they listened to a new voice sing, "I want to see you every day."

Then the door of the house opened and closed. Umm Hanafi said, "My master." She rose and rushed out of the room to turn on the stairway light.

They soon heard the customary taps of his walking stick. When he appeared at the entrance to the sitting room, they all stood up politely. Breathing heavily, he gazed at them a moment before saying, "Good evening."

They replied in unison, "Good evening to you."

Amina went to his room to put on the light, and he trailed after her, exuding an aura of dignified old age.

He sat down to regain his breath. It was only nine o'clock. He was dressed as elegantly as ever. His broadcloth cloak, striped silk caftan, and silk scarf were of the same type as before, but the white in his hair, his gray mustache, his slender, "deserted" body, and his early return were all symptomatic of a new era. Another novel development was the bowl of yogurt and the orange prepared for his supper. He had to avoid alcohol, the appetizers he ate when drinking, red meat, and eggs. Still, the sparkle in his wide blue eyes indicated that his desire for life had not flagged.

He proceeded to remove his clothes with Amina's assistance as usual. Then he put on a wool nightshirt, wrapped up in a robe, donned a skullcap, and sat down cross-legged on the sofa. Amina served him supper on a tray, and he ate without enthusiasm. Afterward she gave him a glass half filled with water, to which he added six drops from a bottle of medicine. He got it down with a frowning expression of disgust. Then he mumbled, "Thanks to God, Lord of the universe."

His doctor had frequently told him that the medicine was a temporary measure but that this new diet would be permanent. The physician had often cautioned him against being reckless or neglectful, for his high blood pressure had become severe, affecting his heart. Experience had taught al-Sayyid Ahmad to heed these instructions, because he had suffered whenever he had ignored them. Every time he had exceeded the limits, he had paid the price. He had finally been forced to give in, eating or drinking only what he was supposed to and coming home by nine. His heart had not given up hope that, by whatever means, he would regain his health and enjoy a pleasant, quiet existence, even though his past life had disappeared forever.

He listened with pleasure to the song coming from the radio. Seated on the pallet, Amina was talking about the cold and the rain that had poured down before noon. Paying no attention to her, he commented happily, "I heard that some of the old songs will be broadcast tonight."

The woman smiled appreciatively, since she liked that kind of music, perhaps most of all because her husband did. Delight sparkled for a few moments in the man's eyes before giving way to listlessness. He could no longer enjoy happy feelings unreservedly without having them suddenly turn sour on him. A confrontation with the facts would awaken him from his happy dream, as reality impinged on him from every direction. The past was nothing but a dream.

What occasion was there for joy, when the days of fellowship, musical ecstasy, and health had departed forever? Delicious food and drink had vanished along with his well-being. Once he had strutted across the earth like a camel, his laughter reverberating from deep inside him, and dawn had found him intoxicated with all sorts of delights. Now he was obliged to return home from his soirees at nine so he could be in bed by ten, and the amounts he ate, drank, and walked were carefully prescribed.

He was the heart and the mainstay of this household, which time had afflicted with sorrows. The wretched Aisha was a thorn in his flesh, for he was incapable of mending the shreds of her life. He could hardly feel comfortable about her condition, since the morrow might find her miserably alone, without a father or a mother. He was also anxious about his own health, which was threatened by various complications of high blood pressure. What he feared most was having his strength fail him, so that he would be forced to lie in bed like a dead man. This had happened to many of his friends and loved ones. These thoughts hovered around him like flies, and he sought refuge with God from their evil torment. Yes, he would hear the old songs and fall asleep to their melodies.

"Leave the radio on even after I'm asleep."

She nodded her head with smiling agreement. Then he sighed and continued: "The stairs are really hard on me!"

"Rest at the landings, sir."

"But it's so humid in the stairwell. What cursed weather we're having this winter. . . ." Then he asked, "I bet you visited al-Husayn as usual despite the cold."

She answered shyly and uneasily, "Hardships seem trivial when I visit him, sir."

"It's all my fault!"

Trying to appease him, she added, "I walk around the holy tomb and pray for your health and well-being."

He was in urgent need of sincere prayers. Every good thing in life had been denied him. Even the cold shower with which he always refreshed his body had been forbidden him, since it was said to be dangerous for his arteries. "God have mercy on us," he thought, "when everything good becomes harmful."

They soon heard the door of the house slam shut. Raising her eyes, Amina murmured, "Kamal."

In a few minutes their son entered the room in his black overcoat, which revealed how thin and tall he was. He looked at his father through gold-rimmed glasses. A compact, bushy black mustache lent him a dignified and manly air. He leaned over to greet his father.

Al-Sayyid Ahmad invited him to sit down and as usual asked with a smile, "Where have you been, Professor?"

Kamal loved this gracious, affectionate tone, which his father had only recently adopted with him. Taking a seat on the sofa, he answered, "I was at the coffeehouse with some friends."

What sort of friends would they be? Kamal appeared exceptionally serious, sober, and dignified for his age, spending most of his evenings in his study. What a difference there was between him and Yasin! Of course, each had his defects. Still smiling, al-Sayyid Ahmad asked, "Did you attend the Wafd Party congress today?"

"Yes. We heard a speech from the leader, Mustafa al-Nahhas. It was a memorable day."

"I was told it would be an important event but wasn't able to go. I gave my ticket to one of my friends. My health's no longer up to the fatigue."

Overcome by sympathetic affection, Kamal stammered, "May our Lord strengthen you."

"Weren't there any incidents?"

"No. The day passed peacefully. For a change, the police were content to watch."

The man nodded his head with relief. Then in a tone of voice that indicated the special significance he attached to the topic, he said, "Let me revert to an old subject. Do you still persist in your mistaken opinion about private lessons?"

Kamal always felt uncomfortable and uneasy when forced to disagree openly with one of his father's ideas. He replied gently, "We've finished discussing that."

"Every day friends ask if you won't give their children private lessons. You shouldn't reject honest work. Private lessons are a source of substantial income for teachers. The men asking for you are some of the most distinguished inhabitants of this district."

Kamal said nothing, but his face showed his polite refusal. His father asked regretfully, "You refuse and waste your time with endless reading and writing for free. Is that appropriate for an intelligent person like yourself?"

At this point Amina told Kamal, "You ought to love wealth as much as you love learning." Then, smiling proudly, she reminded al-

Sayyid Ahmad, "He's like his grandfather. Nothing equaled his love of learning."

Her husband grumbled, "The grandfather again! I mean, was he an important theologian like Muhammad Abduh?"

Although she knew nothing about this distinguished modern reformer, she replied enthusiastically, "Why not, sir? All our neighbors came to him with their spiritual and worldly concerns."

Al-Sayyid Ahmad's sense of humor got the better of him. He laughed and said, "There are more religious scholars like him than you can shake a stick at."

The woman's protest was conveyed by her face, not her tongue. Kamal smiled affectionately but uneasily. He asked their permission to depart and left the room. In the sitting room Na'ima stopped him, wishing to show him her new dress. While she went to get it, he sat down beside Aisha to wait. Like the rest of the family, he indulged Na'ima in order to humor Aisha. But he was also as fond of this beautiful girl as he had been of her mother in the old days. Na'ima appeared with the dress, which he spread out in his hands. He examined it appreciatively and gazed at its owner with love and affection. He was struck by her gentle but extraordinary beauty, which purity and delicacy made magnificently luminous.

Kamal left the room with a heavy heart. It was sad to watch a family age. It was hard to see his father, who had been so forceful and mighty, grow weak. His mother was wasting away and disappearing into old age. He was having to witness Aisha's disintegration and downfall. The atmosphere of the house was charged with warning signs of misery and death.

He ascended the stairs to the top floor, which he called his apartment. He lived there alone, going back and forth between his bedroom and his study, both of which overlooked Palace Walk. He removed his clothes and put on his house shirt. Wrapping his robe around him, he went to the study, where a large desk with bookcases on either side stood near the latticed balcony. He wanted to read at least one chapter of Bergson's *The Two Sources of Morality and Religion* and to revise for the final time his monthly column in the magazine *al-Fikr*. This one happened to be about Pragmatism. The happiest part of his day was the period he devoted to philosophy. Lasting until midnight, it was the time—as he put it—when he felt like a human being. The rest of his day spent as a teacher in al-Silahdar School or in satisfying various needs of daily life was the stamping ground of the animal concealed inside him. That creature's goals were limited to self-preservation and the gratification of desires.

He neither loved nor respected his career but did not openly acknowledge his annoyance with it, especially not at home, for he wished to deprive people of the opportunity of rejoicing at his misfortune. All the same he was an excellent teacher who had won everyone's respect, and the headmaster had entrusted some administrative chores to him. Kamal jokingly accused himself of being a slave, for a slave might have to master work he did not like. The truth was that his desire to excel, which had stayed with him from his youth, compelled him to work hard for recognition. From the beginning he had resolved to win the respect of his pupils and colleagues, and he had achieved that goal. Indeed he was both respected and loved, in spite of his large head and prominent nose. Without any doubt, they—or his painful self-consciousness about them—were primarily responsible for his powerful determination to fashion a dignified persona. Realizing that these features would cause trouble, he had steeled himself to defend them against the plots of troublemakers. He did not escape the occasional gibe or taunt in class or on the playground but countered these attacks with an unflinching resolve softened by his innate sympathy for others. His ability to explain the lessons in a way students could understand and his selection of interesting and engaging topics related to the nationalist movement or to memories of the revolution also swayed public opinion among the pupils in his favor. These factors as well as his firmness when it was necessary nipped rebellion in the bud. At first he had been hurt by the taunts, which were extremely effective at stirring up forgotten sorrows, but he was pleased by the high status accorded him by the youngsters, who regarded him with respect, love, and admiration.

His monthly column in *al-Fikr* magazine had caused him another problem, for he had to worry about the reaction of the headmaster and the other teachers. They might ask if his presentation of ancient and contemporary philosophical ideas that occasionally seemed critical of accepted beliefs and customs was compatible with a teacher's responsibilities. Fortunately none of these colleagues read *al-Fikr*. He realized at last that only a thousand copies of each issue were printed, of which half were exported to other Arab countries. That fact encouraged him to keep writing for the magazine, without fear of attacks or of losing his job.

During these brief nocturnal periods the English-language teacher at al-Silahdar School was transformed into a liberated voyager who traversed the limitless expanses of thought. He read, pondered, and jotted down observations that he later incorporated into his monthly columns. His efforts were motivated by a desire to learn, a love for truth, a spirit of intellectual adventure, and a longing for alleviation of both the nightmare engulfing him and the sense of isolation concealed within him. He escaped his loneliness by adopting Spinoza's notion of the unity of existence and consoled himself for his humiliations by participating in Schopenhauer's ascetic victory over desire. He put his sympathy for Aisha's misery into perspective by devouring Leibniz's explanation of evil and quenched his heart's thirst for love by appealing to Bergson's poetic effusions. Yet this continuous effort did not succeed in disarming the anxiety that tormented him, for truth was a beloved as flirtatious, inaccessible, and coquettish as any human sweetheart. It stirred up doubts and jealousy, awakening a violent desire in people to possess it and to merge with it. Like a human lover, it seemed prone to whims, passions, and disguises. Frequently it appeared cunning, deceitful, harsh, and proud. When he felt too upset to work, he would console himself by saying, "I may be suffering, but still I'm alive. . . . I'm a living human being. Anyone who deserves to be called a man will have to pay dearly in order to live."

Looking over the ledgers, keeping the books, and balancing the previous day's sales were all tasks Ahmad Abd al-Jawad performed as expertly and exactly as ever, but he accomplished them with greater difficulty now that he was old and sick. He looked almost pitiable as he sat hunched over his ledgers, beneath the framed inscription reading "In the Name of God," his gray mustache almost concealed by his large nose, which looked bigger now because of the thinness of his face. The appearance of his assistant, Jamil al-Hamzawi, almost seventy, was even more pathetic, and the moment he finished waiting on a customer, he would collapse, breathless, on his chair.

Ahmad told himself rather resentfully, "If we were civil servants, our pensions would spare us work and effort at our age." Raising his head from the accounts, he announced, "Sales are still off because of the economic crisis."

Al-Hamzawi pursed his pale lips with annoyance and said, "No doubt about it. But this year's better than last year, and that was better than the one before. Praise God in any event."

Merchants called the period commencing with 1930 the days of terror. Isma'il Sidqy had dominated the country's politics, and scarcity had governed its economy. From morning to night there had been news of bankruptcies and liquidations. Throwing up their hands in dismay, businessmen had wondered what the morrow had in store for them. Al-Sayyid Ahmad was definitely one of the lucky ones. Although bankruptcy had threatened him year after year, he had never gone over the brink.

"Yes, praise God in any event."

He noticed that Jamil al-Hamzawi was gazing at him in a strange, hesitant, and embarrassed way. What could be on the man's mind? Al-Hamzawi stood up to move his chair closer to the desk. Then, sitting down again, he smiled uneasily. It was bitterly cold, although the sun was shining brightly. Gusts of wind rattled the doors and windows, making a whistling sound.

Al-Sayyid Ahmad sat up straight and remarked, "Say what you want to. I'm sure it's important."

Lowering his gaze, al-Hamzawi said, "I'm in an awkward position. I don't know how to put it. . . ."

His employer encouraged him: "I've spent more time with you than with my own family. . . . You should feel free to express yourself frankly."

"Our years together are what make it so difficult for me, al-Sayyid, sir."

"Our years together!" he thought. This possibility had never occurred to him.

"You want to . . . really?"

Al-Hamzawi answered sadly, "The time has come for me to retire. God never asks a soul to bear more than it can."

Al-Sayyid Ahmad felt depressed. Al-Hamzawi's retirement was a harbinger of his own. How could he look after the store by himself? He was old and sick.

He looked anxiously at his assistant, who said emotionally, "I'm really sorry. But I'm no longer up to the work. That time has vanished. Still, I've arranged things so you won't be left alone. My place will be taken by someone better able to assist you than I am."

His trust in al-Hamzawi's honesty had relieved him of half of his labors. How could a man of sixty-three start tending a store again from dawn to dusk? He said, "It's when a man retires and sits at home that his faculties begin to fail. Haven't you noticed that in civil servants with pensions?"

Smiling, Jamil al-Hamzawi answered, "In my case, decline has preceded retirement."

Al-Sayyid Ahmad laughed suddenly as if to mask his discomfort and then observed, "You old rascal, you're deserting me in response to your son Fuad's requests."

Al-Hamzawi cried out indignantly, "God protect us! The state of my health is evident to everyone. It is the only reason."

Who could say? Fuad was an attorney in the government judicial service. A person like that would not want his father to continue working as a clerk in a store, not even when the owner had made it possible for him to earn his government post. Yet al-Sayyid Ahmad sensed that his candor had distressed his excellent assistant. So he tried to cover his tracks by asking courteously, "When will Fuad be transferred back to Cairo?"

"This summer, or next summer at the latest. . . ." The moments that followed were heavy with embarrassment until al-Hamzawi, matching his employer's gracious tone, added, "Once he's settled in

Cairo with me, I'll have to think about finding a bride for him. Isn't that so, al-Sayyid, sir? He's my only son out of eight children. I've got to arrange a marriage for him. Whenever I think about this, a refined young lady comes to mind—your granddaughter." He glanced quickly and inquisitively at his employer's face before stammering, "Of course, we're not of your class. . . ."

Al-Sayyid Ahmad found himself forced to reply, "May God forgive us, Uncle Jamil. We've been brothers for ages."

Had Fuad encouraged his father to sound out the situation? To have a position as a government attorney was outstanding, and the most important thing about a person's family was that they be good people. But was this the time to discuss marriage?

"Tell me first of all whether you're determined to retire."

A voice called out from the door of the shop, "A thousand good mornings!"

Although annoyed at having this important conversation interrupted, al-Sayyid Ahmad smiled to be polite and answered, "Welcome! Welcome!" Then he gestured toward the chair al-Hamzawi had vacated, saying, "Please have a seat."

Zubayda sat down. Her body seemed bloated, and her face was veiled by cosmetics. There was no trace of the gold jewelry that had once decorated her neck, wrists, and ears, and nothing remained of her former beauty.

As usual, al-Sayyid Ahmad tried to make her feel at home, but he treated her like any other visitor. His heart was displeased by this call, for whenever she came she burdened him with requests. He asked about her health, and she replied that she was not suffering from anything, "Praise God."

After a moment of silence, he said again, "Welcome, welcome . . ."

She smiled gratefully but seemed to sense the lack of enthusiasm lurking behind his polite remarks. Pretending to be oblivious to the enveloping atmosphere of disinterest, she laughed. Time had taught her how to control herself. She observed, "I don't like to take up your time when you're busy, but you're the finest man I've ever known. Either give me another loan or find someone to buy my house. I wish you'd buy it yourself!"

Ahmad Abd al-Jawad sighed and said, "Me? If only I could. . . . Times have changed, Sultana. I keep telling you frankly how things are, but you don't seem to believe me, Sultana."

She laughed to hide her disappointment and then said, "The sultana's ruined. What can she do?"

"Last time I gave you what I could, but my circumstances won't allow me to repeat that."

She asked anxiously, "Couldn't you find someone to buy my house?"

"I'll look for a buyer. I promise you that."

She answered thankfully, "This is what I expected from you, for you're the most generous of men." Then she added sadly, "The world's not the only thing that's changed. People have changed even more. May God pardon them. In my glory days, they vied to kiss my slippers, but now if they spot me on the street they cross over to the other side."

It was inevitable for a person to be disappointed by something in life, in fact by many things—health, youth, or other people—but where were those days of glory, melodies, and love?

"You're partly to blame, Sultana. You never made any provision for this time of your life."

She sighed sorrowfully and said, "Yes. I'm not like your 'sister' Jalila. She doesn't mind whose reputation is tarnished, as long as she gets rich. She's accumulated a lot of money and several houses. Besides, God has surrounded me by thieves. Hasan Anbar was depraved enough to charge me a whole pound for a pinch of cocaine when it was scarce."

"Curses. . . ."

"On Hasan Anbar? A thousand!"

"No, on cocaine."

"By God, cocaine's a lot more merciful than people."

"No. No, It's really sad that you've succumbed to its evil influence."

With despondent resignation she admitted, "It has sapped my strength and destroyed my wealth. But what can I do? When will you find me a buyer?"

"At the first opportunity, God willing."

She rose, saying reproachfully, "Listen, the next time I visit you, smile as though you really mean it. I can bear insults from anyone but you. I know my requests are a nuisance, but I'm in straits known only to God. In my opinion, you're the noblest man alive."

He told her apologetically, "Don't start imagining things. It's just that I was preoccupied with an important question when you arrived. As you know, a merchant's worries never end."

"May God relieve you of them all."

Escorting her to the door, he bowed his head to show his appreciation for her comment. Then he bade her farewell: "You're really most welcome, any time." He noticed the eloquent look of distress and defeat in her eyes and felt sorry for her. Returning to his seat with a heavy heart, he looked at Jamil al-Hamzawi and remarked, "What a world!"

"May God spare you its evils and treat you to its blessings." But al-Hamzawi's tone grew harsh when he continued: "Still, it's the just reward for a debauched woman."

Ahmad Abd al-Jawad shook his head quickly and briefly as if to protest silently against the cruelty of this moralizing remark. Then resuming the merrier tone of voice he had used before Zubayda's interruption, he asked, "Are you still resolved to desert us?"

The other man answered uneasily, "It's not desertion but retirement. And I'm very sorry about it."

"Words . . . like the ones I used to deceive Zubayda a minute ago."

"God forbid! I'm speaking from my heart. Don't you see, sir, that old age has almost carried me off?"

A customer came into the store, and al-Hamzawi went to wait on him. Then the voice of an elderly man cried out flirtatiously from the doorway, "Who's that person as handsome as the full moon sitting behind the desk?"

Shaykh Mutawalli Abd al-Samad stood there in a crude, tattered, colorless gown and torn red leather shoes, his head wrapped in a camel's-hair muffler. Propping himself up with a staff, he gazed with bloodshot eyes at the wall next to the desk, thinking that he was looking at the proprietor.

In spite of his worries, al-Sayyid Ahmad smiled and said, "Come here, Shaykh Mutawalli. How are you?"

Opening a toothless mouth, the old man yelled, "High blood pressure, go away! Health, return to this lord of men."

Al-Sayyid Ahmad stood up and walked toward him. The shaykh stared in his direction but backed away as if preparing to flee. Then turning around in a circle, he pointed in each of the four directions and shouted, "You'll find relief here . . . and here . . . and here . . . and here." Exiting to the street, he intoned, "Not today. Tomorrow. Or the next day. Say: God knows best." He strode off with long steps that seemed incongruous for a man who looked so feeble.

3 ❧

The extended family returned to its roots every Friday, and the old house came alive with children and grandchildren. This happy tradition had never lapsed. Since Umm Hanafi now held pride of place in the kitchen, Amina was no longer the heroine of the day. Still, the mistress never tired of reminding her family that the servant was her pupil. Amina's desire for praise became more pronounced as she sensed increasingly that she did not deserve it. Although a guest, Khadija always helped with the cooking too.

Shortly before al-Sayyid Ahmad's departure for the store, he was surrounded by family members: Ibrahim Shawkat and his two sons, Abd al-Muni'm and Ahmad, along with Yasin and his children, Ridwan and Karima. They were all subject to a humility that transformed laughter to smiles and conversation to whispers. The older al-Sayyid Ahmad got, the more he delighted in their company. He was critical of Yasin for curtailing visits to the store in exchange for this Friday gathering. Did the mule not understand that his father longed to see him as often as possible?

Yasin's son, Ridwan, had a handsome face with memorable eyes and a rosy complexion. His good looks suggested many different sources, reminding al-Sayyid Ahmad of Yasin, of Yasin's mother, Haniya, and of Muhammad Iffat, a beloved friend and the young man's other grandfather. Ridwan was al-Sayyid Ahmad's favorite grandchild. The boy's sister, Karima, was a little lady of eight. She would surely grow up to be a marvel, if only because of her black eyes, so like those of her mother, Zanuba, that they stirred within the patriarch an embarrassed smile rich with memories.

The decisive feature in the appearance of both Abd al-Muni'm and Ahmad was a lesser version of their grandfather's huge nose, but he could also recognize the small eyes of Khadija, their mother. They were bolder too than the others in addressing him. All these grandsons were pursuing their studies with a success he was proud of, but they seemed too busy with their own affairs to pay much attention to him. While they consoled their grandfather by showing him that his life was being passed on through new generations, they reminded him as well that he was gradually having to relinquish the dominant position he had reserved for himself in the family. He was not as sad as he might have been about this, since age had brought him wisdom along with illness and infirmity. Yet it would have been absurd to imagine that his new insight could prevent a flood of memories from bursting forth. Back in 1890, when he had been their age, he had studied only a little and played a lot, dividing his time between the homes of musicians in al-Gamaliya and the haunts of Ezbekiya. Even then his loyal companions had been Muhammad Iffat, Ali Abd al-Rahim, and Ibrahim al-Far. His father, who had run the store, had scolded his only son a little and pampered him a lot. Life had been a tightly wound scroll crowded with hopes. Then he had married Haniya. . . . But not so fast . . . he should not allow memories to carry him away.

He rose to prepare for the afternoon prayers. This was a sign he would soon depart. After he had changed clothes and left for the store, they all assembled in a congenial chatty mood around the grandmother's brazier for the coffee hour.

Amina, Aisha, and Na'ima occupied the center sofa. The one on the right was taken by Yasin, Zanuba, and Karima. On the left-hand one were seated Ibrahim Shawkat, Khadija, and Kamal. Ridwan, Abd al-Muni'm, and Ahmad had chairs in the center of the room, beneath the electric light. Following his time-honored practice, Ibrahim Shawkat extolled the dishes he had most enjoyed. Even so, during the past few years he had changed the direction of his praise toward the excellent instruction Amina was providing her outstanding pupil, Umm Hanafi.

Zanuba always echoed his words, for she never overlooked an opportunity to ingratiate herself with a member of her husband's family. In fact, ever since her in-laws had opened their doors to her, permitting her to mingle with them, she had shown extraordinary skill in strengthening her ties to them. She considered their welcome an acknowledgement of her status, coming as it did after the years she had lived in isolation like an outcast. The death of a baby had been the pretext for the initial visit, when Yasin's family had come to his home to offer their condolences. Those calls had emboldened her to visit first Sugar Street and then—at a time when al-Sayyid Ahmad was quite ill—Palace Walk. She had even ventured into his room, where they had met like strangers with no past history. Thus Zanuba had become part of al-Sayyid Ahmad's family, calling Amina "Auntie" and Khadija "Sister." She was always exceptionally modest. Unlike other women of the family, she dressed simply when she made her calls, so that she seemed older than she was. Neglected, her beauty began to fade prematurely, and Khadija would never believe she was only thirty-six.

Zanuba had succeeded in gaining everyone's respect, and Amina said of her one day, "No doubt she comes from a good family—even if one or two generations back. It doesn't matter, for she's a good girl and the only one who has been able to live with Yasin."

Khadija seemed to surpass even Yasin in the flabby abundance of flesh and saw no reason to claim she was anything but happy about that. She was delighted with her sons, Abd al-Muni'm and Ahmad, as well as with her generally successful marriage, but to ward off the evil eye of jealousy never let a day go by without some complaint. Her treatment of Aisha had undergone a total change. During the last eight years she had not addressed a single sarcastic or harsh word to her younger sister, not even in jest. In fact, she bent over backwards to be courteous, affectionate, and gracious to Aisha, since she was touched by the widow's misery, frightened that fate might deal her a comparable blow, and apprehensive that Aisha would compare their lots. She had generously insisted that her husband renounce his share of his brother's estate, so that it went in its entirety to Aisha and her daughter, Na'ima. Khadija had hoped her action would be remembered in time, but Aisha was in such a state that she forgot her sister's generosity. This oversight did not keep Khadija from lavishing enough affection, sympathy, and compassion on Aisha to seem a second mother for her younger sister. To feel secure about her own God-granted prosperity, Khadija desired nothing more than Aisha's complaisant affection.

Ibrahim Shawkat took out a pack of cigarettes, and Aisha accepted one gratefully. He helped himself, and they both started smoking. Aisha's excessive dependence on cigarettes and coffee had been the subject of many comments, but her normal response to them was a shrug of her shoulders. Amina limited herself to the prayerful remark: "May God grant her endurance."

Yasin offered the most outspoken advice of any member of the family, for he appeared to think that the death of one of his children gave him this right. Aisha considered his loss inferior to her own and begrudged him any standing in the realm of the afflicted, since his son had died during the first year—unlike Uthman and Muhammad.

Discussion of disastrous losses often seemed to be her favorite pastime, and her distinguished rank in the world of suffering was a consolation to her.

Kamal listened attentively to the conversation Ridwan, Abd al-Muni'm, and Ahmad were having about their future. Yasin's son, Ridwan, said, "We're all in the arts, not science. So the only college worth choosing in the University is Law."

Shaking his huge head, which made him, of the three boys, most resemble Kamal, Abd al-Muni'm Ibrahim Shawkat replied confidently in his powerful voice, "That's easy to understand. But he refuses to!" He pointed at his brother, Ahmad, who smiled ironically.

Also gesturing toward Ahmad, Ibrahim Shawkat seized this opportunity to remark, "He can go into the College of Arts if he wants to, but first he has to convince me of its value. I understand the importance of Law School, but not of Arts."

Kamal looked down rather sadly, stirred by old memories of a debate about the relative merits of the Law School and the Teachers College. He still nourished many of his former hopes, but life kept dealing him cruel blows every day. A government attorney, for example, would need no introduction, but the author of articles in *al-Fikr* magazine might be in even greater need of one than his obscure articles. Ahmad Ibrahim Shawkat left him no time for anxious musings. Looking at him with small protruding eyes, the boy said, "I'll let Uncle Kamal answer for me."

Ibrahim Shawkat smiled to hide his embarrassment, and with little enthusiasm Kamal said, "Study what you feel is most appropriate for your talents."

Ahmad turned his slender head to look victoriously from his brother to his father, but Kamal added, "Still you ought to realize that Law School opens up a wider range of good career opportunities for you than Arts. If you choose the Arts Faculty, your future will lie in teaching, which is a difficult profession with little prestige."

"I'm planning a career in journalism."

"Journalism!" shouted Ibrahim Shawkat. "He doesn't know what he's saying."

Ahmad complained to Kamal, "In our family, they see no distinction between guiding thought and guiding a cart."

Smiling, Ridwan observed, "The great intellectual leaders in our country have been Law School graduates."

Ahmad replied proudly, "I'm thinking of quite a different type of intellectual leadership."

Scowling, Abd al-Muni'm Shawkat said, "Unfortunately I know what you have in mind. It's frightening and destructive."

Looking at the others as if to ask for their support, Ibrahim Shawkat told Ahmad, "Look before you leap. You're only in the fourth year. Your inheritance won't be more than a hundred pounds a year. Some of my friends complain bitterly that their university-educated children are unfit for any kind of work or else employed as clerks at minuscule salaries. Once you've thought about all this carefully you're free to choose for yourself."

Yasin intervened to suggest, "Let's hear Khadija's opinion. She was Ahmad's first instructor. Who is better qualified to select between the selfish instruction in one's own rights provided by Law and the altruistic and humane influence of Arts?"

They all smiled, including Amina, who was busy with her coffee-pot. Even Aisha smiled. Encouraged by her sister's good humor, Khadija retorted, "Let me tell you a cute story. Late yesterday afternoon—you know it gets dark early in winter—I was returning to Sugar Street from al-Darb al-Ahmar when I sensed that a man was following me. Then under the vault of the old city gate he passed me and asked, 'Where are you going, beautiful?' I turned and replied, 'I'm on my way home, Mr. Yasin.'"

The sitting room exploded with laughter. Zanuba directed a telling look at Yasin, one that blended criticism with despair. Motioning for them to be still, he asked, "You don't think I'm that blind, do you?"

Ibrahim Shawkat cautioned, "Watch your tongue!"

Although only eight, Karima grasped her father's hand and laughed as if she had understood the point of her aunt's story.

Zanuba's commentary on the situation was: "It's the worst things that make a person laugh."

Giving Khadija a furious look, Yasin said, "You've gotten me into hot water, girl. . . ."

Khadija replied, "If anyone present is in need of the humane influences of Arts, it's you, not my crazy son Ahmad."

Zanuba agreed, but Ridwan defended his father, claiming he had been falsely accused. Ahmad kept his eyes fixed on Kamal, as though resting his hopes on his uncle.

Abd al-Muni'm glanced stealthily at Nai'ma, who looked like a white rose leaning against her mother. Her pale delicate face blushed whenever she sensed his small eyes looking at her.

Finally Ibrahim Shawkat spoke, changing the course of the conversation: "Ahmad, think how Law School has allowed al-Hamzawi's son to become an important government attorney." Kamal felt that this comment contained criticism directed against him.

Breaking her silence for the first time, Aisha said, "He would like to get engaged to Na'ima."

After the pause that greeted this news, Amina added, "His father mentioned it to her grandfather yesterday."

Yasin asked seriously, "Has Father agreed?"

"It's still early for such questions."

Glancing at Aisha, Ibrahim Shawkat inquired cautiously, "What does Mrs. Aisha think of this?"

Without looking at anyone, Aisha answered, "I don't know."

Studying her sister closely, Khadija remarked, "But it's all up to you."

Kamal wanted to put in a good word for his friend and said, "Fuad's really an excellent fellow."

Ibrahim Shawkat asked circumspectly, "Aren't his folks rather common?"

In his forceful voice, Abd al-Muni'm Shawkat replied, "Yes. One of his maternal uncles is a donkey driver and another's a baker. He has a paternal uncle who is an attorney's secretary." Then he added as a reluctant concession, "But none of this detracts from the man's worth. A person should be judged for what he is, not for his family."

Kamal realized that his nephew wanted to assert two truths no matter how contradictory: first the baseness of Fuad's origins and second the fact that a humble background does not diminish a person's value. He understood that Abd al-Muni'm was both attacking Fuad and repenting for this unfair attack, because of his strong religious convictions. Surprisingly, the assertion of these rival claims relieved Kamal, sparing him the embarrassment of expressing them himself. Like his nephew, he did not believe in the class system. Yet he was as inclined as Abd al-Muni'm to criticize Fuad and to belittle his friend's position, which he knew was far grander than his own.

Amina was clearly uncomfortable with this attack. She said, "His father's a fine man. He has served us honestly and sincerely his whole life."

Khadija found the courage to reply, "But if this marriage takes place, Na'ima may find herself mixing with people who are beneath her. Family origin is everything."

Her opinion was championed by the last person anyone would have expected when Zanuba said, "You're right! Family origin is everything."

Yasin was upset. He looked swiftly at Khadija, wondering how she would react to his wife's endorsement. What would she think of it? Would it remind her of the troupe and its female entertainers? He cursed Zanuba secretly for her empty braggadocio. Feeling obliged to say something to make up for his wife's remark, he observed, "Remember, you're talking about a government attorney...."

Emboldened by Aisha's silence, Khadija said, "It's my father who made him one. Our wealth has made him what he is."

With sarcasm sparkling in protruding eyes that were reminiscent of his late Uncle Khalil's, Ahmad Shawkat retorted, "We're more indebted to his father than he is to us."

Pointing a finger at him, Khadija said critically, "You're always subjecting us to these incomprehensible remarks."

Sounding as if he hoped to terminate this discussion, Yasin commented, "Don't wear yourselves out. Papa will have the final say."

Amina distributed the cups of coffee, and the eyes of the young men gravitated to Na'ima, who sat beside her mother. Ridwan told himself, "She's a sweet and lovely girl. I wish it were possible for us to be friends and companions. If we could walk together in the street, people would have trouble saying which of us was better-looking."

Ahmad thought, "She's very beautiful but seems glued to her mother and has had little education."

Abd al-Muni'm reflected silently, "Pretty, a homemaker, and intensely religious—her only defect is her frailty. But even that's attractive. She's too good for Fuad." Then, breaking out of his internal monologue, he said, "Na'ima, tell us what you think."

The pale face blushed, frowned, and then smiled. Thrust into this awkward situation, the girl pitted a smile against her frown to free herself of both. Then she said shyly, "I don't have an opinion about this. Leave me alone!"

Ahmad remarked sarcastically, "False bashfulness...."

Aisha interrupted him, "False?"

Correcting himself, he said, "This kind of modesty has gone out of style. If you don't speak up, Na'ima, you'll find that your life's over and that all the decisions have been made for you."

Aisha replied bitterly, "We're not used to talk like this."

Paying no attention to his mother's warning look, Ahmad complained, "I bet our family's four centuries behind the times."

Abd al-Muni'm asked scornfully, "Why precisely four?"

His brother answered nonchalantly, "I was being polite."

Khadija shifted the conversation to Kamal by asking, "And you! When are you getting married?"

Kamal was caught off guard by this inquiry, which he attempted to evade by saying, "That's an old story!"

"And a new one at the same time. . . . We won't abandon it until God unites you with a decent girl."

Amina followed this last part of the conversation with redoubled interest. Kamal's marriage was her dearest wish. She hoped fervently that he would turn her wish into a reality. Then she could rest her eyes on a grandchild fathered by her only living son. She said, "His father has proposed brides to him from the best families, but he always finds some excuse or other."

"Flimsy arguments! How old are you, Mr. Kamal?" asked Ibrahim Shawkat with a laugh.

"Twenty-eight! It's too late now."

Amina listened to the figure incredulously, and Khadija said angrily, "You love to make yourself out older than you are."

Since he was her youngest brother, revelation of his age indirectly disclosed hers. Although her husband was sixty, she hated to be reminded that she was thirty-eight. Kamal did not know what to say. In his opinion this was not a subject to be settled with a single word, but he always felt compelled to explain his position. So he said apologetically, "I work all day at school and every evening in my office."

Ahmad said enthusiastically, "What a fantastic life, Uncle . . . but even so, a man needs to marry."

Yasin, who knew more about Kamal than any of the others, said, "You shrug off commitments so that nothing will distract you from your search for the truth, but truth lies in these commitments. You won't learn about life in a library. Truth is to be found at home and in the street."

Doing his best to escape, Kamal said, "I've grown accustomed to spending my salary each month down to the last millieme. I don't have any savings. How can I get married?"

Khadija blocked his escape by retorting, "Make up your mind to get married, and then you'll figure out how to prepare for it."

Laughing, Yasin observed, "You spend every millieme so you won't be able to get married."

"As if the two were equivalent," Kamal thought. But why did he not marry? That was what people expected and what his parents wanted. When he had been in love with Aïda, marriage had seemed absurdly out of reach. After that, love had been replaced by thought,

which had greedily devoured his life. His greatest delight had come
in finding a beautiful book or in getting an article published. He had
told himself that a thinker does not and should not marry. He looked
aloft and imagined that marriage would force him to lower his gaze.
He had been—and still was—pleased to be a thoughtful observer
who avoided, whenever possible, entry into the mechanics of life. He
was as stingy with his liberty as a miser is with money. Besides,
women no longer meant anything to him beyond a lust to be gratified. He was not exactly wasting his youth, since he did not let a
week go by without indulging in intellectual delights and physical
pleasures. If these reasons were not enough, he was apprehensive
and skeptical about everything. Marriage seemed to be something a
person should believe in.

Kamal said, "Relax. I'll get married when I feel like it."

Zanuba smiled in a way that made her look ten years younger and
asked, "Why don't you want to marry now?"

Almost in exasperation, Kamal replied, "Marriage is an anthill.
You're making a mountain out of it."

But deep inside he believed that marriage was a mountain, not an
anthill. He was overcome by a strange feeling that one day he would
give in to marriage and that his fate would then be sealed.

He was rescued by Ahmad's comment: "It's time for us to go up
to your library."

Welcoming the suggestion, Kamal rose and headed for the door,
trailed by Abd al-Muni'm, Ahmad, and Ridwan. As usual, they would
borrow some books during this visit to the old house.

Kamal's desk in the center of the room under an electric light was
flanked by bookcases. He sat down there to watch the young men
read the titles of books on the shelves. Abd al-Muni'm selected a book
of essays on Islamic history, and Ahmad took *Principles of Philosophy*.
Then they stood around his desk as he looked silently at each of
them in turn.

Finally Ahmad said irritably, "I'll never be able to read as much as
I want until I master at least one foreign language."

Glancing at a random passage in his book, Abd al-Muni'm muttered, "No one knows Islam as it truly is."

Ahmad remarked sarcastically, "My brother discovers the truth of
Islam in the Khan al-Khalili bazaar from a man of the people."

Abd al-Muni'm shouted at him, "Hush, atheist!"

Looking at Ridwan questioningly, Kamal asked, "Aren't you going
to choose a book?"

Abd al-Muni'm answered for his cousin, "He's too busy reading the Wafd Party newspapers."

Gesturing toward Kamal, Ridwan said, "Our uncle has this in common with me."

His uncle believed in nothing but was a Wafdist all the same. Similarly, he doubted truth itself but worked pragmatically with other people. Looking from Abd al-Muni'm to Ahmad, he asked, "Since you support the Wafd Party too, what's strange about this? All Egyptian patriots are Wafdists. Isn't that so?"

In his confident voice, Abd al-Muni'm answered, "No doubt the Wafd is the best of the parties, but considered in the abstract it's not completely satisfying."

Laughing, Ahmad said, "I agree with my brother on this. To be more precise, it's the only thing we do agree on. And we may even disagree about the extent of our satisfaction with the Wafd Party. But the most important thing is to question nationalism itself. Yes, there is no argument about the need for independence, but afterward the understanding of nationalism must develop until it is absorbed into a loftier and more comprehensive concept. It's not unlikely that in the future we'll come to regard martyrs of the nationalist movement as we now do victims of foolish battles between tribes and clans."

"Foolish battles! You fool!" Kamal thought. "Fahmy did not die in a foolish battle. But how can you be certain?" Despite these reflections he said sharply, "Anyone slain for a cause greater than himself dies a martyr. The relative worth of causes may vary, but a man's relationship to a cause is a value that does not."

As they left the study, Ridwan told Abd al-Muni'm, "Politics is the most significant career open to a person in a society."

When they returned to the coffee hour, Ibrahim Shawkat was commenting to Yasin, "We rear our children, guide them, and advise them, but each child finds his way to a library, which is a world totally independent of us. There total strangers compete with us. So what can we do?"

4 ❧

The streetcar was packed. There was not even room left for riders to stand. Although squeezed in among the others, Kamal towered over them with his lanky physique. He assumed the other passengers were also heading for the celebration of this national holiday, the thirteenth of November. He looked around at their faces with friendly curiosity.

Convinced that he believed in nothing, he still celebrated these holidays like the most ardent nationalist. Buoyed by their common destination and mutual Wafdist allegiance, strangers discussed the political situation with each other. One said, "Commemoration of our past struggle is a struggle in every sense of the word this year. Or it ought to be."

Another observed, "It should provide a response to Foreign Secretary Hoare and his sinister declaration."

Aroused by the reference to the British official, a third shouted, "The son of a bitch said, '. . . we have advised against the re-enactment of the Constitutions of 1923 and 1930.' Why is our constitution any business of his?"

A fourth reminded the crowd, "Don't forget what he said before that: 'When, however, we have been consulted we have advised . . .' and so on."

"Yes. Who asked for his advice?"

"Ask this government of pimps about that."

"Tawfiq Nasim! Have you forgotten him? But why did the Wafd enter into a truce with him?"

"There's an end to everything. Wait for the speech today."

Kamal listened and even took part in the discussion. Strangely enough, he felt just as excited as the others. This was his eighth commemoration of Jihad—or Struggle—Day. Like the others, he felt bitter about the political experiments of the preceding years.

"I experienced the reign of Muhammad Mahmud, who suspended the constitution for three years in the name of modernization, usurping the people's liberty in exchange for a promise to reclaim swamps and marshlands. I lived through the years of terror and political shame that Isma'il Sidqy imposed on the nation. The people placed their confidence in these men and sought their leadership, only to find them odious executioners, protected by the truncheons and bullets of English constables. Conveyed in one language or another, their message for the Egyptian people has been: 'You're minors. We are your guardians.' The people plunged into one battle after another, emerging breathless from each. Finally they adopted a passive stance of ironic forbearance. Then the arena was empty except for Wafdists and tyrants. The people were content to watch from the sidelines, whispering encouragement to their men but not offering any assistance."

His heart could not ignore the life of the Egyptian people. It was aroused by anything affecting them, even when his intellect wandered off into a fog of doubt.

He got out of the streetcar at Sa'd Zaghlul Street and joined an informal procession heading toward the pavilion erected for the holiday celebrations near Sa'd Zaghlul's home, the House of the Nation. At ten-meter intervals they encountered groups of soldiers with stern but dull faces. They were under the command of English constables. Shortly before reaching the pavilion, he saw Abd al-Muni'm, Ahmad, Ridwan, and a young man he did not know standing together, talking. They came up to greet him and stayed with him for some time. Ridwan and Abd al-Muni'm had been law students for about a month, and Ahmad had begun the final year of secondary school.

In the street Kamal could view them as "men." At home he always thought of them as young nephews. Although Ridwan was exceptionally handsome, his companion, whom he introduced as Hilmi Izzat, was equally good-looking. They demonstrated the truth of the saying: "Birds of a feather flock together."

Ahmad was a source of delight for Kamal, who could always anticipate some entertainingly novel observation or action from him. Of all his nephews, he felt closest spiritually to this one. Although he was shorter and plumper, there was a physical resemblance between Abd al-Muni'm and Kamal, who could love the young man for that reason, if for no other. It was this nephew's certainty and fanaticism he found offensive.

Approaching the huge pavilion, Kamal looked around at the swarming crowds of people, pleased by the astonishing numbers. After gazing at the platform where the people's spokesman would soon deliver an address, he took his seat. His presence at a crowded gathering liberated a new person from deep inside his alienated and isolated soul, a new individual who was throbbing with life and enthusiasm. While his intellect was temporarily sealed up as if in a bottle, psychic forces ordinarily suppressed burst forth, eager for an existence filled with emotions and sensation. They were incentives for him to strive harder and to hope. At times like these, his life was revitalized, his natural impulses were free to express themselves, and his loneliness melted away. He felt linked to the people around him, as if sharing in their lives and embracing their hopes and pains. It would have been unnatural for him to adopt this life permanently, but it was necessary every now and then to keep him from feeling divorced from the daily routines of the people. For the time being he would postpone consideration of the problems of matter, spirit, physics, or metaphysics, in order to concentrate on what these people loved and hated . . . the constitution, the economic crisis, the political situation, and the nationalist cause. There was nothing strange about shouting slogans like "The Wafd creed is the nation's creed!" after having spent the previous night contemplating the absurdity of existence. The intellect can rob a person of peace of mind. An intellectual loves truth, desires honor, aims for tolerance, collides with doubt, and suffers from a continuous struggle with instincts and passions. He needs an hour when he can escape through the embrace of society from the vexations of his life. Then he feels reinvigorated, enthusiastic, and youthful.

In the library he had a few outstanding friends like Darwin, Bergson, and Russell, but in this pavilion there were thousands of friends. If they seemed mindless, they still collectively embodied a commendable natural alertness. In the final analysis, such people were as responsible as intellectual giants for shaping the events of history. In his political life Kamal loved and hated; he felt pleased and annoyed. Yet as an intellectual skeptic, he thought nothing mattered. Whenever he confronted this contradiction, he was overwhelmed by anxiety. No sector of his life was free from contradictions and therefore from anxiety.

For this reason, his heart yearned intensely to achieve a harmonious unity both perfect and happy. Where was this unity to be found? He felt that the life of thought was unavoidable for him so long as he had a mind with which to think. Yet that did not keep him from considering the opposite style of life toward which all his suppressed and ignored vital impulses pushed him as if toward a secure rock surrounded by surging water.

Perhaps for causes like these Kamal found this gathering splendid. The larger the crowd got, the more magnificent everything seemed.

He waited for the leaders to appear with as much fervor and impatience as the rest of the audience.

Abd al-Muni'm and Ahmad sat next to each other, but Ridwan and his friend Hilmi Izzat were either strolling back and forth in the central aisle of the pavilion or standing at the entrance, where they chatted with some of the officials in charge of the festivities. The two certainly were influential young men. The crowd's whispers created a general hubbub. From the far seats occupied by young people there rose a clamor punctuated by yells. Then a loud cry was heard from outside, making heads turn toward the entrance. Everyone stood up and released a deafening roar. Mustafa al-Nahhas appeared on the dais, where he greeted the multitudes with his sincere smile and mighty hands.

Kamal watched the Wafd Party leader with eyes that had temporarily lost their skeptical look, although he wondered how he could believe in this man after ceasing to believe in everything else. Was it because the man was a symbol of independence and democracy? In any case, the warm relationship between the leader and the public was obvious and worth seeing. It had doubtless been a significant factor in the formation of Egyptian nationalism.

The atmosphere was charged with enthusiasm and ardor. The officials wore themselves out quieting the audience so that a reciter could chant some appropriate verses from the Qur'an, including "Prophet, goad the Believers to fight" (8:65). People had been waiting for this call, and their shouts and applause rang out in response to it. Some of the more sedate deplored the outburst and demanded that the audience be silent out of respect for God's Book. Their protest awakened old memories for Kamal of a time when he had been numbered among these pious souls. He smiled and immediately was reminded of his special world, so full of pairs of contradictions canceling out each other that it seemed empty.

The leader rose to deliver his address, which was clear, effective, and delivered in a resonant voice. Lasting for two hours, it concluded with an open call for the use of force and an unambiguous appeal for revolution. The crowd's excitement reached a fever pitch. People stood on the chairs and yelled with wild enthusiasm. Kamal shouted as passionately as anyone else. He forgot he was a teacher who was expected to maintain his dignity. He imagined that he had been transported back to the glorious revolutionary days he had heard about but had not been privileged to experience. Had the speeches back then been as forcefully delivered? Had the crowds received them with comparable enthusiasm? Had death seemed insignificant for those reasons? No doubt Fahmy had been in a gathering like this once and had then rushed off to death and immortality or annihilation. Was it possible for a skeptic to become a martyr?

"Perhaps patriotism, like love," he thought, "is a force to which we surrender, whether or not we believe in it."

The passionate outbursts were intense. The chants were ardent and menacing. Chairs rocked with the motion of the men standing upon them. What would be the next step? Before anyone knew what was happening, throngs of people were heading outside. As he left his place, Kamal looked around, searching for his young relatives, but found no trace of them. He left the pavilion by a side door and then walked briskly toward Qasr al-Ayni Street to get there before the crowd. On his way he passed by the House of the Nation and, as always, gazed at it, moving his eyes from the historic balcony to the courtyard, which had witnessed such momentous events in the nation's history. The building had an almost magical fascination for him. Here Sa'd Zaghlul had stood. Here Fahmy and his comrades had stood. On this street bullets had lodged in the breasts of the martyrs. His people were in perpetual need of a revolution to combat the waves of oppression that prevented their rebirth. Periodic revolutions were necessary to serve as a vaccine against this dread disease, for tyranny was the nation's most deeply entrenched malady.

Kamal's participation in this patriotic holiday had successfully reinvigorated him. Nothing mattered to him except the need for Egypt to reply emphatically and decisively to Hoare's declaration. He held his tall, slender body erect and his large head high as his feet pounded against the pavement. He had lofty affairs and significant deeds on his mind as he passed by the American University campus. Even a teacher occasionally had to join a revolution with his students. He smiled almost in despair. He was an instructor with a big head, destined to teach the fundamentals of English and nothing more, even though this language had introduced him to countless mysteries. His body occupied a tiny space on the swarming surface of the earth, while his imagination spun round in a whirlpool embracing all the secrets of nature. In the morning he asked what this word meant and how to spell that one. In the evening he pondered the meaning of his existence—this riddle that follows one puzzle and precedes another one. In the morning his heart was ablaze with rebellion against

the English but in the evening it was chastened by a general feeling
of brotherhood for all mankind as he felt inclined to cooperate with
everyone in order to confront the puzzle of man's destiny.

He shook his head rather forcefully as if to expel these thoughts.
As he approached al-Isma'iliya Square he could hear people shouting.
He realized that the demonstrators had reached Qasr al-Ayni Street.
The combative spirit animating his breast made him hesitate. Perhaps
he would join in the day's demonstrations after all. For too long the
nation had patiently endured the blows it received. Today it was
Tawfiq Nasim, yesterday Isma'il Sidqy, and before that Muhammad
Mahmud. This ill-omened chain of despots stretched back into pre-
history. "Every bastard has been deluded by his own power and has
claimed to be the chosen guardian for us children. . . . Not so fast!
The demonstration is raging ahead furiously, but what's this?"

Disturbed, Kamal turned to look back. The sound he heard shook
his heart. As he listened intently, the noise of shots rang out once
more. He could see demonstrators in the distance, milling around
chaotically. Groups of people were rushing toward the square, while
others headed for the side streets. English constables on horseback
were galloping in the direction of the demonstrators. The shouting
grew louder. Screams mixed with angry voices, and the firing became
more intense. Kamal's heart pounded as, overcome by a troubled
rage, he worried with each beat about Abd al-Muni'm, Ahmad, and
Ridwan. Turning right and then left, he noticed a coffeehouse at the
corner nearby and made for it. The doors were almost closed, and on
entering he remembered the pastry shop in al-Husayn district where
he had first heard gunfire.

There was pandemonium everywhere. Initially the rapid firing was
frightening, but then the shots became less frequent. The sound of
breaking glass was audible as well as the neighing of horses. An
increase in volume of the furious voices showed that rebellious bands
were dashing at breakneck speed from one location to the next. An
elderly man entered the café. Before anyone could ask him what he
had seen, he exclaimed, "The constables' bullets rained down on the
students. Only God knows how many were hit." He sat down,
breathing hard, and then added in a trembling voice, "It was treachery pure and simple. If their goal had been to break up the demonstration, they would have fired into the air from their distant
positions. But they escorted the demonstration with calculated calm
and then stationed themselves at the intersections. Suddenly they
drew their revolvers and began firing. They shot to kill, showing no

mercy. Young boys fell writhing in their own blood. The English were beasts, but the Egyptian soldiers were no less brutal. It was a premeditated massacre, my God."

A voice called out from the rear of the room, "My heart told me that today would end badly."

Another answered, "These are evil times. Since Hoare announced his declaration, people have been expecting momentous events. Other battles will follow. I promise you that."

"The victims are always students, the most precious children of the nation, alas."

"But the shooting has stopped. Hasn't it? Listen."

"The main part of the demonstration is at the House of the Nation. The shooting will continue there for hours to come."

But the square was silent. Minutes dragged by heavily, charged with tension. Darkness began to fall, and the lamps in the coffeehouse were lit. There was total silence, as if death had overtaken the square and the surrounding streets. When the double doors of the coffeehouse were opened wide, the square—empty of pedestrians and vehicles—was visible. A column of steel-helmeted policemen on horseback circled it, preceded by their English commanders.

Kamal kept wondering about the fate of his nephews. When traffic in the square hesitantly picked up again, he left the coffeehouse and hurried off. He did not return home until he had first visited Sugar Street and Palace of Desire Alley to reassure himself that Abd al-Muni'm, Ahmad, and Ridwan were safe.

Alone in his library, his heart filled with sorrow, distress, and anger, he did not read or write a single word. His mind was still roaming around the House of the Nation, thinking of Hoare, the revolutionary speech, the patriotic chants, and the screams of the victims. He found himself trying to recall the name of the pastry shop where he had hidden long ago, but memory failed him.

The sight of Muhammad Iffat's house in al-Gamaliya was a familiar and beloved one for Ahmad Abd al-Jawad. The massive wooden door looked like the entrance to an ancient caravansary. The high wall hid everything but the tops of lofty trees. Shaded by these mulberry and sycamore trees and dotted with small henna and lemon trees as well as various types of jasmine, the courtyard garden was marvelous. Equally amazing was the pool in the center. And then there was the wooden veranda stretching along the width of the garden.

Muhammad Iffat stood on the veranda steps, waiting to welcome his guest as he pulled his cloak tighter around him. Ali Abd al-Rahim and Ibrahim al-Far were already seated beside each other. Ahmad greeted his chums and followed Muhammad Iffat to the couch at the center of the veranda, where they sat down together. They had all lost their girth, except for Muhammad Iffat, who looked bloated and had a red face. Ali Abd al-Rahim had gone bald, and the others' hair was streaked with white. Wrinkles spread across their faces. Ali Abd al-Rahim and Ibrahim al-Far appeared to have aged more than the other two. The redness of Muhammad Iffat's face seemed almost to suggest a vascular disorder.

Although Ahmad had lost weight and his hair was turning white, he had retained his unblemished good looks. He loved this assembly and admired the view of the garden, which extended all the way to the high wall on al-Gamaliya Street. He leaned his head back a little as if to allow his large nose to inhale the fragrance of jasmine and henna. He closed his eyes occasionally to concentrate on hearing the chirps of the small birds flitting about in the branches of the mulberry and sycamore trees. Still, the most sublime feeling entertained by his heart just then was one of brotherhood and friendship for these men. When his wide blue eyes gazed at their beloved faces, which were masked by age, his heart overflowed with sorrow and sympathy, not only for them but for himself. The most nostalgic of them about the past, he was enthralled by anything he could remember about the beauty of youth, its passionate emotions, and his chivalrous escapades.

Ibrahim went to a nearby table to fetch the backgammon set, asking, "Who will play with me?"

Ahmad, who rarely joined in their games, said disapprovingly, "Wait a bit. We shouldn't lose ourselves in that from the very beginning."

Al-Far replaced the box. Then a Nubian servant brought in a tray with three teas and one whiskey and soda. Muhammad Iffat smiled as he took the whiskey glass and the others helped themselves to tea. This allocation, repeated every evening, often made them laugh. Waving his glass and gesturing toward their tea, Muhammad Iffat said, "May God be merciful to time, which has refined you."

Sighing, Ahmad Abd al-Jawad responded, "It has refined all of us and you more than the others, for you always were an exceptionally coarse fellow."

At approximately the same time one year they had all received identical medical advice to give up alcohol, but Muhammad Iffat's physician had allowed him one glass a day. Back then Ahmad Abd al-Jawad had assumed that his friend's doctor was more lenient than his own. He had gone to see this man, but the physician had advised him firmly and earnestly, "Your condition is different from your friend's." When the others had learned about this visit to Muhammad Iffat's doctor, it had provoked many jokes and comments.

Ahmad laughed and said, "You certainly must have given your doctor a big bribe to persuade him to let you have this one drink."

Al-Far moaned as he stared at the glass in Muhammad Iffat's hand and said, "By God, I've almost forgotten its intoxication."

Ali Abd al-Rahim jested, "You've destroyed your repentance by saying this, ruffian."

Al-Far asked his Lord's forgiveness and then murmured submissively, "Praise God."

"We've sunk to the point of envying one glass. Whatever has become of our ecstatic intoxications?"

Laughing, Ahmad Abd al-Jawad said, "If you repent, let if be of something evil, not of a blessing, you sons of dogs."

"Like all preachers, you have a tongue in one world and a heart in another."

Making his voice loud enough to suggest a change of subject, Ali Abd al-Rahim asked, "Men, what do you think of Mustafa al-Nahhas? This man was not influenced by the tears of an ailing and elderly king. He refused to forget for one second his highest objective, the 1923 constitution."

Muhammad Iffat cracked his fingers and said delightedly, "Bravo! Bravo! He's even more resolute than Sa'd Zaghlul. Although he saw that the tyrannical king was sick and tearful, al-Nahhas stood up to him with rare courage and repeated, with all the authority of the nation behind him, 'The 1923 constitution first.' So the constitution was reinstated. Who would have imagined that?"

Ibrahim al-Far nodded his head admiringly and said, "Picture this scene: King Fuad, broken by age and ill health, places his hand affectionately on the shoulder of Mustafa al-Nahhas and calls for the formation of a coalition government. Al-Nahhas is unmoved. He does not forget his duty as a trusted leader or abandon for one moment the constitution, which royal tears had almost drowned. Unimpressed by any of this, he says resolutely and courageously, 'The 1923 constitution first, Your Majesty.' "

Mimicking his friend's tone of voice, Ali Abd al-Rahim said, "Or impalement, Your Majesty."

Laughing, Ahmad Abd al-Jawad said, "I swear by the One whose fates tantalize us here with whiskey we're not allowed to drink—what a magnificent stand to take!"

Muhammad drained his glass and then said, "This is 1935. Eight years have passed since Sa'd's death and fifteen since the revolution. Yet the English are everywhere, in the barracks, the police, the army, and various ministries. The foreign capitulations that make every son of a bitch a respected gentleman are still operative. This sorry state of affairs must end."

"And don't forget butchers like Isma'il Sidqy, Muhammad Mahmud, and King Fuad's henchman al-Ibrashi. . . ."

"If the English leave, none of these other men will matter and the constant change of governments will cease."

"Yes. If the king wants to make trouble behind the scenes then, he won't find anyone to help him."

Muhammad Iffat added, "The king will be left with two choices. Either he respects the constitution or he says goodbye."

Ibrahim al-Far asked rather skeptically, "Would the English forsake him if he sought their protection?"

"If the English agree to evacuate Egypt, why would they continue to protect the king?"

Al-Far asked, "Will the English really agree to evacuate?"

Speaking with confident pride in his political acumen, Muhammad Iffat replied, "They caught us off guard with Hoare's declaration. Then there were the demonstrations and the martyrs, may God be compassionate to them. Finally there came the invitation to form a coalition government and the 1923 constitution was restored. I assure you that the English now want to negotiate. . . . It's true that no one knows how this sorry situation will be sorted out, under what circumstances the English will leave, or how the influence of resident expatriates can be ended. But we have boundless confidence in Mustafa al-Nahhas."

"Is the exchange of a few words around a table going to end fifty-three years of foreign occupation?"

"The words have been preceded by the shedding of innocent blood. . . ."

"Even so. . . ."

With a wink, Muhammad Iffat replied, "They'll find themselves in an awkward position, given the grave international situation."

"They can always come up with someone to protect their interests. Isma'il Sidqy's still alive."

In a knowing tone, Muhammad Iffat responded, "I've spoken with many informed people and have found them optimistic. They say that the world is threatened by a crushing war, that Egypt is a potential target, and that it's in the best interests of both sides to reach an honorable settlement." After stroking his belly he continued with smug self-assurance: "Here's some important news for you. I've been promised the nomination for al-Gamaliya district in the forthcoming elections. Al-Nuqrashi himself promised me."

The faces of his friends shone with delight. When it was Ali Abd al-Rahim's turn to comment, he said with mock seriousness, "The only thing wrong with the Wafd Party is that they occasionally nominate beasts as deputies."

Ahmad Abd al-Jawad pretended to defend the Wafd against this charge. "What should the Wafd do? It wants to represent the entire nation. Some of the people are good citizens, and others are trash. What better representatives for trash can you have than beasts?"

Muhammad Iffat punched him in the side as he retorted, "You're a sly old fox! You and Jalila are exactly alike. You're a pair of old foxes!"

"I'd be happy to see Jalila nominated. She could sweep the king himself off his feet if she had to."

Smiling, Ali Abd al-Rahim commented, "I ran into her the day before yesterday near her cul-de-sac. She's still as magnificently massive as the ceremonial camel litter bound for Mecca, but age has eaten away at her and relieved itself all over her."

Al-Far added, "She's become a noted madam. Her house is a hotbed of activity, night and day. Even after the piper dies, her fingers keep on playing."

Ali Abd al-Rahim laughed for a long time and then said, "Passing by her house one day, I saw a man slip inside when he thought no one was looking. Who do you think it was?" With a wink in the direction of Ahmad Abd al-Jawad, he continued: "The dutiful Kamal Effendi, instructor at al-Silahdar School."

Muhammad Iffat and al-Far roared with laughter while Ahmad Abd al-Jawad, his eyes wide with astonishment and alarm, asked in a daze, "My son Kamal?"

"Yes indeed. His overcoat wrapped around him, he paraded along in a most genteel manner sporting his gold-rimmed spectacles and bushy mustache. He walked with such sedate dignity that it was hard to believe he was the son of our court jester. He turned into her establishment as solemnly as if entering the holy mosque in Mecca. Under my breath I said, 'Don't wear yourself out, bastard.' "

They laughed loudly. Ahmad Abd al-Jawad had not recovered yet from his stupor but attempted to overcome it by joining in the laughter.

Staring Ahmad in the face, Muhammad Iffat asked suggestively, "What's so amazing about this? Isn't he your son?"

Shaking his head with wonder, Ahmad Abd al-Jawad replied, "I've always thought him polite, refined, and cool. He spends so much time in his library reading and writing that I've been afraid he would become isolated from the world. He expends far too much effort on worthless things."

Ibrahim al-Far joked, "Who knows, perhaps there's a branch of the National Library in Jalila's house."

Ali Abd al-Rahman ventured, "Or perhaps he retreats to his library to read ribald classics like *The Shakyh's Return*. What do you expect from a man who began his career with an essay claiming that man is descended from an ape?"

They laughed again, and Ahmad Abd al-Jawad chuckled along with them. He had learned from experience that if he tried to be serious at a time like this he would become an easy target for jokes and jests. Finally he said, "This must be why the damned fellow has avoided marriage so studiously that I was beginning to have doubts about him."

"How old is your little boy now?"

"Twenty-nine."

"My goodness! You ought to get him married. Why is he so reluctant?"

Muhammad Iffat belched, stroked his belly, and then observed, "It's the fashion now. Girls crowd into the streets, and men don't trust them anymore. Haven't you heard Shaykh Hasanayn sing, 'What startling things we see: the gentleman and the lady both at the barbershop'?"

"Don't forget the economic crisis and the uncertain future facing young people. University graduates accept civil service jobs at only ten pounds a month, if they're lucky enough to find one."

With obvious anxiety, Ahmad Abd al-Jawad said, "I'm afraid that he's learned Jalila was my mistress or that she knows he's my son."

Laughing, Ali Abd al-Rahim asked, "Do you suppose she asks her customers for references?"

With a wink, Muhammad Iffat commented, "If the hussy knew who he was, she'd tell him his father's life story from A to Z."

Ahmad Abd al-Jawad snorted, "God forbid!"

Ibrahim al-Far asked, "Do you think a fellow who can discern that his original ancestor was an ape will have difficulty discovering that his father's a debauched fornicator?"

Muhammad Iffat laughed so loud that he started coughing. After a few moments of silence he remarked, "Kamal's appearance is truly deceptive ... sedate, calm, prim—a teacher in every sense of the word."

In a gratified tone of voice, Ali Abd al-Rahim said, "Sir, may our Lord preserve Kamal and grant him a long life. Anyone who resembles his father can't go wrong."

Muhammad Iffat commented, "What's important is whether he's a Don Juan like his father. I mean, is he good at handling women and seducing them?"

Ali Abd al-Rahim replied, "I doubt it. I imagine he preserves his grave and dignified appearance until the door is closed behind him and the lucky girl. Then he removes his clothes with the same grave dignity and throws himself upon her with grim earnestness. Afterward he dresses and leaves with precisely the same solemnity, as though delivering an important lecture to his students."

"From the loins of Don Juan has sprung a dunce!"

Ahmad Abd al-Jawad asked himself almost resentfully, "Why does this seem strange to me?" He would try to forget about it. Seeing al-Far go to fetch the backgammon set, he proclaimed without any hesitation that it was time for them to play. Even so, his thoughts kept revolving around this news. He consoled himself with the reflection that he had raised Kamal conscientiously and had seen him get a University degree and become a respected teacher. Now the boy could do whatever he wanted. In view of his son's lanky build and enormous head and nose, perhaps it was lucky that he had learned how to have a good time. If there were any justice in the world, Kamal would have married years ago, and Yasin never would have married at all. But who could claim to understand such mysteries?

Then al-Far asked him, "When did you last see Zubayda?"

After thinking it over, Ahmad answered, "Last January. About a year ago. The day she came to the store to ask me to find a buyer for her house."

Ibrahim al-Far remarked, "Jalila bought it. Then that crazy Zubayda fell in love with a cart driver. But he left her destitute. Now she's living in a room on the roof of the house belonging to the performer Sawsan. She's such a ghost of her former self, it's pitiful."

Ahmad Abd al-Jawad shook his head sorrowfully and murmured, "The sultana in a rooftop shack! Glory to the unchanging One!"

Ali Abd al-Rahim commented, "A sad end, but hardly unexpected."

A laugh of lament escaped from Muhammad Iffat, and he said, "God have mercy on people who place their trust in this world."

Then al-Far invited them to play, and Muhammad Iffat challenged him. They quickly turned their attention to backgammon, as Ahmad Abd al-Jawad said, "Let's see whose luck is like Jalila's and whose resembles Zubayda's."

6 ❧

Kamal was sitting with Isma'il Latif at Ahmad Abduh's coffeehouse in the same alcove Kamal and Fuad al-Hamzawi had used as students. Although the December weather was cold, it was warm inside this subterranean establishment. With the entrance closed, all openings to the surface of the earth were sealed, and the air inside was naturally warmer and more humid. But for his desire to be with Kamal, Isma'il Latif would not have patronized this place. Of the old group, he was the only one who still kept in touch, although exigencies of employment had forced him to move to Tanta, where he had obtained a position as an accountant, following his graduation from the School of Commerce. Whenever he returned to Cairo on holiday he telephoned Kamal at al-Silahdar School and arranged to meet at this historic spot.

Kamal gazed at this old friend, taking in his compact build and the sharp features of his tapering face. He was pleasantly surprised by what he heard about Isma'il's polite, dignified, and upright behavior. The notorious paradigm of reckless and boorish impudence had become an exemplary husband and father.

Kamal poured some green tea into his companion's glass and then served himself. Smiling, he said, "You don't seem to care for Ahmad Abduh's coffeehouse."

Craning his neck in his familiar way, Isma'il replied, "It really is unusual, but why not choose somewhere aboveground?"

"In any case it's an eminently suitable place for a respectable person like you."

Isma'il laughed and nodded his head as if to admit that—after a wild youth—he now deserved recognition for his respectability.

To be polite, Kamal asked, "How are things in Tanta?"

"Great! During the day I work nonstop at the office and in the evening I'm at home with my wife and children."

"How are the offspring?"

"Praise God. Their relaxation always comes at the expense of our fatigue. But we praise Him no matter what."

Motivated by the curiosity any reference to family life inspired in

him, Kamal asked, "Have you really found the kind of true happiness
with them that advocates of family life forecast?"

"Yes. I have."

"In spite of the fatigue?"

"In spite of everything."

Kamal looked at his friend with even greater interest. This was a
new person, quite distinct from the Isma'il Latif he had known from
1921 to 1927, that extraordinary era when he had lived life to the
fullest, when not a minute had passed without some profound pleasure or intense pain. It had been a time of true friendship represented
by Husayn Shaddad, of sincere love personified by Aïda, and of ve-
hement enthusiasm derived from the torch of the glorious Egyptian
revolution. It had also been a time of drastic experiments prompted
by doubt, cynicism, desire. Isma'il Latif was a symbol of the former
era and a significant clue to it. But how remote his friend was from
all that today. . . .

Isma'il Latif conceded almost grumpily, "Of course, there's always
something for us to worry about—like the new cadre system at work
and the freeze on promotions and raises. You know I enjoyed an
easy life under my father's wing. But I got nothing from his estate,
and my mother consumes all of her pension. That's why I consented
to work in Tanta—to be able to make ends meet. Would a man like
me agree to it otherwise?"

Kamal laughed and said, "Nothing used to be good enough for
you."

Isma'il smiled with what appeared to be conceit and pride at his
memorable life, which he had renounced voluntarily.

Kamal asked, "Aren't you tempted to recapture some of the past?"

"Certainly not. I've had enough of all that. I can tell you that I've
never regretted my new life. I just need to use a little cleverness from
time to time to get some money from my mother, and my wife has
to play the same game with her father. I still like to live comfortably."

Kamal could not keep himself from observing merrily, "You
showed us how and then abandoned us. . . ."

Isma'il laughed out loud, and his earnest face assumed much of its
mischievous look of the old days. He asked, "Are you sorry about
that? No. You love this life with a curious devotion, even though
you're a temperate person. In a few playful years I did more than
you'll ever do during a whole lifetime." Then he added in a serious
tone, "Get married and change your life."

Kamal said impishly, "This matter deserves serious thought."

Between 1924 and 1935 a new Isma'il Latif had come into existence. Curiosity seekers should search out this novelty. Still, he was
the one old friend left. France had seduced Husayn Shaddad away
from his homeland. Similarly, Hasan Salim had established himself
outside of Egypt. Unfortunately Kamal had no contact with either of
them anymore. Isma'il Latif had never been a soul mate. But he was
a living memory of an amazing past, and for that reason Kamal could
glory in his friendship.

"I also take pride in his loyalty. I derive no spiritual delight from
his companionship, but he's living proof of the existence of that past.
I desire to establish the reality of that era as eagerly as I desire life
itself. I wonder what Aïda's doing now. Where is she in this wide
world? How was my heart ever able to recover from the sickness of
loving her? All those events are marvels of their kind."

"I'm impressed, Mr. Isma'il. You deserve every success."

Isma'il glanced at his surroundings, inspecting the ceiling, lanterns,
alcoves, and the dreamy faces of the patrons, who were absorbed in
their conversations and games. Then he asked, "What do you like
about this place?"

Kamal did not answer but remarked sadly, "Have you heard? It
will soon be demolished so a new structure can be built on its ruins.
This historic spot will vanish forever."

"Good riddance! Let these catacombs disappear so a new civiliza-
tion can rise above them."

"Is he right?" Kamal wondered. "Perhaps ... but the heart feels
strongly about certain things. My dear coffeehouse, you're part of
me. I have dreamt a lot and thought a lot inside you. Yasin came to
you for years. Fahmy met his revolutionary comrades here to plan
for a better world. I also love you, because you're made from the
same stuff as dreams. But what's the use of all this? What value does
nostalgia have? Perhaps the past is the opiate of the Romantic. It's a
most distressing affliction to have a sentimental heart and a skeptical
mind. Since I don't believe in anything, it doesn't matter what I say."

"You're right. I advocate demolition of the pyramids if some future
use is discovered for the stones."

"The pyramids! What's the relationship of the pyramids to Ahmad
Abduh's coffeehouse?"

"I'm referring to all historic relics. I mean let's destroy all of them
for the sake of today and tomorrow."

Isma'il Latif laughed. He craned his neck, as he had in the past
when challenged, and replied, "You've occasionally supported the

opposite point of view. As you know, I read *al-Fikr* magazine from time to time, for your sake. I told you frankly once before what I think of it. Yes, your essays are difficult, and the whole journal is dry, may God grant us refuge. I had to stop buying it, because my wife found nothing in it she wanted to read. Forgive me, but that's what she asserted. I say I've occasionally seen you write the opposite of what you're proposing now. But I won't claim to understand much of what you write. Don't tell anyone, but I don't understand even a little of it. Speaking of this, wouldn't it be better for you to write like popular authors? If you do, you'll find a large audience and make a lot of money."

In the past Kamal had rebelliously and stubbornly scorned such advice. Now he despised it but did not rebel against it. Yet he wondered whether he should be so disdainful, not because he thought the disdain misplaced, but because he worried at times about the value of what he wrote. He was even uneasy about this worry. He was quick to confess to himself that he was fed up with everything and that the world, having lost its meaning, seemed at times to resemble an obsolete expression.

"You never did approve of my way of thinking."

Isma'il guffawed and said, "Do you remember? What days those were!"

Those days had passed. Their fires burned no longer. But they were treasured away like the corpse of a loved one or like the box of wedding candies he had hidden in a special place the night of Aïda's marriage.

"Don't you hear from Husayn Shaddad or Hasan Salim?"

Isma'il raised his thick eyebrows and replied, "That reminds me! Things have happened during the year I've been away from Cairo. . . ." With increasing concern he continued: "I learned on my return from Tanta that the Shaddad family has ended."

Oppressive, rebellious interest erupted in Kamal's heart, and he suffered terribly as he struggled to conceal it. He asked, "What do you mean?"

"My mother told me that Shaddad Bey went bankrupt when the stock market swallowed up his last millieme. Destroyed, he could not stand the blow and killed himself."

"What awful news! When did this happen?"

"Some months ago. The mansion was lost along with all his other possessions—that mansion where we spent unforgettable times in the garden. . . ."

What times, what a mansion, what a garden, what memories, what forgotten pain, and painful forgetfulness. . . . The elegant family, the great man, the mighty dream. . . . Was not his agitation more pronounced than the situation warranted? Was his heart not pounding more violently than these once forgotten memories deserved?

Kamal said sorrowfully, "The bey has killed himself. The mansion has been lost. What's become of the family?"

Isma'il replied angrily, "Our friend's mother has only fifteen pounds a month from a mortmain trust and has moved into an unpretentious flat in al-Abbasiya. My mother, who went to visit them, wept upon her return when describing the woman's condition . . . that lady who once lived in unimaginable luxury. Don't you remember?"

Of course he remembered. Did Isma'il think he had forgotten? He remembered the garden, the gazebo, and the felicity of which the breezes there sang. He remembered happiness and sorrow. Indeed he felt truly sorrowful just then. Tears were ready to well up in his eyes. It would not do for him to mourn the threatened destruction of Ahmad Abduh's coffeehouse anymore, for everything was destined to be turned head over heels.

"That's really sad, and it makes me feel even worse that we didn't do our duty and present our condolences. Don't you imagine Husayn returned from France?"

"No doubt he came back after the incident, as well as Hasan Salim and Aïda. But none of them is in Egypt now."

"How could Husayn go off again, leaving his family in this condition? What's he got to live on, now that his father's money is gone?"

"I heard he married over there. It's not unlikely that he's found work during his long stay in France. I don't know anything about that. I haven't seen him since we both said goodbye to him. How much time has elapsed since then? Approximately ten years . . . isn't that so? That's ancient history, but this upset me a lot."

"A lot . . . a lot," the words echoed inside Kamal. His tears were still trying to escape. He had not cried since that era and had forgotten how to. As his heart dissolved in sorrow, he recalled a time when it had chosen sorrow for its emblem. The news shook him so violently that the present dispersed entirely to reveal the person whose life had been pure love and pure sorrow. Was this the end of the old dream?

"Bankruptcy and suicide!" It almost seemed predestined that this family would teach him that even gods fall. Bankruptcy and suicide

... if Aïda was still living luxuriously because of her husband's position, what had become of her lofty pride? Had the events reduced
her little sister to . . . ?"

"Husayn had a young sister. What was her name? I remember
occasionally, but it escapes me most of the time."

"Budur. She lives with her mother and shares all the difficulties of
the new life."

"Imagine Aïda living in reduced circumstances . . . a life like those
of the men sitting here," Kamal thought. "Does Budur have to wear
darned stockings? Does she ride the streetcar? Will she marry an
employee of some firm?" But how did any of this concern him?

"Oh . . . don't deceive yourself. Today you're sad. Whatever intellectual posture you adopt concerning the class system, you feel a
frightening despair over this family's fall. It's painful to hear that your
idols are wallowing in the dirt. At any rate, the fact that nothing
remains of your love is gratifying. Yes, what's left of that bygone
love?"

Although he thought that no trace remained, his heart pounded
with strange affection when he heard any of the songs of that age,
no matter how trite the lyrics or the tunes. What did this mean?

"But not so fast. A memory of love, not love itself, was at work.
We're in love with love, regardless of our circumstances, and love it
most when we are deprived of it. At the moment, I feel adrift in a
sea of passion. A latent illness may release its poison when we're
temporarily indisposed. What can we do about it? Even doubt, which
puts all truths into question, stops cautiously before love, not because
love is beyond doubt, but out of respect for my sorrow and from a
desire that the past should be true."

Isma'il returned to this tragedy, narrating many of its details. Finally he seemed to tire of it. In a tone that indicated he wished to
end the saga he said, "Only God is permanent. It's really distressing,
but that's enough misfortune for us now."

Feeling a need for silent reflection, Kamal did not attempt to draw
him out. What Isma'il had said was quite sufficient. To his own astonishment, Kamal wept silently with invisible tears shed by his
heart. Although once afflicted by love's malady, he had recovered
completely. He told himself in amazement, "Nine or ten years! What
a long time and yet how short. . . . I wonder what Aïda looks like
now."

He wished terribly that he could gaze at her long enough to discover the secret of that magical past and even the secret of his own

personality. He saw her now only as a fleeting image in a familiar old song, a picture in a soap advertisement, or when in his sleep he whispered with surprise, "There she is!" But what he actually observed was nothing more than glimpses of a film star or an intrusive memory. He would wake up. What reality was there to it then?

He did not feel like sitting here any longer. His soul yearned for an adventuresome journey through the unseen spiritual realm. So he asked Isma'il, "Will you accept my invitation to have a couple of drinks in a nice place where we won't be seen?"

Isma'il chortled and replied, "My wife's waiting for me to take her to visit her aunt."

Kamal was not concerned about this rejection. For a long time he had been his own drinking companion. The two men continued chatting about one thing and another as they left the coffeehouse. In the middle of that conversation, Kamal remarked to himself, "When we're in love, we may resent it, but we certainly miss love once it's gone."

"It's pleasant sitting here . . . although my resources are limited. From this warm spot you can see people coming and going . . . back and forth from Faruq Street, the Muski, and al-Ataba."

But for the stinging cold of January, this Casanova would not have taken shelter behind the coffeehouse window, reluctantly abandoning the excellent outdoor vantage point the establishment claimed on the opposite sidewalk.

"But spring will come. . . . Yes, it will, even though our resources are limited. Sixteen years or more stuck at the seventh grade of the civil service. . . . The store in al-Hamzawi was sold for a minuscule sum. Even though the rental unit in al-Ghuriya is large, it brings in only a few pounds. The house in Palace of Desire Alley is my residence and refuge. Ridwan has a rich grandfather, but Karima's totally dependent on me . . . the head of a household with a lover's heart. Unfortunately my resources are limited."

His roving eyes suddenly came to rest on a lanky young man with a compact mustache and gold-rimmed glasses. Wearing a black overcoat, the fellow was on his way from the Muski to al-Ataba. Yasin straightened up as though preparing to rise but did not stir from his seat. If the young man had not seemed in a such a hurry, Yasin would have stepped out to invite his brother to sit with him. Kamal was an excellent person to talk to when one was feeling low. Although almost thirty, he had never thought of getting married.

"Why was I in such a hurry to marry? Why did I jump right back in before recovering from the first bout? But who doesn't have something to complain of, whether married or single? Ezbekiya was a delightful place for fun, but it's been ruined. Today it's a meeting place for the dregs of society. All you have left from the world of pleasures is the diversion of observing this intersection and then of pursuing some easy quarry, at best an Egyptian maid who works for a foreign family. Usually she'll be clean, with a refined appearance. Yet her dominant characteristic will undeniably be her questionable morals. She's often found at the vegetable market in al-Azhar Square."

His coffee finished, he sat by the closed window, gazing out at the street. His eyes followed all the good-looking women, recording their images, whether they wore the traditional black wrap or a modern overcoat. He observed their individual attractions and their overall appearance with unflagging diligence. Some evenings he sat there until ten. At other times he stayed only long enough to drink his coffee before rising to hurry off in pursuit of prey he sensed would be responsive and cheap—as if he were a dealer in secondhand goods. Most of the time he was content just to watch. He might trail after a beauty without harboring any serious ambitions. Only occasionally was he overwhelmed enough by desire at the sight of a dissolute maid or of a widow over forty to pursue her in earnest. He was no longer the man he had once been, not merely because of the heavy burdens on his income but also because his fortieth year had arrived, an uninvited and unwelcome guest.

"What an alarming fact! White hairs at my temples! I've told the barber repeatedly to deal with it. He says one white hair is nothing to be concerned about, but they keep popping up. Down with both of them—the barber and white hair! He prescribed a reliable dye, but I'll never resort to that. When my father turned fifty, he didn't have a single white hair. What am I compared to my father? And not only with regard to white hair. . . . He was a young man at forty, a young man at fifty. But I . . . My Lord, I've not been more intemperate than my father. . . . Give your head a rest and exercise your heart. Do you suppose the life of Harun al-Rashid was really as filled with sensual pleasures as reports would have it? . . . Where does Zanuba fit into all this? Considered in the abstract, marriage is a bitch of a deception, but it's a powerful enough force to make you cherish the deception as long as you live. Nations will be overthrown, and eras will pass away. Yet the fates will always produce a woman going about her business and a man seriously pursuing her. Youth is a curse, but maturity's a string of curses. Where can a heart find any relaxation? . . . Where? . . . The most wretched thing that could happen in this world would be having to ask in a stupor one day, 'Where am I?' "

He left the coffeehouse at nine-thirty and proceeded slowly across al-Ataba to Muhammad Ali Street. Then, entering the Star Tavern, he greeted Khalo, who stood behind the bar in his traditional stance. The bartender returned Yasin's greeting with a broad smile, which revealed yellow front teeth with gaps between them. He gestured with his chin toward the interior, as if to inform this customer that friends were waiting for him there. The hall running beside the bar ended in a suite of three connected rooms that resounded with raucous laughter. Yasin went to the last of the three. It had but one window, which offered through its iron bars a view of al-Mawardi Alley. Three tables were dispersed in the corners. Two were empty, and the third was surrounded by Yasin's friends, who greeted him jubilantly, as they did every evening. Despite his complaints, Yasin was the youngest of the group. The oldest was an unmarried pensioner, who sat next to a head clerk in the Ministry of Waqfs, or mortmain trusts. Present also were a personnel director from the University and an attorney whose rental income spared him from having to practice law. The excessive reliance of these men on alcohol was apparent in their bleary gaze and in their complexions, which were either flushed or exceedingly pale. They made their way to the tavern between eight and nine and did not leave it until the wee hours of the morning, after imbibing the nastiest, cheapest, and most intoxicating drinks available. Yasin did not keep them company the whole time or did so only rarely. He normally spent two or three hours with them.

As usual the elderly bachelor greeted him with the salutation "Welcome, Hajji Yasin." The old man persisted in calling him a hajji, or pilgrim, not because Yasin had been to Mecca, but because of his Qur'anic name.

The attorney, the most alcoholic, observed, "You're so late, hero, that we said you must have stumbled upon a woman who would deprive us of your company all night long."

The bachelor commented philosophically, "There's nothing like a woman to come between one man and another."

Yasin, who had taken a seat next to him and the head clerk from trusts, jested, "There's no need to worry about that with you."

Lifting his glass to his mouth, the old man said, "Except for a few devilish moments when a girl of fourteen may tempt me."

The head clerk retorted, "Talking about it in January is one thing, but doing it in February is another."

"I don't understand what you mean by this rude remark."

"I don't either!"

Khalo brought Yasin a drink and some lupine seeds. Accepting the drink, Yasin said, "See what January's like this year!"

The personnel director commented, "God creates many different conditions. This year January has brought cold weather but has removed Tawfiq Nasim for good."

The attorney shouted, "Save us from politics! We always have politics for an appetizer when we're getting drunk and that spoils the effect. Find some other subject."

The personnel director said, "Actually our lives are nothing but politics."

"You're a personnel director in the sixth grade of the civil service. What does politics have to do with you?"

The director answered vehemently, "I've been at the sixth level for a long time, if you don't mind. Since the days of Sa'd Zaghlul."

The elderly bachelor said, "I reached the sixth level years ago in the era of Mustafa Kamil. In honor of his memory I retired at that rank. . . . Listen, wouldn't it be better for us to get drunk and sing?"

On the verge of draining his glass, Yasin said, "First let's get drunk, pop."

Yasin had never experienced a deep friendship, but wherever he went—coffeehouses or bars—he had pals. He made friends quickly and found friends even more quickly. He had frequented these men ever since developments in his financial situation had prompted him to make this bar his regular spot for evening relaxation. He chatted on intimate terms with the others, although he never met any of them outside of this setting and made no effort to do so. Alcoholism and frugality brought them together. The personnel director outranked the others but had many dependents. The attorney had sought out this bar because of its reputation for serving potent drinks, after normal ones had ceased to have much effect on him. Then he had gotten accustomed and habituated to the establishment.

Feeling drunk enough to become talkative, Yasin threw himself into the riotous maelstrom that swept through the place, surging into every corner. The elderly bachelor was Yasin's favorite. He never tired of teasing the old man, especially with allusions to sex, and the bachelor would caution Yasin not to indulge himself too much, reminding him of his domestic responsibilities.

Yasin's boastful retort was: "My family is made for this. My father's like that, and my grandfather before him was as well."

When Yasin repeated this statement now, the attorney jestingly asked him, "And what about your mother? Was she like that too?"

They laughed a lot, and Yasin laughed with them. But his tormented heart plunged in his chest. He drank more than usual and, in spite of his intoxication, imagined that he was collapsing. The place, the drink, the day—nothing felt right to him.

"Everywhere I go people are secretly making fun of me. What am

I, compared to my father? Nothing makes a person so miserable as an increase in age or a decrease in wealth. But drinking provides considerable relief. It pours forth gentle sociability and attractive solace, making every mishap seem trivial. So say, 'How happy I am.' The lost real estate will never return nor will my vanished youth. But alcohol can be an excellent lifetime companion. I was weaned on it as a callow youth. Now it's cheering up my manhood. When covered with white hair, my head will quiver with alcohol's ecstatic intoxication. So no matter what hardships I suffer, I will never lose heart. Tomorrow when Ridwan's established as a man and Karima struts off as a bride, I'll drink several toasts to happiness here in al-Ataba al-Khadra Square. How happy I am!"

Then the group was singing, "What humiliations the prisoner of love experiences. . . ." After that they did a loud and tumultuous rendition of "That girl in the neighboring valley." Men in the other rooms and in the lobby took up the song too. When it was finished, the silence was deafening.

The personnel director began discussing the resignation of Tawfiq Nasim and asked about the pact designed to protect Egypt from the danger Italy posed for her as a troublesome neighbor occupying Libya. But the assembly quickly sang in response, "Let down the curtain around us . . . to keep the neighbors from peeking." Although the elderly man had drunk to excess, participating fully in the rowdiness, he protested against this impudent response and accused them of being silly about a serious matter. Their answer was to sing in unison, "Is your opposition real or feigned?" Then the old man was forced to laugh and to join in wholeheartedly once more.

Yasin left the tavern at midnight, reaching his home in Palace of Desire Alley around one in the morning. As usual each night he walked through the rooms of his apartment as though on an inspection tour. He found Ridwan studying in his room, and the young man looked up from his law book to exchange a smile with his father. The love between them was profound. Ridwan also had great respect for Yasin, even though he realized that his father was always intoxicated when he returned home this late. Yasin was extremely appreciative of his son's good looks and also admired his intelligence and industry. He saw Ridwan as a future public prosecutor who would raise his father's status, give him cause for pride, and console him for many things.

Yasin asked, "How are your studies?" Then he pointed to himself as if to say, "I'm home, if you need me." Ridwan smiled, and the eyes he had inherited from his paternal grandmother, Haniya, lit up. His father asked, "Will it bother you if I play something on the phonograph?"

"It won't disturb me, but the neighbors are sleeping at this hour."

As he left the room Yasin said scornfully, "I hope they sleep well."

Passing by the "children's" bedroom, he found Karima sound asleep in her little bed. On the other side of the room Ridwan's bed was empty, waiting for him to finish studying. Yasin thought of waking his daughter up to joke with her but remembered how she grumbled when awakened in the night and gave up the idea. He went toward his room. The most wonderful night of the week in this house was without doubt that preceding the Friday holiday. Each Thursday evening when he got home, regardless of the hour, he would not hesitate to invite Ridwan to keep him company in the sitting room. Then he would awaken Karima and Zanuba. Starting up the phonograph, he would chat and joke with them until early the next morning. He was very fond of his family, especially Ridwan. It was true that he did not make any effort—or did not have the time—to supervise or guide them. He left their care to Zanuba and her instinctive good sense. Even so, he had never wished to play the cruel role with them that his own father had with him. The idea of creating in Ridwan's heart the feelings of terror and fear he had felt for his own father was deeply abhorrent to Yasin. In fact, he would not have been able to do it, even if he had wanted to. When he gathered them around him after midnight he would openly express his warm affection for them in a double intoxication derived from alcohol and love. While jesting and conversing with them he might tell droll anecdotes about the drunks he had encountered at the bar. He paid no attention to the effect these could have on their innocent souls and waved aside Zanuba's discreet attempts to signal him to desist. He seemed unselfconscious and acted spontaneously without reserve or caution.

As usual he found Zanuba half asleep in their room. It was always like this. Before he entered, he could hear her snoring. By the time he reached the middle of the room she was moving and opening her eyes. In her sarcastic voice she said, "Praise God for your safe return." Then she rose to help him take off his clothes and fold them. Unadorned, she appeared older than she was. He frequently thought she looked as old as he did. But she had become his companion, and their lives had become intermeshed. This former entertainer had succeeded in staying married to him, a feat no lady had accomplished before her. His wedded life was firmly anchored. At first there had

been fights and loud quarrels, but she had always shown how much
she cherished their marriage. In the course of time she had become a
mother. When her son had died, leaving her with only Karima, that
loss had made her redouble her efforts to safeguard her married life,
especially once her beauty began to fade and she was threatened by
premature aging. Time had taught her how attractive patience and
conciliation are and how to perfect the role of a lady in every sense
of the word. She went to such extremes in this regard that she dressed
very simply when she went out. Her efforts eventually won a certain
degree of respect for her on Palace Walk and Sugar Street. She had
the good judgment to treat her stepson Ridwan exactly like Karima,
showing both of them great tenderness and affection, even though
she did not feel any love for the boy, especially after she lost the
only son she bore Yasin. No longer a beauty, she was still careful to
wear attractive clothes and to be clean and neat.

Yasin smiled as he watched her fix her hair in front of the mirror.
Although she occasionally annoyed him to the point of anger, he
sensed that she had truly become a precious part of his life, someone
he could never do without.

Since she was shivering, she got a shawl, complaining, "It's so
cold! Do yourself a favor and don't spend your evenings out during
the winter."

He answered sarcastically, "As you know, alcohol changes the season. Why tire yourself by waking up?"

She fumed, "What you say is as tiresome as what you do."

In his nightshirt he looked like a blimp. Rubbing his hand over his
belly, he gazed at the woman with satisfaction. His black eyes sparkled. Then he laughed suddenly and said, "If you could have seen
me exchanging greetings with the officers ... The ones on the late
patrol have become my dear friends."

Sighing, she muttered, "I'm overjoyed."

8 ☙

The sight of Yasin's son, Ridwan, striding through al-Ghuriya at a deliberate pace was really enough to turn heads. Seventeen years old, he had attractive dark eyes and a medium build with a slight tendency to be stocky. His attire was so dapper it attracted attention. His rosy complexion was attributable to his mother's family, the Iffats. He had a radiant charm, and his gestures betrayed the conceit of a person whose good looks were no secret to him. When he passed by Sugar Street, he turned his face with its faint smile in that direction, as his aunt Khadija and her sons, Abd al-Muni'm and Ahmad, came to mind. The thought of them evoked little reaction save apathy. He had never felt tempted even once to take either of his cousins as a friend in the true meaning of the word. Soon he had passed through Bab al-Mutawalli, the ancient city gate. Then turning into al-Darb al-Ahmar, he went down it until he reached an old house, where he knocked on the door and waited.

The door opened to reveal the face of Hilmi Izzat, who was a childhood friend, a colleague in Law School, and a rival in good looks. Hilmi beamed at the sight of him. They embraced and exchanged a kiss, as they always did when they met. On their way up the stairs, Hilmi commended his friend's tie and the way it matched his shirt and socks. They were both known for their elegance and good taste, and their interest in clothing and fashion was matched by their enthusiasm for politics and studying law. Their destination was a large room with a high ceiling. The presence of a bed and a desk in it indicated that it served for both sleeping and studying. Indeed the two young men frequently stayed up late studying there and then stretched out to sleep side by side in the great bed with its black posts and mosquito netting. It was nothing new for Ridwan to spend a night away from home. Since childhood, he had accepted invitations to pass days at a time in various different homes, like those of his grandfather Muhammad Iffat in al-Gamaliya or of his mother, Zaynab—whose only child he remained, even though she had long since married Muhammad Hasan—in al-Munira. Because of this, his father's natural tendency to be nonchalant, and the secret relief his stepmother, Zanuba, took in anything that kept him away from home even temporarily, Ridwan encountered no opposition to his desire to stay overnight with his friend when they were studying for an examination. Eventually the practice became so common that no one paid any attention to it.

Hilmi Izzat had been raised in a similar atmosphere of indifference. His father, a police officer in charge of a station, had died ten years before. Hilmi's six sisters had married, and he lived alone with his aged mother. She had difficulty controlling him, and he soon came to dominate the entire household. The widow lived on her husband's small pension and the rent from the first floor of her ancient house. The family had not had an easy life since the father's death, but Hilmi had been able to continue his studies and to enroll in Law School. All that time he had managed to keep up appearances. For Hilmi there was no pleasure equal to that of seeing his friend, and no period of work or relaxation was truly enjoyable unless Ridwan was present. Then Hilmi would feel a burst of energetic enthusiasm.

Hilmi invited Ridwan to have a seat on the sofa next to the door of the latticed balcony and, sitting down beside him, began to think of a topic of conversation. There were so many subjects to choose from. . . . But the despondent look in Ridwan's eyes cooled Hilmi's fervor. He gazed at Ridwan questioningly. Guessing what was wrong, he muttered, "You've been to visit your mother. . . . I bet you've just been there."

Ridwan realized that his facial expression had given him away. With a vexed look in his eyes, he nodded his head, without speaking.

"How is she?" Hilmi asked.

"Great." Then he sighed and added, "But that man called Muhammad Hasan! Do you know what it means to have a stepfather?"

Hilmi said consolingly, "Many people have stepparents. There's nothing shameful about it. Besides, that happened a long time ago."

Ridwan cried out angrily, "No, no, no! He's always at home. The only time he leaves is to go to his job at the ministry. For once, I'd like to visit her when she's alone. He takes it upon himself to play the role of my father and adviser. Damn him. He never misses an opportunity to remind me that he's my father's boss in the records office and doesn't hesitate to criticize my father's conduct at work. But I don't let it pass in silence." He was quiet for a minute while he got control of his emotions. Then he continued: "My mother was a fool to agree to marry this man. Wouldn't it have been better for her to return to my father?"

Hilmi knew about Yasin's notorious behavior. With a smile he recited, "How many laments passion has brought me. . . ."

Waving his hand to show his disagreement, Ridwan said, "So what! Women's taste is a frightening mystery. What's even more disastrous is that she seems happy with him."

"Don't dwell on things that upset you."

Ridwan answered sadly, "How amazing! A vast part of my life is miserable. I detest my mother's husband and dislike my father's wife. The atmosphere is charged with hatred. Like my mother, my father made a bad choice. But what can I do about it? My stepmother is nice to me, but I don't think she loves me. How vile this life is!"

An elderly servant brought in some tea. Ridwan welcomed it with relish, since he had been stung by bitter February winds on the way there. They were silent as they dissolved the sugar in the tea. The expression on Ridwan's face changed, announcing the end of his gloomy recital.

Hilmi welcomed this and said with relief, "I'm so used to studying with you that I no longer know how to do it by myself."

Ridwan responded to this affectionate comment with a smile but suddenly asked, "Do you know about the decree that was issued concerning the delegation for the negotiations?"

"Yes. But many people are making a big stink about the atmosphere surrounding the negotiations. It seems that Italy, which poses a threat to our borders, is the real focus of the negotiations. For their part, the English pose a threat if the agreement fails."

"The blood of our martyrs is not cold yet, and we have fresh blood to spill."

Hilmi shook his head as he remarked, "What people are saying is that the fighting's over and the talking has begun. What do you think?"

"At any rate the Wafd constitute an overwhelming majority within the delegation. Picture this. When I asked Muhammad Hasan, my stepfather, his opinion of the situation, he replied sarcastically, 'Do you really think the English can leave Egypt?' This is the man my mother consented to marry."

Hilmi Izzat laughed out loud and asked, "Does your father's opinion differ?"

"My father hates the English. That's enough."

"Does he hate them from the depths of his heart?"

"My father does not hate or love anything from the depths of his heart."

"I'm asking what you think. Are you confident?"

"Why not? How long can this situation drag on? Fifty-four years of British occupation? Phooey! I'm not the only one who is miserable."

Hilmi Izzat took a last sip of tea. Then he smiled and said, "I think you were speaking to me with this kind of enthusiasm when he caught sight of you."

"Who?"

Hilmi smiled mysteriously and replied, "When you get excited you blush and that makes you look especially handsome. No doubt he saw you talking to me at one of those happy moments the day our student delegation went to the House of the Nation to call for unity. Don't you remember?"

With an interest Ridwan did not attempt to conceal he said, "Yes. But who is he?"

"Abd al-Rahim Pasha Isa!"

Ridwan thought a little before murmuring, "I saw him once from a distance."

"Well, this was the first time he noticed you."

There was an inquisitive look on Ridwan's face. Hilmi went on: "After you left, he asked me about you, requesting that I introduce you to him as soon as possible."

Ridwan smiled and then said, "Tell me everything you know."

Patting his friend's shoulder, Hilmi said, "He called me over and with his normal effervescence—by the way, he is very entertaining —asked, 'Who was that beauty conversing with you?' I told him you were a fellow student in the Law School, a longtime friend, and named so-and-so. With evident interest he asked, 'When will you introduce him to me?' Pretending not to understand the reason for his interest, I asked in turn, 'Why, Pasha?' He burst out with feigned anger—his lively wit occasionally carries him to such extremes—and said, 'To give him a lesson in religion, you son of a bitch.' I laughed till he put a hand over my mouth."

During the pause that followed they could hear the wind howling outside. A shutter banged against the wall. Then Ridwan spoke up: "I've heard a lot about him. Does he live up to his billing?"

"And more."

"But he's an old man!"

With inaudible laughter sparkling on his face, Hilmi Izzat said, "That's hardly significant, for he's an important man who is debonair and influential. It may well be that his age makes him more useful than if he were young."

Ridwan smiled again and asked, "Where does he live?"

"In a quiet villa in Helwan."

"It must be swarming with petitioners from all classes of society. . . ."

"We'll be his disciples. Why not? He's a senior statesman and we're novices."

Ridwan asked rather cautiously, "How about his wife and children?"

"What an ignoramus you are! He's single. He's never been married and has no taste for that kind of life. He was an only child and lives alone with his servants, like a branch torn from a tree. Once you've met him, you'll never be able to forget him."

They exchanged a long, smiling, conspiratorial look. Finally Hilmi said a bit anxiously, "Please ask me, 'When are we going to visit him?'"

Looking at the tea leaves in his glass, Ridwan repeated, "When are we going to visit him?"

9 ⤳

Located at the corner of al-Najat Street in Helwan, the home of Abd al-Rahim Pasha Isa was of exemplary simplicity and elegance. A one-story brown villa three meters high, it was entered through a gentlemen's parlor and was surrounded by a flower garden. The house, the street, and the neighborhood were refreshingly quiet. Seated on a bench by the gate were the doorman—a Nubian with a handsome face and a slender figure—and the chauffeur, an attractive youth with rosy cheeks.

Looking toward the parlor, Hilmi Izzat whispered to Ridwan, "The pasha has kept his promise. We're the only visitors today!"

Hilmi Izzat was known to the doorman and the chauffeur, who stood up to greet him politely. When he joked with them, they showed no embarrassment about bursting into laughter.

Although dry, the weather was bitterly cold. They went into a magnificent reception hall with a large picture of Sa'd Zaghlul in ceremonial attire on the center wall. Hilmi Izzat turned toward a mirror extending all the way to the ceiling on the right-hand wall to cast a long and searching look at his appearance. Ridwan was quick to join him, examining his own reflection with equal care. At last Hilmi Izzat said, "Two splendid moons in suits and fezzes. All those who love the Prophet's handsome appearance should pray for him."

They sat down beside each other on a gilded sofa with a stunning blue cover. After a few minutes they heard something behind the curtain hanging in the large doorway beneath the portrait of Sa'd Zaghlul. His heart beating with excitement, Ridwan turned to look that way. A man wearing a pleasant cologne and an elegant black suit appeared at once. Clean-shaven, slender, and rather tall, he had fine features marked by age, a dark brown complexion, and small languid eyes. His fez was slanted so far forward that it almost touched his eyebrows. Calm and dignified, he came toward them with slow steady steps. He had a reassuring but awe-inspiring impact on the young man's heart. Silent until he stopped before the two boys, who stood up to greet him, he examined them with a penetrating look that rested on Ridwan long enough to make the young man's eyelids

twitch. Then the pasha smiled suddenly. The attractive affability shining from his face lessened the distance between them until it was
indiscernible. Hilmi held out his hand, which the man took and held.
The pasha puckered up his lips and waited. Noticing what he had in
mind, Hilmi quickly presented his cheek, which the man kissed.

The pasha looked in Ridwan's direction and said in a delicate tone,
"Don't take offense, my son. This is my way of greeting people."

Ridwan held out his hand shyly. The man took it and laughingly
asked, "And your cheek?"

Ridwan blushed. Pointing to himself, Hilmi cried out, "Your Excellency, you need to negotiate that with his guardian."

Abd al-Rahim Pasha laughed and contented himself with a handshake. After inviting them to have a seat, he sat down in a large
armchair nearby. With a smile he said, "You have a damn fool for a
guardian, Ridwan—isn't that your name? Welcome! I noticed you
fraternizing with this naughty boy. I wanted to meet you, because I
was enchanted by your manners. And you've been good enough not
to begrudge me this pleasure."

"I'm happy to have the honor of meeting you, Your Excellency."

Turning a large gold ring around the finger of his left hand, the
man said, "Asking God's forgiveness, my son . . . don't use any titles
or honorific expressions. I don't like that at all. An endearing spirit
and a soul that's sincere and pure are what really interest me. This
business of 'Pasha' and 'Your Excellency,' well . . . we're all descended from Adam and Eve. The fact is that your manners pleased
me, and I wanted to invite you to my home. So you're most welcome.
You're Hilmi's classmate in Law School. Isn't that so?"

"Yes, sir. We've been classmates since Khalil Agha Elementary
School."

The man raised his white eyebrows in admiration and said, "Childhood friends!" Then, nodding his head, he continued: "Excellent, excellent! Perhaps like him you're from al-Husayn district?"

"Yes, sir. I was born in the home of my grandfather, Mr. Muhammad Iffat, in al-Gamaliya. I live now with my father in Palace of
Desire Alley."

The man said with a joy that was almost delirious, "Cairo's ancient
districts . . . grand places! Would you believe that I lived there for a
long time with my late father—in Birguwan. I was my parents' only
child and a rascal. I frequently got the boys together in a procession,
and we'd go from neighborhood to neighborhood, leaving a trail of
devastation behind us. Woe to any poor soul whom fate sent our

way. My father would get extremely angry and chase after me with
a stick. . . . Son, you said that your grandfather is Muhammad Iffat?"

Ridwan replied proudly, "Yes, Sir."

The pasha thought for a moment before saying, "I remember
seeing him once at the home of the deputy for al-Gamaliya. He's an
outstanding person and a sincere nationalist. He was almost nominated to run in the forthcoming elections, but his friend the former
deputy beat him out at the last minute. The recent coalition necessi-
tates a certain amount of goodwill so that our brothers in the Liberal
Constitutionalists can win a few seats. You're with Hilmi in Law
School. . . . Beautiful! Law is the master of all the other disciplines.
Its study requires true brilliance. To have a fine future, just strive to
do your best."

When he made these last remarks, his tone was encouraging and
even promising. Ridwan's heart pulsed with lofty and fervent aspi-
rations as he responded, "We've never failed an exam during our
academic careers."

"Bravo! That's the foundation. Then comes a position as a government attorney, to be followed by a judgeship. There will always be
someone to open closed doors for industrious young men. A judge's
life is an excellent one. Its mainstays are a lively intelligence and a
wakeful conscience. By the grace of God I was an honest judge. I left
the bench to enter politics. Patriotism occasionally forces us to give
up work we love. Yet even today you will find people who swear by
my fairness and integrity. Set your sights on being industrious and
fair. Then you'll be free to do what you want in your private life. Do
your duty and act as you please. If you fail to do your duty, people
will see only your faults. Haven't you observed the pleasure some
busybodies take in saying that such and such a minister has this
defect and that the poet so-and-so has the following disease? Fine . . .
but not all the victims of these slanders are cabinet ministers or poets.
So be a minister or a poet first, and then do what you want. Don't
overlook this lesson, Professor Ridwan."

Quoting the medieval poet al-Mutanabbi, Hilmi said mischievously, " 'The noble man is the one whose faults can be counted.'
Isn't that so, Your Excellency?"

Leaning his head toward his right shoulder, the man said, "Of
course. Glory to the One who alone is perfect. Man is very weak,
Ridwan. But he must be strong in the other parts of his life. Do you
understand? If you want, I'll tell you about the great men of our

nation. You won't find any without some failing. We'll discuss this at length and study the lessons we can derive from it, in order to have a life amply endowed with achievement and happiness."

Hilmi looked at Ridwan, saying, "Didn't I tell you that the pasha's friendship is a limitless treasure?"

Abd al-Rahim Isa told Ridwan, who could hardly keep his eyes off the man, "I love learning. I love life. I love people. My practice is to offer a young man a hand until he grows up. What is there in the world that's better than love? If we run into a legal problem, we must solve it together. When we think about the future, we shall do that together. If we feel like resting, we should rest together. I've never known a man as wise as Hasan Bey Imad. Today he's one of a select group of prominent diplomats. Never mind that he's one of my political enemies. When he concentrates on a subject, he masters it. Yet when music makes him ecstatic, he dances nude. The world can be a delightful place, if you're wise and broad-minded. Aren't you broad-minded, Ridwan?"

Hilmi Izzat immediately answered for him, "If he's not, we're prepared to broaden it for him."

The pasha's face beamed with a childlike smile that revealed his insatiable appetite for pleasure. He said, "This boy's a rapscallion, Ridwan! But what can I do? He's your childhood friend, the lucky fellow. I'm not the one who invented the saying 'Birds of a feather flock together.' You must be a rapscallion too. Tell me about yourself, Ridwan. Oh! You've let me say more than I intended while remaining silent—like an astute politician. Yes? Tell me, Ridwan. What do you love and what do you hate?"

Then the servant entered, carrying a tray. He was a clean-shaven youth like the doorman and the chauffeur. As they drank the water flavored with orange blossoms, the pasha asked, "Water like this is what the people of al-Husayn district drink, isn't it?"

Ridwan smilingly murmured, "Yes, sir."

Nodding his head ecstatically, the pasha said, "People of al-Husayn, help us!"

They all laughed. Even the servant smiled as he left the chamber. Then the pasha resumed his questioning: "What do you love? What do you hate? Speak frankly, Ridwan. Let me make it easier for you to answer. Are you interested in politics?"

Hilmi Izzat said, "We're both members of the student committee."

"This is the first reason for us to be close. Do you like literature?"

Hilmi Izzat replied, "He's fond of Shawqi, Hafiz, and al-Manfaluti."

The pasha chided him, "You be still. Brother, I want to hear his voice."

They laughed. Smiling, Ridwan said, "I could die for Shawqi, Hafiz, and al-Manfaluti."

" 'I could die for' ... What an expression! You only hear it in al-Gamaliya. Is the name of your district derived from *gamal*, or beauty, Ridwan? You must be a fan of verses like 'Silver gold,' 'In the still of the night,' 'Who is it?' and 'Removing one branch, he lays down another....' My God, my God! This is another reason for us to be close friends, beautiful Gamaliya. Do you like singing?"

"He adores ..."

"You be still."

They all laughed once more. Ridwan said, "Umm Kalthoum."

"Excellent. I may prefer the older style of singing, but all singing's beautiful. I love both 'the profound and the witty' as that medieval skeptic al-Ma'arri put it. Or, I could die for it, as you would say, sir. Very fine. What a delightful evening!"

The telephone rang, and the pasha went to answer it. Putting the receiver to his ear, he said, "Hello.... Greetings, Your Excellency the pasha.... What's so amazing about that? Didn't Isma'il Sidqy himself sit on a negotiating team once as one of the nation's leaders? ... I told the leader my candid opinion. It's also that of other Wafdists like Mahir and al-Nuqrashi.... I'm sorry, Pasha. I can't. I haven't forgotten that King Fuad once opposed my promotion. He's the last person to talk about ethics. In any case I'll see you at the club tomorrow. Goodbye, Pasha."

The man returned with a frown but on seeing Ridwan's face almost immediately cheered up and continued their conversation: "Yes, Mr. Ridwan. We've gotten acquainted, and it's been beautiful. I advise you to be industrious. I advise you not to lose sight of your duty or your ideals. Now let's talk about music and having a good time."

Ridwan looked at his watch. The pasha appeared alarmed and said, "Anything but that! The clock is an enemy of friendly reunions."

Ridwan stammered rather uneasily, "But we're late, Your Honor the pasha."

"Late! Do you mean late for me, at my age? You're mistaken, son. I still love to enjoy talk, beauty, and singing until one in the morning. We haven't begun the soiree yet. We've only recited the preliminary blessing: In the name of God the compassionate, the merciful. Don't object. The automobile is at your command until morning. I've heard that you stay out all night when you're studying for an examination. So let's study together. Why not? I'd find it delightful to review an introduction to general law or some Islamic law. By the way, who teaches you Islamic Shari'a law? Shaykh Ibrahim Nadim—may God grant him a good evening—was a very sporting fellow. Don't be astonished! One day we'll write the history of all the important men of the age. You must understand everything. Our night will be a loving, friendly one. Tell me, Hilmi, what's the most appropriate drink for a night like this?"

Hilmi replied confidently, "Whiskey and soda with grilled meat."

The pasha laughed and asked, "Scoundrel, how can you drink grilled meat?"

Every Thursday after lunch Khadija's entire family gathered in a fashion that scarcely ever changed. Assembled in the sitting room were the father, Ibrahim Shawkat, and the two sons, Abd al-Muni'm and Ahmad. It was rare for Khadija to be without some project, and she embroidered on a tablecloth while she sat with them. After a prolonged and heroic struggle against time, Ibrahim Shawkat had finally begun to show his age. His hair was turning white, and he looked a little bloated. Except for this, his health was still enviably good.

Smoking a cigarette, he took his place between his sons with calm assurance. His protruding eyes had their customary look of languid indifference. The two boys kept up a stream of conversation with each other, their father, or their mother, who participated without looking up from her work. She seemed a massive chunk of flesh. There was nothing in the domestic atmosphere to ruffle Khadija's peace of mind. Since the death of her mother-in-law, there had been no one to challenge her control over her home. She performed her chores with unflagging zeal. As plumpness was the key to her beauty, she took extraordinary care to maintain her weight. She attempted to impose her guidance on everyone, especially her husband and their two sons. The man had given in, but Abd al-Muni'm and Ahmad each went his own way, appealing to her love to free themselves from her domination. Some years before she had succeeded in convincing her husband to respect the precepts of Islam. The man had begun praying and fasting and had become accustomed to this. Abd al-Muni'm and Ahmad had grown up with these observances, but for the past two years Ahmad had ceased to perform his religious duties. He would dodge his mother's attempts to interrogate him or excuse himself on some pretext or other.

Ibrahim Shawkat loved and admired his sons greatly. He seized every opportunity to praise the string of successes that had brought Abd al-Muni'm to Law School and Ahmad to the final stage of his secondary education. Khadija also boasted about these achievements, saying, "This is all the fruit of my concern. If I had left the matter up to you, neither of them would have amounted to anything."

It had recently been established that, from want of practice, Khadija had forgotten how to read and write, and this discovery had made her the target of Ibrahim's jests. Finally her sons had suggested that they should teach her what she had forgotten in order to repay her for the helping hand she boasted of giving their education. Their proposal had made her a little angry but had also made her laugh a lot. She summed up her feelings about the situation in one sentence: "A woman does not need to read or write unless she's exchanging letters with a lover."

She appeared to be happy and content with her family, although she did not think that Abd al-Muni'm and Ahmad ate enough. Their thinness enraged her, and she said disapprovingly, "I've told you a thousand times to use chamomile to improve your appetites. You must eat properly. Don't you see how well your father eats?"

Looking at their father, the two young men smiled. Ibrahim said, "Why don't you use yourself as the example? You eat like a food grinder."

Smiling, she replied, "I'll let them decide which of us to imitate."

Ibrahim protested, "Lady, your envious eye has injured me. That's why the dentist suggested I have my teeth extracted."

With a tender look in her eyes, she said, "Don't be upset. Once they're out, you won't have any more problems or pain, God willing."

Ahmad told her, "Our neighbor in the second-floor apartment would like to postpone payment of his rent until next month. He met me on the stairs and made that request."

Frowning at him, she asked, "What did you tell him?"

"I promised I'd speak to my father."

"And did you speak to your father?"

"I'm speaking to you now."

"We don't share the apartment with him. Why should he share our money? If we give him a break, the tenant in the first-floor apartment will follow his lead. You don't know what people are like. Don't get involved in things that don't concern you."

Glancing at his father, Ahmad asked, "What do you think, Papa?"

Ibrahim Shawkat smiled and said, "Spare me the headache. Talk to your mother. . . ."

Ahmad addressed his mother again: "If we're lenient with a man in difficult circumstances, we won't go hungry."

Khadija said resentfully, "His wife has already spoken to me, and I agreed to let them pay later. So don't trouble your mind about it.

But I explained to her that paying the rent is as obligatory as paying for food and drink. Is there anything wrong in that? I'm occasionally criticized for not making friends with women in the neighborhood, but when you know people the way I do, you praise God for solitude."

With a wink of his eye Ahmad asked, "Are we better than other people?"

Scowling, Khadija replied, "Yes ... unless you know something about yourself that would make me think otherwise."

Abd al-Muni'm commented, "In his opinion, he's the best possible man, and his opinion is the only one that counts. All wisdom has been granted to him."

Khadija said sarcastically, "It's also his opinion that tenants should be able to lease apartments without paying the rent."

Laughing, Abd al-Muni'm said, "He's not convinced that some people should have absolute ownership rights to houses."

Shaking her head, Khadija remarked, "I pity such worthless ideas."

Ahmad glared at his brother, but Abd al-Muni'm shrugged his shoulders scornfully and said, "Straighten your mind out before you get angry."

Ahmad protested, "It would be better if we didn't try to debate each other."

"Right. Wait till you grow up."

"You're only a year older than me. No more than that...."

"A person a day older than you is a year wiser."

"I don't believe in that saying."

"Listen, there's only one thing that concerns me. It's for you to start praying with me again."

Khadija nodded her head sadly as she said, "Your brother's right. Usually when people grow up they grow wiser, but you ... I seek refuge with God from you. Even your father prays and fasts. How could you have done this to yourself? I worry about it night and day."

In a powerful and profusely self-confident voice Abd al-Muni'm said, "To be blunt, his mind needs a thorough cleansing."

"It's just that ..."

"Listen, Mother. This young man has no religion. This is what I've begun to believe."

Ahmad waved his hand as if angered and asked loudly, "Where do you get the right to judge a man's heart?"

"Your acts betray your secret thoughts." Then, hiding a smile, he added, "Enemy of God!"

Without abandoning his assured composure, Ibrahim Shawkat said, "Don't make false accusations against your brother."

Looking at Ahmad but addressing Abd al-Muni'm, Khadija said, "Don't deprive your brother of the dearest thing a person can have. How could he be anything but a Believer? If only his mother's relatives wore turbans, they would be recognized as religious scholars. His maternal great-grandfather had a career in religion. When I was growing up everyone around me prayed devoutly and served God, as if we were living in a mosque."

Ahmad said sarcastically, "Like Uncle Yasin!"

A laugh escaped from Ibrahim Shawkat. Pretending to be annoyed, Khadija retorted, "Speak respectfully about your uncle. What's wrong with him? His heart is filled with belief, and our Lord guides him. Look at your grandfather and grandmother."

"And Uncle Kamal?"

"Your uncle Kamal is watched over by al-Husayn. You don't know anything."

"Some people don't know anything. . . ."

Abd al-Muni'm asked defiantly, "Even if everyone else neglected their religion, would that be any excuse for you?"

Ahmad replied calmly, "In any case, you shouldn't worry about it. You won't ever be held responsible for my sins."

Then Ibrahim Shawkat said, "Stop your quarreling. I wish you could be like your cousin Ridwan."

Khadija stared at him disapprovingly. It was more than she could bear that anyone would prefer Ridwan to her sons. To explain himself, Ibrahim said, "That young man has contacts with top politicians. He's bright and seems guaranteed a glorious future."

Khadija said furiously, "I don't agree with you. Ridwan's an unlucky boy, like anyone else who has been deprived of his mother's care. The fact is that 'Mrs.' Zanuba thinks nothing of him. I'm not deceived by her good treatment of him. It's simply a political stratagem like those of the English. For this reason the poor boy has no real home. He spends most of his time away from the apartment. And his contacts with important men are meaningless. He's a student in the same year as Abd al-Muni'm. What's the point of this weighty remark? You don't know how to pick your examples."

Ibrahim gave her a look, as if to say, "It's impossible for you ever to agree with me." Then he continued with his explanation: "Things aren't the same for young people today. Politics has changed everything. Each important figure surrounds himself with young protégés. An ambitious youth wishing to make his way in the world must find a patron he can rely on. Your father's status is based on his close ties to important men."

Khadija said haughtily, "My father is sought out by people eager to get to know him. He doesn't curry favor with people. As for politics, it doesn't concern my boys. If they had known their uncle who sacrificed his life for the nation, they would learn for themselves what I mean. It's 'Long live so-and-so' or 'Down with someone else,' while people's sons are perishing. If Fahmy had lived, he would be one of the greatest judges today."

Abd al-Muni'm said, "Everyone has to find his own way. We won't imitate anyone. If we wanted to be like Ridwan, we could be."

Khadija said, "That's right!"

Ibrahim told Abd al-Muni'm, "You're just like your mother . . . no difference at all between you."

There was a knock on the door and the servant came to announce the tenant from the first floor. As she started to rise, Khadija said, "I wonder what she wants. . . . If she wishes to put off paying her rent, it will take all the policemen from the Gamaliya station to separate us."

The Muski was very congested. Already teeming with more than its normal pedestrian traffic, it was being flooded by currents of human beings from al-Ataba. The April sun cast fiery rays from a cloudless sky, and Abd al-Muni'm and Ahmad were sweating profusely as they made their way through the throngs with more than a little effort.

Taking his brother's arm, Ahmad said, "Tell me what you feel."

Abd al-Muni'm thought a little and then replied, "I don't know. Death is always terrifying, especially a king's death. The funeral procession was more crowded than any I'd seen before. Since I didn't witness Sa'd Zaghlul's funeral, I can't compare the two. But it seems to me that most of the onlookers were mourning. Some of the women were weeping. We Egyptians are an emotional people."

"But I'm asking about your own feelings."

Abd al-Muni'm thought again while trying to keep from bumping into people. Finally he said, "I didn't love him. None of us did. So I wasn't sad. Yet I wasn't happy either. I followed the bier without feeling anything one way or the other about the man, but the thought of such a mighty person in a coffin affected me. A sight like that was bound to move me. God's sovereignty is universal. He is alive and eternal. I wish people would realize that. If the king had died before the political situation changed, great multitudes would have rejoiced. And you—what are your feelings?"

Smiling, Ahmad said, "I have no love for tyrants, no matter what the political situation."

"That's excellent. But what about the sight of death?"

"I don't care for sick romanticism."

Abd al-Muni'm asked angrily, "Then were you pleased?"

"I hope to live long enough to see the world cleansed of all tyrants, no matter what the title or description."

They were silent for a time, fatigue having gotten the best of them. Then Ahmad asked, "What happens next?"

With the confident tone for which he was known, Abd al-Muni'm answered, "Faruq is just a boy. He's not as crafty or as vindictive as his father. If all goes well, with successful negotiations and a return of the Wafd to power, things will calm down and the era of conspiracies will vanish. It seems that the future will be good."

"And the English?"

"If the negotiations are successful, they will become our friends and, consequently, the alliance between the palace and the English against the Egyptian people will be terminated. Then the king will be forced to respect the constitution."

"The Wafd Party is better than the other ones."

"No doubt ... but it hasn't governed long enough to demonstrate its abilities fully. Experience will soon reveal its true potential. I agree it's better than the others, but our ambitions don't stop there."

"Of course not! I believe that rule by the Wafd Party is a good starting point for much greater developments. That's all there is to it. But will we really reach an agreement with the English?"

"If there isn't an agreement, then we'll return to a situation like that under Sidqy. Our nation has an inexhaustible supply of traitors. Their main task is always to discipline the Wafdists whenever we say no to the English. They are certainly watching for another opportunity, even if they're aligned with the nationalists at present. Sidqy, Muhammad Mahmud, and men like them are just waiting. That's the tragedy."

On reaching New Street they suddenly found themselves facing their grandfather, Ahmad Abd al-Jawad, who was heading toward the Goldsmiths Bazaar. They went over and greeted him respectfully.

He smiled and asked, "From where, to where?"

Abd al-Muni'm answered, "We were watching the funeral of King Fuad."

The smile still on his lips, the man said, "Thank you for your thoughtful condolences."

After shaking hands, they went their separate ways. Ahmad watched for a moment as his grandfather walked off. Then he said, "Our grandfather's charming and elegant. His cologne has a pleasant fragrance."

"Mother recounts amazing tales about his tyranny."

"I don't think he's a tyrant. That's incredible."

Abd al-Muni'm laughed and said, "Even King Fuad himself by the end of his days seemed pleasant and charming." They both laughed and proceeded on to Ahmad Abduh's coffeehouse.

In the room opposite the fountain, Ahmad saw a shaykh with a long beard and penetrating eyes. He sat in the center of a group of young men, who watched him attentively. Ahmad stopped and told his brother, "Your friend Shaykh Ali al-Manufi.... 'The earth casts out its burdens' [Qur'an, 99:2]. So I must leave you here."

Abd al-Muni'm invited him: "Come sit with us. I'd love for you to get to know him and to hear him speak. Dispute with him as much as you want. Many of the fellows around him are students from the University."

Freeing his arm from his brother's, Ahmad said, "No, sir. I almost got into a fight with him once. I don't like fanatics. Goodbye."

Abd al-Muni'm stared at him critically and said sharply, "Goodbye. May our Lord guide you." Then he joined the assembly presided over by Shaykh Ali al-Manufi, head of al-Husayn Primary School. The man stood up to greet him, and the young people sitting there also rose and embraced him. When the shaykh sat down, they all resumed their seats. Examining Abd al-Muni'm with piercing eyes, the shaykh commented, "We didn't see you yesterday."

"Studying."

"Industry is an acceptable excuse. Why did your brother leave you to go off by himself?"

Abd al-Muni'm smiled but did not reply. Shaykh Ali al-Manufi remarked, "Our Lord is the guide. Don't wonder about him. Our founder, Hasan al-Banna, encountered many skeptics who today are some of his sincerest disciples. When God wants to guide a people, Satan has no power over them. We are God's soldiers, spreading His light and combating His enemies. More than others, we have given our spirits to Him. Soldiers of God, how happy you are!"

One of the congregation observed, "But the kingdom of Satan is large."

Shaykh Ali al-Manufi scolded, "Look at this fellow who's afraid of Satan's world when he's in God's presence.... What shall we say to him? We are with God, and God is with us. So what should we fear? What other soldiers on earth enjoy your power? What weapon is more effective than yours? The English, French, Germans, and Italians rely primarily on their material culture, but you rely on true belief. Belief can dent steel. Faith is stronger than any other force on earth. Fill your pure hearts with belief, and the world belongs to you."

Another young man commented, "We believe, but we're a weak nation."

The shaykh clenched his fist as he cried out, "If you feel weak, then your faith has decreased without your being aware of it. Faith creates power and induces it. Bombs are made by hands like yours.

They are the fruit of power, not its cause. How did the Prophet conquer the whole Arabian peninsula? How did the Arabs conquer the entire world?"

Abd al-Muni'm answered fervently, "Faith and belief."

Then someone else asked, "But how can the English be so powerful? They're not Believers."

The shaykh smiled and ran his fingers through his beard as he said, "Anyone strong believes in something. They believe in their nation and in 'progress.' But faith in God is superior to any other kind of belief. It's only fitting that people who believe in God should be stronger than those believing in the physical world. We Muslims have at our disposal a buried treasure. We must extract it. We need to revive Islam and to make it as good as new. We call ourselves Muslims, but we must prove it by our deeds. God blessed us with His Book, but we have ignored it. This has brought down humiliation upon us. So let us return to the Book. This is our motto: a return to the Qur'an. That was what our leader called for at the beginning in Isma'iliya, and from that time on his message has been sinking deep into people's spirits, winning over villages and hamlets, filling every heart."

"But wouldn't it be wise for us to stay out of politics?"

"Our religion consists of a creed, a code of law, and a political system. God is far too merciful to have left the most troublesome aspects of human affairs devoid of any regulation or guidance from Him. Actually, that's the subject of our lesson for tonight. . . ."

The shaykh was ebullient. His approach was to affirm some truth, which they would then discuss, as disciples asked questions and he replied. Most of his remarks centered on quotations from the Qur'an and from the collections of hadith reports of the Prophet's words and deeds. He spoke as if preaching, indeed preaching to all the patrons of the coffeehouse.

From his seat at the far end of the room, where he was drinking green tea, Ahmad could hear the shaykh. There was a sarcastic smile on the young man's lips, as he incredulously attempted to measure the gulf separating him from this zealous group. Angry and scornful, he grew so irritated that he thought of asking the shaykh to lower his voice and to stop disturbing the other patrons. But he abandoned that idea as soon as he remembered his brother was one of the shaykh's disciples. Finally, he saw no alternative to leaving the coffeehouse, rose resentfully, and left.

Abd al-Muni'm returned to Sugar Street around eight. The fury of the weather had abated, making for a pleasant evening with some of the freshness of spring. The lesson was still ringing in his head and heart, but he felt mentally and physically exhausted. As he crossed the courtyard in the darkness, heading for the stairway, the door of the first-floor apartment opened. By the light escaping from inside he saw a figure slip out, close the door, and precede him up the stairs. His heart pounded, and his blood pulsed through him like tiny insects inflamed by hot weather. Even in the shadows he could see her waiting for him at the first landing. She glanced at him as he stared up at her, not averting his gaze.

It was amazingly easy for young people to deceive their parents. This young girl had stepped out of her apartment on the pretext of visiting the neighbors. And she would visit them, but only after participating in a dangerous flirtation on the dark landing. He found that his head was empty of ideas, for all the thoughts he had been wrestling with had disappeared like a puff of smoke. He was transfixed by a single desire—to satisfy the craving that would not leave his nerves and limbs alone. His sincere faith seemed to have fled in anger or to have taken refuge deep inside him, where it snarled resentfully, although the sound of its complaints was drowned out by the hissing of lust's flames.

Was she not his girl? Of course she was. The alcoves of the courtyard, the stairwell, and the corner of the roof overlooking Sugar Street could all testify to this. No doubt she had been watching for him to return so that she could meet him at just the right moment. She had taken all this trouble for his sake. He hurried on cautiously until he stood facing her on the landing. There was hardly any distance separating them. The fragrance of her hair tantalized him, and her breath tickled his neck.

He gently caressed her shoulder as he whispered, "Let's go to the second landing. It's safer than here."

She made no reply but headed up the steps, and he cautiously followed behind. At the second landing, halfway between the two floors, she stopped, leaning her back against the wall, and he stood right in front of her. When he put his arms around her, she resisted for a second out of force of habit before warming to his embrace.

"Darling. . . ."

"I was waiting for you at the window. Mother has been busy getting ready for the Shamm al-Nasim holiday."

"Best wishes for our spring festival. Now let me taste spring on your lips."

Their lips met in a long, famished kiss. Then she asked, "Where were you?"

With wrenching suddenness he remembered the lesson on politics in Islam. But he answered, "With some friends at the coffeehouse."

In a tone of protest she said, "The coffeehouse! When there's only a month before the examination?"

"I know what I have to do to prepare for it. . . . But now I'll kiss you again to punish you for thinking ill of me."

"Your voice is too loud. Have you forgotten where we are?"

"We're in our home, in our room. The landing is our room!"

"This afternoon, when I was going to my aunt's, I glanced up in hopes of seeing you at the window, but your mother was looking down at the alley, and our eyes met. I trembled with fear."

"What were you afraid of?"

"I imagined that she knew I was looking for you and that she had discovered my secret."

"You mean 'our secret.' It's the same bond that links both of us together. Aren't we now a single entity?"

Racked by unruly desire, he hugged her violently to his chest as if, in his desperate capitulation to lust, he was attempting to flee the faint voices of protest lodged deep inside him. Blazing fires seared him. He was seized by a force capable of dissolving the two of them into a single swirling vortex.

The silence was broken by a sigh and then by heavy breathing. He finally became aware that he and she were separate beings and that the darkness sheltered two figures. Then he heard her ask shyly in a gentle whisper, "Shall we meet tomorrow?"

With a resentment he did his best to conceal, he replied, "Yes . . . yes. You'll find out when. . . ."

"Tell me now."

As his annoyance grew increasingly hard to bear, he said, "I don't know when I'll have time tomorrow."

"Why not?"

"Goodbye for now. I heard a sound."

"No! There wasn't any sound."

"Nobody should find us like this."

He patted her shoulder as if it were a dirty rag and freed himself from her arms with affected tenderness. Then he quickly climbed the stairs. His parents were in the sitting room listening to the radio. The door of the study was closed, but the light shining through its little window indicated that Ahmad was studying. Saying, "Good evening," to his parents, he went to the bedroom to remove his clothes, bathe, and cleanse himself in the manner prescribed by Islam, before returning to his room to pray. Afterward he sat cross-legged on the prayer rug and lost himself in deep meditation. There was a sad look to his eyes, his breast was aflame with grief, and he felt like crying. He prayed that his Lord would come to his aid to help him combat temptation and to drive Satan away, that Satan he encountered in the shape of a girl who inspired a raging lust in him.

His mind always said, "No," but his heart, "Yes." The fearful struggle he experienced invariably ended with defeat and regret. Every day was a test and every test an experience of hell. When would this torment end? His entire spiritual effort was threatened with ruin, as though he were building castles in the sky. Sinking into the mud, he could not find any secure footing. He wished his remorse could bring back the past hour.

13 ❧

In Ghamra, Ahmad Ibrahim Shawkat finally found his way to the building of *al-Insan al-Jadid* (The New Man) magazine. Situated halfway between streetcar stops, the structure had two stories and a basement. From the wash hanging on the balcony, he realized at once that the top floor was an apartment. There was a sign with the magazine's name on the door downstairs. The basement was the printshop, for he could see its machines through the bars of the windows. He climbed the four steps and asked the first person he met— a worker carrying proofs—for Mr. Adli Karim, the magazine's editor. The pressman pointed to the end of an unfurnished hall and a closed door with a sign reading: "Editor in Chief." Ahmad walked that way, thinking he might see a receptionist, but reached the door without finding one. After a moment's hesitation he knocked gently. Then he heard a voice inside say, "Come in." Ahmad opened the door and entered. From the far end of the room, two wide eyes stared at him questioningly from beneath bushy white eyebrows.

Closing the door behind him, he said apologetically, "Excuse me. One minute. . . ."

The man replied gently, "Yes. . . ."

Ahmad went up to the desk, which was stacked with books and papers, and greeted the gentleman, who rose to welcome him. When the editor sat down again, he invited Ahmad to have a seat. The young man felt relief and pride at being able to view the distinguished master from whose magazine and books he had gained so much enlightenment during the past three years. Ahmad gazed at the pale face, which seemed even whiter because of the man's white hair. Age had left its mark on this visage. The only remaining traces of youth were deep eyes that sparkled with a penetrating gleam. This was his master, or his "spiritual father," as Ahmad called him. Now the young man was in the chamber of inspiration with its walls hidden behind bookshelves that stretched all the way to the ceiling.

The editor said curiously, "You're welcome. . . ."

Ahmad answered suavely, "I've come to pay for my subscription."

Reassured by the favorable impression his words had made, he added, "And I'd like to find out what happened to the article I sent the magazine two weeks ago."

Mr. Adli Karim smiled as he inquired, "What is your name?"

"Ahmad Ibrahim Shawkat."

The editor frowned as he tried to place the name and then said, "I remember you. You were the first subscriber to my magazine. Yes. And you brought three other ones. Isn't that so? I remember the name Shawkat. I think I sent you a letter of thanks on behalf of the magazine."

This pleasant memory made him feel even more at home, and Ahmad said, "The letter I received referred to me as 'the magazine's first friend.'"

"That's true. *The New Man* is devoted to principle and needs committed friends if it is to compete with all the picture magazines and the journals controlled by special interests. You are a friend of the magazine and most welcome. But haven't you honored us with a visit before?"

"Of course not. I only got my baccalaureate this month."

Adli Karim laughed and said, "You assume a person must have the baccalaureate to visit the magazine?"

Ahmad smiled uneasily and replied, "Certainly not. I mean I was young."

The editor commented seriously, "It's not right for a reader of *The New Man* to judge a person by his age. In our country there are men over sixty who have youthful minds and young people in the spring of life with a mentality as antiquated as if they had lived a thousand years or more. This is the malady of the East." Then he asked in a gentler tone, "Have you sent us other articles before?"

"Three that were ignored and then this last article, which I was hoping you would print."

"What's it about? Forgive me, but I receive dozens of articles every day."

"Le Bon's theories of education and my comments on them."

"In any case, if you look for it in the adjoining room where the correspondence is handled, you'll discover its fate."

Ahmad started to rise, but Mr. Adli gestured for him to remain seated and said, "The magazine's more or less on vacation today. I hope you'll stay and talk a little."

Ahmad murmured with profound gratitude, "I'd be delighted, sir."

"You said you got the baccalaureate this year. How old are you?"

"Sixteen."

"Precocious. Excellent. Is the magazine widely read in the secondary schools?"

"No, unfortunately not."

"I realize that. Most of our readers are at the University. In Egypt, reading's considered a cheap entertainment. We won't develop until we accept that reading is a vital necessity." After a pause he asked, "What's the attitude of secondary-school students?"

Ahmad looked at him inquisitively, as if wanting clarification of the question, and the man said, "I'm asking about their political affiliation, since that's more obvious than other things."

"The overwhelming majority are Wafdists."

"But is there any talk of the new movements?"

"Young Egypt—Misr al-Fatat? It's insignificant. You could count its supporters on your fingers. The other parties have no followers except for relatives of the leaders. Then there is a minority that's not interested in any of the parties. Some, and I'm among them, prefer the Wafd to the others but hope for a more perfect one."

With satisfaction the man said, "This is what I wanted to know. The Wafd is the people's party and represents an important and natural step in our development. The National Party is Turkish, religious, and reactionary. The Wafd Party has crystallized and purified Egyptian nationalism. It has also been a school for nationalism and democracy. But the point is that the nation is not and must not be content with this school. We want a further stage of development. We desire a school for socialism. Independence is not the ultimate goal. It's a way to obtain the people's constitutional, economic, and human rights."

Ahmad cried out enthusiastically, "What a fine statement!"

"But the Wafd must be the starting point. Young Egypt is a criminal, reactionary, Fascist movement. It's just as dangerous as the reactionary religious groups. It's nothing more than an echo of German and Italian militarism, worshipping power, demanding dictatorial control, and disparaging human values and human dignity. Like cholera and typhoid, reactionary movements are endemic to this region and need to be eradicated."

Ahmad said zealously, "We in the *New Man* group believe this firmly."

The editor nodded his large head sorrowfully and said, "That's why the magazine is a target for reactionaries of every stripe. They accuse me of corrupting the young."

"Just as they once denounced Socrates."

With a gratified smile, Mr. Adli Karim said, "What's your goal? I mean, which college of the University are you heading for?"

"Arts."

The editor sat up straight and remarked, "Literature is one of the greatest tools of liberation, but it can also be employed for reactionary ends. So watch your step. From the mosque university of al-Azhar and from the Dar al-Ulum teachers college have come a sickening type of literature that has left generations of Egyptians with rigid minds and broken spirits. But no matter what, science is the foundation of modern life. . . . Don't be surprised that a man who is considered a literary figure should tell you this frankly. We must study the sciences and absorb the scientific mentality. A person who doesn't know science is not a citizen of the twentieth century, even if he is a genius. Artists too must learn their share of science. It's no longer just for scientists. Yes, the responsibility for comprehensive and profound knowledge of the field as well as for research and discoveries in it belongs to the scientists, but every cultured person must illuminate himself with its light, embrace its principles and procedures, and use its style. Science must take the place that prophecy and religion had in the ancient world."

Ahmad endorsed his master's statement: "That's why the message of *The New Man* is the development of a society based on science."

Adli Karim replied with interest, "Yes. Each of us must do his part, even if he finds himself alone in the arena."

Ahmad nodded his head, and the other man continued: "Study literature as much as you want, but pay more attention to your own intellectual development than to the selections you're asked to memorize. And don't forget modern science. In addition to Shakespeare and Schopenhauer, your library must contain Comte, Darwin, Freud, Marx, and Engels. Be as zealous about this as if you were religious, and remember that each age has its prophets. The prophets of this era are the scientists."

The editor's smile indicated that the conversation was coming to an end. Ahmad rose and stretched out his hand. He said goodbye and left the room, feeling joyously alive. Outside, in the hall, remembering his subscription and the article, he looked for the other room, knocked on the door to announce himself, and entered. He saw that there were three desks in the room. Two were empty, and a girl was sitting at the third. He had not been expecting this and stopped in his tracks. He looked at her inquisitively and apprehensively. She was around twenty, with a dark brown complexion, black eyes, and black hair. There was a resolute look about her delicate nose, pointed chin, and thin lips, but that did not detract from her beauty.

Scrutinizing him, she asked, "Yes?"

To justify his presence he said, "My subscription." He paid the amount and took the receipt. Then, overcoming his nervousness, he said, "I sent an article to the magazine, and Mr. Adli Karim told me it would be here."

She invited him to have a seat in front of her desk and asked, "The title of the article, please?"

Still uncomfortable about dealing with this girl, he replied, "Education According to Lè Bon."

She opened a file and flipped through some papers until she pulled out the essay. When Ahmad glimpsed his handwriting, his heart pounded. From where he sat he tried to read the red notation upon it, but she saved him the trouble, remarking, "The note says, 'To be summarized and published in the section for readers' letters.' "

Ahmad was disappointed. He looked at her for a few moments without saying anything. Then he asked, "In which issue?"

"The next one."

After some hesitation he asked, "Who will summarize it?"

"I will."

He felt annoyed but asked, "Will it bear my name?"

She laughed and answered, "Naturally. There is usually a statement to the effect that we have received a letter from the writer ..." She looked at the signature on the article and continued: "Ahmad Ibrahim Shawkat. Then we provide a full summary of your ideas."

He hesitated a little before saying, "I would have preferred for you to publish it in its entirety."

Smiling, she replied, "Next time, God willing."

He looked at her silently and asked, "Are you an employee here?"

"As you can see!"

He was tempted to ask what her qualifications for the position were, but his courage failed him at the last moment. So he inquired, "What is your name, please, so I can ask for you by telephone, if I need to."

"Sawsan Hammad."

"Thank you very much."

He stood up and bade her farewell with a wave of his hand. Before departing, he turned back to say, "Please summarize it carefully."

Without looking up she replied, "I know my job."

Regretting his words, he left the room.

Kamal was in his study wearing a loose-fitting house shirt when Umm Hanafi came to tell him, "Mr. Fuad al-Hamzawi is with my master." He rose and hurried downstairs.

So Fuad had returned to Cairo after a year's absence. The distinguished public prosecutor from Qena district was home again. The friendship and affection that filled Kamal's heart were marred by an uncomfortable feeling. His relationship with Fuad was still marked by a struggle between loving affection and jealous aversion. No matter how hard he tried to elevate himself intellectually, his instincts always forced him back down to the petty mundane level. As he descended the stairs he sensed that this visit would awaken happy memories but also rub the scabs off wounds that had almost healed. When he passed through the sitting room, where the coffee hour—consisting of his mother, Aisha, and Na'ima—was in session, he heard his mother whisper, "He'll ask for Na'ima's hand."

Sensing his presence, she turned to tell him, "Your friend's inside. He's so charming. . . . He wanted to kiss my hand, but I wouldn't let him."

Kamal found his father sitting cross-legged on the sofa and Fuad in a chair opposite. The old friends shook hands, and Kamal said, "Praise God for your safe return. Welcome, welcome! Are you on vacation?"

Smiling, al-Sayyid Ahmad answered, "No, he's been transferred to Cairo. He's finally been moved back here after a lengthy absence in Upper Egypt."

Sitting down on the sofa, Kamal said, "Congratulations! Now we hope to see you more often."

Fuad answered, "Naturally. As of the first of next month we'll be living in al-Abbasiya. We've leased an apartment near the Wayliya police station."

Fuad's appearance had not changed much, but he looked healthier. He had filled out, his complexion was rosier, and his eyes still had the familiar sparkle of intelligence.

Al-Sayyid Ahmad asked the young man, "How is your father? I haven't seen him for a week."

"His health isn't as good as we'd wish. He's still sad about leaving the shop. But hopefully the person he found to take his place is doing a good job."

Al-Sayyid Ahmad laughed and said, "The shop now requires my constant attention. Your father, may God grant him a complete recovery and good health, took care of everything."

Fuad sat up and placed one leg over the other. This gesture attracted Kamal's attention and distressed him, for he considered it disrespectful to his father, even though al-Sayyid Ahmad gave no sign of having noticed. Was this how things were developing? Yes, Fuad was a prominent member of the judicial service, but had he forgotten who it was who sat facing him? Lord, as if that was not enough, he took out a cigarette case and offered it to al-Sayyid Ahmad, who graciously declined. Fuad's judicial career had really made him forget himself, but it was sad that his forgetfulness should extend to the person who had financed his career. Fuad's grateful memories seemed to have vanished in thin air as quickly as the smoke from his fancy cigarette. His gestures appeared quite natural and unaffected, for he was an executive who had grown accustomed to taking charge.

Al-Sayyid Ahmad told Kamal, "Congratulate him on his promotion too."

Smiling, Kamal said, "Congratulations! That's great. I hope I'll soon be able to offer you my best wishes for being named a judge."

Fuad answered, "That's the next step, God willing."

Once a judge he might allow himself to piss in front of the man who sat before him now. The grade-school teacher would remain just that. Kamal would have to content himself with his bushy mustache and the tons of culture weighing down his head.

Looking at Fuad with great interest, al-Sayyid Ahmad inquired, "How is the political situation?"

Fuad answered with satisfaction, "The miracle has happened! A treaty has been signed in London. I could not believe my ears when I heard the radio announce Egypt's independence and the termination of the four restrictions Britain had placed on our independence in the last treaty. Who would have anticipated this?"

"Then you're happy with the treaty?"

Nodding his head as though personally responsible for the decision, Fuad replied, "On the whole, yes. Some oppose it for legitimate

reasons and others do so in bad faith. When we consider the circumstances in which we find ourselves and remember that despite the
bitterness of the Sidqy era our people endured it without rebelling
against him, we must consider the treaty a positive step. It abolishes
the 'reserved points' limiting Egyptian independence, prepares the
way for an end to the capitulations granting special privileges to
foreigners, limits the future presence of foreign troops, and restricts
them to a certain region. Without any doubt, it's a great step forward."

Al-Sayyid Ahmad was more enthusiastic and less knowledgeable
about the treaty than Fuad. He would have liked the young man to
agree more decisively with him, and when that did not happen, he
insisted, "In any case, we must remember that the Wafd have restored the constitution to the nation and brought us independence,
even if this has taken some time."

Kamal reflected that Fuad had always been lukewarm about politics. Perhaps he still was. But he did seem to favor the Wafd.

"For a long time I was politically engaged in a most emotional
way," Kamal reflected. "But now I don't believe in anything. Not
even politics is exempt from my insatiable doubt. Yet no matter what
my intellect does, my heart pounds with nationalist fervor."

Fuad laughingly remarked, "In periods of unrest, the judicial system quails, and the police take precedence. Thus times of unrest are
also times of police power. If the Wafd returns to rule, the judicial
system will regain its rightful place and activities of the police will
be limited. The natural state of affairs is for the law to have the final
say."

Al-Sayyid Ahmad commented, "Can we forget the Sidqy era? Soldiers used truncheons to assemble citizens on election days. Many of
our distinguished friends were ruined and went bankrupt as a result
of their loyalty to the Wafd. And then we see this 'devil' become a
member of the negotiating team, posing as a nationalist liberal."

Fuad replied, "Circumstances required a united front, one that
would have been incomplete had it not included this 'devil' and his
supporters. It's the end result that counts."

Fuad lingered there for some time, sipping coffee, while Kamal
examined his friend, noticing the elegant white silk suit, which had a
red rose decorating its lapel, and the forceful personality that he had
acquired to match his position. Deep inside, Kamal felt that, in spite
of everything, he would be happy to have this young man ask for

Na'ima's hand, but Fuad did not touch on this subject. He seemed ready to depart and soon told al-Sayyid Ahmad, "It must be time for you to leave for the store. I'll stay and chat with Kamal, but I'll visit you before going to Alexandria. I've decided to spend the rest of August and part of September at the beach." Then he rose, said good-bye to his host with a handshake, and left the room, preceded by Kamal.

They climbed the stairs to the top floor and settled themselves in the study. Fuad smiled as he looked around at the books on the shelves. He asked, "May I borrow a book from you?"

Hiding his lack of enthusiasm, Kamal answered, "I'd be delighted. What do you normally read during your free time?"

"I have the poetry collections of Shawqi, Hafiz Ibrahim, and Mutran as well as some books by al-Jahiz and al-Ma'arri. I'm especially fond of al-Mawardi's *Culture for This World and the Next*, not to mention works of contemporary authors. This, along with a few books by Dickens and Conan Doyle ... but my commitment to the law consumes most of my time."

Fuad rose to walk around and inspect the books, reading their titles. Completing his circle, he snorted, "A purely philosophical library! There's nothing to interest me here. I read *al-Fikr* magazine and have followed your essays in it over the years. But I don't claim to have read all of them or to remember anything from them. A philosophical discussion is heavy reading, and a public prosecutor is burdened with work. Why don't you write on popular topics?"

Kamal had heard his works belittled so often that he had almost grown accustomed to it and felt little distress about it. For him, doubt devoured everything, including any sorrow over such criticism. What was fame? What was popularity? Kamal was actually pleased to hear that Fuad found the articles useless for diversion in his spare time.

Kamal asked, "What do you mean by 'popular topics'?"

"Literature, for example."

"I've read many charming works since we were together, but I'm not a novelist or a poet."

Fuad laughed and said, "Then stay in philosophy, all by yourself. Aren't you a philosopher?"

"Aren't you a philosopher?" This expression had been etched into his mind ever since Aïda's lips had tossed it at him on Palaces Street. He shuddered from the terrifying impact it still made on his heart but concealed his emotional turmoil by laughing loudly. He remembered

the days when Fuad had been devoted to him, following him around
like a shadow. Now Kamal was looking at an important man, who
deserved his affection and loyalty.

"What have you done with your life?" he asked himself.

Fuad was examining his friend's mustache. Suddenly he laughed
and said, "If only . . ." When Kamal's eyes inquired what this meant,
Fuad continued: "We're both almost thirty, and neither of us has
married. Our generation is rife with bachelors. It's a crisis generation.
Are you still resolutely opposed to marriage?"

"I haven't budged."

"I don't know why, but I believe that you will never marry."

"You've always been very perceptive."

Smiling warmly as though to apologize in advance for what he
was going to say, Fuad commented, "You're an egotistical man. You
insist on maintaining total control over your life. Brother, the Prophet
married, and that did not prevent him from having a sublime spiritual
life." Then, laughing, he emended his statement: "Excuse me for using the Prophet as an example. I almost forgot that you . . . But not
so fast. You're no longer the same old atheist. Now you even doubt
atheism. This represents a gain for belief."

Kamal replied calmly, "Let's skip the philosophizing. You don't
enjoy it. Tell me why you haven't married yet, since this is what you
think of the single life."

He immediately sensed that he should not have brought up this
topic, for fear his friend would consider it a hint to ask for Na'ima's
hand. But Fuad gave no sign of having understood his words in this
manner. Instead, he laughed aloud—although without abandoning
his dignified demeanor—and answered, "You know, I've only recently started to enjoy the seamy side of life. Unlike you, I wasn't
corrupted early in life. I haven't had enough fun yet."

"Will you marry when you have?"

As if to brush aside the temptation to prevaricate, Fuad waved his
hand backwards through the air and confessed, "Since I've waited
this long, I need to be patient a little longer, until I become a judge,
for example. Then I'll be able to marry the daughter of a cabinet
minister if I want."

"You son of Jamil al-Hamzawi!" Kamal exclaimed to himself. "The
bridegroom of a cabinet official's daughter . . . her mother-in-law
would be from the working-class district of al-Mubayyada. Even
though he justified the presence of evil in the world, I defy Leibniz
to justify this."

Kamal said, "You consider marriage a . . ."

Before he could complete this statement, Fuad laughingly interrupted: "At least that's better than not considering it at all."

"But happiness . . ."

"Don't philosophize! Happiness is a subjective art. You may find bliss with the daughter of a cabinet minister and nothing but misery with a girl from your own background. Marriage is a treaty like the one al-Nahhas signed yesterday. It involves haggling, realistic appraisals, shrewdness, perspicacity, gains and losses. In our country this is the only door to advancement. Last week a man not yet forty was appointed a senior judge for the appeals court, while I could devote a lifetime of diligent and tireless service to the judicial system without ever attaining such an exalted position."

What was the primary-school teacher to say? He would spend his entire life at the sixth level of the civil service, even if philosophy did fill his head to overflowing.

"Your position should save you from having to resort to such stratagems."

"If it weren't for strategic alliances of this kind, no prime minister would ever be able to assemble a cabinet."

Kamal laughed lifelessly and observed, "You're in need of some philosophy. You would benefit from a spoonful of Spinoza."

"Sip as much of it as you want, but spare us. Tell me where a man can have a good time and find something to drink. In Qena I had to take my pleasures cautiously, on the sly. A position like mine forces a man to be discreet and private. The constant struggle between us and the police means that we must be extra careful. A public prosecutor has a tedious and sensitive job."

"We're returning to talk that threatens to make me explode with bitterness," Kamal noted to himself. "Compared to yours, my life seems disciplined and refined, but it's also the greatest possible test in life for my skeptical philosophy."

"My circumstances," Fuad continued, "bring me together with many important people, and they invite me to their mansions. I feel obliged to refuse their invitations in order to avoid any possible conflict of interest in the performance of my duties. But their mentality is such that they don't understand this. All the leading citizens of the region accuse me of being a snob, although I am entirely innocent of the charge."

Although saying, "Yes," agreeably to his friend, Kamal thought, "You're a conceited snob who is solicitous about his position."

"For similar reasons I lost favor with the police force. Dissatisfied with their crooked procedures, I attempted to entrap them. I had the law on my side, while they had the brutality of the Middle Ages on theirs. Everyone hates me, but I'm right."

"You're right," Kamal reflected. "That's what I've always known about you. You're shrewd and honest. But you don't and can't love anyone. You don't cling to what's right simply because it is right but out of conceit, pride, and a feeling of inferiority. This is what men are like. I run into people like you even in lowly callings. A man who is both pleasant and forceful is a myth. But what value does love have? Or idealism? Or anything?"

They talked for a long time. When preparing to leave, Fuad leaned toward Kamal and whispered, "I'm new in Cairo. You naturally know of an establishment—or probably several ... one that's very private, naturally...."

Smiling, Kamal replied, "A teacher, like a public prosecutor, must always take care to be discreet."

"Excellent. We'll get together soon. I'm busy arranging the new apartment now, but we'll have to spend some evenings together."

"Agreed."

They left the room together, and Kamal accompanied his friend all the way to the street. Passing by the first floor on his return, he met his mother, who stood waiting for him at the door. She inquired anxiously, "Didn't he say anything to you?"

He understood what she meant, and that tormented him terribly. But he pretended not to understand and asked in turn, "About what?"

"Na'ima?"

He answered resentfully, "Absolutely not."

"Amazing!"

They exchanged a long look. Then Amina continued: "But al-Hamzawi spoke to your father about it."

Concealing his fury as best he could, Kamal said, "Perhaps he spoke without having consulted his son."

Amina retorted angrily, "What a silly idea. Doesn't he know how lucky he would be to get her? Your father should have reminded him who he is."

"Fuad's not to blame. Perhaps his father, with all the best intentions, spoke rashly, without thinking it over."

"But he must have told his son. Did Fuad refuse ... that boy who was transformed into a distinguished civil servant by our money?"

"There's no need to talk about that."

"Son, this is unimaginable. Doesn't he know that accepting him into our family does us no honor?"

"Then don't be upset if it doesn't happen."

"I'm not upset about it. But I'm angered by the insult."

"There has been no insult. It's just a misunderstanding."

He returned to his room, sad and embarrassed, telling himself, "Na'ima's a beautiful rose. Yet, since I'm a man whose only remaining merit is love of truth, I must ask whether she is really a good match for a public prosecutor. Although he comes from a modest background, he will be able to find a spouse who is better educated, from a more distinguished family, wealthier, and prettier too. His good-natured father was too hasty. But he's not to blame. Still, Fuad's remarks to me were impudent. He certainly is impertinent. He's bright, honest, competent, insolent, and conceited, although it's not his fault. It's the result of the factors dividing men from each other. They infect us with all these maladies."

15 ⚤

Al-Fikr magazine occupied the ground floor of number 21 Abd al-Aziz Street. The barred window in the office of its proprietor, Mr. Abd al-Aziz al-Asyuti, overlooked the tenebrous Barakat Alley, and therefore the light inside was left on both night and day. Whenever Kamal approached the magazine's headquarters, the gloomy premises and shabby furniture reminded him of the status of thought in his land and of his own position in his society. Mr. Abd al-Aziz greeted him with an affectionate smile of welcome. This was hardly surprising, for they had known each other since 1930, when Kamal had begun sending the magazine his essays on philosophy. During the past six years his collaboration with the editor had been mutually supportive, if unremunerated. In fact, the magazine paid none of its writers for their efforts, which were undertaken solely for the advancement of philosophy and culture.

Abd al-Aziz welcomed all volunteer contributors, even specialists in Islamic philosophy, which was his own field. After receiving an Islamic education at al-Azhar university, he had traveled to France, where he spent four years doing research and auditing lectures without obtaining a degree. His real estate holdings, which provided him with a monthly income of fifty pounds, spared him from having to earn a living. He had founded *al-Fikr* magazine in 1923 and had kept publishing it, even though the profits were not commensurate with the labor he poured into it.

Kamal had scarcely taken a seat when a man his own age entered. Wearing a gray linen suit, he was tall and thin, although less so than Kamal, and had a long profile, taut cheeks, and wide lips. His delicate nose and pointed chin lent a special character to his full face. Smiling, he came forward with light steps and stretched out his hand to Mr. Abd al-Aziz, who shook it and presented the visitor to Kamal: "Mr. Riyad Qaldas, a translator in the Ministry of Education. He has recently joined the group writing for *al-Fikr*, infusing fresh blood into our scholarly journal with his monthly summaries of plays from world literature and his short stories."

Then he introduced Kamal: "Mr. Kamal Ahmad Abd al-Jawad. Perhaps you've read his essays?"

The two men shook hands, and Riyad said admiringly, "I've read them for years. They are essays of value, in every sense of the word."

Kamal thanked him cautiously for this praise. Then they sat down on neighboring chairs in front of the desk of Mr. Abd al-Aziz, who remarked, "Mr. Riyad, don't wait for him to return your compliment and say that he has read your valuable stories. He never reads stories."

Riyad laughed engagingly and revealed gleaming regular teeth with a gap between the middle incisors. "Don't you like literature?" he asked. "Every philosopher has a special theory of beauty arrived at only after an exhaustive examination of various arts—literature included, naturally."

Rather uneasily, Kamal ventured, "I don't hate literature. For a long time, I've used it for relaxation, enjoying both poetry and prose. But I have little free time."

"That must mean you've read what short stories you could, since modern literature consists almost entirely of short stories and plays."

Kamal replied, "Over the years I've read a great number, although I . . ."

Smiling in a knowing way, Abd al-Aziz al-Asyuti interrupted: "It's up to you, Mr. Riyad, to convince him of the truth of your new ideas. For the moment it will suffice if you realize that he's a philosopher whose energies are concentrated on thought." Then, turning toward Kamal, he asked, "Do you have your essay for this month?"

Kamal brought out an envelope of medium size and silently placed it in front of the editor, who took it. After extracting the article and examining it he said, "On Bergson? . . . Fine!"

Kamal explained, "The idea is to give an overview of the role his philosophy has played in the history of modern thought. Perhaps later I'll follow up on it with some detailed studies."

Riyad Qaldas was listening to the discussion with interest. Gazing at Kamal in an endearing way, he asked, "I've read your articles for years, starting with the ones you did on the Greek philosophers. They have been varied and occasionally contradictory, since they have presented rival schools of philosophy. I realize that you're a historian of ideas. Yet all the same I've tried in vain to discover your own intellectual position and the school of philosophy with which you're affiliated."

Abd al-Aziz al-Asyuti observed, "We're relative newcomers to the field of philosophical studies. So we must commence with general presentations. Perhaps in time Professor Kamal will develop a new philosophy. Possibly, Mr. Riyad, you'll become one of the adherents of Kamalism."

They all laughed. Kamal removed his spectacles and began to clean the lenses. He was capable of losing himself rapidly in a conversation, especially if he liked the person and if the atmosphere was relaxed and pleasant.

Kamal said, "I'm a tourist in a museum where nothing belongs to me. I'm merely a historian. I don't know where I stand."

With increasing interest Riyad Qaldas replied, "In other words, you're at a crossroads. I stood there for a long time before finding my way. But I wager there's a story behind your current posture. Usually it's the end of one stage and the beginning of another. Haven't you believed strongly in various different causes before reaching this point?"

The melody of this conversation revived the memory of an old song that was rooted in Kamal's heart. This young man and this conversation. . . . The previous barren years had been completely devoid of spiritual friendship. Kamal had grown accustomed to addressing himself whenever he needed someone to talk to. It had been a long time since anyone had been able to awaken a spiritual response like this in him . . . not Isma'il Latif, not Fuad al-Hamzawi, not any one of the dozens of teachers. Had the time come for the place vacated by Husayn Shaddad's departure to be filled?

He put his glasses on again. Smiling, he said, "Of course there's a story. Like most people, I began with religious belief, which was followed by belief in truth. . . ."

"I remember that you discussed materialist philosophy with suspicious zeal."

"My enthusiasm was sincere, but later I was troubled by skeptical doubts."

"Perhaps rationalism was the answer."

"I quickly felt skeptical about that too. Systems of philosophy are beautiful and tranquil castles but unfit to live in."

Abd al-Aziz smiled and said, "These are the words of one of their denizens."

Kamal shrugged his shoulders to dismiss that remark, but Riyad continued questioning him: "There's science. Perhaps it could save you from your doubts."

"Science is a closed world to those of us who know only its most obvious findings. Besides, I've learned that there are distinguished scientists who question whether scientific truth matches our actual world. Some find the laws of probability perplexing. Others are averse to asserting that there is any absolute truth. So I became even more tormented by doubt."

Riyad Qaldas smiled but made no comment. Then Kamal continued: "I've even plunged into modern spiritualism and its attempts to contact the other world. That made my head revolve in a frightening emptiness, and it's still spinning. What is truth? What are values? What is anything? Occasionally when I do the right thing I feel the prickings of conscience that I normally experience on doing something wrong."

Abd al-Aziz laughed out loud and said, "Religion has taken its revenge on you. You fled it to pursue higher truths only to return empty-handed."

Apparently more from politeness than conviction, Riyad Qaldas commented, "This skeptical stance is rather delightful. You observe and ponder everything with total freedom, acting like a tourist."

Addressing Kamal, Abd al-Aziz said, "You're a bachelor in both your thought and your life."

Kamal noted this chance phrase with interest. Was his single status a consequence of his philosophy or vice versa? Or were both a product of some third factor?

Riyad Qaldas said, "Being single's a temporary condition. Perhaps doubt is too."

Abd al-Aziz replied, "But it seems he's averse to ever getting married."

Amazed, Riyad asked, "What's incompatible about love and doubt? What's to prevent a lover from getting married? A persistent refusal to marry cannot be justified by doubt, which admits no persistence in anything."

Without believing it himself, Kamal asked, "Doesn't love require a certain amount of faith?"

Riyad Qaldas answered laughingly, "Of course not. Love is like an earthquake, rocking mosque, church, and brothel equally."

"An earthquake?" Kamal asked himself. "What an appropriate comparison! An earthquake destroys everything and then drowns the world in deathly silence."

"What about you, Mr. Qaldas?" Kamal inquired. "You have praised doubt. Are you a skeptic?"

Abd al-Aziz laughed and said, "He's doubt incarnate."

They roared with laughter. Then Riyad, as though to introduce himself, commented, "I was a skeptic for a long time before renouncing it. I no longer have any doubts concerning religion, because I've abandoned it. But I believe in science and art. I always shall, God willing."

Abd al-Aziz asked sarcastically, "The God you don't believe in?"

Smiling, Riyad Qaldas answered, "Religion is a human artifact. We know nothing about God. Who can really say he doesn't believe in God? Or that he does? The prophets are the only true Believers. That's because they see and hear Him or converse with messengers bringing His revelations."

Kamal inquired, "Yet you believe in science and art?"

"Yes."

"There's some basis for belief in science. But art? I'd rather believe in spiritualism than in the short story, for example."

Riyad stared at him critically but said calmly, "Science is the language of the intellect. Art is the language of the entire human personality."

"What a poetic statement!"

Riyad received Kamal's sarcasm with an indulgent smile and replied, "Science brings people together with the light of its ideas. Art brings them together with lofty human emotions. Both help mankind develop and prod us toward a better future."

"What conceit!" Kamal exclaimed to himself. "He writes a two-page short story every month and imagines that he's helping mankind progress. But I'm as nauseating as he is, for I summarize a chapter from Høffding's *History of Modern Philosophy* and then deep inside claim to be the equal of Fuad Jamil al-Hamzawi, public prosecutor for al-Darb al-Ahmar. But how would life be bearable otherwise? Are we insane, wise, or merely alive? To hell with everything!"

"What do you say about scientists who do not share your enthusiasm for science?"

"We should not interpret the modesty of science as weakness or despair. Science provides mankind with its magic, light, guidance, and miracles. It's the religion of the future."

"And the short story?"

For the first time it became clear that Riyad was offended, even though he attempted not to let it show. Kamal corrected himself almost apologetically, "I mean art in general."

Riyad Qaldas asked emphatically, "Can you live in absolute isolation? People need confidential advice, consolation, joy, guidance, light, and journeys to all regions of the inhabited world and of the soul. That's what art is."

At this juncture Mr. Abd al-Aziz said, "I have an idea. Let's get together with some of our colleagues once a month to talk about intellectual concerns. Then we can publish our discussion under the title 'Debate of the Month.' "

Looking at Kamal affectionately, Riyad Qaldas said, "Our debate will continue. Or that's what I hope. Shall we consider ourselves friends?"

Kamal replied with sincere enthusiasm, "Most certainly! We must meet as often as possible."

Pervaded by happiness because of this new friendship, Kamal sensed that an exalted side of his heart had been awakened after a profound slumber. He was more convinced than ever of the important role friendship played in his life. It was vital and indispensable for him. Without it, he was like a thirsty man perishing in the desert.

The new friends parted at al-Ataba, and Kamal returned by the Muski. Although it was nearly 8 P.M., the air he breathed in was hot enough to be stifling. He slowed down on reaching al-Gawhari Alley, which he entered. Then he stepped into the third house on the right, climbing the stairs to the second floor. After he rang the bell, a little window in the door opened, revealing the face of a woman over sixty. She welcomed him with a smile, which showed off her gold teeth, and admitted him.

"Welcome to my lover's son!" she exclaimed. "Welcome to my brother's son!"

He followed her to a sitting room surrounded by bedrooms. The two sofas were placed opposite each other. Between them were a small carpet gleaming with gold and silver thread, a table, and a water pipe. The fragrance of incense permeated the room.

The woman was plump, but old enough to be fragile, and her head was wrapped in a spangled kerchief. Although decorated by kohl, her eyes had a heavy look indicative of drug abuse. The wrinkles of her face revealed traces of her former beauty and of an enduring wantonness. Sitting down cross-legged on the sofa near the water pipe, she gestured for him to sit beside her.

Obeying her, he smiled and asked, "How is Mrs. Jalila?"

She protested, "Call me 'Aunt' "

"How are you, Auntie?"

"Superb, son of Abd al-Jawad." Then she shouted in a harsh voice, "Girl! Nazla!"

In a few minutes the maid brought two full glasses, which she placed on the table. Jalila directed: "Drink! . . . How often I said that to your father in those sweet bygone days. . . ."

As Kamal picked up a glass he remarked jovially, "It's really sad that I arrived too late. . . ."

She gave him a punch that made the gold bracelets covering her arm jangle. "Shame on you! Would you have wished to ravage what your father adored?" Then she added, "But what are you compared to your father? He had already married a second time when I met him. He married young, as was the custom then. But that did not prevent him from keeping me company for a period that was the sweetest of my life. Then he left me for Zubayda, may God take her by the hand. And there were dozens of other women besides us, may God be indulgent with him. But you're still a bachelor, and even so you only visit my house once a week, Thursday evenings. Shame on you! What ever happened to virility?"

The father he heard about from her was not the one he knew personally. This was not even the father Yasin had described to him. Jalila's lover had been a passionate and impetuous man with a heart untroubled by qualms. What was Kamal compared to that man? Even when he visited this brothel each Thursday, only alcohol could release him from his worries long enough for him to enjoy "love" here. Without its intoxication, he would have felt the brothel's atmosphere to be devastatingly grim. That first night, when fate had led him to this house, had been unforgettable. He had seen this woman for the first time, and she had invited him to sit with her until a girl was ready. When he had revealed his full name during the course of the conversation, she had cried out, "Are you the son of al-Sayyid Ahmad Abd al-Jawad whose store is in al-Nahhasin?"

"Yes. Do you know my father?"

"A thousand welcomes to you!"

"Do you know my father?"

"I know him far better than you do. We were lovers, and I performed at your sister's wedding. In my time, I was as famous a singer as Umm Kalthoum in your gray days. Ask anyone about me."

"It's an honor to meet you, ma'am."

"Pick any of my girls you like. Benevolent folks like us don't bill each other."

So his first girl in this house had been a gift from his father. That evening Jalila had looked at his face for so long he had felt embarrassed. Only fear of being rude had kept her from expressing her astonishment, for what resemblance was there between this boy's bizarre head and amazing nose and his father's exquisite and ruddy face? During a lengthy conversation with her he had learned about his father's secret history, peculiarities, amazing deeds, romantic adventures, and hidden qualities.

"I'm so bewildered," Kamal reflected. "I've always wavered between instinct's searing flame and mysticism's cool breeze."

He replied, "Don't exaggerate, Auntie. I'm a teacher, and teachers like to be discreet. Don't forget that during the vacation I visit you several times a week. Wasn't I here the day before yesterday? I visit you whenever . . ."

"Whenever I'm tormented by anxiety," he confessed to himself. "Anxiety drives me to you far more often than lust."

"Whenever what, my dear?"

"Whenever I don't have to work."

"Say anything but that. Down with this age of yours. Our coins were made of gold. Yours are nickel and copper. We had live entertainment. You have the radio. Our men were descended from Adam's loins. Yours come from Eve's womb. What do you have to say about that, you teacher of girls?"

She took a drag on the water pipe and then sang:

> *Teacher of girls, show them how*
> *To play instruments and sing.*

Kamal laughed, leaned toward her, and kissed her cheek, half affectiously and half flirtatiously.

She cried out, "Your mustache pricks. God help Atiya!"

"She loves pricks."

"By the way, yesterday we had the honor of a visit from a prominent police officer. I'm not bragging. All our clients are distinguished gentlemen. Or do you consider your visits here to be charitable contributions?"

"Madam Jalila, your very name means 'glorious,' and you certainly are that."

"I love it when you're drunk. Intoxication liberates you from your schoolmasterly earnestness and makes you a little more like your father. But tell me. Don't you love Atiya? . . . She loves you!"

How could these hearts, hardened by the coarseness of life, love anyone? Yet what experience did he have of hearts generous with love or eager for it? The daughter of the snack shop owner had been in love with him, but he had ignored her. He had loved Aïda, but she had spurned him. In his living dictionary, the only meaning for love was pain . . . an astonishing pain that set the soul on fire. By the light of its raging flames amazing secrets of life became visible, but it left behind only rubble.

He commented ironically, "May you find health and love too!"

"She's only been in this line of work since her divorce."

"Praise God! He alone is praised for hateful things."

"Praise to Him in all circumstances."

He smiled sardonically. Grasping what his smile implied, she protested, "Do you begrudge me my enthusiasm for praising God? That's enough from you, son of Abd al-Jawad. Listen, I don't have a son or a daughter. I'm fed up with the world. Forgiveness is from God."

It was interesting that the woman's conversation was so frequently interspersed with this melody celebrating asceticism. Kamal glanced at her stealthily as he drained his glass. For him, alcohol's magic effect began with the first drink. He found himself recalling a bygone age when drinking had brought him a heavenly bliss. How many of his joys had vanished. . . . At first lust had been both a rebellion and a victory for him. Then it had eventually been transformed into a whore's philosophy. Time and habituation had extinguished its delirium. It was also frequently marred by the agony of a man wavering between heaven and earth—before doubt had reduced heaven to earth's level.

The doorbell rang, and Atiya entered. Her body was full, supple, and fair. Her shoes and her laughter both resounded noisily. She kissed the madam's hand. Casting a smiling glance at the two empty glasses, she teased Kamal, "You've been unfaithful to me!"

She leaned down to the madam's ear and whispered to her. Then, giving Kamal a laughing look, she vanished into the bedroom on the madam's right. Jalila punched Kamal and told him, "Go along, light of my eye."

Picking up his fez, he headed for the bedroom. Nazla immediately caught up with him, carrying a tray with a bottle, two glasses, and some appetizers. Atiya instructed her, "Bring us two pounds of kebab from al-Ajati's restaurant. I'm hungry!"

He took off his jacket and made himself comfortable by stretching out his legs. As he sat watching her, she removed her shoes and dress. Then at the mirror she straightened her chemise and combed her hair. He loved her body, which was so full, supple, and fair. What did Aïda's body look like? Frequently when he remembered her, it seemed that she had no body. Even when he recalled her grace, slenderness, and brown skin, these physical characteristics took their place in his spirit as pure ideas. As for the customary kind of memories concerned with bodily attributes like breasts, legs, or buttocks, he could not remember his senses ever having paid attention to them. Today, if a beautiful woman whose only attractions were a graceful slenderness and a swarthy complexion was presented for his admiration he would not even offer twenty piasters for her. So how had his love for Aïda been possible? Why was his memory of her so firmly protected by veneration and adoration, even though he scorned all her qualities?

"It's hot. Darn it."

"Once the alcohol gets into our systems, we won't care if the weather's hot or cold."

"Stop eating me with your eyes. Take off your glasses!"

"A divorced woman with children," he brooded. "She masks gloomy melancholy with boisterous behavior. These greedy nights carelessly swallow her femininity and her humanity. Her every breath blends together fake passion and loathing. It's the worst form of bondage. Thus, alcohol provides an escape from suffering as well as from thought."

She plopped down beside him and prepared to pour their drinks, reaching her soft hand out to the bottle, which was sold in this establishment for twice what it was worth. Everything here was expensive except women, except for human beings. Without alcohol to distract one from humanity's disdainful glare, reunions like this would be impossible. But life is full of prostitutes of various types. Some are cabinet ministers and others authors.

As his second drink went to work inside him the harbingers of forgetfulness and delight arrived. "I've craved this woman for a long time, even without being conscious of it. Lust is a tyrannical master. Love is something entirely different. When liberated from lust, it appears in the most amazing garb. If one day I'm permitted to find love and lust united in a single human being, a desirable stability will be achieved. I still see life as a set of mismatched parts. I'm searching for a marriage that will affect both the private and public aspects of my life. I don't know which is more basic, but I'm certain that I'm miserable, despite having created a life that assures me both intellectual pleasures and bodily delights. A train, too, rolls forcefully down the tracks without having any idea of where it has been or where it is going. Lust is a tyrannical beauty readily felled by disgust. The heart cries out as it vainly searches in agonizing despair for eternal bliss. Complaints are endless. Life is a vast swindle. To be able to accept this deception gracefully, we must assume that life contains some secret wisdom. We're like an actor who, while conscious of the deceit implicit in his role onstage, worships his craft."

He downed his third drink in a single gulp, sending Atiya into gales of laughter. She loved to get drunk, even though it had a bad effect on her. If he did not stop her in time, she would become rowdy, twitch, weep, and throw up. The liquor had gone to his head, and he quivered with excitement. He gazed at her with a beaming face. She was simply a woman now, not a problem. Problems no longer seemed to exist. Existence itself—the most troublesome issue in life —had stopped being a problem.

"Just drink some more and lose yourself in her kisses," he thought.

"You're so charming," he told her, "when you laugh for no reason at all."

"If I seem to laugh for no reason, I hope you'll understand that some reasons are too important to be mentioned."

17

Wrapped up in his overcoat, Abd al-Muni'm returned home to Sugar Street, bracing himself against the bitter winter cold. Although it was only six, darkness had fallen. When he reached the entry to the staircase, the door of the first-floor apartment opened and out slipped the lithe figure that had been waiting for him. His heart pounded and his fiery eyes watched her advance as he climbed the stairs with light steps, taking care not to make any sound. He was torn between his desire, which tempted him to yield, and his will, which urged him to take control of a nervous system apparently bent on betraying and destroying him. He remembered, only then, that she had made a date with him for this evening and that he could have come home earlier or later, thus avoiding the encounter. He had forgotten all about it. How forgetful he was! There was no time for deliberation and reflection. He would have to wait until he was alone in his room, until a moment that would mark triumphant victory or miserable defeat.

Nothing could make him forget his endless struggle. Throwing himself into this trial, he mounted the stairs behind her without having reached any decision. At the landing, he imagined her figure had swelled so large that it filled space and time to bursting.

With some difficulty, he concealed his anxiety and hid his determination to resist temptation when he said, "Good evening."

The voice replied affectionately, "Good evening. Thank you for heeding my advice to wear your overcoat."

He was touched by her tenderness, and the words he was about to cast at her melted in his mouth. Trying to mask his confusion, he said, "I was afraid it might rain."

She raised her head as though to look at the sky and remarked, "It will rain sooner or later. You can't see a single star in the sky. I had trouble recognizing you when you turned into our street."

He collected his unruly faculties and observed as if to caution her, "It's cold and extremely humid in the staircase."

With a directness the girl had learned from him, she replied, "I don't feel the cold when I'm near you."

The heat welling up inside him made his face burn. His condition suggested that he was going to err again, his best intentions notwith-standing. He summoned all his willpower in an effort to master the tremor sweeping through his body.

"Why don't you speak?" she asked.

Sensing her hand gently squeeze his shoulder, he could not stop himself from putting his arms around her. He began with one long kiss and then showered her with more, until he heard her say breath-lessly, "I can't bear to be apart from you!"

He kept on hugging her, as he warmed to her embrace. She whis-pered in his ear, "I wish I could stay like this forever."

Tightening his grip on her, he said in a trembling voice, "I'm sorry!"

In the darkness she drew her head back a little and asked, "About what, darling?"

He replied hesitantly, "The mistake we're making."

"By God, what mistake?"

He gently freed himself from her and removed his overcoat, which he folded and started to place on the railing. But at the last terrifying moment he changed his mind, draped it over his arm, and took a step backwards, breathing heavily. His willpower was able to halt his pro-gressive surrender to lust, and that changed everything. When her hand sought to return to his neck, he grabbed hold of it. Then he waited until his breathing had returned to normal and said calmly, "This is a great error."

"What error? I don't understand."

"A young girl not yet fourteen," Abd al-Muni'm chided himself, "and you're toying with her to satisfy a merciless desire. This flirta-tion will lead to nothing. It's merely an amusement that will draw down God's wrath and anger on you."

"You must try to understand," he said. "Would we be able to tell everyone what we're doing?"

"Tell everyone?"

"Don't you see you would be forced to deny it? If we can't talk about it, then it must be a despicable error."

He felt her hand search for him again. He climbed the first step of the next flight of stairs, confident that he had passed safely out of the danger zone. "Admit that we're doing something wrong. We mustn't continue to make this mistake."

"I'm amazed to hear you talk like this."

"Don't be. My conscience can no longer tolerate this mistake. It torments me, making it hard for me to pray."

"She's silent," he thought. "I've hurt her, may God forgive me.

How painful! But I won't give in. Praise God that desire didn't lead you to commit an even greater error."

"What's happened must teach us not to do anything like this in the future. You're young. You've made a mistake. Don't ever yield to temptation again."

In a sobbing voice she protested, "I haven't done anything wrong. Are you planning to desert me? What are your intentions?"

In full command of himself now, he answered, "Go back to your apartment. Don't do anything you would have to conceal. Don't ever meet anyone in the dark."

The shaky voice asked, "Are you deserting me? Have you forgotten what you said about our love?"

"Those were a fool's words. You were mistaken. Let this be a lesson for you. Beware of the dark, for it could be your ruin. You're young. How come you're so daring?"

Her sobs reverberated in the gloom, but that made no impression on his heart. He was intoxicated by the stern delight of victory.

"Heed my words. Don't be angry. Remember that if I were really a scoundrel I wouldn't have been satisfied with anything less than ruining you. Goodbye."

He bounded up the stairs. The torment was over. Remorse would no longer be able to sink its teeth into him. But he should remember what his mentor Shaykh Ali al-Manufi said: "You cannot conquer the devil by ignoring the laws of nature." Yes, he had to remember that. He quickly changed into his house shirt. Then as he left the room he told his brother, Ahmad, "I want to talk privately with Father in the study. Please give us a little time to be alone."

When Abd al-Muni'm asked his father to join him there, Khadija raised her head to inquire, "Good news?"

"I want to talk to Father first. Then it will be your turn."

Ibrahim Shawkat trailed after his son silently. The man had recently gotten a new set of dentures. His languid complacency had returned, after he had been forced to confront life in a toothless condition for six whole months. They sat down beside each other, and the father asked, "Good news, God willing?"

Without any hesitation or introduction, Abd al-Muni'm said, "Father, I want to marry."

The man stared at his son's face and then knit his brows jovially as though he had not understood. After shaking his head in a baffled way, he remarked, "Marriage? There's a right time for everything. Why are you speaking about this now?"

"I want to get married now."

"Now? You're only eighteen. Won't you wait until you get your degree?"

"I can't."

Then the door opened, and Khadija entered. "What's happening behind this door?" she asked. "Are there secrets you can tell your father but not me?"

Abd al-Muni'm frowned nervously. Ibrahim, who scarcely understood the meaning of his own words, answered, "Abd al-Muni'm wants to get married."

Khadija scrutinized her husband as though fearing he had gone insane. She cried out, "Get married! What do I hear? Have you decided to leave the University?"

In an angry, forceful voice, Abd al-Muni'm responded, "I said I want to marry, not that I'm dropping out of school. I'll continue my studies as a married man. That's all there is to it."

Looking back and forth from one to the other, Khadija asked, "Abd al-Muni'm, are you really serious?"

He shouted, "Absolutely!"

The woman struck her hands together and riposted, "The evil eye has struck you. What's happened to your brain, son?"

Abd al-Muni'm stood up angrily. He asked, "What brings you here? I wanted to speak privately with my father first, but you don't know what patience is. Listen! I want to get married. I have two more years before I finish my studies. Father, you can support me for these two years. If I weren't sure of that, I would not have made this request."

Khadija said, "God's grace! They've destroyed his mind."

"Who has?"

"God knows best who they are. I'll let Him take care of them. You shouldn't have any doubts as to their identity, and we'll soon learn."

The young man told his father, "Don't listen to her. Even now I have no idea what girl will be mine. Choose her yourselves. I want a suitable bride, any bride."

Flabbergasted, she asked him, "Do you mean there's not some special girl who is the cause of this whole calamity?"

"Absolutely not. Believe me. Choose for me yourself."

"Why are you in such a hurry then? I'll select someone for you. Give me a little time. Say a year or two?"

Raising his voice, he said, "I'm not joking. Leave me alone. He understands me better than you do."

His father asked him calmly, "Why the rush?"

Lowering his gaze, Abd al-Muni'm answered, "I can't wait any longer."

Khadija inquired, "How come thousands of other young men like you can?"

The boy told his father, "I'm not willing to do what they do."

Ibrahim thought a little. To put an end to this scene he said, "That's enough for now. We'll continue this discussion another time."

Khadija started to say something, but her husband stopped her and took her by the hand. The couple left the study to resume their places in the sitting room, where they went over the topic, considering it from every angle. After a lot of give-and-take, Ibrahim felt inclined to support his son's request. He took it upon himself to convince his wife. Once she had accepted the notion in principle, Ibrahim said, "We have Na'ima, my niece. We won't need to tire ourselves out searching for a bride."

Capitulating, Khadija said, "I'm the one who persuaded you to renounce your share of your late brother's estate for Aisha's sake. So I have no objection to the choice of Na'ima as a bride for my son. I'm very concerned about Aisha's happiness, as you know. But I'm afraid of her melancholy brooding and am very apprehensive about her eccentric behavior. Haven't you hinted to her repeatedly that we would like Na'ima to marry Abd al-Muni'm? All the same I think she was ready to accept Jamil al-Hamzawi's son when al-Hamzawi proposed it."

"That's ancient history. A year or more has passed since then, and praise God nothing has come of it. No matter how good a position he has, it would have done me no honor to have a young man like that marry my niece. As far as I'm concerned, a man's family origin is everything, and Na'ima is very dear to us."

Sighing, Khadija agreed, "Very, very dear. What do you suppose my father will say about this foolishness when he learns of it?"

Ibrahim replied, "I'm sure he'll welcome it. Everything about it seems like a dream, but I won't regret it. I'm positive that it would be an unforgivable error to ignore Abd al-Muni'm's request, so long as it's within our power to grant it."

18

No changes worth mentioning had taken place at the old house on Palace Walk, but the neighbors—Hasanayn the barber, Darwish the bean seller, al-Fuli the milkman, Abu Sari', who ran the snack shop, and Bayumi, who sold fruit drinks—had all learned in one way or another that al-Sayyid Ahmad's granddaughter was to marry her double first cousin Abd al-Muni'm today. Al-Sayyid Ahmad did not break with his time-honored traditions, and the day passed like any other one. Only members of the family were invited, and the day's major activity was preparation of the dinner banquet.

It was at the beginning of summer, and they were all assembled in the parlor: al-Sayyid Ahmad Abd al-Jawad, Amina, Khadija, Ibrahim Shawkat, Abd al-Muni'm, Ahmad, Yasin, Zanuba, Ridwan, and Karima. The only two family members missing were Na'ima, who was adorning herself on the top floor, and Aisha, who was helping her. Sensing that his presence might dampen their spirits at this festive family reunion, al-Sayyid Ahmad went off to his room shortly after welcoming everyone and waited there for the religious official to arrive.

He had liquidated his business and sold the store, choosing to retire, not merely because he was sixty-five but also because Jamil al-Hamzawi's resignation had forced him to assume much of the work at a time when he was no longer up to it. Thus he had decided to retire, contenting himself with his savings and what he had gotten from closing out his store. He calculated that this amount would suffice for the rest of his days. His retirement had been an important milestone in the life of the family. Kamal had begun to wonder whether they had not underestimated the role Jamil al-Hamzawi had played in all their lives and especially in their father's.

Alone in his room, al-Sayyid Ahmad silently pondered the events of the day, as if he could not believe that the bridegroom was his grandson Abd al-Muni'm. He had been amazed and incredulous the day Ibrahim Shawkat had raised the matter with him.

"How could you allow your son to speak to you so bluntly and to impose his will on you?" he had wanted to know. "Fathers like you are spoiling the next generation."

He would have said no, had it not been for the delicacy of the circumstances. Out of consideration for Aisha's misery, he had renounced his customary stubbornness, since he could not bear to disappoint her, especially after all the little comments provoked by Fuad al-Hamzawi's silence. If Na'ima's marriage would lessen the anguish of Aisha's heart, then welcome to it. His distress had prompted him to grant his consent, and he had allowed children to force their wishes on adults and to marry before finishing their education. He had summoned Abd al-Muni'm and had made him promise to complete his studies. Citing passages from the Qur'an and from reports of the Prophet's life, Abd al-Muni'm had offered an eloquent defense, setting his grandfather's mind at ease, while arousing in the patriarch feelings of both admiration and contempt. So today the schoolboy was getting married, while Kamal had not yet thought of it—although al-Sayyid Ahmad had once refused even to announce the engagement of his late son Fahmy, who had died before enjoying the prime of his youth. The cosmos seemed to have turned upside down. Another extraordinary world had sprung up in its place.

"We're strangers even among our own kinsfolk," he thought. "Today, schoolboys marry. Who knows what they'll do tomorrow?"

In the parlor, Khadija was concluding a lengthy monologue: "And that's why we moved everyone out of the second floor. Tonight it will look its best when it receives the newlyweds."

Yasin told her impishly, "You have everything it takes to be an outstanding mother-in-law. But you'll be unable to exploit your extraordinary talents with this bride."

Although she fully understood his allusion, she ignored it and said, "The bride is my daughter and my sister's daughter."

To soften the impact of Yasin's jest, Zanuba commented, "Mrs. Khadija is a perfect lady." Khadija thanked her. Despite a secret dislike for this sister-in-law, Khadija responded thankfully and respectfully to her ingratiating remarks, for Yasin's sake.

Karima at ten was already pretty enough for Yasin to make proud forecasts about her future feminine charms. Abd al-Muni'm was conversing with his grandmother, Amina, who was always impressed by his piety. She would occasionally interrupt his comments to invoke God's blessings on him.

Kamal teased Ahmad: "Are you getting married next year?"

"Unless I follow your example, Uncle."

Zanuba, who was listening, said, "If Mr. Kamal will give me permission, I promise to have him married off in a matter of days."

Pointing to himself, Yasin said, "I'm ready to let you find a bride for me."

Shaking her head scornfully, she replied, "You've been married more than enough. You've had your share of brides and your brother's share too."

Attracted by the topic of this conversation, Amina told Zanuba, "If you get Kamal married, I'll trill with joy for the first time in my life."

When he tried to picture his mother trilling joyfully, Kamal laughed. Then he imagined himself in the place of Abd al-Muni'm, waiting for the Islamic notary, and fell silent. The thought of marriage stirred up a whirlpool of emotions deep inside him as surely as winter's humidity troubles the breathing of an asthmatic. Although he categorically rejected the idea of marriage, he could not ignore it. His heart was free, but he found this emptiness as nerve-racking as being in love. If he did decide to marry now, his only recourse would be the traditional process beginning with a matchmaker and ending with a household, children, and immersion in the mechanics of daily life. After that, no matter how much a person wanted to, he would scarcely be able to find time for reflection. Kamal would always view marriage with a strange mixture of longing and aversion.

"The end of your life will be nothing but loneliness and despair," he warned himself.

The truly happy person that day was Aisha. For the first time in nine years she had put on a pretty dress and had braided her hair. Now with dreamy eyes she was looking at her daughter, who was as beautiful as a moonbeam. As her tears began to flow, Aisha hid her own pale withered face from her daughter. At that moment, finding her weeping, Amina gave Aisha a critical look and said, "It's not right for Na'ima to leave the house with a sad heart."

Aisha sobbed, "Don't you see that she's alone today, without a father or a brother?"

Amina replied, "That makes her mother all the more important. May our Lord grant the mother a long life, for the girl's sake . . . and she's going to her aunt and uncle. Besides, she has God, the creator of the whole universe, to watch over her."

Drying her eyes, Aisha said, "From daybreak on, I'm inundated with memories of my departed loved ones. I can see their faces. Once she's gone I'll be all alone."

Amina scolded her, "You're not alone!"

Na'ima patted her mother's cheek and asked, "How can I leave you, Mama?"

Aisha smiled and answered sympathetically, "Your new household will show you how."

Na'ima said anxiously, "You'll visit every day. You've avoided going anywhere near Sugar Street, but from now on you'll have to change that."

"Of course. Do you doubt it?"

Then Kamal came to tell them, "Get ready. The marriage clerk has arrived."

His eyes fastened on Na'ima admiringly. "How beautiful, delicate, and ethereal," he thought. "What role can animal desires and needs play in this exquisite creature?"

On learning that the marriage contract had been executed, they all exchanged congratulations. Then a shrieking trill of joy shattered the somber decorum of the household and reverberated through its still reaches. Their astonished faces discovered Umm Hanafi standing at the end of the sitting room.

When it was time for the dinner banquet and the guests started making their way to the table, Aisha found that she had no appetite and felt depressed, for she could think of nothing but the imminent separation.

Umm Hanafi announced that Shaykh Mutawalli Abd al-Samad was sitting on the ground in the courtyard and that he had asked for some supper, especially for a good selection from the different meat dishes. Al-Sayyid Ahmad laughed and ordered her to prepare a tray and carry it to him. Immediately thereafter, they heard the shaykh's voice calling up from the courtyard, praying that his beloved Ahmad ibn Abd al-Jawad would have a long life. He could also be heard asking the names of al-Sayyid Ahmad's children and grandchildren so he could offer prayers on their behalf too.

Smiling, al-Sayyid Ahmad commented, "What a pity! Shaykh Mutawalli has forgotten your names. May God be indulgent with the infirmities of old age."

Ibrahim Shawkat said, "He's a hundred, isn't he?"

Ahmad Abd al-Jawad agreed. Then the shaykh's voice cried out, "In the name of the martyr al-Husayn, be generous with the meat."

Al-Sayyid laughed and said, "His holy powers are concentrated on meat today."

When it was time to say farewell, Kamal went down to the courtyard before the others to avoid the spectacle. Although Na'ima was only moving to Sugar Street, that deeply troubled her heart and her mother's. Kamal himself felt skeptical about this wedding, for he doubted that Na'ima was strong enough for married life. In the courtyard he saw Shaykh Mutawalli Abd al-Samad sitting on the ground under the electric light attached to the wall of the house to illuminate the area. The old man's legs were stretched out, and he had removed his sandals. Wearing a discolored white shirt that went down to his ankles and a white skullcap, he leaned against the wall as if sleeping off his meal. Kamal noticed water flowing down the man's legs and realized that he was incontinent. Resounding like a whistle, the man's breathing was clearly audible. Kamal stared at him with a mixture of disdain and disgust. Then a thought made him smile in spite of himself. He reflected, "Perhaps in 1830 he was a pampered child."

19

The very next day Aisha went to call at Sugar Street. During the nine previous years, except for a few visits to Palace of Desire Alley when Yasin had lost a child, she had left the old house only to visit the cemetery. She stopped for a moment at the entrance to look around, and her eyes filled with tears. Uthman's and Muhammad's feet had frequently run and skipped there by the doorway. The courtyard had once been decorated for her glorious wedding. That was the reception room where Khalil had smoked his water pipe and played backgammon or dominoes. Here the sweet fragrance of the past was redolent of lost love and tenderness. She had been so joyful that her happiness had been proverbial. Called the merry soprano, she had been accused of flirting with her mirror and of consorting with her dressing table. Her husband had uttered sweet nothings and the children had scampered about ... in those bygone days. She dried her eyes so she would not meet the bride that way. These eyes were still blue, even though the eyelashes had fallen out and the eyelids seemed withered. She found the apartment newly outfitted and painted, resplendent with the bride's furnishings, on which a considerable amount had been spent. Wearing a diaphanous white frock, her golden hair hanging down to her knees, Na'ima greeted her mother. The bride was serene, charming, and immaculate, and her perfume had a haunting fragrance.

Their long affectionate embrace lasted until Abd al-Muni'm, calmly waiting his turn in a blue-green robe that enveloped his silk house shirt, protested, "That's enough! Just say hello to each other. A nominal separation like this merits nothing more."

Then he embraced his aunt and escorted her to a cozy chair. As she sat down, he remarked, "We were just thinking of you, Aunt. We have decided to invite you to come live with us."

Aisha smiled as she answered, "Anything but that. I'll visit you every day. This will give me an excuse for a walk. I really need more exercise."

With his customary candor, Abd al-Muni'm said, "Sweet Na'ima has told me that you can't bear to stay here for fear of being over-come by memories. But a Believer need not fall prey to sad thoughts. What happened was God's will, and it was a long time ago. God has sent us as a consolation for you."

"Though this young man," Aisha reflected, "is frank and good-hearted, he is cavalier about the impact of his words on wounded hearts."

"Of course, Abd al-Muni'm," she said. "But I'm comfortable at home. It's better this way."

Then Khadija, Ibrahim, and Ahmad entered and shook hands with Aisha. Khadija told her sister, "If I had realized this would make you start visiting us again I would have had them married even before they were old enough."

Aisha laughed. Reminding Khadija of distant times, she asked, "A single kitchen? Or does the bride demand to be independent of her mother-in-law?"

Khadija and Ibrahim both laughed. In a tone that was not free of insinuation, Khadija answered, "Like her mother, she isn't concerned about such silly things."

For his sons' sake, Ibrahim explained Aisha's obscure reference: "The battles between your mother and mine began with the kitchen, which my mother monopolized. Your mother demanded one of her own."

The bridegroom asked in amazement, "Mother, did you fight over a kitchen?"

Laughing, Ahmad said, "Do the struggles between nations have grander causes than that?"

Ibrahim remarked ironically, "Your mother is as powerful as England. While mine ... well, may God have mercy on her."

Kamal arrived. He was wearing an elegant white suit, but his face was distinguished as always by his protruding forehead, enormous nose, gold spectacles, and thick but compact mustache. He was car-rying a large package that promised to be a fine present. As she smilingly examined it, Khadija cautioned him, "Watch out, brother. If you don't go ahead and marry, you'll always be taking presents to other people without getting anything in return. There's a whole family of young people about to get married. We have Ahmad, and Yasin has Ridwan and Karima. Start making plans now to do what's right."

Ahmad asked his uncle, "Has the school vacation begun?"

Removing his fez and gazing at the beautiful bride, Kamal replied, "There's only a short period left while we monitor and correct the elementary-level examination."

Na'ima disappeared and returned shortly with a silver tray filled with sweets of various different types and flavors. For a time nothing was heard but the noise of lips smacking and mouths sucking. Then Ibrahim started to recount what he remembered of his own wedding, the reception, and the male and female vocalists. Aisha listened with a smiling face and a sad heart. Kamal also followed this narrative with great interest, since it reminded him of things he remembered and of others he had forgotten and wanted to learn about.

Laughing, Ibrahim said, "Al-Sayyid Ahmad was just the same as he is today or even more severe. But my mother, may God be compassionate to her, declared decisively, 'Al-Sayyid Ahmad can do anything he wishes at his house. But in our home we'll celebrate as much as we want.' And that's what happened. Al-Sayyid Ahmad was accompanied to the wedding by his friends, may God be gracious to them all. I remember that Ridwan's grandfather, Mr. Muhammad Iffat, was one of them. They sat in the reception room, far removed from the commotion."

Khadija added, "Jalila, the most renowned performer of her time, entertained that evening."

As he thought of the aged madam, who still boasted of her successes in his father's era, Kamal felt like smiling.

Stealing a look at Aisha, Ibrahim remarked, "We used to have our own private singer in the house. Her voice was more beautiful than that of any professional musician. She made us think of Munira al-Mahdiya at her prime."

Aisha blushed and replied quietly, "Her voice has been silent for a long time. She's forgotten how to sing."

Kamal said, "Na'ima sings too. Haven't you heard her?"

Ibrahim answered, "I understand she does, but I haven't heard her yet. The truth is that we've had more opportunities to observe her piety than her singing. Yesterday I told her, 'Your husband is one of the most pious Believers, but you must postpone your prayers and devotions for a while.'"

They all laughed. Then Ahmad taunted his brother, "The only thing your bride hasn't done yet is join the followers of Shaykh Ali al-Manufi."

The bridegroom retorted, "It was our shaykh who first advised me to marry."

Ahmad continued to tease his brother: "It seems the Muslim Brethren have made marriage a plank in their political platform."

Turning to Kamal, Ibrahim said, "You were very young then—I mean when I got married. And you had a lot more hair than today. You accused me and my brother of stealing your sisters and never forgave us."

"I was a blank page then," Kamal thought. "My struggles of conscience were not yet recorded there. They speak of married bliss. Haven't they heard what grumbling spouses say about it? I cherish Na'ima too much for me to tolerate a husband's growing tired of her. What is there in life that doesn't turn out to be a fraud?"

Commenting on her husband's statement, Khadija said, "We thought you were accusing our bridegrooms because you loved us. But eventually it became clear that you spoke from a hatred for marriage that you've had since you were a child."

Kamal laughed along with the others. He loved Khadija, and his affection was strengthened by his knowledge that she loved him dearly. Although upset by the young bridegroom's fanaticism, he liked and admired Ahmad. Kamal was fleeing matrimony but rather enjoyed having Khadija remind him of it at every opportunity. Profoundly influenced by the conjugal atmosphere that surrounded him, intoxicating his heart and senses, he felt a longing, although not for anyone or anything in particular. He wondered, as if for the first time, "What's keeping me from getting married? . . . My intellectual life, as I once claimed? Today I doubt the worth of both thought and the thinker. Is it fear, vengeance, masochism, or some reaction to my former love? My life provides evidence to support any of these hypotheses."

Ibrahim Shawkat asked Kamal, "Do you know why I'm sorry you're a bachelor?"

"Yes?"

"I'm convinced you'd be an exemplary husband if you did marry, for you're a family man by nature. You're organized, upright, and a respected civil servant. No doubt somewhere on this earth there's a girl who deserves you, and you're depriving her of her opportunity."

Even mules occasionally spoke words of wisdom . . . a girl somewhere in the world, but where? Yet he was unfairly accused of being upright, for he was nothing but a sinful and hypocritical pagan inebriate. A girl somewhere on the earth, presumably not in Jalila's brothel on al-Gawhari Alley. . . . Why were pains struggling with each other in his heart? How could one describe the kind of perplexity from which the only refuge was drink and lust? It was said that if you marry and have children, you will be immortal. He yearned in the worst possible way for all forms and varieties of immortality. In his despair would he finally resort to this trite and instinctual method? There was always hope that death would bring no pain to disturb his eternal repose. Death appeared frightening and senseless, but with life having lost all meaning, death seemed the only true pleasure left. How extraordinary it was that scholars devoted themselves to the advancement of science in their laboratories. How amazing it was that leaders jeopardized their careers for the sake of the constitution. But people who wandered aimlessly in their anxious torment—God's mercy on them.

Kamal looked from Ahmad to Abd al-Muni'm with a mixture of admiration and delight. The new generation was making its difficult way to well-defined goals without doubt or anxiety. He asked himself, "What's the secret of my enervating disease?"

Ahmad said, "I'm inviting the newlyweds, my parents, and my aunt to join me in a box at al-Rihani's theater this Thursday."

Khadija asked, "Al-Rihani?"

Ibrahim explained, "The actor who plays Kishkish Bey!"

Khadija laughed and said, "Yasin was almost thrown out of our house soon after he was first married because he took Ridwan's mother to see Kishkish one night."

"That's the way things were back then," Ahmad said, dismissing the implicit criticism. "Nowadays my grandfather wouldn't object to my grandmother's going to see Kishkish Bey."

Khadija replied, "Take the newlyweds and your father. The radio's enough for me."

Aisha said, "And coming to your house is sufficient entertainment for me."

Khadija launched into a rendition of the tale of Yasin and Kishkish Bey. Kamal happened to glance at his watch and remembered his appointment with Riyad Qaldas. So he rose and asked their permission to leave.

20

"Are you really able enjoy the beauties of nature only a few days before the examination?" one student asked another in a group sitting spread out in a semicircle on a green hill at the top of which stood a wooden pavilion occupied by more students. As far as the eye could see there were clusters of palms and flower beds separated by mosaic walks.

The second student answered, "Just as surely as Abd al-Muni'm Shawkat can get married shortly before it."

Abd al-Muni'm, who was seated toward the center of the semicircle near Ahmad Shawkat, said, "Contrary to what you think, a married student has the best possible chance of passing."

Sitting next to Ridwan Yasin at the other side of the semicircle, Hilmi Izzat remarked, "That's if the husband is one of the Muslim Brethren."

Ridwan laughed and revealed his pearly teeth, although this discussion depressed him. The whole subject of marriage awakened his anxieties, for he did not know whether he would embark on this adventure. The apparent necessity of marriage made it all the more terrifying, since it did not correspond to either his physical or his spiritual longings.

A student asked, "Who are the Muslim Brethren?"

Hilmi Izzat replied, "A religious group with the goal of reviving Islam, intellectually and practically. Haven't you heard of their circles that have been established in all the districts?"

"Does it differ from the Young Men's Muslim Association?"

"Yes."

"How?"

Pointing to Abd al-Muni'm Shawkat, he answered, "Ask the Muslim Brother."

In his powerful voice, Abd al-Muni'm said, "We're not merely an organization dedicated to teaching and preaching. We attempt to understand Islam as God intended it to be: a religion, a way of life, a code of law, and a political system."

"Is talk like this appropriate for the twentieth century?"

The forceful voice answered, "And for the hundred and twentieth century too."

"Confronted by democracy, Fascism, and Communism, we're dumbfounded. Then there's this new calamity."

Laughing, Ahmad observed, "But it's a godly calamity!"

There was an outburst of laughter, and Abd al-Muni'm glared at his brother angrily. Ridwan Yasin thought his cousin's words ill chosen and said, " 'Calamity' isn't the right word."

The same student asked Abd al-Muni'm, "Do you stone people who disagree with you?"

"Young people are given to deviant views and dissolute behavior. They deserve far worse than stoning, but we don't stone anyone. Instead we provide guidance and direction through moral suasion and example. There is a fine illustration in my own household, for I have a brother who is ripe for stoning. Here he is laughing about it in front of you and showing disrespect to his Creator, may He be glorified."

Ahmad laughed, and Hilmi Izzat told him, "If you feel threatened by your brother, I invite you to live with me in al-Darb al-Ahmar."

"Are you as bad as he is?"

"Certainly not. But we Wafdists are a tolerant bunch. The senior adviser to our leader is a Coptic Christian. That's what we're like."

The other student continued to question Abd al-Muni'm: "How can you advocate nonsense like this in the same month that the foreign capitulations have been abolished?"

Abd al-Muni'm asked in return, "Should we give up our religion in order to please foreigners?"

Approaching the same topic from a totally different angle, Ridwan Yasin remarked, "The capitulations were abrogated. I wonder what critics of the treaty can say now?"

"Those critics are insincere," Hilmi Izzat declared. "They're just envious and spiteful. True and total independence can only be seized by armed combat. How could they hope to achieve more by negotiating than we have?"

A voice remarked angrily, "Allow us to wonder about the future."

"What point is there in discussing the future in May with the examination staring us in the face? Spare us. After today to give myself time to study I'm not coming back to the college."

"Not so fast. There aren't any positions waiting for us. What future is there for Law or Arts students? You can either loaf around or take some job as a clerk. Go ahead and wonder about your futures, if you want."

"Now that the capitulations favoring foreigners have been abolished, doors will start to open."

"Doors? There are more people than doors!"

"Listen: Al-Nahhas broadened the system of admissions to the University after many had been arbitrarily excluded. Won't he also be able to find jobs for us?"

Then tongues fell silent and faces looked off toward the far end of the park, where a flock of four young women approached from the University en route to Giza. It was hardly possible to identify them, but as they were advancing with deliberate speed there was hope of a closer look. The path they were following circled around the spot where the young men sat before it turned off to the left. When the women came into plain view, their names and those of their faculties were on the boys' lips. There was a woman from Law and three from Arts.

Looking at one of them, Ahmad said to himself, "Alawiya Sabri." The name galvanized him. She was a young woman with an Egyptian version of Turkish beauty. Slender and of medium height, she had a fair complexion and coal-black hair. Her wide black eyes had lofty eyelids, and her eyebrows met in the center. She was distinguished by her aristocratic demeanor and refined gestures. Moreover, she was a classmate in the first university year. He had learned—and there is no end of information that an inquiring mind may acquire—that she had put her name down for sociology, just as he had. Although he had not yet had a chance to exchange a single word with her, she had aroused his interest at first sight. For years he had gazed admiringly at Na'ima, but she had never shaken him to the core. This girl was truly remarkable, and he looked forward to a platonic and possibly a romantic relationship with her.

Once the flock was out of sight again, Hilmi Izzat said, "Soon the Arts Faculty is going to resemble a women's college."

Looking from one to another of the Arts students in the semicircle, Ridwan Yasin warned, "Don't trust the friendship of law students who visit you frequently in your college between lectures. Their intentions are quite reprehensible." He laughed loudly, even though he was anything but happy then. Talking about the girls made him uneasy and sad.

"Why are girls so interested in the Arts Faculty?"

"Because the teaching profession offers them more opportunities than most others."

Hilmi Izzat said, "That's true, but there's also something feminine about instruction in the arts. Rouge, manicures, kohl for eyes, poetry, and stories all fall into one category."

Everyone laughed, even Ahmad, and despite their vigorous protests the other Arts students joined in. Ahmad retorted, "This unfair judgment applies equally to medicine. For a long time nursing has been considered a woman's job. The truth not yet firmly established in your souls is that men and women must be believed to be equal."

Smiling, Abd al-Muni'm said, "I don't know whether we praise or censure women when we call them our equals."

"If it's a question of rights and duties, then it's praise, not blame."

Abd al-Muni'm continued: "Islam holds men and women to be equal except with regard to inheritance."

Ahmad responded sarcastically, "Even in slavery it has treated them equally."

Abd al-Muni'm protested furiously, "You don't know anything about your religion. That's the tragedy."

Turning to Ridwan Yasin, Hilmi Izzat smilingly inquired, "What do you know about Islam?"

Another student asked Hilmi, "And how about you?"

Abd al-Muni'm asked his brother, Ahmad, "What knowledge of yours lets you blather on so?"

Ahmad replied calmly, "I know it's a religion, and that's enough for me. I don't believe in religions."

Abd al-Muni'm asked disapprovingly, "Do you have some proof that all religions are false?"

"Do you have any proof they're true?"

Raising his voice enough to make the young man sitting between the two brothers look from one to the other of them with some agitation, Abd al-Muni'm said, "I do. Every Believer does. But allow me to ask you first what you live by."

"My own personal beliefs . . . in science, humanity, and the future. These beliefs entail various duties intended to help establish a new order on earth."

"You destroy everything that makes man a human being."

"Say rather that the survival of a creed for more than a thousand years is not a sign of its strength but of the degradation of some human beings, for this flies in the face of life's normal process of renewal. Conduct and ideas appropriate for me when I was a child should change now that I am a man. For a long time people worshipped nature and other human beings. We can overcome our servitude to nature through science and inventions. Slavery to other human beings should be opposed by progressive theories. Anything else is a brake obstructing the free movement of humanity's wheel."

Disgusted by the thought that Ahmad was his brother, Abd al-Muni'm remarked, "It's easy to be an atheist. It's a simple, escapist solution, allowing you to shirk a Believer's responsibilities to his Lord, to himself, and to other people. No proof for atheism is any stronger than those for faith. Thus we do not choose by our intellects but by our conduct."

Ridwan interjected, "Don't let yourselves get carried away by the fury of your debate. Since you're brothers, the best thing would be for you to take the same side."

Hilmi Izzat, who was afflicted at times by inexplicable moments of rebelliousness, burst out, "Faith! Humanity! The future! . . . What rubbish! The only possible system is one based entirely on science. There is only one thing we need to believe in, and that is the extermination of human weakness in all its manifestations, no matter how stern our science seems. The goal is to bring humanity to an ideal condition, pure and powerful."

"Are these the new principles of the Wafd Party, subsequent to the treaty?"

Hilmi Izzat laughed, and this restored him to his normal good humor. Ridwan explained, "He's really a Wafdist but occasionally entertains bizarre and alien notions. He advocates killing everyone, when it may simply mean that he didn't sleep well the night before."

The reaction to this fierce quarrel was universal silence, which pleased Ridwan. His eyes roamed around, following some kites that circled overhead or gazing at the groups of palm trees. Everyone else felt free to express his opinion, even if it attacked his Creator. Yet he was compelled to conceal the controversies raging in his own soul, where they would remain a terrifying secret that threatened him. He might as well have been a scapegoat or an alien. Who had divided human behavior into normal and deviant? How could an adversary also serve as judge? Why were wretched people so often mocked?

Ridwan told Abd al-Muni'm, "Don't be angry. Religion has a Lord to protect it. As for you, in nine months at the most, you'll be a father."

"Is that so?"

Trying to appease his brother, Ahmad joked, "It's easier for me to confront God's wrath than yours."

Ahmad told himself, "Whether he's angry or not, when he returns to Sugar Street he'll find a sympathetic breast waiting for him. Is it ridiculous to think I'll return one day to find Alawiya Sabri waiting for me on the first floor of our house?"

He laughed, but no one suspected the true reason for his mirth.

21

There appeared to be an unusual flurry of activity at the home of
Abd al-Rahim Pasha Isa. Many people were standing in the garden
or sitting on the veranda, and there was a constant flow of men
arriving or departing. Hilmi Izzat nudged Ridwan Yasin's arm as they
neared the house and observed with relief, "Contrary to the claims
of their newspapers, we are not without our supporters."

As the two made their way inside, some of the young men shouted,
"Long live solidarity!" Ridwan's face became flushed from excitement. He was as zealous a rebel as the others but wondered anxiously
whether anyone suspected the nonpolitical side to his visits. Once
when he had confided his fears to Hilmi Izzat, the latter had said,
"Only cowards get suspected. Proceed with head held high and resolute steps. People preparing for public life shouldn't pay too much
attention to what others think of them."

Sitting in the reception room was a crowd of students, workers,
and members of the Wafd organization. Abd al-Rahim Pasha Isa,
looking uncustomarily grim, serious, and stern, sat at the front of the
room with the aura of an important statesman. When the two young
men approached, he rose to greet them gravely. After shaking hands,
he gestured for them to be seated.

One of the men sitting there resumed a discussion he had interrupted when the two arrived: "Public opinion was shocked to learn
the names of the members of the new cabinet, for they did not find
al-Nuqrashi's among them."

Abd al-Rahim Pasha Isa replied, "We suspected something as soon
as the cabinet resigned, especially since the dispute had become so
well known that it was even the talk of the coffeehouses. But al-
Nuqrashi is not like other members of the Wafd. The party has
sacked many, but no one with so much support. Al-Nuqrashi is entirely different. Don't forget that al-Nuqrashi implies Ahmad Mahir
too. They are the Wafd—the Wafd Party that has struggled, dis-
puted, and fought. Ask the gallows, prisons, and bombs. This time
the disagreement is not one that will dishonor those who leave the
Wafd, for the regime's integrity and the bombing case are both in

question. If the worst happens and the party is split, those who remain will be the deserters, not al-Nuqrashi and Mahir."

"Makram Ubayd has finally shown his true colors."

This statement sounded odd to Ridwan. It was hard for him to believe that such a prominent leader would be attacked this way by stalwart Wafdists.

Someone else remarked, "Makram Ubayd is the source of all this trouble, Your Excellency."

Abd al-Rahim Pasha replied, "The others are just as guilty."

"But he's the one who can't abide his rivals. He wants to control al-Nahhas all by himself. Once Mahir and al-Nuqrashi are out of the way, there will be no one to oppose him."

"If he could get rid of al-Nahhas, he would."

An elderly man sitting there said, "Please, don't exaggerate. The streams may return to their banks."

"After a cabinet has been formed without al-Nuqrashi?"

"Everything is possible."

"That would have been possible in Sa'd Zaghlul's era, but al-Nahhas is an obstinate man. When he's made up his mind. . . ."

At this point a man rushed in. The pasha greeted him at the center of the room. As they embraced each other warmly, the pasha asked, "When did you return? How's Alexandria?"

"Great . . . great! Al-Nuqrashi was welcomed at the Sidi Gabir station by unprecedented popular acclaim. Swarms of educated people shouted their heartfelt greetings. In their fury, they called rebelliously for integrity in government. They cried out, 'Long live al-Nuqrashi, the honest leader. Long live al-Nuqrashi, Sa'd's true successor.' Many shouted, 'Long live al-Nuqrashi, leader of the nation.' "

The man was speaking in a loud voice, and several of those listening repeated his slogans until Abd al-Rahim Pasha had to gesture for them to be calm. Then the man continued: "Public opinion is angry about the cabinet, outraged that al-Nuqrashi has been ousted from it. Al-Nahhas has done himself irreparable harm by consenting to support the devil against this pure angel."

Abd al-Rahim Pasha observed, "We're in August now. The University reopens in October. The showdown should come then. We must start preparing for the demonstrations. If al-Nahhas doesn't return to his senses, he can go to hell."

Hilmi Izzat said, "Rest assured that a great number of student demonstrations will converge on al-Nuqrashi's home."

Abd al-Rahim Pasha commented, "Everything needs to be organized. Meet with your student supporters and make your preparations. Moreover, according to my information, an incredible number of deputies and senators will side with us."

"Al-Nuqrashi was the founder of the Wafdist committees. Don't forget that. Telegrams of support pile up in his office from dawn to dusk."

Ridwan wondered what was happening to the world. Would the Wafd Party be divided again? Was Makram Ubayd truly responsible for this? Were the best interests of the nation really compatible with a split in the party that had represented it for eighteen years?

The exchange of views lasted a long time as the men assembled there discussed how to make their views known and how to run the demonstrations. Then they started to leave. At last only the pasha, Ridwan, and Hilmi Izzat remained. Invited by their host to move to the veranda, they followed him outside. The three sat around a table and were immediately served lemonade. Shortly thereafter a man in his forties appeared at the door. From previous visits Ridwan recognized him as Ali Mihran, an aide to the pasha. The man's appearance showed a natural inclination toward frivolity and mirth. He was accompanied by a young fellow in his twenties with a handsome countenance. Unruly hair, long side curls, and a broad necktie suggested that this stranger was an artist by profession. With a smile on his lips, Ali Mihran advanced, kissed the pasha's hand, and shook hands with the two visitors. Then he introduced the newcomer: "Mr. Atiya Jawdat, a young but gifted singer. Your Excellency, I've mentioned him to you before."

Putting on his glasses, which he had laid on the table, the pasha examined the young man carefully. Smiling, he said, "Welcome, Mr. Atiya. I've heard a lot about you. Perhaps we'll hear you yourself this time."

The singer invoked God's blessings on the pasha and sat down, while Ali Mihran leaned over the pasha to ask, "How are you, Uncle?" That was what he called the pasha when formalities could be ignored.

Grinning, the man replied, "A thousand times better than you are."

With uncustomary earnestness, Ali Mihran said, "At the Anglo Bar people are whispering about a possible nationalist cabinet headed by al-Nuqrashi. . . ."

The pasha smiled diplomatically and murmured, "We're not in line for the cabinet."

With anxious interest Ridwan inquired, "What grounds are there for these rumors? I naturally can't imagine that al-Nuqrashi would plot like Muhammad Mahmud or Isma'il Sidqy to bring down the government."

Ali Mihran said, "A plot? No. At present it's merely a question of convincing a majority of the senators and deputies to join us. Don't forget that the king is on our side. Ali Mahir goes about his work deliberately and wisely."

Ridwan asked dejectedly, "Will we end up being the king's men?"

Abd al-Rahim Pasha observed, "That sounds bad, but the expression means something different now. Faruq is quite unlike his father, King Fuad. Circumstances have changed. The present king is an enthusiastic young nationalist. He's the one wronged by al-Nahhas's unfair attacks."

Ali Mihran rubbed his hands together gleefully as he said, "When do you suppose we'll be congratulating the pasha on his cabinet post? Will you choose me to assist you in the ministry just as you've had me help you with your other affairs?"

Laughing, the pasha said, "No, I'll appoint you director general of prisons, for that's your natural milieu."

"Prison? But they say it's for brutes."

"It takes in other types too. Don't worry about it." Suddenly overcome by annoyance, he cried out, "That's enough politics! Change the mood, please." Turning toward Mr. Atiya, he asked, "What are you going to sing for us?"

Ali Mihran interjected, "The pasha is a connoisseur who delights in music and good times. If your singing appeals to him, you'll find the way open for you to have your songs broadcast."

Atiya Jawdat said gently, "I've recently set to music some lyrics entitled 'They bound me to him,' composed by Mr. Mihran."

Staring at his aide, the pasha asked, "How long have you been writing songs?"

"Didn't I spend seven years at the seminary of al-Azhar, immersed in the study of Arabic and its meters?"

"What's the relationship between al-Azhar and your naughty songs? 'They bound me to him'! Who is he, my dear seminarian?"

"The answer's hiding behind your beard, Your Excellency."

"You son of an old hag!"

Ali Mihran summoned the butler, and the pasha asked, "Why are you calling him?"

"To set up for the music."

Rising, the politician said, "Wait till I perform the evening prayers."

Mihran smiled wickedly and asked, "When we touched in greeting, didn't that end your state of ritual cleanliness?"

22

Leaning on his stick, Ahmad Abd al-Jawad left his house with slow steps. Things had changed. Since the liquidation of his store, he left home but once a day, for he tried to spare himself the stress that climbing the stairs put on his heart. Although it was only September, he had chosen wool garments. His thin frame could no longer bear the brisk weather his plump and powerful body had once enjoyed. The stick, which had been his companion since he was a young man, when it had been a symbol of virility and of elegance, now helped support him as he plodded along slowly. Even this level of exertion was a trial for his heart. All the same he had not lost his dapper good looks. He still dressed quite splendidly, used a fragrant cologne, and took full advantage of the charm and dignity of old age.

When he drew near the store, his eyes glanced toward it involuntarily. The sign that had borne his name and his father's for years and years had been removed, and the appearance and use of the establishment had changed. It had become a fez shop, where new ones were sold and old ones blocked. The copper forms and the heating apparatus were up in front. He imagined he saw a placard, invisible to everyone else, informing him that his time had passed . . . his time for serious endeavors, hard work, and pleasure. Retreating into retirement, he had turned his back on hope, finding himself face to face with old age, ill health, and the need to idle his time away. He had always been full of love for the world and its pleasures. Often he still was, but now his spirits sank. He had considered faith itself one of the joys of life and a reason for embracing the world. He had never—not even now—pursued the kind of ascetic piety that turns its back on the world and concerns itself solely with the afterlife. The store was no longer his, but how could he erase its memory from his mind, when it had been the hub of his activities, the focus of his attention, the meeting place for his friends and lovers, and the source of his renown and prestige?

"You may console yourself by saying, 'We've found husbands for the girls and reared the boys. We've lived to see our grandchildren.

We have enough money to keep us till we die. We've experienced
life's delights for years.' Has it really been years? 'Now the time has
come for us to show our gratitude, and it is our obligation to thank
God always and forever.' But oh how nostalgic I feel. . . . May God
forgive time—time, which by the mere fact of its uninterrupted existence betrays man in the worst possible way. If stones could speak,
I would ask this site to inform me about the past, to tell me if this
body could really crush mountains once. Did this sick heart beat
regularly then? Did this mouth do anything but laugh? Was pain an
unknown emotion? Was this the image of me treasured by every
heart? . . . Again, I ask God to forgive time."

When his deliberate pace finally brought him to the mosque of al-
Husayn, he removed his shoes and entered, reciting the opening
prayer of the Qur'an. He made his way to the pulpit area, where he
found Muhammad Iffat and Ibrahim al-Far waiting for him. They all
performed the sunset prayer together and then left the mosque, heading for al-Tambakshiya to visit Ali Abd al-Rahim. Each of them had
retired due to ill health, but they were in better shape than Ali Abd
al-Rahim, who was bedridden.

Sighing, al-Sayyid Ahmad said, "I imagine that soon the sole way
I'll be able to get to the mosque is by riding."

"You're not the only one!"

Then al-Sayyid Ahmad added anxiously, "I'm dreadfully afraid I'll
be confined to bed like Mr. Ali. I pray that God will favor me with
death before my strength gives out."

"May our Lord spare you and the rest of us every misfortune."

As if frightened by the thought, he commented, "Ghunaym
Hamidu lay paralyzed in bed for about a year. Sadiq al-Mawardi suffered the same kind of torment for months. May God grant us a
speedy end when the time comes."

Muhammad Iffat laughed and said, "If you let gloomy thoughts get
the better of you, you'll be nothing but a woman. Declare that there
is only one God, brother."

When they reached the home of Ali Abd al-Rahim, they went to
his room. Before they could say anything, he blurted out unhappily,
"You're late, may God forgive you."

The vexation of the bedridden man was visible in his eyes. The
only time he ever smiled was when they were with him. He complained, "All day long my only occupation is listening to the radio.
What would I do if it had not yet been introduced to Egypt? I enjoy

everything that's broadcast, even lectures I can barely understand. All
the same we're not so old that we should be suffering like this. Our
grandfathers married new wives at this age."

Ahmad Abd al-Jawad's sense of humor got the better of him, and
he observed, "That's an idea! What do you think about us taking
another wife? Perhaps that would bring back our youth and cure what
ails us."

Ali Abd al-Rahim smiled but refrained from laughing for fear he
would break into a fit of coughing that would strain his heart. "I'm
with you!" he said. "Select a bride for me. But tell her frankly that
the bridegroom can't move and that it's all up to her."

As though suddenly remembering something, al-Far told him,
"Ahmad Abd al-Jawad will see a great-grandchild before you do. May
our Lord prolong his life."

"Congratulations in advance, son of Abd al-Jawad."

Al-Sayyid Ahmad frowned as he replied, "Na'ima is pregnant, but
I have some misgivings. I still remember what was said about her
heart when she was born. I've tried without success to forget that for
a long time."

"What an ungrateful soul you are! Since when do you put your
faith in the prophecies of physicians?"

Laughing, al-Sayyid Ahmad answered, "Since I'm kept awake till
dawn whenever I eat anything they've forbidden me."

Ali Abd al-Rahim asked, "What about our Lord's compassion?"

"Praise to God, Lord of the universe." Then he added, "I'm not
oblivious to God's mercy, but fear spawns fear. Ali, the fact is that
I'm more worried about Aisha than Na'ima. All my anxieties in life
converge on Aisha, that miserable darling. When I leave her, she'll
be alone in the world."

Ibrahim al-Far commented, "Our Lord is always present. He is the
ultimate guardian for everyone."

They were silent for a time. Finally Ali Abd al-Rahim's voice cur-
tailed the silence: "It will be my turn after yours to see a great-
grandchild."

Al-Sayyid Ahmad laughed and said, "May God forgive girls for
making parents and grandparents old before their time."

Muhammad Iffat cried out, "Old man, admit you're old and stop
being so obstinate."

"You mustn't raise your voice for fear my heart will hear you and
act up. It's like a spoiled child."

Shaking his head sorrowfully, Ibrahim al-Far said, "What a year we've had.... It's been rough. It hasn't left any of us in good shape—as if ill health had booked an appointment with us."

"In the words of Abd al-Wahhab's song, 'Let's live together and die together.' "

They all laughed. Ali Abd al-Rahim changed his tone and asked seriously, "Is it right? I mean what al-Nuqrashi did?"

Ahmad Abd al-Jawad frowned as he answered, "I hoped so much that things would return to normal.... I ask the forgiveness of God Almighty."

"A fraternal bond developed through a lifetime of shared struggle went up in smoke."

"Nowadays all good deeds go up in smoke."

Ahmad Abd al-Jawad continued: "Nothing has made me so sad as al-Nuqrashi's departure from the Wafd. He should not have carried the dispute that far."

"What fate do you suppose awaits him?"

"The inevitable one, for where are rebels like al-Basil and al-Shamsi today? This valiant leader has sealed his own fate and taken Ahmad Mahir down with him."

Then Muhammad Iffat said nervously, "Spare us this story. I'm about ready to renounce politics."

Al-Far had an idea and asked with a smile, "If we were forced— God forbid it—to take to our beds, like Mr. Ali, how would we meet and converse with each other?"

Muhammad Iffat murmured, "God's will be done—not yours!"

Ahmad Abd al-Jawad laughed and replied, "If the worst happens, then we'll talk to each other by radio, the way Papa Soot talks to the children when he does his show."

They laughed together. Muhammad Iffat took out his watch to consult it. Ali Abd al-Rahim became alarmed and said, "You'll stay with me until the doctor comes, so you can hear what he has to say —may he and his days be cursed."

23

The shops in al-Ghuriya were closing. There were few people in the street, and the cold was intense. It was the middle of December, and winter had arrived early. Kamal had no difficulty tempting Riyad Qaldas to visit the district of al-Husayn. Although not a native of the area, the young man loved strolling through it and sitting in its coffeehouses. More than a year and a half had passed since their first meeting at *al-Fikr* magazine, and not a week had gone by without their seeing each other once or twice. During the school vacation they got together almost every evening at either the magazine, the house on Palace Walk, Riyad's home in Manshiya al-Bakri, the cafés of Imad al-Din Street, or the grand coffeehouse of al-Husayn, to which Kamal had retreated after Ahmad Abduh's historic one had been destroyed and permanently erased from existence.

They were both happy with this friendship, and Kamal had once told himself, "I missed Husayn Shaddad for years. His place remained empty until Riyad Qaldas took it." When he was with Riyad, Kamal's spirit came to life and was filled with an explosion of energy sparked by their intellectual exchange. This was true despite their marked—if complementary—differences from each other. They were both conscious of a mutual affection but never referred to it openly. Neither said to the other, "You're my friend" or "I can't imagine life without you," but this was the truth of the matter. The cold weather did not diminish their desire to walk, and they had decided to proceed on foot to their favorite café on Imad al-Din Street.

Riyad Qaldas was upset that evening. He said passionately, "The constitutional crisis has concluded with the rout of the people. Al-Nahhas' removal is a defeat for the nation in its historic struggle with the palace."

Kamal answered sorrowfully, "It's clear now that Faruq's as bad as his father."

"Faruq's not the only one responsible. The traditional enemies of the people have engineered this debacle. It's the work of Ali Mahir and Muhammad Mahmud. Lamentably Ahmad Mahir and al-Nuqrashi, these two populist leaders, joined ranks with the enemies of the people. If the nation were cleansed of traitors, the king would not find anyone to help him suppress the rights of the people." After a short silence he continued: "The English aren't playing an active role now, but the people and the king are at loggerheads. Independence isn't everything. There is also the people's sacred prerogative to enjoy their rights and their sovereignty—to live as free men, not slaves."

Unlike Riyad, Kamal was not deeply engaged in politics, but his doubts had not been able to destroy it for him, as they had so many other interests. It retained an emotional vitality for him. His heart believed firmly in the rights of the people, no matter how divided his intellect was on the subject, espousing at times "the rights of man," and on other occasions proclaiming, "It's all a question of the survival of the fittest. The masses are the common herd." It might also wonder, "Isn't Communism an experiment worth exploring?" His heart had not been purged of the populist sentiments with which he had grown up, and these were mixed with memories of Fahmy.

Politics was an essential element of Riyad's intellectual activity. He asked, "Is it possible for us to forget the humiliating reception Makram Ubayd got in the square in front of Abdin Palace or al-Nahhas's criminal ouster, that insulting calumny, like spit in the face of the nation? Blind hatred makes some applaud it, alas."

"You're just angry because of what happened to Makram Ubayd," Kamal teased.

Without any hesitation Riyad replied, "All of us Copts are Wafdists. That's because the Wafd Party represents true nationalism. It's not a religious, Turkish-oriented bunch like the National Party. The Wafd is a populist party. It will make Egypt a nation that provides freedom for all Egyptians, without regard to ethnic origin or religious affiliation. The enemies of the people know this. That's why the Copts were targeted for barefaced oppression throughout the Sidqy era. Now we'll be experiencing that again."

Kamal welcomed this candor, which demonstrated the depth of their friendship. All the same he felt like teasing Riyad some more: "Here you are, talking about Coptic Christians, when you believe in nothing but science and art. . . ."

Riyad fell silent. They had reached al-Azhar Street, where the cold wind gusted rather fiercely. As they walked along they came to a pastry shop, and Kamal invited Riyad to have some with him. They each got a modest plateful and stepped to the side of the shop to eat. Then Riyad said, "I'm both a freethinker and a Copt. Indeed I'm both a Copt and a man without any religion. I frequently feel that Christianity is my community, not my faith. If I analyzed this feeling, I might entertain some reservations about it. But not so fast . . . isn't it cowardly to ignore my people? There's one thing that can help me overcome this quandary, and that is to devote myself to the kind of sincere Egyptian patriotism envisaged by Sa'd Zaghlul. Al-Nahhas is a Muslim by way of religion, but he's also a nationalist in every sense of the word. He makes us think of ourselves as Egyptians, whether we are Muslims or Copts. I could lead a happy life with an untroubled mind by focusing on thoughts like these, but a real life is at the same time a responsible one."

Kamal's breast was agitated by emotion and his thoughts wandered as he smacked his lips over the pastry. Riyad's appearance, which was so purely Egyptian that it reminded him of a pharaonic portrait, stirred various reflections: "Riyad's point can't be denied. I'm torn between the dictates of my intellect and of my heart, and so is he. How can a minority live in the midst of a majority that oppresses it? Different sacred scriptures are commonly compared according to the level of happiness they provide to human beings, and that is most clearly represented by the amount of aid they give the oppressed."

Kamal said, "Forgive me. I've never had to deal with racism. From the very beginning my mother trained me to love everyone, and I grew up in the revolutionary atmosphere that was free of ethnic prejudices. So I have had no experience with this problem."

As they resumed their walk, Riyad said, "One would hope there wouldn't be any problem at all. I'm sorry to have to tell you bluntly that we grew up in homes with plenty of gloomy memories. I'm not a Coptic chauvinist, but anyone who neglects human rights, whether at home or at the ends of the earth, has neglected the rights of all mankind."

"That's beautifully put. It's not surprising that truly humanitarian manifestos originate frequently in minority circles or with people whose consciences are troubled by the problems of minorities. But there are always some fanatics."

"Always. Everywhere. Men have only recently evolved from animals. Your fanatics consider us cursed infidels. Our fanatics consider you infidel usurpers. They call themselves descendants of the kings of ancient Egypt and people who were able to preserve their religion by paying the poll tax levied on non-Muslims."

Kamal laughed out loud. Then he said, "That's precisely what the two sides say. Do you suppose the origin of this dispute is religion or a human proclivity for dissension? Muslims don't all agree with each other and neither do Christians. You will find that there have long been disagreements between Shi'i Muslims and Sunni Muslims, Hijazi Muslims and Iraqi Muslims, Wafdists and Constitutionalists, students in the humanities and in the sciences, and supporters of the rival Ahli and Arsenal soccer teams. But in spite of this contentious streak in human nature, we are deeply upset when we read newspaper accounts of an earthquake in Japan. Listen, why don't you treat this subject in your stories?"

"The problem of Copts and Muslims. . . ." Riyad Qaldas was quiet for a time. Then he said, "I'm afraid it would be misunderstood." After another period of silence he added, "And don't forget that, in spite of everything, we're enjoying our golden age. At one time Shaykh Abd al-Aziz Jawish suggested that Muslims should make shoes from our hides."

"How can we eradicate this problem?"

"Fortunately it has been absorbed by the problems of the people as a whole. Today the Copts' problem is the people's problem. We are oppressed when everyone else is. When the people are free, we are."

"Happiness and peace," Kamal thought. "That's the goal we dream of. Your heart lives by love alone. When will your mind find its proper way? When will I be able to say, 'Yes, yes!' with the certainty of my nephew Abd al-Muni'm? My friendship with Riyad has taught me to read his stories. But how can I believe in art at the very time that I find philosophy inadequate and inhospitable?"

Glancing stealthily in his direction, Riyad suddenly asked Kamal, "What are you thinking about now? . . . Tell me the truth."

Understanding the reason for his friend's question, Kamal answered candidly, "I was thinking about your stories."

"Weren't you distressed by my bluntness?"

"Me! God forgive you."

Riyad laughed a bit apologetically and then inquired, "Have you read my latest story?"

"Yes. It's nice. But I can't help thinking that art isn't serious work. Of course, I need to point out that I don't know whether work or play is more significant in life. You have advanced training in the sciences and perhaps know as much about them as anyone who is not actually a scientist, but all your efforts are squandered on writing stories. I wonder occasionally how science has helped you."

Riyad Qaldas replied vigorously, "I have transferred from science to art a sincere devotion to the truth, a willingness to confront the facts no matter how bitter they are, an impartiality of judgment, and finally a comprehensive respect for all creatures."

These were grand words, but what relationship did they have to comic stories? Riyad Qaldas looked at him and, reading the doubt in his expression, laughed aloud. Then Riyad said, "You have a low opinion of art. My only consolation is that there's nothing on earth that escapes your doubts. We understand with our minds but live with our hearts. Despite your skeptical stance, you love, work together with other people, and share in the political life of your nation. Whether we are conscious of it or not, behind each of these initiatives there is a principle that is no less powerful than faith. Art is the interpreter of the human world. Besides that, some writers have produced works forming part of the international contest of ideas. In their hands art has become one of the weapons of international progress. There is no way that art can be considered a frivolous activity."

"Is this a defense of art or of the artist?" Kamal asked himself. "If the man who sells melon seeds had a talent for debating, he would prove that he plays a significant role in the life of mankind. It's quite possible that everything has an intrinsic merit. Similarly, it's not out of the question that everything, without exception, is worthless. Millions of people are breathing their last at this moment, and yet a child's voice is raised to bewail the loss of a toy and a lover's moans resound throughout existence to broadcast the torments of his heart. Should I laugh or weep?"

Kamal remarked, "With regard to what you said about the international competition of ideas, let me tell you that it's being played out on a small scale in our family. One of my nephews is a Muslim Brother and one a Communist."

"Sooner or later this struggle will be reflected in some form everywhere. We don't live in a vacuum. Haven't you thought about these issues?"

"I read about Communism when I studied materialist philosophy, and similarly I've read books about Fascism and the Nazis."

"You read and understand. You're a historian with no history. I hope you observe the day you emerge from this condition as your true birthday."

Kamal was offended by this remark, not only because of its stinging criticism but also because of the truth it contained. To avoid commenting on it, he said, "Neither the Communist nor the Muslim Brother in our family has a sound knowledge of what he believes."

"Belief is a matter of willing, not of knowing. The most casual Christian today knows far more about Christianity than the Christian martyrs did. It's the same with you in Islam."

"Do you believe in any of these ideologies?"

After some reflection, Riyad replied, "It's clear that I despise Fascism, the Nazi movement, and all other dictatorial systems. Communism might be able to create a world free from the calamities of racial and religious friction and from class conflicts. All the same, my primary interest is my art."

In a teasing tone, Kamal asked, "But more than a thousand years ago Islam created this ideal world you've mentioned."

"But it's a religion. Communism is a science. Religion is nothing more than a myth." Then, smiling, he added, "The problem is that we interact with Muslims, not with Islam."

They found Fuad I Street very crowded despite the cold weather. Riyad stopped suddenly and asked, "What would you think about having macaroni with an excellent wine for supper?"

"I don't drink in places where a lot of people will see me. If you want, we could go to Ukasha's café."

Riyad Qaldas laughed and said, "How can you bear to be so sedate? Spectacles, mustache, and traditional mores! You've liberated your mind from every fetter, but your body is bound with chains. You were created—at least your body was—to be a teacher."

Riyad's reference to his body reminded Kamal of a painful incident. He had attended the birthday party of a colleague, and they had all become intoxicated. Then a guest had launched a verbal attack on him, pointing out his head and nose, and everyone had laughed. Whenever he thought of his head and nose he also remembered Aïda and the past—Aïda, who had first made him self-conscious about his features. It was amazing that when love receded, nothing came to take its place. All that remained were bitter dregs.

Riyad pulled at his arm and said, "Let's go drink some wine and talk about literature. Then afterward we'll go to Madam Jalila's house in al-Gawhari Alley. If you call her 'Auntie,' I will too."

24

There was a flurry of activity at Sugar Street, or more precisely in the apartment of Abd al-Muni'm Shawkat. Gathered in the bedroom around Na'ima's bed were Amina, Khadija, Aisha, Zanuba, and a nurse-midwife. In the parlor, sitting with Abd al-Muni'm were his father Ibrahim, his brother Ahmad, Yasin, and Kamal. Yasin was teasing Abd al-Muni'm: "Arrange things so that the next birth doesn't come when you're preparing for an exam."

It was the end of April. Abd al-Muni'm was tired, delighted, and anxious in equal measure. Screams provoked by labor pains carried through the closed door, and the entire spectrum of pain was present in these shrill cries.

Abd al-Muni'm remarked, "Pregnancy has exhausted her and has left her incredibly weak. Her face is so pale that all the blood seems to have drained away."

Yasin belched contentedly and then said, "This is normal. It's always this way."

Smiling, Kamal observed, "I still remember when Na'ima was born. It was a difficult delivery, and Aisha suffered terribly. I was very upset and stood here with her late husband, Khalil."

Abd al-Muni'm asked, "Do you mean to tell me that difficult deliveries are hereditary?"

Gesturing heavenward with his finger, Yasin said, "He can make everything easy."

Abd al-Muni'm said, "We got a nurse-midwife who is known throughout the entire district. My mother would have preferred to have the woman who delivered us, but I insisted on having a trained professional. There's no doubt that she is cleaner and more skillful."

Yasin replied, "Naturally. Although, as a whole, childbirth is in God's hands. He controls it."

Lighting a cigarette, Ibrahim Shawkat said, "Her labor pains began early in the morning. Now it's almost five P.M. The poor dear is as insubstantial as a shadow. May our Lord come to her aid."

Then glancing with languid eyes at the other men, particularly at his sons, Abd al-Muni'm and Ahmad, he said, "Oh, if only you would remember the pain a mother endures. . . ."

Laughing, Ahmad said, "How can you expect a fetus to remember anything, Papa?"

The man scolded his son: "When it's a question of gratitude, there's no need to depend solely on memory."

The screams stopped. The bedroom was silent, and everyone looked in that direction. After a few moments, his patience exhausted, Abd al-Muni'm rose, went to the door, and knocked. The door was opened just enough to reveal Khadija's plump face. He gave her a questioning look and tried to poke his head inside. But she blocked him with the palms of her hands and said, "God hasn't granted a delivery yet."

"It's taking a long time. Could it be false labor?"

"The midwife knows better than we do. Calm down and pray for a safe delivery."

She closed the door. The young man resumed his seat next to his father, who justified Abd al-Muni'm's anxiety: "You'll have to excuse him. This is his first time."

Wishing to distract himself, Kamal took out *al-Balagh*, the newspaper that had been folded up in his pocket, and started to leaf through it. Then Ahmad said, "The results of the last election were announced on the radio." Smiling scornfully, he added, "How ridiculous they were. . . ."

His father asked casually, "How many Wafdists were elected?"

"Thirteen, if I remember correctly."

Addressing his uncle Yasin, Ahmad said, "I guess you're happy, Uncle, for Ridwan's sake?"

Yasin shrugged his shoulders and replied, "He's not a cabinet minister or a deputy. So how does that affect me?"

Laughing, Ibrahim Shawkat said, "The Wafdists thought the age of rigged elections was over, but the reformers are more corrupt than the sycophants they replaced."

Ahmad said resentfully, "It's clear that in Egypt the exception is the rule."

"Even al-Nahhas and Makram were defeated. Isn't that a joke?"

At this point Ibrahim Shawkat said rather sharply, "But no one can deny they were rude to the king. Kings have a certain stature. That wasn't the right way to do things."

Ahmad responded, "To wake up from its long torpor, our country needs a strong dose of disrespect for kings."

Kamal remarked, "But these dogs are returning us to a form of absolute rule hidden behind a counterfeit parliament. At the end of this experiment, we'll find that Faruq's as powerful and tyrannical as Fuad, or worse. And all this is the fault of some of our compatriots."

Yasin laughed. As if to clarify and explain the point, he said, "Although when Kamal was a boy he loved the English as dearly as Shahin, Adli, Tharwat, and Haydar did, afterward he turned into a Wafdist."

Looking at Ahmad most of all, Kamal said earnestly, "The elections were rigged. Everyone in the country knows that. All the same they have been recognized officially, and the country will be governed according to their results. What this means is that people will become convinced that their representatives are thieves who stole their seats in parliament, that the cabinet ministers also stole their posts, that the whole government is bogus and fraudulent, and that theft, fraud, and deception are legitimate and officially sanctioned. So isn't an ordinary man to be excused if he renounces lofty principles and morality and believes in deceit and opportunism?"

Ahmad replied enthusiastically, "Let them rule. There's a positive side to every wrong. It's better for the people to be humiliated than for them to be intoxicated by a government they love and trust, if it does not fulfill their true wishes. I've often thought about this, and as a result I have more appreciation for the reign of despots like Muhammad Mahmud and Isma'il Sidqy."

Kamal noticed that Abd al-Muni'm was not taking his usual part in the conversation. Wishing to draw him out, Kamal said, "Why don't you tell us your opinion?"

Smiling vacuously, Abd al-Muni'm answered, "Let me listen today."

Yasin laughed and said, "Pull yourself together. If the baby finds you looking so glum, it will think twice about staying." He shifted restlessly, and Kamal interpreted this as a prelude to an excuse for leaving. Yes, it was time for Yasin to take up his post at the coffeehouse. His evening adventures followed a schedule that nothing could alter.

Kamal thought he would depart with his brother, since there was no reason for him to stay either. Ready to make his move, Kamal watched Yasin carefully. Then a harsh and violent scream burst forth from Na'ima's room, conveying the deepest form of human emotion. One fierce shriek followed another in rapid succession. All eyes were fixed on the door, and the men fell silent. Finally Ibrahim whispered hopefully, "Perhaps it's the end of the labor, God willing."

Was that it? But the screaming continued, and the men felt disheartened. Abd al-Muni'm looked quite pale. Na'ima's room was silent once more, although only for a time. When the screams resumed they sounded hollow, as though expelled by a hoarse throat and an exhausted chest in the throes of death.

Since Abd al-Muni'm clearly needed encouragement, Yasin told him, "You're not hearing anything you wouldn't at any other difficult delivery."

"Difficult! Difficult! But why should it be difficult?"

The door was opened by Zanuba, who came out, closing it behind her. They stared at her. Walking over to Yasin, she stopped in front of him and said, "Everything's fine, but as a precaution the midwife wants you to ask Dr. Sayyid Muhammad to come."

Jumping to his feet, Abd al-Muni'm said, "Then no doubt her condition requires it. Tell me what's wrong."

In a calm, confident voice, Zanuba replied, "Everything's fine. If you want to reassure us, hurry to get the doctor."

Wasting no time, Abd al-Muni'm went immediately to his room to finish dressing. Ahmad followed him, and they went off together to fetch the doctor. Then Yasin asked his wife, "What's going on in there?"

Her face betraying her anxiety for the first time, Zanuba said, "The poor dear's very tired, God help her."

"Hasn't the midwife said anything?"

In a resigned tone, Zanuba answered, "She says she wants the doctor."

Leaving a heavy cloud of anxiety behind her, Zanuba returned to the bedroom. Yasin wondered aloud, "How far is this doctor?"

Ibrahim Shawkat replied, "In the building over your coffeehouse in al-Ataba."

A scream rang out and struck them dumb. Had the labor pains resumed? When would the doctor arrive? There was another resounding scream. The tension increased. And then Yasin cried out in alarm, "That's Aisha's voice!"

Listening intently, they recognized Aisha's shriek. Ibrahim went to the door and knocked. When Zanuba opened it, her face exceedingly pale, he asked apprehensively, "What's the matter? What's the matter with Mrs. Aisha? Wouldn't it be best for her to leave the room?"

Swallowing, Zanuba replied, "Absolutely not. The situation is extremely serious, Mr. Ibrahim."

"What's happened?"

"All of a sudden . . . she . . . look . . ."

In less than a second the three men were at the door of the room, looking in. Na'ima was covered to her chest. Her aunt, her grandmother, and the midwife were around the bed. Na'ima's mother stood in the center of the room, staring at her daughter from afar with eyes that did not seem to focus on anything, as if she was in a daze. Na'ima's eyes were closed, and her breast was heaving up and down as though it had slipped free of its ties to her still body. Her face was white, with a deathly pallor.

The midwife shouted, "The doctor!"

Amina began to exclaim, "Lord! . . ."

In a terrified voice, Khadija called out, "Na'ima . . . answer me."

Aisha said nothing, as if the matter had no relationship to her whatsoever.

"What's happening?" Kamal wondered. Stunned, he asked his brother. But Yasin did not reply.

"What a difficult delivery!" Kamal thought. He glanced around at Aisha, Ibrahim, and Yasin, and his heart sank. Their expressions could mean only one thing.

They all went into the room. It was no longer a delivery room, or they would not have entered. Aisha was in an extreme state, but no one said anything to her. Na'ima opened her eyes, which seemed glazed. When she moved as if wanting to rise, her grandmother helped her sit up and embraced her. The girl gasped and moaned. Suddenly, she cried out as if appealing for help, "Mama . . . I'm going . . . I'm going." Then her head fell on her grandmother's breast.

The room came alive with a noisy commotion. Khadija slapped her cheeks. Directing her words to the girl's face, Amina recited the Muslim credo: "There is no god but God, and Muhammad is the Messenger of God."

Aisha gazed out the window overlooking Sugar Street, focusing her eyes on some unknown spot. Then her voice rang out like a death rattle: "What is this, my Lord? What are You doing? Why? Why? I want to understand."

Ibrahim Shawkat went to her and stretched out his hand, but she pushed it away with a nervous gesture and said, "Don't any of you touch me. Leave me alone. Leave me. . . ." Glancing around at them, she said, "Please leave. Don't say a word. Is there anything you could say? Words won't help me. Na'ima's dead, as you can see. She was all I had left. There's nothing for me in the world now. Please go away."

It was pitch-black when Yasin and Kamal returned to Palace Walk. Yasin said, "It will be very hard for me to break the news to your father."

Drying his eyes, Kamal replied, "Yes."

"Don't cry. My nerves can't take any more. . . ."

Sighing, Kamal said, "She was very dear to me. Brother, I'm sad. And poor Aisha!"

"That's the ultimate calamity. Aisha! We'll all forget in time, but not Aisha."

" 'We'll all forget'?" Kamal asked himself. "I think her face will stay with me to the end of my days, although I've already had one extraordinary experience with forgetting. . . . It can be a great blessing, but when will its balm arrive?"

Yasin continued: "I had my reservations when she got married. Don't you know? When she was born, the doctor predicted that her heart was not strong enough for her to live past twenty. Your father almost certainly remembers."

"I don't know anything about this. Did Aisha know?"

"Certainly not. It's ancient history. There's no escaping God's decree."

"How unfortunate you are, Aisha!"

"Yes. The poor dear is really unlucky."

25 ~

Ahmad Ibrahim Shawkat sat in the reading room of the University library concentrating on the book in front of him. Only a week was left before the examination, and he had exhausted himself studying for it. He heard someone enter and sit down behind him. Turning around curiously, he saw Alawiya Sabri. Yes, it was the girl herself. Perhaps she was sitting there to wait for the book he had. At that moment his eyes met two black ones. He turned his head back to its original position, with heart and senses in a state of intoxication. There could be no doubt that she had begun to recognize him. And she must have realized he was in love with her. Things like that could not be hidden. Besides, wherever she turned, in a class or in al-Urman Gardens, she would often find him glancing at her stealthily.

Her presence distracted him from his reading, but his delight was too great to be measured. Ever since he had learned that, like him, she would be majoring in sociology, he had hoped they would get acquainted the next year. There were too many students in the first university year for him to meet her then. Whenever he had been this close to her before there had been many people watching. He would go to the reference shelves, pretend to look at a book there, and greet her on the way. He cast a glance around him and found some students scattered around the room, but not more than he could count on the fingers of one hand. He rose without any hesitation and walked down the aisle between the seats. As he passed her, their eyes met, and he bowed his head in a polite greeting. The impact of the surprise was apparent in her expression, but she nodded to acknowledge his greeting and looked back at her work.

He wondered whether he had made a mistake, but concluded he had not, since she had been his classmate all year long. It was his duty to greet her when they met face to face like this in a place that was almost deserted. He proceeded on to the bookcase containing the encyclopedia. Choosing a volume, he turned the pages without reading a word. His joy at her having returned his greeting was enormous. The fatigue left him, and he felt full of energy. How beautiful she was! He felt such admiration for her and was so attracted to her that she was all he could think of. Everything about her indicated that she came from a "family," as people said. What he was most afraid of was that her gracious manners might conceal some snobbish pride. He could truthfully claim that he too came from a "family," if he had to. Weren't the Shawkats a "family"? Of course . . . and they had properties. One day he would have both a salary and a private income. His mouth parted in a sarcastic smile. A private income, a salary, and a family! What had become of his principles? He felt rather embarrassed. In its passions the heart is oblivious to precepts. People fall in love and get married in ways that are incompatible with their principles, without stopping to wonder about it. They are forced to reshape their ideals, just as a foreigner is forced to speak a country's language to achieve his ends. Besides, class and property were two existing realities that he had not created himself, no more than his father or grandfather had. He bore no responsibility for them. A combination of struggle and science could wipe out these absurdities that separated people from each other. It might be possible to change the class system, but how could he change the past that had decreed he would come from a family with a comfortable private income? It was absurd to think that socialist principles should interfere with love for an aristocrat when Karl Marx himself had married Jenny von Westphalen, whose grandfather, a chief aide to the Duke of Bruns-wick, had married into a family of Scottish barons. They had called her the "Enchanted Princess" and "Queen of the Ball." Here was another enchanting princess, who—if she danced—would be queen of the ball.

After returning the volume to the shelf, he walked back toward his place, filling his eyes with her figure, upper back, delicate neck, and the braided hair that adorned the rear of her head. What a beautiful sight! He passed by her quietly and regained his seat. In only a few minutes he heard her light footsteps. Assuming that she was leaving, he looked back regretfully but saw her approaching. When parallel with him, she stopped somewhat nervously. He could not believe his eyes.

"Excuse me," she said. "Could I get the history lectures from you?"

He rose and stood at attention like a soldier, blurting out, "Certainly."

She said apologetically, "I couldn't follow what the British profes-

sor was saying as well as I should have. I'm unclear about many of
the most important points. I don't look up the sources for the subjects
I'm not going to major in. I don't have time. . . ."

"I understand. I understand."

"I was told that you have a complete set of notes and have lent
them to students, who get what they missed from them."

"Yes. I'll bring them for you tomorrow."

"Thank you very much." Then, smiling, she added, "Don't think
I'm lazy, but my English is mediocre."

"Never mind. I'm mediocre in French. Maybe we'll have some
opportunities to cooperate. But forgive me. Please sit down. You
might want to see this book: *Introduction to the Study of Society* by
Hankins.

She replied, "Thanks, but I've gone over it several times. You say
your French is mediocre. Perhaps you need my psychology notes?"

Without any hesitation he responded, "I'd be grateful, if you don't
mind."

"So tomorrow we'll exchange notes?"

"With pleasure. But forgive me . . . won't you find that most of
the instruction in sociology is in English?"

"You know I've chosen sociology?"

He smiled as if to hide his embarrassment, although he felt none,
and answered simply, "Yes."

"How did you happen to find that out?"

He said boldly, "I asked someone."

She pressed her crimson lips together. Then she continued as if
she had not heard his reply: "Tomorrow we'll exchange notes."

"In the morning."

"See you then, and thanks."

Before she could depart he said, "I'm happy to have met you. See
you tomorrow."

He remained on his feet until she had disappeared out the door.
When he sat back down, he noticed that some of the young men
were looking at him curiously. But he was tipsy with happiness. Had
the conversation been a response to his obvious admiration for her
or had it been occasioned by a pressing need for his notes? He had
never had a chance to get acquainted with her before. Whenever he
had seen her, she had been with a group of friends. This was his first
opportunity, and almost miraculously he had obtained what he had
wanted for so long. A word from the lips of a person we love is apt
to make everything else seem insignificant.

26 ❧

No matter how hard he tried to stay calm, Yasin seemed anxious. To both his colleagues and himself he had pretended for a long time that he did not care about anything—not his rank, his salary, or even which party was in power. If promoted to the sixth level, he would only get two pounds more a month, and he spent so much. . . . They said that an increase in his rank would mean a promotion for him from review clerk to head of section. But when had Yasin ever shown any interest in administration? All the same, he felt worried, especially after Muhammad Effendi Hasan, head of the bureau and husband of Ridwan's mother, Zaynab, was summoned to a meeting with the deputy minister to give his opinion of his employees one final time before the list of promotions was signed. Muhammad Hasan? The man was vengeful by nature and would have treated Yasin badly from the beginning had it not been for Mr. Muhammad Iffat. Could such a man give Yasin a good report? Taking advantage of his supervisor's absence to hurry to the telephone, Yasin called the Law School for the third time that day and asked for Ridwan Yasin.

"Hello, Ridwan? It's your father."

"Hello. Everything's great." The boy's voice was confident. He had been working on his father's behalf.

"All that remains is for the promotions to be signed?"

"Have no fear. The minister himself recommended you. Some deputies and senators spoke to him, and he promised that everything would be fine."

"Doesn't the affair require one last recommendation?"

"Not at all. As I told you, the pasha already congratulated me on your promotion this morning. You have every reason to be confident."

"Thanks, son. Goodbye."

"Goodbye, Papa. Congratulations in advance."

He put down the receiver, left the room, and ran into his colleague and competitor for this promotion, Ibrahim Effendi Fath Allah, who approached carrying some files. They greeted each other circumspectly. Then Yasin said, "Let's be good sports about this, Ibrahim Effendi. Whatever the result is, let's receive it with good grace."

The man said angrily, "On condition that you play fair."

"What do you mean?"

"The selection should be based on merit, not influence."

"What strange ideas you have! Isn't influence necessary to obtain any kind of position in this world? You do your best, and I'll do mine. Whoever is destined to receive the promotion will get it."

"I have more seniority than you do."

"We've both been in the civil service for a long time. One year more or less won't make any difference."

"In one year many people are born and many others die."

"Whether a person is born or dies is all a question of his destiny."

"What about qualifications?"

"Qualifications? Are we constructing bridges or building power plants? What qualifications are required for our clerical work? We both have the elementary certificate. In addition to that, I'm a man of culture."

Ibrahim Effendi laughed sarcastically and replied, "Culture? Greetings to the cultured gentleman! Do you think the poems you've memorized make you cultured? Or is it the style you use in drafting letters for the bureau ... the kind a person would employ when retaking the elementary certificate examination. I'll leave my fate to God."

The two men parted on bad terms, and Yasin returned to his desk. The room was large. On both sides there were rows of desks that faced each other. The walls were lined with shelves crammed with files. Some of the clerks were busy with their papers, but others chatted or smoked. Meanwhile messengers carrying files came or left.

Yasin's neighbor told him, "My daughter will do the baccalaureate examination this year. I'll sign her up for the Teacher Training Institute, and then I'll be able to stop worrying about her. It doesn't cost anything, and there will be no difficulty finding her a job after she graduates."

Yasin said, "You've done the best thing."

The man asked him argumentatively, "What do you have planned for Karima? By the way, how old is she?"

Although irritated, Yasin relaxed his face into a smile and said, "Eleven. She'll take the elementary-school certificate examination next summer, God willing." After counting out the months on his fingers, he continued: "We're in November, so there are seven more months until it's over and done with."

"If she does well in elementary school, she'll succeed in secondary school too. Girls today are a safer bet in school than boys."

Secondary school? . . . That was what Zanuba wanted. Certainly not . . . he could not bear to have a daughter stroll off to school with bouncing breasts . . . and what about the fees?

"We don't send our girls to secondary school. Why not? Because they're not going to take jobs."

A third man asked, "Does talk like this make sense in 1938?"

"In our family, they'll be saying it in 2038."

A fourth clerk laughed as he said, "Admit you'd have to choose between spending money on her and on yourself. The coffeehouse in al-Ataba, the bar on Muhammad Ali Street, and 'Love for young women has sapped my strength.' That's the true story."

Yasin laughed and then said, "May our Lord protect her. But as I said, we don't educate girls beyond the elementary certificate."

A cough resounded from the corner of the room closest to the entrance. Yasin turned in that direction and then stood up, as if he had remembered something important. He went over to the cougher's desk. Sensing Yasin's presence, the man looked up, and Yasin leaned down to say, "You promised to tell me how to make the elixir."

The man moved his ear closer to Yasin, asking, "What?"

Since he was afraid to raise his voice, Yasin was distressed by the man's difficulty in hearing him. A loud voice from the middle of the room announced, "I bet he's asking you about the prescription for the aphrodisiac that's going to send all of us to the grave."

Yasin retreated to his desk in disgust. Paying no attention to his embarrassment, the man said in a voice everyone could hear, "I'll tell you how to make it. Get the peel of a mango, boil it rapidly until the mixture attains the consistency of honey, and take a spoonful of it before breakfast."

They all laughed, but Ibrahim Fath Allah remarked sarcastically, "That's swell, but wait till you're promoted to the sixth level. See if that doesn't perk you up."

Laughing, Yasin asked, "Does a man's rank help him in this area?"

His neighbor, who was laughing too, replied, "If this theory was correct, then Uncle Hasanayn, our office boy, should be the Minister of Education."

Ibrahim Fath Allah clapped his hands together and, pointing to Yasin, asked, "Brothers, this man is nice and pleasant, a good fellow, but does he do a millieme's worth of work? Give me your honest opinion."

Yasin said scornfully, "A minute of my work is equivalent to a day's work by you."

"The real story is that the director goes easy on you and that you rely on your son's intervention in this bleak era."

Determined to infuriate his rival, Yasin said, "By your life, I'll have an advocate in every era. Now it's my son. If the Wafd returns to power, you'll find I have my nephew and my father. Tell me what advocates you have."

Looking up toward the ceiling, the other man answered, "I have our Lord."

"Glory to Him, I have Him too. Isn't He everyone's Lord?"

"But He's not fond of patrons of drinking establishments on Muhammad Ali Street."

"Does that mean He likes dope addicts?"

"There's no more revolting creature than a drunkard."

"Cabinet ministers and ambassadors drink. Don't you see pictures in the papers of them drinking toasts? But have you ever seen a diplomat at an official party offer opium to someone in celebration of the signing of a treaty, for example?"

Trying to stop laughing, Yasin's neighbor said, "Hush, fellows, or the rest of your civil service will be performed in prison."

Pointing to his adversary, Yasin shot back, "By your life, even in prison he would loathe me and brag about his seniority."

Then Muhammad Hasan returned from his meeting with the deputy minister. There was universal silence as all faces watched him go to his office without pausing to look at anything. The clerks exchanged inquisitive glances. Probably one of the rivals was now head of his section. But which was the lucky one? The door of the director's office opened. The director's bald head appeared, and he called out in an emotionless voice, "Yasin Effendi." Yasin rose and directed his huge body toward the office as his heart pounded.

The director scrutinized him with a strange look and then said, "You've been promoted to the sixth level."

Relieved and delighted, Yasin replied, "Thank you, sir."

In a rather dry tone the man continued: "It's only fair to tell you frankly that someone else deserves it more than you do. But strings were pulled on your behalf."

Yasin was annoyed, as he often was when with this man. He retorted, "Strings! So what? Is anything big or small accomplished without the use of influence? Does anyone get promoted in this bureau or this ministry, yourself included, without influence?"

The other man restrained his rage and said, "You're nothing but a headache for me. You get promoted without deserving it and then resent the least remark, no matter how appropriate. Don't blame us. Congratulations. Congratulations, sir. I just hope you'll pull yourself together. You're head of your section now."

Encouraged by the way the director had backed down, Yasin, without modifying his own sharp tone, replied, "I've been a civil servant for more than twenty years. I'm forty-two. Do you think the sixth level is too good for me? Boys are appointed at this rank merely because they've graduated from the University."

"The important thing is for you to pull yourself together. I hope I'll find you as reliable as the others. When you were the school disciplinarian at al-Nahhasin School, you were a diligent and exemplary employee. Had it not been for that incident long ago ..."

"That's ancient history. There's no need to mention it now. Everyone makes mistakes."

"You're a mature adult. If you play around, it will be hard to carry out your duties. When you stay out late every night, what condition is your brain in the next morning when you're supposed to work? I want you to shoulder your responsibilities. That's all there is to it."

Yasin was offended by the reference to his conduct and said, "I won't let anyone comment on my private life. Once I'm outside the ministry I'm free to do what I want."

"And inside it?"

"I will do as much work as any other section head. I've toiled enough over the years to suffice for the rest of my life."

When Yasin returned to his desk, despite the anger raging in his breast, he sported a smile. As the news spread, he was showered with congratulations.

Ibrahim Fath Allah leaned over to whisper spitefully to his neighbor, "His son! That's the whole story. Abd al-Rahim Pasha Isa ... you understand? Disgusting!"

27

Seated in a large chair on the latticed balcony, al-Sayyid Ahmad Abd al-Jawad gazed alternately at the street and at *al-Ahram*, the newspaper spread across his lap. The gaps between the spindles of the latticework allowed patches of light to fall on his ample house shirt and on his skullcap. He had left the door to his room open so he could hear the radio from the sitting room. He appeared gaunt and wasted, and the dull look in his eyes suggested sorrowful resignation. From his perch on the balcony, he seemed to be discovering the street for the first time. In the past, he had never experienced it from this angle. Back then, he had slept most of the time he was at home. Nowadays the only amusement he had left, except for the radio, was sitting on the balcony and peering out between the spindles to the north and the south. It was a lively, charming, and entertaining street. Moreover, it had a special character distinguishing it from al-Nahhasin, which he had observed for roughly half a century from his shop, the one he had owned. Here were the establishments of Hasanayn the barber, Darwish the bean seller, al-Fuli the milkman, Bayumi the drinks vendor, and Abu Sari', who grilled snacks. Known for their location on this street, they were also the features by which Palace Walk was identified.

"What good companions and neighbors ... I wonder how old these men are. Hasanayn the barber has a good build, the kind that rarely shows a man's age. Almost nothing about him has changed except his hair, but he's certainly over fifty. God's grace has preserved these men's health. And Darwish? Bald ... he always was. But he's in his sixties. What a powerful body he has! I was like that when I was sixty, but now I'm sixty-seven. That's old! I've had my clothes cut down to fit what's left of my body. When I look at the photo hanging in my room, I can't believe I'm that same person. Poor blind al-Fuli is younger than Darwish. Without his apprentice, he wouldn't be able to make his rounds. Abu Sari' is an old man. Old? But he's still working. None of them has given up his shop. It's a shattering experience for a man to abandon his store. Afterward all you have left is sitting in your house, staying home day and night. If only I could go out for an hour every day! I have to wait for Friday and then I need both my stick and Kamal to assist me. Praise God, Lord of the universe, in any case. Bayumi's the youngest of them and the luckiest. His prominence began with Maryam's mother, and mine ended with her. Today he owns the most modern building in the neighborhood. That's what became of Mr. Muhammad Ridwan's home. Where it once stood, Bayumi has built a juice shop lit by electricity. A man's good fortune may start with a woman's treachery. Glory to God who gives all things. May His wisdom be exalted. Everything's been modernized. The roads have been paved with asphalt and illuminated with streetlights. Remember how pitch-black the nights were when you used to return home? What a long time it's been since you did that! Every shop has electricity and a radio. Everything's new, except me, an old man of sixty-seven who can only leave his home once a week. Even then I'm short of breath. My heart! It's all the fault of my heart that loved, laughed, rejoiced, and sang for so many years. Today it dictates calm, and there's no way to reject its decree. The doctor said, 'Take your medicine, stay home, and keep to the diet I've prescribed.' I told him, 'Fine. But will that make me strong again? Or give me back at least some of my strength?' He replied, 'Warding off further complications is the most we can hope for. Any exertion or movement puts you at risk.' Then he laughed and wanted to know, 'Why do you want to regain your strength?' Yes, why? It's ridiculous and pathetic."

All the same, al-Sayyid Ahmad had answered, "I want to be able to come and go."

The physician had commented, "Every condition has its own special pleasures—like sitting quietly. Read the newspapers, listen to the radio, enjoy your family, and on Friday ride to the mosque of al-Husayn. That's enough for you."

"The matter's in God's hands," he thought. "Mutawalli Abd al-Samad is still stumbling about in the streets. . . . He says, 'Enjoy your family.' Amina no longer stays home. Our roles have been reversed. I'm confined to the latticed balcony while she roams around Cairo, going from mosque to mosque. Kamal sits with me for fleeting moments, as if he were a guest. Aisha? Alas, Aisha, are you alive or dead? And then they want my heart to recover and to feel contented."

"Master . . ."

He turned around and saw Umm Hanafi carrying a small tray with a bottle of medicine, an empty coffee cup, and a glass half filled with water.

"Your medicine, master."

Kitchen fragrances wafted from the black dress of this woman who in the course of time had become one of the family. Picking up the glass, he poured out enough water to fill the cup halfway and then, after removing the medicine bottle's stopper, added four drops to the water in his cup. In anticipation of the taste, he made a face and then swallowed.

"May it bring you health, master."

"Thanks. Where's Aisha?"

"In her room. May God grant her forbearance."

"Call her, Umm Hanafi."

In her room or on the roof ... what difference did it make? The radio's cheerful songs were in ironic contrast to the mournful atmosphere of this otherwise silent dwelling. Al-Sayyid Ahmad had been confined to the house for only the last two months. A year and four months had passed since Na'ima's death. When the man had asked to listen to the radio in view of his urgent need for entertainment, Aisha had replied, "Of course, Papa. May God find ways to console you for being forced to stay home."

Hearing the rustling of a dress, he turned and saw Aisha approaching in her black attire. Although the weather was warm, she had a black scarf wrapped around her head. Her fair complexion had a strange blue cast to it. "That's a symptom of her depression," he thought. Then he said tenderly, "Get a chair and sit with me a little."

But she did not budge and replied, "I'm comfortable like this, Papa."

The recent past had taught him not to try to make her change her mind about anything. "What were you doing?"

A blank expression on her face, she answered, "Nothing, Papa."

"Why don't you go out with your mother and visit the blessed shrines? Wouldn't that be better than staying at home alone?"

"Why should I visit shrines?"

He seemed astonished by her response but said calmly, "You could entreat God for solace."

"God is with us here in our house."

"Of course. I mean you shouldn't spend so much time alone, Aisha. Visit your sister. Visit the neighbors. Find some amusements for yourself."

"I can't bear to see Sugar Street. I have no friends. I don't know anyone anymore. I can't stand to visit people."

Turning his face away, the man said, "I want you to be brave and to take care of your health."

"My health!" she exclaimed almost incredulously.

He persisted: "Yes. What's the point of sorrow?"

In spite of her agitated condition, she did not abandon the decorum she observed with him and replied, "What's the point of life, Papa?"

"Don't say that. God's reward for you will be great."

Bowing her head to hide the tears in her eyes, she replied, "I want to go to Him to receive my reward. It won't come in this world, Papa." She started to withdraw quietly but before leaving the balcony stopped a moment as if she had remembered something and asked, "How's your health today?"

He smiled and answered, "Fine, praise God, but what's important is your health, Aisha." Then she was gone.

How could he relax in this house? He glanced down at the street again, and finally his eyes came to rest on Amina, who was returning from her daily circuit. Modestly attired in a coat and a white veil, she proceeded at a slow pace. How she had aged! Since he remembered that her mother had lived to a ripe old age, he was not especially concerned about his wife's health. But here she was at sixty-two looking at least ten years older than that.

It was quite a while before she arrived and asked him, "How are you, master?"

Raising his voice loud enough to allow the desired sharpness to reverberate in it, he said, "How are you yourself? God's will be done! You've been out since early this morning, lady."

She smiled and replied, "I visited the shrines of al-Sayyida Zaynab and of al-Husayn. I prayed for you and for everyone else."

Now that she was home, his composure and peace of mind returned, for he sensed he could request anything he wanted without hesitation. "Is it right for you to leave me alone all this time?"

"You gave me permission, master. I haven't been gone long. It's necessary, master. We're badly in need of prayer. I entreated my master al-Husayn to give you back your health so you can go and come as you wish. And I also prayed for Aisha and the others."

She got a chair and sat down. Then she asked, "Have you taken your medicine, master? I told Umm Hanafi . . ."

"I wish you had told her to do something nicer for me than that."

"It's for your good health, master. At the mosque I heard a beautiful talk by Shaykh Abd al-Rahman. Master, he spoke about atonement for sin and how misdeeds can be wiped away. His words were very beautiful, master. I wish I could remember as well as I once did."

"Your face is pale from your walk. It's just a matter of time before you become one of the doctor's regular patients."

"Lord protect us! I only go out to visit the tombs of members of the Prophet's family. So how could any harm befall me?" Then she added, "Oh, master, I almost forgot. They're talking about the war everywhere. They say that Hitler has attacked."

The man asked with interest, "Are you certain?"

"I heard it not once but a hundred times. 'Hitler attacked. . . . Hitler attacked.' "

To make her think she was not telling him anything he did not already know, the man observed, "People have been expecting this from one moment to the next."

"God willing, it won't affect us, will it, master?"

"Did they say only Hitler and not Mussolini? Didn't you hear that other name too?"

"Just Hitler's name."

"Will it affect us?" he asked himself. "Who knows?"

"May our Lord be gracious to us," he said. "If you hear someone selling a special edition of *al-Balagh* or *al-Muqattam* newspapers, buy one."

"It's like the days of Kaiser Wilhelm and the zeppelin. Do you remember, master? Glory to God the everlasting."

28 ❧

As Khadija later observed, it was a "momentous" family reunion. When the door of her apartment opened, Yasin, wearing a white linen suit with a red rose in the lapel and brandishing an ivory-handled fly whisk, filled the aperture. His huge body almost created a draft of air as he advanced, followed by his son, Ridwan, who had on a silk suit of exemplary elegance and beauty. Then came Zanuba in a gray dress, radiating the modest decorum that had become an inseparable part of her. Finally there was Karima in an exquisite short-sleeved blue dress that revealed the uppermost part of her chest. Although she was only thirteen, her virginal femininity had blossomed and she seemed outrageously attractive. In the parlor they were received by Khadija, Ibrahim, Abd al-Muni'm, and Ahmad.

Yasin wasted no time in asking, "Have you ever heard anything like this? My son is secretary to the chief of the ministry where I'm employed as a section head in the records office. The very earth rises to greet him when he passes, while people are barely aware of my existence."

Although his words were couched in the language of protest, his proud satisfaction with his son was obvious to everyone. After receiving his degree in May, Ridwan had been appointed a secretary to the cabinet minister in June, starting out in the civil service at the sixth level, when most college graduates joined at the eighth as clerks. Abd al-Muni'm, who had received his degree at the same time, still did not know what the future held in store for him.

Feeling a bit jealous, Khadija smiled and said, "Ridwan is a friend of the men in power, but children are only as good as their parents."

With a delight he did not succeed in concealing, Yasin asked, "Didn't you see the photograph of him and the minister in *al-Ahram* yesterday? It's gotten so we don't know how to address him."

Pointing to Abd al-Muni'm and Ahmad, Ibrahim Shawkat said, "These boys are a disappointment. They waste their lives in bitter but meaningless debates, and their best contacts are Shaykh Ali al-Manufi, who runs the al-Husayn Primary School, and that scum of the earth Adli Karim, publisher of a journal called *Light* or *Smut* or who knows what."

Even though he tried to appear calm, Ahmad was infuriated. His uncle Yasin's conceit upset him as much as his father's slighting remarks. Abd al-Muni'm's anger, which under different circumstances might easily have flared up, was dampened by the expectations this family visit had aroused. Glancing surreptitiously at Ridwan's face, he wondered what his cousin was thinking. His heart felt that this visit was an auspicious one, for his relatives would probably not have come unless they were bearing good news.

Responding to Ibrahim's comments, Yasin remarked, "If you ask my opinion, I think you have fine sons. Isn't there a proverb that says, 'The sultan is the one person you don't find waiting by the sultan's door.' "

Yasin's attempt to hide his delight was a complete failure, and he convinced no one that he actually believed what he was saying. All the same, pointing to Ridwan, Khadija remarked, "May our Lord grant him any good that comes to them and spare him whatever misfortunes they experience."

At last, Ridwan turned to Abd al-Muni'm and said, "I hope to be able to offer you my congratulations soon. . . . ."

Blushing, Abd al-Muni'm looked inquisitively at his cousin. Ridwan added, "The minister promised to give you an appointment in the Bureau of Investigations."

The members of Khadija's family were impatient to hear all the details and fixed their eyes on Ridwan in hopes of discovering further substantiating signs. The young man continued: "Most probably at the beginning of next month."

Expanding on his son's words, Yasin said, "It's a judicial position. In our records office two young men with university degrees have been appointed to clerical jobs at the eighth level with salaries of only eight pounds a month."

It was Khadija who had asked Yasin to talk to his son about Abd al-Muni'm. So she said gratefully, "Our thanks to God and to you, brother." Turning to Ridwan, she added, "And it goes without saying that we are very appreciative of the favor Ridwan has done us."

Ibrahim added his own thanks to hers, saying, "Absolutely! Ridwan is Abd al-Muni'm's brother and a fine one too."

To remind them of her presence, the smiling Zanuba remarked, "Ridwan and Abd al-Muni'm truly are brothers. There's no question about that."

Abd al-Muni'm, who for the first time felt bashful in Ridwan's presence, asked, "Was he serious about it?"

Yasin answered importantly, "The minister's word! I'm following up on it."

Ridwan said, "I'll take care of any problems that might arise in the personnel office. I have many friends there, even though it's said that employees of the personnel office don't have a friend in the world."

Ibrahim Shawkat sighed and observed, "Praise God who spared us from embarking on a career and from dealing with personnel officers."

Yasin said, "You live like a king, as is only right for a person named after God's friend, the prophet Abraham."

But Khadija retorted scornfully, "May our Lord never decree that a man should stay home."

Zanuba, as usual, intervened with a pleasant word: "To be forced to stay home is a curse, but a man with a private income has a sultan's life."

A mischievous gleam in his eyes, Ahmad said, "Uncle Yasin has a private income and a civil service position too."

Yasin laughed out loud and replied, "I have a civil service post and that's all, if you please. My private income! That's over and done with. How can anyone with a family like mine hold on to his fortune?"

Khadija cried out in dismay, "Your family!"

To end this conversation, which was beginning to get on his nerves, Ridwan turned to Ahmad and said, "God willing, you'll find us ready to serve you next year when you get your degree."

Ahmad answered, "Thank you very much, but I'm not entering government service."

"How so?"

"A civil service job would kill a person like me. My future lies outside the government."

Khadija wanted to remonstrate with her son but chose to postpone the argument to another time. Smiling, Ridwan said, "If you change your mind, you'll find me at your service."

To show his gratitude, Ahmad raised his hand to his head. Then the maid brought in glasses of cold lemonade. During the moment of silence as they began to sip their drinks, Khadija happened to glance at Karima. She seemed to be noticing the girl for the first time since reassuring herself about Abd al-Muni'm. She asked her niece tenderly, "How are you, Karima?"

In a melodious voice the girl replied, "Fine, thanks, Auntie."

Khadija was about to extol her niece's beauty, but caution restrained her. This was not the first time Zanuba had brought her daughter to visit them since the girl had been staying home after finishing her elementary certificate. Khadija told herself that there was something suspicious about it. Karima was Zanuba's daughter, but Yasin was her father. That fact made the matter a delicate one.

Abd al-Muni'm was too engrossed with his future position to give Karima the attention she deserved, although he was well acquainted with her. Moreover, he had not yet recovered from the death of his wife. And there was no space left in Ahmad's heart.

Yasin said, "Karima's still sorry she didn't go to secondary school."

Frowning, Zanuba said, "I'm even sorrier than she is."

Ibrahim Shawkat commented, "The effect the exertion of studying has on girls concerns me. Besides, a girl is going to end up at home. It's only a year or two before Karima will be married off to some lucky fellow."

"You should have your tongue cut out," Khadija observed silently. "He brings up dangerous topics without paying any attention to the consequences. What a situation! Karima is Yasin's daughter and sister to Ridwan, who has done us this important favor. Perhaps there are no grounds for this anxiety, and I'm just imagining things. But why does Zanuba visit us so often, bringing Karima along with her? Yasin's too busy to think up plots, but that woman was raised in a troupe of performers. . . ."

Zanuba responded, "That's what people used to say. But now all girls go to school."

Khadija said, "In our district there are two girls who are studying for advanced degrees, but God knows they are no beauties."

Yasin asked Ahmad, "Aren't some of the girls in your department beautiful?"

Ahmad's heart pounded as the image nestling in his heart appeared before his mind's eye. He answered, "The love of learning is not restricted to ugly girls."

Looking toward her father with a smile, Karima said, "It's all a question of who a girl's father is."

Yasin laughed and said, "Bravo, daughter! That's how a good girl talks about her father. That's how your aunt used to speak to your grandfather."

Khadija said sarcastically, "It really does make a difference who your father is."

Zanuba quickly replied, "Don't blame the girl. Oh, if you could hear the way he talks to his children. . . ."

Khadija said, "I know."

Yasin commented, "I'm a man with his own ideas about child rearing. I'm their father and their friend. I wouldn't want any of my children to tremble from fear when they're with me. Even now I'm ill at ease in my father's presence."

Ibrahim Shawkat said, "May God strengthen him and console him for having to stay home. Al-Sayyid Ahmad is a generation all by himself. There's not another man like him."

Khadija said critically, "Tell him!"

As if to apologize for not being like his father, Yasin agreed, "My father is an entire generation all by himself. Alas, he and his friends are now confined to their homes—men for whom the whole world wasn't big enough."

Ridwan said in an aside to Ahmad, "With the entry of Italy into the war, Egypt's situation has become extremely grave."

"Perhaps these mock air raids will turn into real ones."

"But are the English strong enough to turn back the expected Italian advance? No doubt Hitler will leave the task of taking the Suez Canal to Mussolini."

Abd al-Muni'm asked, "Will America just stand by and watch?"

"Russia holds the true key to the situation."

"But she's allied with Hitler."

"Communism is the enemy of the Nazis, and the evil threatening the world from a German victory is greater than that from a victory by the democracies."

"They have darkened the world," Khadija complained. "May God darken their lives. What are all these things we never knew before? Air-raid sirens! Antiaircraft guns! Searchlights! These calamities could turn a man's hair white before his time."

With mild sarcasm, Ibrahim retorted, "At any rate, in our family nobody goes gray prematurely."

"That's only true of you."

Ibrahim was sixty-five now, but compared to al-Sayyid Ahmad, who was only three years his senior, he seemed decades younger.

When the visit was ending, Ridwan instructed Abd al-Muni'm: "Come see me at the ministry."

Once the door was closed behind the departing guests, Ahmad told Abd al-Muni'm, "Be careful not to barge in on him unannounced. Find out how to behave when visiting a minister's secretary."

His brother did not reply or even look his way.

Ahmad had little trouble finding the villa of his sociology professor, Mr. Forster, in the Cairo suburb of al-Ma'adi. On entering, he realized that he was a bit late and that many of the other students had already arrived for this party, which the professor was giving before he returned to England. Ahmad was welcomed by the host and his wife, and the professor introduced Ahmad to her as one of the best students in the department. Then the young man joined the others, who were sitting on the veranda. All levels of the sociology program were represented. As one of the small group promoted to the final year, Ahmad shared with those peers a sense of excellence and of achievement. None of the women students had appeared yet, but he was confident that they would come or at least that his "friend" would, since she also lived in al-Ma'adi. Glancing at the garden, he saw a long table set on a grassy lawn, which was bordered on two sides by willow and palm trees. Lined up on the table were teapots, containers of milk, and platters of sweet confections and pastries.

He heard a student ask, "Shall we observe British manners or swoop down on the table like vultures?"

Another replied rather sadly, "Oh, if only 'Lady' Forster weren't present."

It was late afternoon, but the weather was pleasant, June's reputation for sultriness notwithstanding. In no time at all the eagerly awaited flock was at the door. As if by design, the only four women students in the department all came together. Wearing a fitted pure-white dress that seemed one with the rest of her charming person—except for her coal-black hair—Alawiya Sabri came into view, striding jauntily forward. At that moment Ahmad, whose secret had long since gotten out, felt a teasing foot rub against his to alert him to her presence, as if there were any need for that. He kept his eyes on the women until they found seats on the veranda in a corner that had been vacated for them.

Mr. Forster and his wife appeared, and, pointing to the girls, Mrs. Forster asked, "Would you like to be introduced?"

Their response was resounding laughter. Extraordinarily lively although nearly fifty, the professor said, "It would be far better if you'd introduce them to me."

The guests laughed noisily once more, and Mr. Forster continued: "At about this time each year we leave Egypt for a holiday in England, but this year we don't know whether we'll see Egypt again or not. . . ."

His wife interrupted: "We don't even know if we'll manage to see England!"

They realized that she was referring to the danger posed to shipping by submarines, and more than one voice called out, "Good luck, ma'am."

The host added, "I'll carry away with me beautiful memories of our life at the Faculty of Arts and of this tranquil and lovely area of al-Ma'adi. I'll always remember you fondly, even your tomfoolery."

To be polite, Ahmad replied, "The memory of you will stay with us forever and will continue to develop as our intellects do."

"Thank you." Then, smiling, the professor told his wife, "Ahmad is an academic at heart, even though he has ideas of a kind that often cause trouble in this country."

One of Ahmad's fellow students explained, "That means he's a Communist."

The smiling hostess raised her eyebrows, and Mr. Forster commented in a tone that conveyed more than his words themselves, "I'm not the one who said that. Your comrade did." Then, standing up, he announced, "It's time for tea. We mustn't let the moment slip away from us. Later there will be an opportunity for conversation and entertainment."

The tea party was catered by Groppi's, a famous Cairo establishment, and its waiters stood nearby, ready to serve the guests. "Lady" Forster sat between the girls on one side, and the professor was at the center on the other. To explain the seating arrangement, he said, "We would have liked to mix you up more but decided to respect Eastern etiquette. Isn't that right?"

Without any hesitation, one of the male students answered, "This, unfortunately, is what we've noticed, sir."

A servant poured tea and milk, and the feast began. Ahmad observed furtively that Alawiya Sabri was the most proficient of the girls in Western table manners and the most relaxed. She seemed accustomed to social life and as much at ease as if in her own home.

Watching her eat pastries was even sweeter than eating them himself. She was his dear friend who reciprocated his friendship without encouraging him to cross its boundaries.

He told himself, "If I don't seize the opportunity that today offers, I may as well give up."

Mrs. Forster raised her voice to advise them, "I hope you won't let the thought of war rationing make you shy about eating the pastries."

A student commented, "It's a lucky break that the authorities haven't restricted tea yet."

Mr. Forster leaned over toward Ahmad, who was sitting to his left, and inquired, "How do you spend your holidays? I mean, what do you read?"

"A lot of economics and a little politics. I write some articles for magazines too."

"I'd advise you to go on for a master's degree when you finish this one."

After chewing what was in his mouth, Ahmad replied, "Perhaps later on, but I'll start out working as a journalist. That's been my plan for years."

"Excellent!"

His dear friend was conversing easily with Mrs. Forster. How quickly she had perfected her English! The roses and other blooms were as saturated with red and their other colors as his heart was with love. In a world that was truly free, love would blossom like a flower. Only in a Communist country could love be a totally natural emotion.

Mr. Forster said, "I'm sad I won't be able to continue my study of Arabic. I would like to read Majnun's poems in praise of Layla without having to rely on one of you."

"It's a pity that you won't be able to study it anymore."

"Unless circumstances permit, later on."

"You may find yourself obliged to learn German," Ahmad reflected. "Wouldn't it be amusing if London were the scene of demonstrations calling for the evacuation of foreign forces and you took part in them? The seductive charm of the English can be attributed to their manners, but that of my dear friend is unique. The sun will soon set, and night will find us together in an isolated spot for the first time. If I don't seize this opportunity, I may as well give up."

He asked his professor, "What will you be doing once you return
to London?"

"I've been invited to work in broadcasting."

"Then we won't be deprived of hearing your voice."

"A polite statement," Ahmad told himself, "is excusable at a party
ornamented by my friend, but we only listen to the German broad-
casts. Our people love the Germans, if only because they hate the
English. Colonialism is the final stage of capitalism. The situation
created by our professor's party merits some thought. Although we
justify it in the spirit of intellectual inquiry, there is a conflict between
our love for this professor and our loathing for his nationality. Hopefully the war will polish off both the Nazi movement and colonialism.
Then I can concentrate entirely on love."

They returned to their seats on the veranda, where the lamps had
been lit. "Lady" Forster said at once, "Here's the piano. Won't someone play for us?"

A student entreated her, "Won't you please perform for us?"

She rose with the graceful agility of youth, which was many years
behind her, and sat down at the piano. Opening some sheet music,
she started to play. None of them had any particular familiarity with
Western music or a taste for it, but wishing to be polite and courteous, they listened attentively. From his love, Ahmad attempted to
extract a magical power to unlock the obscure passages of the music.
But he forgot all about the song when he glanced stealthily at the
girl's face. Their eyes met once, and they exchanged a smile seen by
many of the others.

In an intoxicated delight, he told himself, "Yes, if I don't seize my
opportunity today, I may as well give up."

When "Lady" Forster had finished, one of the students played an
Eastern tune. Then they conversed for quite a long time. At about
eight o'clock, the students said goodbye to their professor and set off.
On this night, which seemed remarkably beautiful and compassionate, Ahmad lingered under the canopy of towering trees at a bend in
the road until he saw her approach on her way home alone. Then he
popped out in front of her.

She stopped in astonishment and asked, "Didn't you go off with
the others?"

Exhaling as if to relieve his breast of its turmoil, he replied calmly,
"I let the caravan go on ahead so I could meet you."

"What do you suppose they'll think?"

He answered scornfully, "That's their problem."

She walked slowly forward, and he kept pace with her. Then his long days of patience bore fruit as he said, "Before I leave you I want to ask if you will allow me to request your hand in marriage."

Her beautiful head shot up in reaction to this surprise, but no sound escaped her, as if she could not think of anything to say. The street was empty and the streetlights were dim from the blue paint applied as a precaution for air raids. He asked her again, "Will you give me permission?"

In a faint voice with a hint of censure to it she said, "This is the way you talk, but what an approach.... The fact is that you've stunned me."

He laughed gently and then said, "I apologize for that, although I would have thought the long history of our friendship would have prevented my words from coming as a startling surprise."

"You mean our friendship and our academic collaboration?"

He was not comfortable with her choice of words but said, "I mean my obvious affection that has taken the form of 'friendship and academic collaboration,' as you put it."

In a jolly but shaky voice she inquired, "Your affection?"

With stubborn sincerity he replied, "I mean my love, my unconcealed love. Usually we do not announce it merely to proclaim it but to rejoice at hearing it proclaimed."

To string him along until she could regain her composure, she said, "The whole thing comes as a surprise to me."

"I'm sad to hear this."

"Why? The truth is that I don't know what to say...."

Laughing, he responded, "Say, 'You have my permission.' Then leave the rest to me."

"But, but ... I don't know anything about ... No offense, we really have been friends, yet you've never spoken of ... I mean there has never been an occasion for you to tell me about yourself."

"Don't you know me?"

"Of course I know you, but there are other things one has to know."

"You mean the traditional things? Those questions are best suited to a heart that has never been a prisoner of love." He felt annoyed but this only made him more obstinate. He continued: "Everything will become clear at the proper time."

Regaining control of herself, she asked, "Isn't this the proper time?"

He smiled wanly and replied, "You're right. Are you referring to the future?"

"Naturally."

This "naturally" exasperated him. He had hoped to hear a song and instead had been subjected to the drone of a lecture, but no matter what happened it was important for him to retain his self-confidence. The icy darling did not know how happy it would make him to make her happy.

"Once I graduate, I'll get a job." Then after a few moments of silence he added, "And one day I'll have a substantial private income."

She stammered in embarrassment, "That's not very specific."

Trying to mask his pain with a calm exterior, he replied, "The salary will be in the normal range, and the income will be around ten pounds."

Silence reigned. Perhaps she was weighing matters and thinking them over. This was the way a materialist would understand love. He had dreamt of a sweet intoxication but had not achieved anything close to that. It was amazing that in this country where people allowed emotion to guide their politics they approached love with the precision of accountants.

At last the delicate voice replied, "Let's leave aside the private income, for it's not nice to plan your life around the death of loved ones."

"I wanted to let you know that my father is a man of property."

With a burst of energy to make up for the vacillation preceding it, she said, "We need to be realistic."

"I told you I'd find work. And you'll get a job too."

She laughed in an odd way and replied, "Certainly not. I won't work. Unlike the other women students, I haven't enrolled in the University to obtain a government position."

"There's nothing wrong in having a job."

"Naturally. But my father ... The fact is that we're all agreed on this. I won't work."

As his emotions cooled down, he became pensive. He commented, "So be it. I'll work."

In a voice that she seemed deliberately to be making more tender than usual she said, "Mr. Ahmad, let's postpone this discussion. Give me time to think it over."

He laughed dispiritedly and responded, "We have looked at the question from every angle. Don't you really need more time to draft your rejection?"

She said bashfully, "I must talk to my father."

"That goes without saying. But it should have been possible for us to reach an understanding first."

"I need some time, even if it's not very long."

"It's June now, and you'll be going off to your summer resort. We won't meet again until next October at school."

She insisted, "I must have time to think about it and to consult my family."

"You just don't want to commit yourself."

Then she suddenly stopped walking and remarked with determined resolve, "Mr. Ahmad, you're trying to force me to speak. I hope you'll take my words the right way. I've thought about marriage frequently, not with regard to you but in general terms. I've concluded—and my father agrees with me—that my life won't be successful and that I won't be able to maintain my standard of living unless I have no less than fifty pounds a month."

He swallowed this disappointment, which hurt more than he could ever have expected, even allowing for the worst possible outcome. He asked, "Does any working man, I mean one of an age to marry, make a salary that vast?" When she did not respond, he declared, "You want a rich husband!"

"I'm very sorry, but you have forced me to be blunt."

He answered gruffly, "That's better, at any rate."

"Sorry," she murmured.

Although furious, he made a sincere effort to stay within the bounds of polite behavior. Feeling an overwhelming desire to be blunt with her, he asked, "Would you allow me to give you my frank opinion?"

She shot back, "Certainly not! I know many of your ideas. I hope that we can stay friends."

In spite of his anger, he pitied her condition, an inevitable one for a life that had not been transformed by love. A lady who eloped with one of her servants acted naturally but by traditional standards was judged a deviant. In an imperfect society, a healthy man seems sick and the sick one healthy. He was angry, but his unhappiness was greater than his anger. At any rate she would guess what he thought of her, and there was some consolation in that. When she stretched out her hand to take leave of him, his hand took hers and kept hold of it until he had said, "You claimed you didn't enroll in the University to obtain a job. That's a lovely notion in and of itself. But how have you benefited from the University?"

She raised her chin inquisitively. In a slightly sarcastic tone he concluded, "Forgive my foolish behavior. Perhaps the problem is that you haven't fallen in love yet. Goodbye."

He turned on his heels and walked away rapidly.

30

Isma'il Latif said, "Perhaps bringing my wife to Cairo to have the baby was a mistake. The air-raid siren goes off every night. In Tanta we know almost none of the terrors of this war."

Kamal replied, "These are just symbolic raids. If they really wanted to harm us, no force would be able to stop them."

This was the second meeting for Riyad Qaldas and Isma'il Latif after their introduction the year before. Riyad laughed and told Isma'il, "You're talking to a man who doesn't know what it means to be responsible for a spouse."

Isma'il asked Riyad sarcastically, "And do you know what it's like?"

"I am a bachelor too, but at least I'm not a foe of matrimony."

They were walking along Fuad I Street early one evening. The darkness was relieved only by the meager amount of light escaping from the doors of commercial establishments. Even so, the street was crowded with Egyptians and British soldiers from different parts of the Empire. There was the damp breath of autumn in the air, but people were still wearing summer clothes.

Riyad Qaldas saw some Indian soldiers and commented, "It's sad that a man should be transported such a long distance from his homeland to kill for someone else's sake."

Isma'il Latif mused, "I wonder how these wretches can laugh."

Kamal answered resentfully, "The same way we can—in our bizarre world that reeks of liquor, drugs, and despair."

Riyad Qaldas chuckled and observed, "You're going through a unique crisis. Your whole world is coming apart at the seams. It appears to consist of nothing but a vain grasping at the wind, a painful debate between life's secrets and the soul, ennui, and ill health. I pity you."

Isma'il Latif advised Kamal with great directness, "Get married. I felt the same kind of ennui before I married."

Riyad Qaldas exclaimed, "Tell him!"

As though to himself, Kamal remarked, "Marriage is the ultimate surrender in life's losing battle."

"Isma'il was mistaken in thinking our situations comparable," Kamal mused. "He's a well-behaved animal. But not so fast. . . . Perhaps you're just conceited, and what's there to be conceited about when you're resting on a dunghill of disappointment and failure? Isma'il knows nothing of the world of thought, only the happiness a man derives from his work, spouse, and children. But isn't happiness right to mock your disdain for it?"

Riyad commented, "If I eventually decide to write a novel, you'll be one of the main characters."

Kamal turned toward him with boyish excitement and asked, "What will you make of me?"

"I don't know, but try not to get angry. Many of the readers who find themselves in my stories become irate."

"Why?"

"Perhaps because each of us has an idea he has created of himself. When a writer strips us of that self-image, we object angrily."

Kamal inquired anxiously, "Are you holding back some secret opinions about me?"

His friend immediately reassured him: "Certainly not. But a writer may begin with someone he knows and then forget all of that person's characteristics in creating a new specimen of humanity. The only relationship between the two may be that the first inspired the second. You seem to be an Easterner teetering uncertainly between East and West. He goes round and round until he's dizzy."

"He speaks of East and West," Kamal thought. "But how could he know about Aïda? It may well be that misery has many faces."

Isma'il Latif said as bluntly as before, "All your life, you've made problems for yourself. In my opinion, books are the source of your misfortunes. Why don't you try living a normal life?"

They reached the corner of Imad al-Din Street and, on turning down it, almost ran into a large group of British nationals. Isma'il Latif said, "To hell with them! Why do they look so optimistic? Do you suppose they actually believe their own propaganda?"

"It seems to me," Kamal observed, "that the outcome of the war has already been determined. It will be over by next spring."

Riyad Qaldas said resentfully, "The Nazi movement is reactionary and inhumane. The world's suffering will increase dramatically under their iron rule."

Isma'il replied, "Be that as it may, what's important is to see the English subjugated in the same manner that they subjugated so many of the weaker areas of the world."

Kamal commented, "The Germans are no better than the English."

Riyad Qaldas said, "We have learned to live with the English, and British imperialism is well into its dotage. It is tempered, perhaps, by some humane principles. With the Germans tomorrow, we'll have to deal with a youthful, greedy, conceited, wealthy, and bellicose imperialism. What will we do then?"

Kamal laughed in a way that suggested a change of mood and suggested, "Let's have a couple of drinks and dream of a united world ruled by a single just government."

"We'll definitely need more than two drinks for that."

They found themselves in front of a new bar they had never seen before. It was probably one of those infernal establishments that spring up over night during a war. Glancing inside, Kamal noticed the proprietor was a woman with a fair complexion and a voluptuous Eastern body. Then his feet froze to the pavement. He was unable to move, and his companions had to stop to see what he was looking at.

"Maryam!" Kamal whispered to himself. "It's Maryam, no one but Maryam. Maryam, Yasin's second wife. Maryam, the lifelong neighbor. Here, in this bar, after a long disappearance. Maryam, who was thought to have gone to join her late mother. . . ."

"Do you want to go in here? Let's do. There are only four soldiers inside."

He hesitated, but his courage was not adequate for the occasion. When he had recovered from his astonishment, he said, "Absolutely not."

He cast a parting glance at the Maryam who reminded him now of her mother toward the end of that woman's life, and they proceeded on their way. When had he last seen her? It had not been for at least thirteen or fourteen years. She was a landmark of his past, and he would never forget her. His past, his history, and his essence—they were all a single entity. She had received him in the apartment in Palace of Desire Alley one last time before Yasin divorced her. He could still remember how she had complained about his brother's deviant behavior and reversion to a life of shameless wantonness. On that occasion he had not foreseen the consequences this complaint would have, for it had landed her in this hellish tavern. She had once been the darling daughter of Mr. Muhammad Ridwan and Kamal's friend, as well as a source of inspiration for boyish dreams. His old house had then appeared to be a setting that overflowed with tranquillity and delight. Maryam and Aisha had been roses, but time is an indefatigable enemy of flowers. He could easily have bumped into her at one of these brothels, just as he had first encountered Madam Jalila. If that had happened, he would have found himself in an indescribable quandary. Maryam, who had begun her flirtations with the English, had ended up with them.

"Do you know this woman?"

"Yes."

"How?"

"She's one of those women ... Perhaps she's forgotten me."

"Oh, the bars are full of them: old whores, rebellious servants, every kind of woman."

"Yes. ..."

"Why didn't you go in? She might have welcomed us warmly for your sake."

"She's no longer young, and we have better places."

He had grown old without noticing it. He was halfway into his fourth decade. He seemed to have squandered his share of happiness. When he compared his current misery to that of the past, he did not know which was worse. But what importance did life have, since he was fed up with living? Death truly was the most pleasurable part of life. But what was this sound?

"Air raid!"

"Where shall we go?"

"To the shelter at the Rex Café."

Since there was no place to sit in the shelter, they remained standing in the crowd of Egyptian gentlemen, foreigners, women, and children. People were speaking a number of different languages and dialects. Outside men from the civil defense forces shouted, "Turn off your lights!" Riyad's face looked pale. He hated the ringing sound of the antiaircraft guns.

Kamal teased him, "You may not get a chance to play with my character in your novel."

Laughing nervously as he gestured toward the other people, Riyad answered, "There's a representative sample of humanity in this shelter."

Kamal observed sarcastically, "If only they would band together in good times the way they do when they're frightened. ..."

Isma'il cried out nervously, "Right now my wife must be groping her way down the stairs in the dark. I'm thinking seriously of returning to Tanta tomorrow."

"If we live that long."

"The people of London are really to be pitied."

"But they're the source of all the trouble."

Riyad Qaldas's face grew even paler, but he tried to hide his discomfort by asking Kamal, "I once heard you inquire the way to death's station, so that you could disembark from life's boring train. Will it really seem so trivial to you now if a bomb blasts us to bits?"

Kamal smiled. He was listening with increasing anxiety, for he expected, from one moment to the next, to hear the antiaircraft guns fire with a deafening sound. He answered, "Of course not." Then he continued in a questioning tone: "Perhaps from fear of pain?"

"Is there still some obscure hope for life stirring within you?"

Why did he not kill himself? Why did his life wear a façade of enthusiasm and faith? For a long time his soul had been torn between the two extremes of hedonism and asceticism. He would not have been able to bear a life devoted entirely to the tranquil satisfaction of his desires. Inside him there was also something that made him shy away from the notion of a passive escape from life. Whatever that thing was, perhaps it was what kept him from killing himself. At the same time, the fact that he clung to the agitated rope of life with both hands contravened his lethal skepticism. The resulting condition was a tormented anxiety.

Suddenly the antiaircraft guns burst forth with a continuous volley that scarcely left the chest time to breathe. People did not know what they were seeing or saying. Yet, by the clock, the shooting lasted only two minutes. Afterward everyone awaited the odious return of the frightful noise.

Terror gripped their souls, and there was a heavy silence. Isma'il Latif asked, "When do you suppose the raid will be over? I can imagine all too well the state my wife is in now."

Riyad Qaldas asked, "When will the war end?"

Shortly thereafter the all-clear siren sounded, and the shelter's denizens voiced a profound sigh of relief. Kamal said, "The Italians were just teasing us."

They left the shelter in the dark, like bats, as doors emitted one ghostly figure after another. Then a faint glimmer of light could be seen coming from windows, and the world resumed its normal commotion.

In this brief moment of darkness, life had reminded careless people of its incomparable value.

31

Over the course of time, the old house assumed a new look of decay and decline. Its routine disintegrated, and most of the coffee-hour crowd was dispersed. These two features had been the household's soul and lifeblood. During the first half of the day, when Kamal was away at his school, Amina was off on her spiritual tour of the mosques of the Prophet's grandchildren al-Husayn and al-Sayyida Zaynab, and Umm Hanafi was down in the oven room, al-Sayyid Ahmad would stretch out on the sofa in his room or sit in a chair on the balcony while Aisha wandered aimlessly between the roof terrace and her bedroom. The radio's voice was the only one heard in the sitting room until late in the afternoon, when Amina and Umm Hanafi met there. Aisha would either stay in her room or spend part of the coffee hour with them. Al-Sayyid Ahmad did not leave his room, and even if Kamal returned home early, he retreated to his study on the top floor. At first, the confinement of al-Sayyid Ahmad had been a source of unhappiness, but then he and the others had become accustomed to it. Aisha's grief had been most distressing, but eventually she and the others had grown used to it too.

Amina was still the first to wake. After rousing Umm Hanafi, she performed her ablutions and her prayers. The maid, who was by and large the healthiest of them all, headed on rising for the oven room.

Opening heavy eyes, Aisha would get up to drink successive glasses of coffee and to light one cigarette after another. When summoned to breakfast, she would take only a few morsels. She had allowed her body to waste away to a skeleton covered with a faded skin. Her hair had started to fall out, and she had been forced to consult a doctor to avoid going bald. She had fallen victim to so many ills that the physician had advised having her teeth removed. All that remained of the old Aisha was her name and the habit of looking at her reflection in the mirror, although not to adorn herself. It was simply a custom allowing her to scrutinize her sorrows. Occasionally she seemed to have resigned herself gracefully to her losses, as she sat for longer periods with her mother, took part in the conversation, allowed her withered lips to part in a smile, visited her father to ask after his health, or strolled around the roof garden, tossing grain to the chickens.

On one such occasion her mother said hopefully, "It does my heart good, Aisha, to see you like this. I wish you were always so cheerful."

Drying her eyes, Umm Hanafi said, "Let's go to the oven room and make something special."

But at midnight the mother awoke to the sound of weeping from Aisha's room. She rushed to her daughter, taking care not to wake al-Sayyid Ahmad, and found Aisha sitting up and sobbing in the darkness. Sensing her mother's presence, Aisha grabbed hold of Amina and cried out, "If only I had the baby from her belly as a reminder of her . . . a bit of her! My hands have nothing to hold. The world is empty."

Embracing Aisha, the mother said, "I know more about your sorrows than anyone else. They are so great that any attempt at consolation is meaningless. I would gladly have given my life for theirs. But God's wisdom is lofty and exalted. What point is there to this sorrow, my poor dear?"

"Whenever I fall asleep, I dream of them or of my life in the old days."

"Proclaim that God is one. I've had my own taste of suffering like yours. Have you forgotten Fahmy? Even so, an afflicted Believer asks God for strength. What has happened to your faith?"

Aisha exclaimed resentfully, "My faith!"

"Yes, remember your religion and entreat God for merciful relief, which may come from some totally unexpected source."

"Merciful relief! Where is it? Where?"

"His mercy is so vast it encompasses everything. For my sake, visit al-Husayn with me. Put your hand on the tomb and recite the opening prayer of the Qur'an. Then your fiery suffering will be changed into a refreshing peace just as Abraham's fire was" (Qur'an, 21:69).

Aisha's attitude toward her health was equally mercurial. She would visit doctors diligently and regularly for a time, leading people to think that she had regained her interest in life. Then she would neglect herself and scornfully disregard everyone's advice in a virtually suicidal fashion. Visiting the cemetery was the only custom from which she never once deviated. With happy abandon she spent the income from her husband's and her daughter's bequests on the grave site, transforming it into a lush garden of flowers and fragrant herbs. The day Ibrahim Shawkat came to complete the formalities of the bequest, she had laughed hysterically, telling her mother, "Congratulate me on my inheritance from Na'ima."

Whenever he sensed that she was calm, Kamal would visit her and stay for lengthy periods, humoring her affectionately. He would gaze at her silently for a long time, sadly remembering the exquisite form God had bestowed upon her and examining what had become of it. She was emaciated and sickly, to be sure, but also heartbroken in every sense of the word. The striking similarity between their misfortunes did not escape him. She had lost her offspring, and he had lost his hopes. If she had ended up with nothing, so had he. All the same, her children had been flesh and blood, and his hopes had been deceptive fictions of the imagination.

One day he suggested to them, "Wouldn't it be better if you all went to the air-raid shelter when the siren goes off?"

Aisha replied, "I won't leave my room."

His mother said, "These raids don't harm anyone, and the guns sound like fireworks."

His father called out from the bedroom, "If I were able to go to the shelter, I would go to the mosque or to Muhammad Iffat's house instead."

On another occasion, Aisha rushed down from the roof, all out of breath, to tell her mother, "Something amazing has happened!"

Amina looked at her with hopeful curiosity, and Aisha, who was still panting, explained, "I was on the roof, watching the sun go down. I felt more wretched than ever before. All of a sudden a window of glorious light opened up in the sky. At the top of my lungs I shouted, 'O Lord!' "

The mother's eyes grew wide in amazement. Was this the desired merciful relief or a new abyss of sorrows? She murmured, "Perhaps it's our Lord's mercy, daughter."

Her face radiant with joy, Aisha said, "Yes. I shouted, 'O Lord!' and light filled the whole world."

They all brooded about this event and, with obvious anxiety, kept careful track of developments. Aisha stood for hours at her post on the roof, waiting for the light to break through again. Kamal finally asked himself, "I wonder if this is a finale compared to which death would seem trivial." But fortunately for all of them, she appeared to forget the matter in time and stopped mentioning it. Then she became ever more deeply involved with a private universe of her own creation. She lived there by herself, a solitary figure, whether in her room

or sitting beside them, although at infrequent intervals she would
come back to their world, as if returning from a voyage. Shortly
thereafter she would resume her imaginary travels. She developed a
new habit of speaking to herself, especially when no one else was
present. This made her family quite nervous, but when she spoke to
the dead she recognized that her loved ones had passed away. She
did not think that they were present as specters or ghosts. This com-
promise with reality was a source of some comfort to those around
her.

32

"How cold it is this winter! It reminds me of the one people used as a point of reference for years after. I wonder which it was? My Lord, where is the memory for it, where? My old heart yearns for that winter—even though I can't remember the date—since it's part of the past and such memories coax my tears from their hiding places."

In those days he had awakened early, taken a cold shower even in winter, filled his belly, and then burst forth into the world of people, activity, and freedom. He knew nothing of that world today, except for the reports people gave him, and even these seemed to refer to life on the far side of the planet.

More recently, when he had been able to sit on the sofa in his room or in a chair on the balcony, confinement to the house had seemed irksome. Although he had been free to go to the bathroom when it was necessary and to change his clothes by himself he had cursed staying home. One day a week he had been permitted to leave the house—supported by his stick or riding in a carriage—on a visit to al-Husayn or to the home of a friend. Still, he had often prayed for God to deliver him from this house arrest.

Now he could not get out of bed. The boundaries of his world extended no further than the edges of his mattress. The bathroom came to him, instead of the other way around. He had never imagined such a squalid eventuality, and having to cope with this left a resentful pout on his lips and a bitter taste in his mouth. On the same mattress he stretched out during the day and slept at night. He took his meals on it and answered the calls of nature there, he who had once been proverbial for his neatness and fragrant cologne. This household, which had always yielded to his absolute authority, now looked askance at him, granting him pitying looks when he asked for something or scolding remarks fit for a child. His beloved friends had departed from life in rapid succession, as if by prior arrangement. They had gone, leaving him alone.

"God's compassion on you, Muhammad Iffat!"

Al-Sayyid Ahmad had seen him for the last time one night during Ramadan at a party held in the men's parlor overlooking the garden.

After bidding Muhammad Iffat farewell, he had started off, accompanied to the door by his friend's noisy laughter. He had scarcely made it back to his room when someone had knocked on the door. Ridwan had rushed in, saying, "Grandfather has died, Grandfather."

"Glory to God.... When?... And how?... Wasn't he laughing with us just a few minutes ago?... But he fell flat on his face as he headed for bed. That was how a lifelong friend disappeared. It took Ali Abd al-Rahim three whole days to die. His repeated bouts of coughing were so severe that we had no choice but to pray that God would grant him a peaceful end and relieve our friend of his pain, and thus my soul mate Ali Abd al-Rahim vanished from my world."

He had been able to say farewell to these beloved friends but not to Ibrahim al-Far. The severity of his own ailments had kept him in bed, preventing him from paying a sick call on al-Far, whose servant had eventually come to announce his master's death. Al-Sayyid Ahmad had not even been able to attend the funeral. Yasin and Kamal had paid last respects to the man for him.

"To the compassion of God, you most charming man!"

Even before them, Hamidu, al-Hamzawi, and tens of other friends and acquaintances had died, leaving him alone, as though he had never known anyone. No one visited him. No one paid him a sick call. There would not be a single friend to see him off at his funeral. He was prevented even from praying, for he could maintain the necessary state of ritual purity for only a few hours after a bath, and his guardians granted him one very infrequently. He was denied access to prayer when, plunged into oppressive solitude, he was in the greatest need of communion with God the Compassionate.

His days passed in this manner. The radio played, and he listened. Amina came and went. She was very feeble but had never developed the habit of complaining. She acted as his nurse, and what he feared most was that she would soon need someone to care for her. She was all he had left. Yasin and Kamal would sit with him for an hour and then depart. He wished they would stay with him all the time, but this was a wish he could never express and they could never grant. Only Amina never tired of him. If she went to al-Husayn, it was solely to pray for him. In every other respect, his was an empty world.

For him, the day of Khadija's visit was definitely worth the wait. She would bring Ibrahim Shawkat, Abd al-Muni'm, and Ahmad. They would fill the room with life and dispel its desolation. He would not have much to say, but they would.

Once Ibrahim had requested, "Give the master a rest from your chatter."

But al-Sayyid Ahmad had scolded him: "Let them talk.... I want to hear them!"

He prayed that his daughter would have good health and a long life and made similar invocations to God on behalf of her husband and sons. He knew that she would have liked to supervise his care herself. The affection he could see in her eyes defied description.

One day, with jovial curiosity and avid interest, he asked Yasin, "Where do you spend your evenings?"

Yasin answered bashfully, "Today the English are everywhere. It's like the old days."

"The old days!" he mused. "The days of power and strength, of laughter that shook the walls, of convivial evenings spent in al-Ghuriya and al-Gamaliya, and of people of whom nothing is left but their names. Zubayda, Jalila, and Haniya.... I wonder if you remember your mother, Yasin.... Here's Zanuba and her daughter, Karima, sitting beside Karima's father.... You'll never be able to ask for God's mercy and forgiveness often enough."

"Of the people we used to know, who is still at the ministry, Yasin?"

"They've all retired. I no longer have any news of them."

"Nor do they have any of us," he thought. "All our close friends are dead. Why should we ask about acquaintances? But how lovely Karima is! She's more beautiful than her mother in her day. And she's only fourteen. Na'ima was outstandingly beautiful too."

"Yasin, if you're able to persuade Aisha to visit you, do. Rescue her from her solitude. I'm afraid of its effect on her."

Zanuba responded, "I've asked her time and again to visit Palace of Desire Alley, but she ... May God come to her aid."

There was a gloomy look in the man's eyes when he asked Yasin, "Don't you ever run into Shaykh Mutawalli Abd al-Samad when you're on the street?"

Smiling, Yasin replied, "Occasionally. He hardly recognizes anyone. But he's still walking around on two sturdy feet."

"What a man! Doesn't he ever feel the urge to visit? Or has he forgotten me, just as he forgot my children's names?"

Deserted by his friends, he had befriended Kamal. This late-blooming friendship probably surprised the son, but al-Sayyid Ahmad was no longer the father he had once known. The man became a friend who shared confidences with him and who looked forward to their chats. Al-Sayyid Ahmad said of him regretfully, "A bachelor at thirty-four, he spends most of his life in his study. May God come to his aid." He no longer felt responsible for what became of his son, for from the beginning Kamal had refused to accept anyone's advice. As a result, he had ended up an unmarried teacher and an emotionally crippled recluse. Al-Sayyid Ahmad avoided annoying references to marriage or to the money that could be made from private lessons. He asked God to make his own savings last until his final breath, so that he would never be a burden on his son.

He asked Kamal once, "Do you like this age?"

Kamal smiled nervously and was slow to reply. So the father continued: "Our times were the real ones! Life was easy and pleasant. We had our health and strength. We saw Sa'd Zaghlul and heard the supreme vocalist, Abduh al-Hamuli. What do your days have to offer?"

Fascinated by the implications of the words themselves, Kamal answered, "Every age has its good and bad points."

Shaking his head, which rested against the folded pillow, the father said, "Pretty words, nothing more. . . ."

Then after a period of silence he announced without any preamble, "My inability to perform the prayers hurts me badly, for worship is one of the consolations of solitude. All the same I experience strange moments when I forget all deprivations of food, drink, freedom, and health. I feel such an amazing peace of mind I imagine that I'm in contact with heaven and that there is an unknown happiness compared to which our life and everything about it will seem insignificant."

Kamal murmured, "May our Lord prolong your life and restore your health."

Nodding his head meekly, al-Sayyid Ahmad said, "This has been a good hour. No pain in my chest, no difficulty with breathing . . . the swelling in my leg has started to disappear, and it's time for the listeners' request show on the radio."

Then Amina's voice asked, "Is my master well?"

"Praise God."

"Shall I bring your supper?"

"Supper? Do you call yogurt supper? Oh, bring me the bowl."

33 🍃

Kamal reached his sister's home on Sugar Street at about the time for afternoon prayers and found the whole family gathered in the sitting room. He shook hands with them and said to Ahmad, "Congratulations on your degree!"

In a tone that was anything but jubilant, Khadija replied, "Thank you very much. But come hear the latest. The bey doesn't want to enter the civil service."

Ibrahim Shawkat explained, "His cousin Ridwan is ready to find a position for him, if Ahmad will agree. But he insists on refusing the offer. Talk to him, Mr. Kamal. Perhaps your opinion will sway him."

Kamal removed his fez and, because of the heat, took off his white jacket, which he draped over the back of the chair. Although he had expected a fight, he smiled and said, "I thought today would be reserved for congratulations. But this house can never stop quarreling."

Khadija said self-pityingly, "That's my fate. We're just not like other people."

Ahmad told his uncle, "The matter's quite simple. The only kind of position I could get now would be a clerical one. Ridwan informed me that he could get me appointed to a vacant secretarial post in the records office where Uncle Yasin works. He suggested that I should wait three months until the new school year begins, when I might get a job as an instructor of French in one of the schools. But I don't want a civil service position of any kind."

Khadija cried out, "Tell him what you do want."

The young man answered with straightforward determination, "I'm going to work in journalism."

Ibrahim Shawkat snorted and exclaimed, "A journalist! We used to hear him say this but thought it a harmless joke. He refuses to become a teacher like you and strives to become a journalist."

Kamal said sarcastically, "May God spare him the evil of teaching."

Alarmed, Khadija said, "Would you like to see him employed as a journalist?"

To improve the mood, Abd al-Muni'm remarked, "Government service is no longer everyone's first choice."

His mother retorted sharply, "But you're a government employee, Mr. Abd al-Muni'm."

"In an elite unit. I wouldn't want him to accept a clerical position. And here's Uncle Kamal asking God to save my brother from becoming a teacher like him."

Turning toward Ahmad, Kamal asked, "What type of journalism do you have in mind?"

"Mr. Adli Karim has agreed to accept me provisionally on the staff of his magazine. At first I'll prepare translations. Later on I'll help with the editing."

"But *The New Man* is a cultural journal with limited resources and scope."

"It's a first step. I'll get experience that will make it easier for me to get a more important job. In any case, I won't go hungry even if I have to wait."

Looking at Khadija, Kamal suggested, "Let him do what he wants. He's an educated adult and knows better than anyone else what he should do."

But Khadija would not accept defeat so easily. She kept on trying to convince her son to accept a civil service position, and their voices grew loud and acrimonious. After Kamal intervened to separate them, a heavy silence reigned, and the party's atmosphere was spoiled. Laughing, Kamal said, "I came to drink some punch and celebrate, but instead I've found a somber gathering."

Ahmad was already putting on his coat to leave the house, and, excusing himself, Kamal left with his nephew. As they walked along al-Azhar Street, Ahmad informed his uncle that he was going to the offices of *The New Man* to start work, as he had promised Mr. Adli Karim.

Kamal told him, "Do whatever you want, but avoid offending your parents."

Ahmad laughed and commented, "I love them and revere them, but ..."

"But what?"

"It's a mistake for a man to have parents."

Laughing, Kamal asked, "How can you say that so glibly?"

"I don't mean it literally, but insofar as parents represent bygone traditions. In general, fatherhood acts as a brake. What need do we have of brakes in Egypt when we're hobbling forward with fettered legs?" After reflecting for a moment he added, "A person like me will not know the bitter meaning of struggle as long as he has a home and a father with a private income. I don't deny that I enjoy it, but at the same time I feel embarrassed."

"When do you expect to start getting paid for your work?"

"The editor hasn't set a date. . . ."

They parted at al-Ataba al-Khadra Square, and Ahmad continued on to *The New Man*. Mr. Adli Karim greeted him warmly and took him into the editorial offices to introduce him: "Your new colleague, Mr. Ahmad Ibrahim Shawkat."

Presenting the other members of the staff to Ahmad, he said, "Miss Sawsan Hammad, Mr. Ibrahim Rizq, and Mr. Yusuf al-Jamil."

They shook hands with Ahmad and welcomed him. Then, to be polite, Ibrahim Rizq said, "His name is well known here at the magazine."

Smiling, Mr. Adli Karim observed, "He was our first subscriber and has grown up with the magazine." Pointing to the desk of Yusuf al-Jamil, he added, "You will use this desk, for its occupant spends little time here."

When Adli Karim left the room, Yusuf al-Jamil invited Ahmad to sit down near his desk. He waited until the young man was seated and then said, "Miss Sawsan will allocate your work. You might as well have a cup of coffee now."

He pressed a buzzer, and Ahmad began to study their faces and the room. Ibrahim Rizq, a middle-aged man of decrepit appearance, looked ten years older than he actually was. Yusuf al-Jamil was a mature young man whose looks suggested an alert intelligence. Glancing at Sawsan Hammad, Ahmad wondered whether she remembered him. He had not seen her since that first encounter in 1936. Their eyes met. Wishing to escape from his silence, he mentioned with a smile, "I saw you here five years ago. . . ." Detecting a look of recognition in her eyes, he continued: "I asked what had happened to one of my articles that had not been published yet."

Smiling, she said, "I can almost remember that. In any case, we've published many of your articles since then."

Yusuf al-Jamil commented, "Articles that reveal a fine progressive spirit."

Ibrahim Rizq said, "People have a heightened awareness today. Out on the street wherever I look I see the phrase 'Bread and liberty.' This is the people's new slogan."

Sawsan Hammad remarked with interest, "It's a most beautiful one. Especially at this time when gloom encompasses the world."

Ahmad understood what her words implied, and with enthusiastic delight his soul responded to this new environment. He replied, "The world certainly is cloaked in darkness, but until Hitler attacks Britain, there's still hope of salvation."

Sawsan Hammad said, "I see the situation from another angle. Don't you suppose that if Hitler attacks Britain, it's probable that both giants will be destroyed or at least that the balance of power will shift to Russia?"

"What if the opposite happens? I mean, what if Hitler subdues the British Isles and achieves an uncontested supremacy?"

Yusuf al-Jamil said, "Napoleon, like Hitler, took on all of Europe, but Russia was his downfall."

In this pure atmosphere, with these liberated comrades and this enlightened and beautiful colleague, Ahmad felt more alive and vigorous than ever before. For some reason he thought of Alawiya Sabri and the tormented year during which he had wrestled with unrequited love until he had finally emerged the victor. From the depths of his heart he had cursed that love morning and evening until it had dispersed into thin air, leaving behind enduring traces of rebellious resentment. She was now home in al-Ma'adi, waiting for a husband with an income of at least fifty pounds a month. The girl here was calling for a Russian victory. What was she waiting for?

Then Sawsan waved a sheaf of papers in his direction as she said gently, "Would you mind?"

He rose and walked over to her desk to begin his new career.

34 ❦

Yusuf al-Jamil came into the office only once or twice a week, since most of his energies were directed toward soliciting advertising and subscriptions. Similarly, Ibrahim Rizq remained in the editorial department for no more than an hour a day before he left for one of the other magazines he helped edit. Most of the time they were alone: Ahmad and Sawsan. Once, when the chief pressman from the printshop came to get some copy, Ahmad was astounded to hear her call him "Father." Afterward, he learned that Mr. Adli Karim himself was related to the man, and this information was a thrilling surprise.

Even more stunning than Sawsan was her diligence. She was the heart of the editorial department and its dynamo. She did far more work than the mere editing of the magazine required, for she was always reading and writing. She seemed serious, bright, and extremely intelligent, and from the very first he was conscious of her forceful personality. So much so that in spite of her attractive black eyes and charmingly feminine body he occasionally imagined himself in the presence of a well-disciplined man with a strong will. Her industry motivated him to work with an assiduous zeal impervious to fatigue and boredom. He had assumed responsibility for translating excerpts from international cultural magazines as well as some significant articles.

One day he complained, "The censors watch us like hawks."

In an irritated and scornful tone, she replied, "You haven't seen anything yet! To its credit, our journal is deemed 'subversive' by the ruling circles."

Smiling, Ahmad said, "Naturally you remember the editorials Mr. Adli Karim wrote before the war."

"During the reign of Ali Mahir, our magazine was closed down once because of an essay commemorating the Urabi rebellion. In it the editor had accused the Khedive Tawfiq of treachery."

One day, in the midst of a conversation on another topic, she asked, "Why did you choose journalism?"

He reflected a little. How much of his soul should he bare to this girl, who, compared to the other women he knew, was one of a kind?

"I didn't go to the University to obtain a government job. I had ideas I wanted to express in print. What better vehicle could there be for that than journalism?"

Her interest in his response delighted him. She countered, "I didn't go to the University. Or, more precisely, I didn't have the opportunity."

He was also enthralled by her candor, which by itself sufficed to show how different she was from other girls. She went on: "I'm a graduate of Mr. Adli Karim's school, an institution no less distinguished than the University. I've studied with him since I finished my baccalaureate. Frankly, I think you've given a good definition for journalism, or the kind of journalism we're engaged in. Yet so far you have expressed your thoughts by relying on others, I mean by translating. Haven't you thought of selecting a genre that suits you?"

He was silent for a time, groping for an answer, as if he had not understood her words. Then he asked, "What do you mean?"

"Essays, poetry, short stories, plays?"

"I don't know. The essay comes to mind first."

In a tone that said more than her words did, she observed, "Yes, but in view of the political situation, it's no longer an easy endeavor. Freethinkers are forced to speak their mind in clandestine publications. An essay is blunt and direct. Therefore it is dangerous, especially when eyes are scrutinizing us. The short story is more devious and thus harder to restrict. It's a cunning art, which has become such a prevalent form it will soon wrest leadership from all the others. Don't you see that there is not a single prominent literary figure who hasn't tried to make a name for himself in this genre, if only by publishing one short story?"

"Yes, I've read most of these works. Haven't you read some of the stories Mr. Riyad Qaldas publishes in *al-Fikr* magazine?"

"He's one of many and not the best."

"Perhaps not. My uncle Kamal Ahmad Abd al-Jawad, who writes for that same magazine, drew my attention to his stories."

Smiling, she asked, "He's your uncle? I've frequently read him, but . . ."

"Yes?"

"No offense, but he's a writer who rambles through the wilderness of metaphysics."

A bit anxiously he asked, "Don't you like him?"

"Liking is something else. He writes a good deal about ancient notions like the spirit, the absolute, and the theory of knowledge.

That's lovely, but such topics provide intellectual entertainment and mental enrichment without leading anywhere. Writing should be an instrument with a clearly defined purpose. Its ultimate goal should be the development of this world and man's ascent up the ladder of progress and liberation. The human race is engaged in a constant struggle. A writer truly worthy of the name must be at the head of the freedom fighters. Let's leave talk about mysterious forces like *élan vital* to Bergson."

"But even Karl Marx began as a budding philosopher who rambled through the labyrinth of metaphysics."

"And he ended up with a scientific understanding of society. That's where we should commence—not from his starting point."

Ahmad was uncomfortable at hearing his uncle criticized in this fashion. Motivated more by a desire to defend his uncle than by anything else, he said, "It's always worthwhile to know the truth, no matter what it is or what effects people think it has."

Sawsan responded enthusiastically, "This thought contradicts what you've written. I bet you're just saying it out of loyalty to your uncle. When a man's in pain, he concentrates on eradicating its causes. Our society is in deep pain. So first and foremost we must stop this pain. After that we can play around and philosophize. Imagine a man musing happily about abstruse points of philosophy while his life's blood drains away. What would you say of a man like that?"

Was this really a fair description of his uncle? He had to admit that her words struck a responsive chord inside him, that her eyes were beautiful, and that despite her strange earnestness she was attractive . . . very attractive.

"Actually, my uncle doesn't pay enough attention to these matters. I've discussed them with him many times and have found him to be a man who studies the Nazi movement as objectively as democracy or Communism, without being for or against any of them. I can't figure out his stance."

With a smile, she said, "He has none. A writer can't conceal his convictions. Your uncle is like all those other bourgeois intellectuals who enjoy reading and pondering things. When considering the 'absolute' they may feel such distress that it hurts, but on the street they nonchalantly walk past people who really are suffering."

He laughed and replied, "My uncle's not like that."

"You know best. The stories of Riyad Qaldas are not what we need either. They are descriptive analyses of reality but nothing more. They provide no guidance or direction."

Ahmad thought a little before remarking, "But he often describes the condition of laborers, both farmers and factory workers. This means that in his stories the proletariat is in the spotlight."

"But he limits himself to description and analysis. Compared to real struggle, his work is passive and negative."

This girl was a firebrand! She appeared to be extremely serious. Where was her feminine side?

"What would you want him to write?"

"Have you read any modern Soviet literature? Have you read anything by Maxim Gorky?"

He smiled but did not reply. There was no reason for him to feel embarrassed. He was a student of sociology, not of literature. Besides, she was several years his senior. How old was she? She might be twenty-four, or older.

She said, "This is the type of literature you should read. I'll lend you some if you want."

"I'd be delighted."

She smiled and said, "But a liberated man must be more than a reader or a writer. Principles relate primarily to the will ... the will above all other things."

Even so, he was aware of her elegance. Although she did not use makeup, she was as fastidious about her appearance as any other girl and her lively breasts were as attractive and fascinating as any other ones. But not so fast ... didn't the principles that he espoused distinguish him from other men?

"Our class is perverse," he thought. "We're unable to see women from more than one perspective."

"I'm delighted to have met you and predict that we will have many opportunities to work together closely."

Smiling in a way that was quite feminine, she said, "You're too kind."

"I really am delighted to have a chance to get to know you."

Yes, he was. But it was important that he not misinterpret his feelings, which might simply be the natural response of a young man like him.

"Be cautious," he advised himself. "Don't create a dilemma for yourself like that one in al-Ma'adi, for the sorrow it provoked has yet to be erased from your heart."

"Good evening, Aunt."

He followed Jalila to her preferred spot in the parlor, and once they were installed on the sofa, she called her maid, whom she watched fetch the drinks, prepare the table, and then depart after finishing these tasks. Turning toward Kamal, Jalila said, "Nephew, I swear that I no longer drink with anyone but you, when you come every Thursday night. I used to enjoy having a drink with your father in the old days. But back then I drank with many others too."

Kamal commented to himself, "I'm in dreadful need of alcohol. I don't know what life would be like without it." Then he told her, "But whiskey has disappeared from the market, Auntie, along with all other wholesome drinks. They say that one of the last German air raids on Scotland scored a direct hit on the warehouse of an internationally known distillery and that rivers of the best whiskey flowed out."

"What I wouldn't give for a raid like that! But before you get drunk tell me how al-Sayyid Ahmad is."

"No better and no worse. Madam Jalila, I hate to see him confined to bed. May our Lord be gracious to him."

"I'd love to visit him. Can't you summon the courage to give him my best wishes?"

"What an idea! That's all we need to provoke Judgment Day."

The old lady laughed and asked, "Do you suppose that a person like al-Sayyid Ahmad is capable of thinking any man pure, especially one of his own brood?"

"Even so, most beautiful of women. . . . To your health."

"And yours. . . . Atiya may be late, since her son is sick."

"She didn't mention that last time."

"No. Her son fell ill this past Saturday. The poor darling—her son is the apple of her eye. When anything happens to him, she loses her head."

"She's a fine woman who has had rotten luck. I've long felt her character convincing evidence that only dire necessity could have forced her to enter this profession."

In a jovial but sarcastic tone Jalila replied, "If a man like you is embarrassed by his honorable profession, why should she find hers satisfying?"

The maid passed back through the room with an incense burner wafting a pleasant scent. The moist autumn breeze entered through a window at the rear of the parlor, and the alcohol was bitter but potent. Jalila's comment about his profession reminded him of something he might otherwise have forgotten to tell her, and he said, "I was almost transferred to Asyut, Auntie. If the worst had happened, I would be packing my bags now to go there."

Striking her hand against her breast, Jalila exclaimed, "Asyut! How do you like those dates! May your worst enemy be sent there. What happened?"

"It has turned out all right, praise God."

"Your father knows more people in the government ministries than there are ants."

He nodded his head as if in agreement but did not comment. She still pictured his father in his old glory and had no way of knowing that when Kamal had informed his father of the transfer al-Sayyid Ahmad had lamented, "No one knows us anymore. What has become of our friends?"

Before telling his father, Kamal had gone to see his old friend Fuad Jamil al-Hamzawi, thinking he might know one of the top men in the Ministry of Education. But the illustrious judge had told him, "I'm very sorry, Kamal. Since I'm a judge, I can't ask anyone for favors."

With enormous embarrassment, Kamal had finally contacted his nephew Ridwan, and that same day the transfer had been rescinded. What an illustrious young man he was! They were both employed by the same ministry at the same rank, but Kamal was thirty-five and Ridwan only twenty-two. But what could a teacher in an elementary school expect? It was no longer possible for him to find consolation from philosophy or from claiming to be a philosopher. A philosopher is not a parrot who merely repeats what other philosophers have said. Any current graduate of the Arts Faculty could write as well as or better than he did. He had once hoped a publisher would bring out a collection of his essays, but those didactic works were no longer of any particular value. How many books there were nowadays.... In that ocean of learning he was an invisible drop. He had grown so weary that boredom oozed from every pore. When would his carriage reach death's station? He looked at the glass in his aunt's hand and then at her face, which clearly revealed her considerable age.

He could not help marveling at her and asked, "What does drinking do for you, Auntie?"

Displaying her gold teeth, she answered, "Do you call what I'm doing now 'drinking'? That time has passed. Liquor no longer has any taste or effect. It's like coffee. Nothing more or less. Toward the beginning of my career I once got so drunk at a wedding party in Birguwan that the members of my troupe were forced to carry me to my carriage at the end of the evening. May our Lord spare you anything like that!"

"Liquor's still the best thing a bad world has to offer," he reflected. Then he asked, "Have you experienced total intoxication? I used to reach it in two glasses. Today it takes me eight. I don't know how many I'll need tomorrow. But it's an absolute necessity, Aunt. Once intoxicated, the wounded heart dances with joy."

"Nephew, you have a sensitive heart that responds joyfully to music, even without any alcohol."

His heart . . . joyful? What of his sorrow . . . that constant companion? What of the ashes left from the bonfire of his hopes? . . . As a bored man, he had no goal beyond filling himself with liquor, in either this parlor or that bedroom, once the woman tending her sick son arrived. He and his favorite prostitute had reached the same point in life—that of a person whose life was not worth living.

"I'm afraid Atiya won't come."

"She'll come. When someone's ill, there's even more need for money."

"What a response!" he thought. But she did not give him a chance to brood about it, for, turning toward him, she examined him with interest for a time. Then she said in a low voice, "It's only a matter of days."

Without understanding what she actually meant, he replied, "May God grant you a long life and never deprive me of you."

Smiling, she said, "I'm going to give up this life."

Astonished, he sat up straight and cried out, "What did you say?"

She laughed and then answered in a mildly sarcastic tone, "Never fear. Atiya will take you to another house as safe as this one."

"But what's happened?"

"I've grown old, nephew, and God has given me more riches than I need. Yesterday, the police raided a nearby brothel and took the madam to the station. I've had enough. I'm planning to repent. I must change my ways before I meet my Lord."

He finished his drink and refilled the glass. Then, as if he did not believe what he had heard, he remarked, "All that's left is for you to board the boat to Mecca and perform the pilgrimage."

"May our Lord give me the power to do what's right."

After wondering about this for a while, he roused himself from his stupor to ask, "Did all this happen suddenly?"

"Of course not. I don't reveal a secret until I'm ready to act on it. I've been thinking about this for a long time."

"You're serious?"

"Absolutely. May our Lord be with us."

"I don't know what to say. But in any case may our Lord give you the strength to do the right thing."

"Amen." Then, laughing, she added, "Relax. I won't close this house until I've made provisions for your future."

He laughed out loud and asked, "Isn't it absurd to think that I could ever find a house where I would feel as much at home as here?"

"You can depend on me to pass you on to a new madam, even if I'm in Mecca."

"Everything seems ridiculous," Kamal thought. "But alcohol will always be the direction toward which sorrowful people turn their prayerful attentions. Circumstances have changed. Fuad Jamil al-Hamzawi's star has risen, and that of Kamal Ahmad Abd al-Jawad has declined. Yet alcohol will always bring a smile to the face of a grieving person. Kamal once amused Ridwan by carrying the young boy on his shoulder. Now the day has come for Ridwan to grasp Kamal in order to keep him from stumbling. Still, alcohol remains a lifeline for melancholy men."

Even Madam Jalila was planning to repent at the very time that he was searching for a new brothel. But liquor would continue to be his last resort.

"An invalid," he concluded, "finds everything boring, even boredom, but alcohol will always be the key to a happy release."

"Whenever I hear good things about you it makes me happy," he told her.

"May God guide you and bring you happiness."

"Perhaps I had better go? . . ."

She placed a finger in front of his mouth to silence him and exclaimed, "God forgive you! This is your house so long as it is mine. And whatever house I settle in will be yours, nephew."

Was he expiating some ancient curse of unknown origin? How could he escape from the anguish engulfing his life? Jalila herself was thinking seriously about transforming her life. Why should he not follow her example? A drowning man either finds a boulder to cling to or drowns. "If life has no meaning, why shouldn't we create a meaning for it?" he asked himself. "Perhaps it's a mistake for us to look for meaning in this world, precisely because our primary mission here is to create this meaning."

Jalila gave him a peculiar look, and he realized too late that he had unconsciously spoken these last words. Laughing, Jalila inquired, "Have you gotten drunk so fast?"

He masked his discomfort with a loud laugh and replied, "Wartime liquor's like poison. Forgive me. When do you suppose Atiya's coming?"

36 ❧

Kamal left Jalila's house at one-thirty in the morning. The world was veiled in a darkness tempered by silence as he slowly made his way to New Street and then turned toward al-Husayn. How long would he live in this sacred district that had lost all of its spiritual significance for him? He smiled wanly. The only remaining vestige of the liquor was a hangover. His blazing desires had died away, and he plodded along lethargically. Often at a time like this when lust had been satisfied, something—not regret or a wish to repent—would scream from his inner depths, imploring and urging him to cleanse and free himself from the grip of physical appetites once and for all, as if the receding waves of desire had laid bare submerged boulders of asceticism. When he raised his head skyward to commune with the stars, an air-raid siren ripped through the stillness of the night. His heart raced fiercely, and his sleepy eyes opened wide. He headed instinctively for the nearest wall, to walk along beside it. Looking up at the sky once more, he saw that searchlights were sweeping across the heavens at great speed. They met at times, only to veer off wildly on separate paths. Still hugging the walls, he increased his pace. He had an oppressive sense of being alone, as though he were the only person left on the face of the earth.

A shrill whistling sound, unlike anything he had ever heard before, plummeted from the sky, and it was followed by an enormous explosion that rocked the earth beneath his feet. Was it near or far? He did not have time to review his information about air raids, since the explosions came in such rapid succession that it took his breath away. There were repeated bursts of antiaircraft fire, and mysterious unidentifiable flashes of light streaked the air like lightning. It seemed to him that the whole earth was flying apart in a burst of sparks. Heedless of his surroundings, he shot off at a gallop toward Qirmiz Alley to shelter under its historic vaults. The guns were firing with an insane rage, as bombs pounded their targets and made the earth shake. After a few terrifying seconds he reached the passageway, which was packed with a multitude of people, whose bodies gave substance to its gloom. Panting, he slipped in among them. In the pervasive darkness, the prevailing sense of terror was voiced by little moans of alarm. From time to time, the entrance and exit to the vaulted section were illuminated by light reflected from the streaks in the sky.

The bombs had stopped falling—or so it seemed—but the antiaircraft guns kept on firing as wildly as before, and their impact on the soul was no less distressing than that of the bombs. There was a babbling confusion of shrieks, sobs, and scolding reprimands from various men, women, and children.

"This raid's not like the others."

"Our ancient district can't take this new kind of raid."

"Spare us your chatter. Say, 'O Lord!' "

"We are saying, 'O Lord!' "

"Be quiet. Be quiet! May God be compassionate to you."

While watching flashes of light illuminate the exit, Kamal saw a new group approach. He thought he recognized his father among them, and his heart pounded. Was it really his father? How could the man have gotten all the way to the alley? Indeed, how could he have gotten out of bed? Kamal pushed through the agitated throngs of people until he reached the end of the vault. In a glimmer of light, he saw the whole family—his father and mother, Aisha, and Umm Hanafi. He made his way to them and then, standing beside them, whispered, "It's Kamal. Are you all right?"

His father did not answer. Utterly exhausted, he was leaning against the wall, between Kamal's mother and Aisha. The mother said, "Kamal? Praise God. This is atrocious, son. It's not like before. We thought the house was going to tumble down on our heads. Our Lord gave your father enough strength to get out of bed and come with us. I have no idea how he made it or how we got here."

Umm Hanafi muttered, "Compassion is from Him. What is this terror? May our Lord be gracious to us."

Suddenly, Aisha cried out, "When will these guns be still?"

Fearing that her voice suggested her nerves were at the breaking point, Kamal went to Aisha and took her hand between both of his, for he had recovered some of his presence of mind on finding himself with people who needed his support. The guns were still firing with a wild rage, but their fury started to abate by barely perceptible degrees. Kamal leaned toward his father and asked, "How are you, Father?"

The man replied in a feeble whisper, "Where were you, Kamal? Where were you when the raid started?"

To set the man's mind at ease, Kamal said, "I was near the alley. How are you?"

In a shaky voice the father said, "God only knows ... how I got out of bed and rushed along the street. God knows ... I wasn't conscious of what I was doing. . . . When will things return to normal?"

"Shall I take off my jacket for you to sit on?"

"No. I can stand, but when will things calm down?"

"The raid seems to have ended. Don't worry about getting up so suddenly. Surprises often work miracles in an illness."

He had hardly finished speaking when the ground trembled from three explosions in a row, and the antiaircraft guns went on the rampage again. The passageway was filled with screams.

"It's right over our heads!"

"Declare the unity of God."

"Don't make things worse than they are with your talk."

Kamal released Aisha's hand to take both of his father's in his grasp. It was the first time in his life he had done that. Al-Sayyid Ahmad's hands were trembling, and Kamal's were too. Umm Hanafi, who had thrown herself on the ground, wailed noisily.

An agitated voice called out irritably, "I've had enough screaming! I'll kill anyone who screams."

But the screaming grew louder, and the gunfire continued. Nervous tension increased as they waited for the next shock wave. This expectation of more explosions had a stifling effect on them, as the firing of the guns went unanswered.

"The bombing's over!"

"It only stops to start up again."

"It's far away. If it were close, the houses around us would not have survived."

"The bombs fell in al-Nahhasin."

"It seems that way to you, but they may have fallen on the ordnance depot."

"Listen, will you? Hasn't the gunfire started to die down?"

It had. Soon firing was audible only in the distance. Then it was intermittent, coming at intervals—of a whole minute eventually. Finally silence descended, spread, and became firmly entrenched. People felt free to talk again, and whispered expressions of tearful hope could be heard. They had so many things to remember as they came back to life and sighed with cautious but anxious relief. Kamal tried in vain to inspect his father's face, for the flashes of light had disappeared and the world was dark.

"Father, things will calm down now."

The man did not answer but wiggled his hands, which his son still grasped, to show that he was alive.

"Are you all right?" Kamal asked. The hands moved once more, and the son felt so sad that he was on the verge of tears.

A siren went off to mark the end of the raid. Afterward, the jubilant shouts heard on all sides were reminiscent of the cries of children after the cannon fires to mark the start of a holiday or to signal the hour for feasting during Ramadan. The alley and the neighboring area were the scene of unlimited commotion as doors and windows banged open, agitated conversations grew loud, and the people packed into the vaulted part of the alley began to move out in waves.

Sighing, Kamal said, "Let's go home."

Placing one arm over Kamal's shoulder and the other over Amina's, al-Sayyid Ahmad walked along between them, a step at a time. They began to wonder how he was and what effect this grim outing would have on him. . . . But he stopped walking and said in a weak voice, "I've got to sit down."

Kamal suggested, "Let me carry you."

The exhausted man protested, "You won't be able to."

Putting one arm around the man's back and the other under his legs, Kamal picked him up. It was not a light load, but little was left of his father in any case. Kamal walked along very slowly, and the others followed him apprehensively.

Aisha suddenly started sobbing. When her father said in a tired voice, "There's no call for a scene," she put a hand over her mouth.

When they reached the house, Umm Hanafi helped Kamal carry the master. They took him upstairs slowly and cautiously. Although he submitted gracefully to this treatment, his stream of mumbled pleas for God's forgiveness betrayed his grief and discomfort. They deposited him carefully on the bed. When the light was turned on, they could see that his face was very pale, as if the exertion had drained his blood. His chest was heaving violently up and down, and his eyes were closed from his exhaustion. He began moaning and moaning. Eventually he got the better of his pain and sank into silence. They stood in a row beside his bed, watching him with apprehensive dread. At last Amina inquired in a trembling voice, "Is my master well?"

He opened his eyes, and took his time looking at the faces, which he did not always seem to recognize. Then he sighed and said in a scarcely audible voice, "Praise God."

"Sleep, master. Sleep to regain your strength."

They heard the ring of the bell outside, and Umm Hanafi went to open the door. They exchanged questioning glances, and Kamal suggested, "Probably someone from Sugar Street or Palace of Desire Alley has come to see if we're all right."

His supposition was confirmed, for Abd al-Muni'm and Ahmad soon entered the room, and they were followed by Yasin and Ridwan. Approaching al-Sayyid Ahmad's bed, they greeted those present. The man glanced at them listlessly. As though speech were beyond him, he contented himself with raising a thin hand to them in greeting. Kamal recounted in an abbreviated form what his father had experienced that alarming night. Then Amina whispered, "An atrocious night—may our Lord never repeat it."

Umm Hanafi remarked, "The movement has tired him, but with some rest he'll recover his strength."

Yasin leaned over his father to say, "You need to sleep. How do you feel now?"

The man gazed with dull eyes at his eldest son and mumbled, "Praise God. My left side doesn't feel good."

Yasin asked, "Should I call a doctor for you?"

The father waved his hand testily and then whispered, "No. It's better if I sleep."

Starting to retreat, Yasin gestured for the family to leave the room, and the man raised his scrawny hand again. They walked out, one after the other, leaving only Amina. Once they were assembled in the sitting room, Abd al-Muni'm asked his uncle Kamal, "What did you do? We hurried down to the reception room in the courtyard."

Yasin volunteered, "We went downstairs to our neighbors' apartment on the ground floor."

Kamal said anxiously, "Fatigue has sapped Papa's strength."

Yasin asserted, "But he'll regain his health by sleeping."

"What can we do if there's another raid?"

No one answered, and there was a heavy silence, until Ahmad complained, "Our houses are ancient. They won't stand up to these raids."

Wishing to dissipate the lingering cloud of despair, since it was upsetting him, Kamal coaxed a smile from his lips and said, "If our houses are destroyed, they'll have the honor of being demolished by the most advanced inventions of modern science."

37

Kamal had barely reached the stairway door after showing out the last visitors of the evening when an alarming din reached his ears from above. His nerves were still on edge, and he feared the worst as he bounded up the steps. The sitting room was empty, but through the closed door of his father's chamber he could hear the loud voices of several people, who were all speaking at once. Rushing to the door, he opened it and entered, expecting something unpleasant but refusing to think what it might be.

His mother's hoarse voice was exclaiming, "Master!"

Aisha was calling curtly for "Papa!"

Mumbling to herself, Umm Hanafi stood riveted to her spot by the head of the bed. When Kamal looked in that direction, he was overcome by desperate alarm and mournful resignation, for he saw that the bottom half of his father's body lay on the bed while the upper half rested on Amina's breast. The man's chest was heaving up and down mechanically as he emitted a strange rattling sound not of this world. His eyes had a new blind look, which suggested that they could not see anything or express the man's internal struggle. Kamal, near the end of the bed, felt that his feet were glued to the floor, that he had lost the ability to speak, and that his eyes had turned to glass. He could think of nothing to say or to do and had an overwhelming sense of being utterly impotent, forlorn, and insignificant. Although aware that his father was bidding farewell to life, Kamal was in all other respects as good as unconscious.

Glancing away from her father's face long enough to look at Kamal, Aisha cried out, "Father! Here's Kamal. He wants to talk to you."

Umm Hanafi abandoned her murmured refrain to say in a choking voice, "Get the doctor."

With angry sorrow, the mother groaned, "What doctor, you fool?"

The father moved as if trying to sit up, and the convulsions of his chest increased. He stretched out the forefinger of his right hand and then that of the left. When Amina saw this, her face contracted with pain. She bent down toward his ear and recited in an audible voice,

"There is no god but God, and Muhammad is the Messenger of God." She kept repeating these words until his hand became still. Kamal understood that his father, no longer able to speak, had asked Amina to recite the Muslim credo on his behalf and that the inner meaning of this final hour would never be revealed. To describe it as pain, terror, or a swoon would have been a pointless conjecture. At any rate it could not last long, for it was too momentous and significant to be part of ordinary life. Although his nerves were devastated by this scene, Kamal was ashamed to find himself snatching a few moments to analyze and study it, as if his father's death was a subject for his reflections and a source of information for him. This doubled his grief and his pain.

The contractions of the man's chest intensified and the rattling sound grew louder. "What is this?" Kamal wondered. "Is he trying to get up? Or attempting to speak? Or addressing something we can't see? Is he in pain? Or terrified? ... Oh. ..." The father emitted a deep groan, and then his head fell on his breast.

With every ounce of her being Aisha screamed, "Father! ... Na'ima! ... Uthman! ... Muhammad!" Umm Hanafi rushed to her and gently shoved her out of the room. The mother raised a pale face to look at Kamal and gestured for him to leave, but he did not budge.

She whispered to him desperately, "Let me perform my last duty to your father."

He turned and exited to the sitting room, where Aisha, who had flung herself across the sofa, was howling. He took a seat on the sofa opposite hers, while Umm Hanafi went back into the bedroom to assist her mistress, closing the door behind her. But Aisha's weeping was unbearable, and rising again, Kamal began to pace back and forth, without addressing any comment to her. From time to time he would glance at the closed door and then press his lips together.

"Why does death seem so alien to us?" he wondered. Once his thoughts were collected enough for him to reflect on the situation, he immediately lost his concentration again, as emotion got the better of him. Even when no longer able to leave the bedroom, al-Sayyid Ahmad had defined the life of the household. It would come as no surprise if on the morrow Kamal found the house to be quite a different place and its life transformed. Indeed, from this moment on, he would have to accustom himself to a new role. Aisha's wails made him feel all the more distraught. He considered trying to silence her but then refrained. He was amazed to see her give vent to her emotions after she had appeared for so long to be impassive and oblivious to everything. Kamal thought again of his father's disappearance from their lives. It seemed almost inconceivable. Remembering his father's condition in the final days, he felt sorrow tear at his heartstrings. When he reviewed the image of their father at the height of his powers and glory, Kamal felt a profound pity for all living creatures. But when would Aisha ever stop wailing? Why could she not weep tearlessly like her brother?

The door of the bedroom opened, and Umm Hanafi emerged. During the moment before it was shut again, he could hear his mother's lamentations. He gathered that she had finished performing her final duty to his father and was now free to cry. Umm Hanafi approached Aisha and told her brusquely, "That's enough weeping, my lady." Turning toward Kamal, she remarked, "Dawn is breaking, master. Sleep, if only a little, for you have a hard day ahead of you."

Then she suddenly started crying. As she left the room, she said in a sobbing voice, "I'll go to Sugar Street and Palace of Desire Alley to announce the dreadful news."

Yasin rushed in, followed by Zanuba and Ridwan. Then the silence of the street was rent by the cries of Khadija, whose arrival caused the household's fires of grief to burn at fever pitch, as wails mixed with screams and sobs. It would not have been appropriate for the men to mourn on the first floor, and they went up to the study on the top floor. They sat there despondently, overwhelmed by a gloomy silence, until Ibrahim Shawkat remarked, "The only power and strength is God's. The raid finished him off. May God be most compassionate to him. He was an extraordinary man."

Unable to control himself, Yasin started crying. Then Kamal burst into tears too. Ibrahim Shawkat said, "Proclaim that there is only one God. He did not leave you until you were grown men."

With morose sorrow and some astonishment Ridwan, Abd al-Muni'm, and Ahmad gazed at the weeping men, who quickly dried their tears and fell silent.

Ibrahim Shawkat said, "It will be morning soon. Let's consider what has to be done."

Yasin answered sadly and tersely, "There's nothing novel about this. We've gone through it repeatedly."

Ibrahim Shawkat responded, "The funeral must suit his rank."

Yasin replied with conviction, "That's the least we can do."

Then Ridwan commented, "The street in front of the house isn't wide enough for a funeral tent that can hold all the mourners. Let's put it in Bayt al-Qadi Square instead."

Ibrahim Shawkat remarked, "But it's customary to install the tent in front of the home of the deceased."

Ridwan replied, "That isn't so important, especially since cabinet ministers, senators, and deputies will be among the mourners."

They realized that he was referring to his own acquaintances. Yasin commented indifferently, "So let's erect it there."

Thinking about the part he was to play, Ahmad said, "We won't be able to get the obituary in the morning papers. . . ."

Kamal said, "The evening papers come out at about three P.M. Let's have the funeral at five."

"So be it. The cemetery's not far, at any rate. There'll be time to have the burial before sunset."

Kamal considered what they were saying with some amazement. At five o'clock the previous day his father had been in bed, listening to the radio. At that time the following day . . . next to Yasin's two young children and Fahmy. What was left of Fahmy? Life had done nothing to diminish Kamal's childhood desire to look inside his brother's coffin. Had his father really been preparing to say something? What had he wanted to say?

Yasin turned toward Kamal to ask, "Were you there when he died?"

"Yes. It was shortly after you left."

"Did he suffer much?"

"I don't know. Who could say, brother? But it didn't last more than five minutes."

Yasin sighed and then asked, "Didn't he say anything?"

"No. He probably wasn't able to speak."

"Didn't he recite the credo?"

Looking down to hide his tearful expression, Kamal replied, "My mother did that for him."

"May God be compassionate to him."

"Amen."

They were silent for a time until finally Ridwan remarked, "The funeral pavilion must be large, if there's to be room for all the mourners to sit."

Yasin said, "Naturally. We have many friends." Then, looking at Abd al-Muni'm, he added, "And there are all the Muslim Brethren." He sighed and continued: "If his friends had been alive, they would have carried his coffin on their shoulders."

The funeral went off according to their expectations. Abd al-Muni'm had the most friends in attendance, but Ridwan's were higher in rank. Some of them attracted attention because they were well known to readers of newspapers or magazines. Ridwan was so proud they were there that his pride almost obscured his grief. The people of the district, even those who had not known al-Sayyid Ahmad personally, came to bid farewell to their lifelong neighbor. The only thing missing from the funeral was the deceased man's friends, who had all preceded him to the other world.

At Bab al-Nasr, as the funeral cortege made its way to the cemetery, Shaykh Mutawalli Abd al-Samad materialized. Staggering from advanced age, he looked up at the coffin, squinted his eyes, and asked, "Who is that?"

One of the men from the district told him, "Al-Sayyid Ahmad Abd al-Jawad, God rest his soul."

The man's face trembled unsteadily back and forth as a questioning look of bewilderment spread across it. Then he inquired, "Where was he from?"

Shaking his head rather sadly, the other man replied, "From this district. How could you not have known him? Don't you remember al-Sayyid Ahmad Abd al-Jawad?"

But the shaykh gave no sign of remembering anything and after casting a final glance at the casket proceeded on his way.

38

"Now that my master has left this house, it's no longer the place I called home for more than fifty years. Everyone around me weeps. I receive the unflagging attentions of Khadija, who is my heart filled with sorrow and memories as well as the heart of everyone who has a heart. In fact, she's my daughter, sister, and, at times, my mother. I do most of my crying surreptitiously, when I'm alone, for I have to encourage them to forget. Their grief is hard for me to bear. God forbid that one of them should be tormented by sorrow. When I'm by myself, my only consolation comes from weeping, and I cry till I exhaust my tears. If Umm Hanafi disturbs my tearful solitude, no matter how unobtrusively, I tell her, 'Leave me and my affairs alone, may God have mercy on you.' She complains, 'How can I when you're in this state? I know how you feel. But you're the mistress and a Believer, indeed the mistress of all women Believers. From you we learn forbearance and submission to God's decree.'

"That's a beautiful thought, Umm Hanafi, but how can a grieving heart hope to comprehend it? This world is no longer any concern of mine. I have no further tasks to perform here. Every hour of my day is linked to some memory of my master. He was the pivot of the only life I've ever known. How can I bear to live now that he has departed, leaving nothing behind him? I was the first to suggest changing the furniture in the dear room. What could I do? Their eyes would gaze at his empty bed, and then they would break into tears. . . . My master is certainly entitled to the tears shed for him, but I can't stand to see them cry. I worry about their tender hearts. I attempt to console them with the same ideas you use on me, Umm Hanafi. I ask them to submit to God and His decree. That's why after the old furniture was taken out I moved into Aisha's room. To keep that room from being abandoned, I transferred the sitting-room furniture and the coffee hour in there. When we gather around the brazier we talk a lot and our conversations are interrupted by tears.

"Nothing preoccupies us so much as getting ready to visit the cemetery, and I myself supervise the preparation of the food we distribute to the poor there. That's just about the only task I don't entrust to Umm Hanafi, to whom I have relinquished so many of my duties ... that dear loyal woman who has certainly earned her place in our family. We both prepare this mercy offering. We cry together. We remind each other of the beautiful days. She's always with me, assisting me with her spirit and her memory. Yesterday when the evening celebrations of Ramadan were mentioned, she launched into a description of what my master did during Ramadan from the time he woke up late in the morning until he returned to have breakfast with us before sunrise the next day. For my part, I mentioned how I used to scurry to the latticed balcony to watch the carriage bring him home and to listen to the laughter of the passengers, those men who have departed to God's mercy, one after the other—just as our sweet days have departed, along with youth, health, and vigor. O God, grant the children a long life and comfort them with its joys.

"This morning I saw our cat under the bed. She was sniffing around where she had nursed her beloved kittens that I gave away to the neighbors. The sight of her, so sad and bewildered, broke my heart and I cried out from the depths of my soul, 'God grant you patience, Aisha.' Poor dear Aisha.... Her father's death has awakened all the old sorrows, and she weeps for her father, her daughter, her sons, and her husband. How hot tears are.... I, who once found the loss of a child such a bitter experience that I seemed to weep away my heart's blood, am today afflicted with the death of my master. My life, which he once filled completely, is empty. Of all my duties, the only one left is preparing the mercy offering I give on his behalf or collecting it from Sugar Street or Palace of Desire Alley. This is all I have.

"No, son. You should find yourself some gathering other than our mournful one, for I fear it will depress you.... Why are you so despondent? Grief is not for men. A man can't bear his normal burdens and sorrow too. Go up to your room and read or write the way you used to. Or get out of the house in the evening and see your friends. Since God created the world, loved ones have left their kin. If everyone fell victim to sorrow, no one would remain alive on the face of the earth. I'm not as forlorn as you think. A Believer should not feel dejected. If God so wills, we'll live and forget. 'There's no way to catch up with the dear one who has gone on ahead until God decrees it.' That's what I tell him, and I go out of my way to appear composed and collected. But when Khadija, the living heart of our household, turns up and weeps with abandon, I can't keep from bursting into tears.

"Aisha told me she'd seen her father in a dream. He was grasping Na'ima's arm with one hand and Muhammad's with the other. Uthman was sitting on his shoulders. He told her he was fine, that they were all fine. She asked about the secret meaning of the window of light she had once seen in the sky only to have it disappear for good. His sole response was the look of censure in his eyes. Then she asked me what the dream meant. How helpless you make your mother feel, Aisha. . . . All the same, I told her that the dear man, although dead, was still concerned about her and, for that reason, had visited her in a dream and had brought her children from paradise so that the sight of them would cheer her. 'So don't spoil their peace of mind by clinging to your sorrow.' I wish the old Aisha would come back, even for an hour. . . . If the people around me would get over their grief, I could devote myself entirely to my duty to grieve profoundly.

"I got Yasin and Kamal together and asked, 'What shall we do with these dear items?' Yasin said, 'I'll take the ring, for it fits my finger. Kamal, you take the watch. And, Mother, the prayer beads are for you. . . . What about his cloaks and caftans?' I immediately mentioned Shaykh Mutawalli Abd al-Samad, the only survivor from the dear man's friends. Yasin said, 'He's as good as dead, for he's oblivious to the world and has no fixed abode.' Frowning, Kamal remarked, 'He no longer knew who Father was. He had forgotten his name and nonchalantly turned away from the funeral procession.' I was shocked and said, 'How amazing! When did that happen?' Even in his last days, my master asked about him. He always loved the shaykh and had seen him only once or twice since his visit to our house the night of Na'ima's wedding. But, my Lord, what's become of Na'ima and of that whole portion of our lives? Then Yasin suggested giving the clothes to the messenger boys in his office and the janitors at Kamal's school because no one deserved the clothes more than poor people like them who would pray for him. And the beloved prayer beads will not leave my hands until I leave this life.

"The tomb is such a pleasant place to visit, even though it stirs my grief. I've frequented it ever since my precious martyred son was taken there. From that time on, I've considered it to be one of the rooms of our house, even though it's at the outskirts of our district. The tomb brings us all together just as the coffee hour once did. Khadija weeps until she's exhausted. Then we're instructed to be silent out of respect for a recitation of the Qur'an. After that they converse for a time. I'm pleased by anything that distracts my loved ones from their sorrow. Ridwan, Abd al-Muni'm, and Ahmad become embroiled in a long argument. Occasionally Karima joins them. That tempts Kamal to participate and brightens the gloomy atmosphere of the grave site. Abd al-Muni'm asks about his martyred uncle. Yasin recounts various stories concerning him. The old days come to life, and forgotten memories are revived. My heart pounds, because I'm at a loss to know how to hide my tears.

"I frequently find Kamal looking despondent. When I ask him about it, he replies, 'His image never leaves me, especially the vision of his death. If only he had had an easier end!'

I told him tenderly, 'You must forget all this.' He asked, 'How can I?' I suggested faith, but he smiled sadly and remarked, 'How I feared him when I was young . . . but in his later years he revealed to me a totally different person, indeed a beloved friend. How witty, tender, and gracious he was . . . unlike any other man.'

"Yasin weeps whenever he happens to remember his father. Kamal's sorrow takes the form of silent dejection, but huge Yasin weeps like a child and tells me, 'He was the only man I ever loved.' Yes, my master was Yasin's father and mother too. The boy was never treated to affection, care, or concern anywhere but under his father's wing. Even the man's fierceness was compassionate. I'll never forget the day he forgave me and invited me back to his house, confirming my mother's hunch, may God be compassionate to her. She kept telling me, 'Al-Sayyid Ahmad is not a man who will permanently ban the mother of his children.' His love united us in the past, just as his memory does now. Our house does not lack for visitors, but my heart is not at rest unless I have Khadija and Yasin around me with their families. Even Zanuba's grief is quite sincere. Beautiful young Karima suggested, 'Grandmother, come home with us. It's time for the celebrations in honor of al-Husayn. You can hear Sufi groups chanting below our house. I know you like that.' I gave her a grateful kiss and told her, 'Daughter, your grandmother's not used to spending the night away from home.' The girl knows nothing of the customs of her grandfather's house in the old days. How beautiful it is to remember them. . . . The latticed balcony was the outer limit of my world. I waited there for my master to return late at night. At the time, he was so mighty that the earth almost shook when he stepped out of the carriage. Vigor virtually leaping from his face, he would fill the room on entering it, he was so big and tall. He won't come home tonight. He'll never come home. Even before his passing, he withered away, stopped going out, and stayed in bed. He grew thin and lost so much weight you could pick him up with one hand. I'll never recover from my grief.

"Aisha said angrily, 'These children haven't grieved for their grandfather and don't grieve for him.' I told her, 'They did grieve, but they're young. It's part of God's compassion for them that they don't get bogged down in their grief.' She retorted, 'See how Abd al-Muni'm can't stop arguing. He never mourned for my daughter. He quickly forgot all about her, as if she had never existed.' I reminded her, 'No, he mourned her for a long time and wept a great deal. Men's grief differs from that of women. A mother's heart is unlike any other one. Who doesn't forget, Aisha? Don't we take comfort in conversation? Aren't we occasionally surprised by a smile? There will come a day when not a tear is shed. Besides, where is Fahmy? What about him?'

"Umm Hanafi asked me, 'Why have you stopped going to al-Husayn?' I replied, 'My soul is indifferent to all the things I used to love. I'll visit my master al-Husayn once the wound is healed.' She inquired, 'What will heal the wound if not a visit to your Master?' This is how Umm Hanafi takes care of me. She is the mistress of our household. If it were not for her, we would not have a home. My Lord, You who are the lord of all creation, You who issue all the ineluctable decrees, to You I pray. I wish you had allowed my master to keep his strength to the end. Nothing caused me so much pain as his confinement to bed—a man for whom the whole world was hardly big enough. He wasn't even able to pray. I regret the suffering endured by his weak heart and the way he was carried home like a child after the raid. These things cause my tears to flow and dam up my grief."

39

"Putting my trust in God, I shall ask for the hand of my cousin Karima."

Ibrahim Shawkat glanced up at his son with some astonishment. Ahmad bowed his head but smiled in a way that showed the news came as no surprise to him. Khadija set aside the shawl she was embroidering to cast a strange look of disbelief at her son. Then, staring at her husband, she asked, "What did he say?"

Abd al-Muni'm repeated: "Putting my trust in God, I shall ask for the hand of your brother's daughter Karima."

To show her bewilderment Khadija spread her hands out and asked, "Has good taste gone out of fashion in this world? Is this an appropriate time to discuss an engagement, regardless of the identity of your intended?"

Smiling, Abd al-Muni'm said, "All times are appropriate for betrothals."

Shaking her head to express her bafflement, she inquired, "And your grandfather?" Then, as she looked from Ahmad to Ibrahim, she continued: "Have you ever heard of anything like this before?"

Abd al-Muni'm remarked a bit sharply, "An engagement . . . not a marriage or a wedding. And my grandfather's been dead four whole months. . . ."

Lighting a cigarette, Ibrahim Shawkat said, "Karima's still young. She looks older than she is, I think."

Abd al-Muni'm answered, "She's fifteen, and the marriage contract would not be signed for a year. . . ."

Khadija asked with bitter sarcasm, "Has Mrs. Zanuba shown you the birth certificate?"

Ibrahim Shawkat and his son Ahmad laughed, but Abd al-Muni'm said earnestly, "Nothing will happen for a year. By that time almost a year and a half will have passed since Grandfather's death, and Karima will be old enough to get married."

"So why are you causing us a headache now?"

"There wouldn't be any harm in announcing the engagement at present."

Khadija inquired scornfully, "Will the engagement go sour if it's postponed for a year?"

"Please don't jest."

Khadija shouted, "If this happens, it will cause a scandal."

With all the composure he could muster, Abd al-Muni'm replied, "Leave Grandmother to me. She'll understand me better than you do. She's my grandmother and Karima's too."

His mother observed gruffly, "She's not Karima's grandmother."

Abd al-Muni'm fell silent, but his expression was sullen. Before he could answer, his father interjected, "It's a question of good taste. It would be better to wait a little."

Khadija cried out furiously, "You mean your only objection is to the timing?"

Pretending not to understand, Abd al-Muni'm asked, "Is there some other objection then?"

Khadija did not answer. When she started embroidering the shawl again, Abd al-Muni'm protested, "Karima's the daughter of your brother Yasin, isn't she?"

Dropping the shawl, Khadija said bitterly, "She truly is my brother's daughter, but you ought to remember as well who her mother is."

The men exchanged apprehensive glances. Abd al-Muni'm burst out acerbically, "Her mother's also your brother's wife."

Raising her voice, she proclaimed, "I know that and regret it."

"That forgotten past! Who remembers it now? She's no longer anything but a respectable lady like you."

In a surly voice she retorted, "That woman's not like me and never will be."

"What's wrong with her? Since we were little children we've known her to be a lady in every sense of the word. When a person repents and lives righteously, his former misdeeds are erased. After that, the only people who would remind him of them are . . ."

He stopped. Shaking her head sorrowfully, she challenged him, "Yes? . . . Tell me what I am! Insult your mother for the sake of this woman who has successfully ensnared you. I've long wondered what lay behind those repeated dinner invitations to Palace of Desire Alley. You've been taken in by it."

After looking angrily from his father to his brother, Abd al-Muni'm inquired, "Is this the way we talk? I'd like to hear what you two think."

Yawning, Ibrahim Shawkat said, "There's no need for all this discussion. Abd al-Muni'm will get married again, if not today then tomorrow. You want that to happen. Karima's our daughter and a lovely, charming girl. There's no need to become agitated."

Ahmad remarked, "Mother, you're always the one who thinks first about pleasing Uncle Yasin."

Exasperated, Khadija replied, "You're all against me, as usual, but the only argument you can think of is 'Uncle Yasin.' Yasin is my brother. His primary fault was not knowing how to pick a bride, and his nephew has inherited this strange defect from him."

Abd al-Muni'm asked in amazement, "Isn't my uncle's wife a friend of yours? Anyone watching the two of you exchange secrets would think you are sisters."

"What can I do when the woman's as shrewd a diplomat as Allenby? But if it had been up to me and I had not been concerned about Yasin, I would not have allowed her to enter my home. What has been the result? Against your better judgment you have been won over by the dinners given to promote her own interests . . . God help us."

Then Ahmad told his brother, "Ask for her hand whenever you want. Mother has an active tongue but a fine heart."

Laughing nervously, she said, "Bravo, son. You two differ about everything—beliefs, religion, politics—but you're united against me."

Ahmad said gleefully, "Uncle Yasin is a favorite of yours, and you'll accord Karima the warmest welcome. The thing is that you would like a bride who isn't a relative so that you, as her mother, can dominate her. Fine . . . it'll be up to me to fulfill this dream for you. I'll bring you a bride you've never heard of so your craving can be satisfied."

"I wouldn't be at all surprised if you brought home a dancer tomorrow. Why are you laughing? This devout young shaykh wants to marry into the family of a professional entertainer. So what should I expect from you, whose religious beliefs are suspect, so help me God?"

"We really do need a dancer in the family."

Then, as though she had just remembered a terribly important matter, Khadija asked, "And Aisha? My Lord, what do you suppose she'll say about us?"

Abd al-Muni'm objected, "What should she say? My wife died four years ago. Does she want me to remain a widower for the rest of my life?"

Ibrahim Shawkat said irritably, "Don't turn an anthill into a mountain. The question is far simpler than you suggest. Karima is Yasin's daughter. Yasin is the brother of both Khadija and Aisha. That suffices. Pshaw! You argue about everything, even weddings."

A smile on his face, Ahmad glanced stealthily at his mother. He continued to observe her until she rose, as if infuriated, and left the room. He told himself, "This bourgeois class is nothing but an array of complexes. It would take an expert psychoanalyst to cure all of its ills, an analyst as powerful as history itself. If luck had given me any kind of break, I would have married before my brother, but that other bourgeois woman stipulated a salary of at least fifty pounds a month. This is how hearts are wounded for considerations that have nothing to do with the heart. I wonder what Sawsan Hammad would think if she knew about my abortive adventure?"

40

The weather was bitterly cold and the dampness of Khan al-Khalili in winter made it a less than ideal destination, but that evening Riyad Qaldas himself had suggested going to the Khan al-Khalili coffeehouse constructed above the site of the old one of Ahmad Abduh. Or, as he put it, "Kamal has finally taught me to appreciate quaint places." From its doorway, which opened out to al-Husayn, this small café, like a corridor with tables lining the two sides, extended back to a wooden balcony that overlooked the new Khan al-Khalili. Drinking tea and taking turns with a water pipe, the friends sat on the right-hand side of the balcony.

Isma'il explained, "I have a few days to pack and then I'll be traveling there."

Kamal asked sadly, "We won't see you for three years?"

"That's right. This is one gamble I have to make. The position offers an enormous salary I couldn't ever imagine getting here, and, besides, Iraq is an Arab country. It's not that different from Egypt."

"I'll miss him," Kamal thought. "He's not a soul mate, but he's my lifelong friend."

Laughing, Riyad Qaldas inquired, "Doesn't Iraq need any translators?"

Kamal asked, "Would you leave home if you had an opportunity like Isma'il's?"

"In the past I wouldn't have hesitated, but not now."

"What distinguishes the present from the past?"

Riyad Qaldas replied merrily, "For you, nothing. For me, everything. It seems I'm soon to join the fraternity of married men."

Astonished by the news, which came without any warning, Kamal felt anxious in a way he could not pinpoint precisely.

"Really? You've never alluded to this before."

"No. It's come about suddenly . . . at the last meeting. When the two of us last met, it wasn't even under consideration."

Isma'il Latif laughed triumphantly. Attempting to smile, Kamal asked, "How did this happen?"

"How? The way it happens every day. A woman teacher came to

visit her brother in the translation bureau. I liked her and, on exploring my prospects, found myself invited to proceed."

As he accepted the hose of the water pipe from Kamal, Isma'il asked jovially, "When do you suppose this fellow will get around to exploring his prospects?"

Isma'il never missed a chance to bring up this stale topic. But there was a more serious side to the matter. All of Kamal's friends who had tried marriage maintained that it was a cage. If this wedding took place, he would probably see Riyad only on rare occasions and his friend might change into a different person, a kind of pen pal. The writer was so gentle and tender, it would not take much to subdue him. But how would Kamal's life be possible without him? If marriage transformed Riyad as radically as it had Isma'il, Kamal could bid farewell to the joys of life.

"When are you getting married?" Kamal asked.

"Next winter, at the latest."

It seemed that the tormented Kamal was fated to lose a best friend time and again. "At that moment, you'll become a different Riyad Qaldas."

"Why? . . . You have a fantastic imagination."

Masking his anxiety with a smile, Kamal asked, "A fantastic imagination? Today Riyad Qaldas is a man whose spirit always wants more while his pocket is happy to go empty. Once you're a husband, your pocket will always need more money and you'll have no opportunity for spiritual fulfillment."

"What an offensive description of the husband! But I don't agree with you."

"How about Isma'il, who is being forced to migrate to Iraq? I'm not making fun of that decision, for it's not only natural but heroic. Yet, at the same time, it's hideous. Picture yourself up to your ears in the problems of daily life, thinking only of how to make ends meet, reckoning your hours by piasters and milliemes. Then the poetic side of life can only seem a waste of time."

Riyad replied scornfully, "Imagination's fantasies inspired by fear. . . ."

Isma'il Latif said, "Oh, if only you would experience marriage and fatherhood. . . . Even today, you have no idea of the true meaning of life."

This view might well be correct, in which case Kamal's life was a silly tragedy. But what was happiness? What exactly did he desire? Even so, the main cause of his distress was the fact that he was once again threatened by a terrifying isolation of the kind he had suffered when Husayn Shaddad had disappeared from his life. What if it were possible for him to find a wife with the body of Atiya and the spirit of Riyad? That was what he really wanted: Atiya's body and Riyad's soul united in a single person whom he could marry. In that way, he would free himself from the threat of loneliness for the rest of his life. This was the challenge.

Riyad remarked impatiently, "Let's not talk about marriage. I've made my decision, and, Kamal, I hope your turn is next. Still there are important political events that demand our attention today."

Although Kamal shared his friend's sentiments, he was unable to shake off his surprise and appeared indifferent to the suggestion, offering no comment.

Isma'il Latif said cheerfully, "Al-Nahhas knew how to avenge his forced resignation of December 1937. He stormed Abdin Palace at the head of a column of British tanks."

To give Kamal a chance to comment, Riyad hesitated briefly. But when his friend was slow to respond, he asked gloomily, "Vengeance? There is little resemblance between the facts and your imagination's depiction of them."

"So what are the facts?"

After glancing at Kamal in a fruitless attempt to induce him to speak, Riyad continued: "Al-Nahhas is not a man who would conspire with the English in order to get returned to power. Ahmad Mahir's crazy. He's the one who betrayed the people and joined ranks with the king. Then he strove to hide the weakness of his position by making a stupid declaration and calling in the press to hear it." Riyad looked at Kamal to see what he thought. This political discussion had finally begun to attract some of his attention, but he felt inclined to disagree with Riyad, if only a little.

"It's clear that al-Nahhas has saved the situation," Kamal said. "I have no doubts whatsoever about his patriotism. A man his age doesn't turn traitor to obtain a position he's held five or six times before. But has he behaved in the ideal manner?"

"You're a skeptic, and there's no end to your doubts. What behavior would have been ideal?"

"He should have persisted in his rejection of the British ultimatum for him to become prime minister. Regardless of the outcome, he should not have yielded."

"Even if the king had been deposed and a British military government had taken control of the country?"

"Yes."

Huffing furiously, Riyad exclaimed, "We're having a pleasant chat over a water pipe. But a statesman has to shoulder tremendous responsibilities. In these delicate wartime conditions, how could al-Nahhas have agreed to let the king be deposed and the country be ruled by an English soldier? If the Allies are victorious—and we must realize that this is possible—then we would be counted among the defeated enemies. Politics isn't poetic idealism. It's realist wisdom."

"I still believe in al-Nahhas, but perhaps he's made a mistake. I don't say he's a conspirator or a traitor. . . ."

"The responsibility rests with those troublemakers who supported the Fascist cause behind the backs of the English—as if the Fascists would respect our independence. Don't we have a treaty with the English? Doesn't honor oblige us to keep our word? Besides, are we not democrats who should be interested in seeing the democratic nations triumph over the Nazis, since they place us at the bottom level of the world's peoples and races and stir up antagonism between the different races, nationalities, and religious groups?"

"I'm with you on all that, but when he yielded to the British ultimatum our independence was reduced to a legal fiction."

"The man protested the ultimatum, and the British deferred to him."

Isma'il laughed out loud and then said, "How admirable the protest was!" But he soon added in earnest, "I agree with what he did. If I had been in his place I would have done the same thing. He was humiliated and forced out of power, even though he had a majority. And he's known how to exact revenge. The fact is that our independence is nothing but a fiction. What purpose would be served by having the king deposed and our country governed by an English military ruler?"

Riyad's expression looked even glummer. But Kamal smiled and said with odd detachment, "Others have made mistakes, and al-Nahhas is having to deal with the consequences of those errors. No doubt he has saved the situation. He's saved the throne and the country. Moreover, all's well that ends well. If, after the war, the English remember appreciatively what he did, no one will bring up the ultimatum of the fourth of February."

After clapping his hands to order more charcoal for the water pipe, Isma'il scoffed, "If the English remember his good deed! I tell you right now they'll sack him long before that."

Riyad said with conviction, "The man has stepped forward to assume the greatest responsibility in the most trying circumstances."

Smiling, Kamal replied, "Just as you will step forward to assume the greatest responsibility of your life."

Riyad laughed. Rising, he said, "If you'll excuse me," and headed off toward the rest room. Then Isma'il leaned in Kamal's direction and gleefully remarked, "Last week a bunch you surely remember visited my mother."

Looking at him inquisitively, Kamal asked, "Who?"

Smiling in a knowing way, the other man answered, "Aïda."

For Kamal this name had an odd ring that eclipsed all the emotions it might otherwise have evoked. At first this name appeared to have emerged from deep inside him, not from his friend's lips. Nothing could have been more unexpected, and for some moments the name seemed meaningless. Who was Aïda? Which Aïda was it? That was all ancient history. How many years had passed since he had heard that name? Since 1926 or 1927 . . . sixteen years . . . long enough for a boy to reach the prime of adolescence, fall in love, and experience heartbreak. He really had grown old. Aïda? How did this memory affect him? It had no impact on him—aside from a sentimental interest mixed with emotions like those of a person who remembers a former painful and critical condition as his hand probes the scars of a surgical operation. He murmured, "Aïda?"

"Yes. Aïda Shaddad. Don't you remember her? The sister of Husayn Shaddad."

Becoming nervous under Isma'il's scrutiny, he said evasively, "Husayn! I wonder what's new with him."

"Who knows?"

He was conscious of how ridiculous his subterfuge was, but what could he do when he sensed that his face was starting to burn in spite of the intensely cold February weather? Although the comparison was a bit odd, love seemed to him to resemble nothing so much as food. "When it's on the table," he mused, "we are intensely aware of it. We are still conscious of it to a lesser degree as we digest it. But when it has been incorporated into our blood, our relationship to it is quite different. Then it is absorbed into the cells, and they are renewed. Eventually no trace of it remains, except perhaps for an inner echo we term 'forgetfulness.' A person may unexpectedly encounter a familiar voice, which will move this forgetfulness toward the level of consciousness. Then somehow he will hear this echo." If this was not correct, then why was he so shaken? Of course, he might pine for Aïda, not because he had once loved her—for that relationship had vanished never to return—but because she represented love, which he had often sorely missed over the years. She was nothing but a symbol, like a deserted ruin that evokes exalted historic memories.

Isma'il continued: "We talked for a long time—Aïda, my mother, my wife, and I. She narrated for us how she and her husband—in fact, all the other diplomats—retreated from the advancing German forces until they ended up taking refuge in Spain. They are finally being transferred to Iran. Then we reviewed the past and laughed a lot."

No matter how dead his love was, his heart felt an intoxicating longing. Inside him, chords once silent reverberated softly and sadly. He asked, "What does she look like now?"

"She's possibly forty. No, I'm two years older than she is. Aïda's thirty-seven. She's filled out a little but is still slender. Her face looks just about the same, except for the earnest and serious expression of her eyes. She said she has a son of fourteen and a daughter who is ten."

So this was Aïda then. She was not a dream, and he had not imagined his time with her. There had been moments when that part of his past had seemed an illusion. She was a wife and a mother. She remembered the past and laughed a lot. But what was her true image? How much of it did he still retain in his memory? Impressions might easily be transformed during their stay in one's memory. He would have liked to get a good look at this person, in order to discover the secret that had enabled her to exert such enormous influence on him in the past.

Riyad returned to his seat. Although Kamal feared that Isma'il would drop this topic, he continued: "They asked about you!"

Looking from one friend to the other, Riyad realized that they were involved in a private conversation and turned his attentions to the water pipe.

Kamal felt that the phrase "They asked about you" posed as great a threat to his immune system as the most virulent germs. Doing his utmost to appear natural, he inquired, "Why?"

"They asked about one and another of their friends from the old days. Then they asked about you. I said, 'He's a teacher in al-Silahdar School and a great philosopher who publishes articles that I don't understand in *al-Fikr* magazine, which I don't even open.' They laughed and then asked, 'Has he gotten married?' And I answered, 'Absolutely not.'"

Kamal found himself asking, "What did they say then?"

"Something—I don't remember what—diverted us from this topic."

The dormant disease threatened to flare up again. Anyone who has had tuberculosis must beware of catching a cold. The phrase "They asked about you" resembled a children's song, for its meaning was as simple as its impact on the soul was profound. Circumstances may arise for a soul to relive in all its fury a former emotional state that then dies away again. Thus, for a fleeting moment Kamal felt he was that lover from the past, resonating with love's joyous and mournful melodies. But he was not in serious jeopardy, for he was like a sleeping man who is distressed by a dream and yet senses with relief that what he sees is not real. All the same, he wished at that moment for a heavenly dispensation allowing him to meet her, if only for a few minutes, so she could confess that she had reciprocated his affection for a day or even part of one and that what had kept them apart had been the difference in their ages or something similar. If this miracle ever came to pass, it would repay him for all his pains, past and present, and he would consider himself a happy person, aware that his life had not been in vain. But wishful thinking like this was as false an awakening as that of death. He should content himself with forgetfulness. That would be a victory, even if tinged with defeat. He should let his consolation be the fact that he was not the only person to suffer failure in life.

He asked, "When are they leaving for Iran?"

"They were to leave yesterday, or at least that's what she said during her visit."

"How did she take her family's disaster?"

"I naturally avoided the subject, and she did not refer to it."

Pointing straight ahead, Riyad Qaldas exclaimed, "Look!" Glancing toward the left-hand side of the balcony, they observed a strange-looking woman in her seventh decade. Skinny and barefoot, she was attired in an ankle-length shirt like a man's and wore a skullcap from which no wisp of hair protruded. Her scalp was either bald or diseased, and her face was so coated with makeup that it appeared ridiculous and disgusting. Her front teeth were missing, and her eyes radiated beaming messages of affectionate ingratiation in all directions.

Riyad asked with interest, "A beggar?"

Isma'il replied, "A crazy woman, more likely."

She stood looking at the empty chairs on the left. Then choosing one, she sat down. When she noticed that they were looking at her, she smiled broadly and said, "Good evening, men."

Riyad responded warmly to her greeting, "Good evening, my good woman."

She emitted a laugh that, as Isma'il said, reminded him of the Ezbe-kiya entertainment district in its days of glory. Then she answered, " 'Good woman'! Yes, I am that, if you mean 'good' as in 'good times.' "

The three men laughed. Encouraged by this reaction, she said enticingly, "Treat me to tea and a pipe, and God will make it up to you."

Riyad clapped his hands together energetically to place her order. Leaning toward Kamal's ear, he whispered, "This is the way some stories begin."

The old woman laughed delightedly and said, "What old-fashioned generosity! Are you members of the wartime rich, my sons?"

Laughing, Kamal replied, "We're members of the wartime poor, in other words civil servants, my good woman."

Riyad asked her, "What is your distinguished name?"

Raising her head with ludicrous pride, she responded, "The celebrated Sultana Zubayda, in person."

"The Sultana?"

"Yes," she continued jovially. "But my subjects have all died."

"May God have mercy on them."

"God have mercy on the living. It's enough for the dead that they're in the presence of God. Tell me who you are."

A smiling waiter brought her a water pipe and tea. Then, approaching the three friends, he asked, "Do you know her?"

"Who is she?"

"The entertainer Zubayda, the most famous vocalist of her time, but age and cocaine have reduced her to the state you see today."

It seemed to Kamal that he had heard the name before. The interest of Riyad Qaldas intensified, and he urged his friends to introduce themselves as she had requested, in order to encourage her to talk.

Isma'il presented himself: "Isma'il Latif."

Giggling and sipping her tea before it could grow cold, she remarked, "Long live names! Even when a charming one like this doesn't fit the person. . . ."

They laughed, and Isma'il cursed her in a low voice she could not hear. But Riyad said, "Riyad Qaldas."

"An infidel? I had one of you for a lover. He was a merchant in the Muski, and his name was Yusuf Ghattas. He was a world-beater. I used to crucify him on the bed till dawn."

She laughed along with them, her pleasure obvious from her face. Then she turned her eyes to Kamal, who said, "Kamal Ahmad Abd al-Jawad."

She was bringing the glass of tea to her lips. Her hand stopped in midair as she experienced a fleeting moment of lucidity. Staring at his face, she asked, "What did you say?"

Riyad Qaldas answered for him, "Kamal Ahmad Abd al-Jawad."

She took a drag on the water pipe and said as if to herself, "Ahmad Abd al-Jawad! But there are lots of people with the same name, as many as there once were piasters." Then she asked Kamal, "Is your father a merchant in al-Nahhasin?"

Kamal was astonished and replied, "Yes."

She stood up and walked toward them. Coming to a stop in front of him, she roared with a laughter that seemed to exceed by far the powers of her emaciated skeleton. Then she exclaimed, "You're Abd al-Jawad's son! O son of my precious companion! But you don't resemble him! This really is his nose, but he was as handsome as the full moon shining by night. Just mention the Sultana Zubayda to him, and he'll tell you more than enough about me."

Riyad and Isma'il burst into laughter. Kamal smiled as he tried to conquer his disquiet. Only then did he remember that long ago Yasin had told him the story—in fact the many stories—about his father and Zubayda the entertainer.

She asked Kamal, "How is al-Sayyid Ahmad? It's been ages since I moved out of your neighborhood, which spurned me. Now I'm one of the people of Imam al-Shafi'i. But I get homesick for al-Husayn and visit on rare occasions. I was ill for so long that the neighbors got disgusted with me. If they had not been afraid of censure, they would have thrown me into the grave alive. How is my master?"

Kamal replied rather despondently, "He passed away four months ago."

She frowned a little and said, "To God's mercy ... what a pity! He was a man unlike any other."

She returned to her seat and suddenly laughed loudly. Shortly thereafter the proprietor of the coffeehouse appeared at the entry to the balcony and warned her: "That's enough laughter! 'When we did not scold him the first time, he brought in his jenny.' The gentlemen are to be praised for their generosity to you, but if you're rowdy again, I'll show you the door."

She kept quiet until he left and then smiled at the men. "Are you like your father or not?" she asked Kamal as she made a lewd gesture with her hand.

The friends laughed, and Isma'il said, "He's not even married yet!"

In a bantering tone of disbelief, she said, "It's clear that you're trying to make a sucker out of me."

They laughed. Riyad rose and went to sit beside her. He remarked, "We're honored by your company, Sultana. But I want to hear about the days of your reign."

41

Twenty minutes before the lecture was to begin, Ewart Hall at the American University was almost full. According to Riyad Qaldas, Mr. Roger was a noted professor and especially memorable when discussing Shakespeare. There had been a suggestion that the lecture would contain political allusions, but that was hardly worth considering when the speaker was Mr. Roger and the topic William Shakespeare. Even so, Riyad was glum and despondent. Had he not invited Kamal, he would have stayed away. His distress was entirely natural for a man as preoccupied by politics as he was. With obvious passion, he whispered to Kamal, "Makram Ubayd has been expelled from the Wafd! Why are all these outrageous things happening?"

Kamal, who also still felt stunned by the news, shook his head dejectedly without any comment.

"It's a national catastrophe, Kamal. Things should not have deteriorated this far."

"Yes, but who was responsible?"

"Al-Nahhas! Makram Ubayd may be high-strung, but the corruption that has infiltrated the government is a fact that should not be hushed up."

Smiling, Kamal replied, "Let's not talk about corruption in government. Makram's revolt was less about corruption than about his loss of influence."

With a trace of resignation, Riyad asked, "Would a committed nationalist like Makram abandon the struggle on account of a transitory emotion?"

Kamal could not restrain his laughter as he replied, "You've abandoned your struggle for the sake of a transitory emotion."

Without smiling, Riyad insisted, "Answer me!"

"Makram has an emotional personality like a poet's or a singer's. If he can't be everything, he'd rather be nothing at all. He discovered that his authority was shrinking and rebelled by openly criticizing instances of favoritism and by making an issue of it in the cabinet. So he precluded any chance for reconciliation and cooperation. It's regrettable."

"And what's the result?"

"No doubt the palace blesses this new split in the Wafd Party and will embrace Makram at an appropriate time, just as it has embraced other rebels in the past. From now on, we will see Makram playing a new role with the minority parties and palace agents. Otherwise, he will be out of the picture. They may hate him as much as they do al-Nahhas, or worse, and there are some who hate the Wafd because of Makram. But they will embrace him in order to destroy the Wafd. What happens then is anybody's guess."

Frowning, Riyad said, "A hideous picture! Both men were at fault, al-Nahhas and Makram. My heart senses that no good will come of this." Then in a lower voice he continued: "The Copts will have no one to turn to. Or they will seek protection from their archenemy, the king, and his defense of them will not last long. If the Wafd is now treating us as unfairly as the other parties have, what is to become of us?"

Pretending not to understand, Kamal inquired, "Why do you exaggerate the importance of this incident? Makram is not all the Coptic Christians, and the Copts aren't Makram. He's a political figure who has lost power, but the nationalist principles of the Wafd Party will never be abandoned."

Riyad shook his head sadly and answered sarcastically, "The papers may assert this, but what I'm saying is the truth. The Copts feel that they have all been expelled from the Wafd. They are searching for security, and I fear they will never find it. Politics has recently handed me a new puzzle similar to the one I've had with religion. I have spurned religion with my intellect and yet from ethnic loyalty have felt sympathetic to it with my heart. In exactly the same way, I will spurn the Wafd with my heart and feel sympathetically inclined toward it with my intellect. If I say I'm a Wafdist, I betray my heart. If I say I'm opposed to the Wafd, I cheat my intellect. It's a catastrophe I never dreamed of. Apparently Copts are destined to live forever with split personalities. If all of us were a single individual, he would go mad."

Kamal felt vexed and hurt. It seemed to him that all the different ethnic groups into which humanity was divided were acting out an ironic farce that would have a dreadful ending. In a voice betraying little conviction he said, "The problem ceases to exist if you think of Makram as a politician and not as the entire Coptic community."

"Do the Muslims themselves think of him merely as a politician?"

"I do."

Despite Riyad's despair, a smile flickered across his lips as he said, "I'm talking about Muslims. How does this relate to you?"

"Aren't our situations identical, yours and mine?"

"Yes, but with one difference: you don't belong to a minority." Smiling, he continued: "If I had lived when Egypt was first conquered by the Muslims and had been able to foretell the future, I would have urged all Copts to convert to Islam." Then he protested, "You're not listening to me!"

Kamal was not. His eyes were fixed on the entrance to the auditorium. Looking in that direction, Riyad saw a girl in the bloom of youth wearing a simple gray dress, apparently a student. She took a seat at the front, in the section reserved for women.

"Do you know her?"

"I'm not sure."

They had to stop talking, for the speaker had appeared on the stage and hearty applause resounded through the hall. Then the ensuing silence was so profound that a cough would have seemed an outrage. The president of the American University gave an appropriate introduction, and the professor began to speak. Kamal spent most of his time gazing at the girl's head inquisitively. He had noticed her by accident when she entered, and the sight of her had surprised him, wrenching him away from the train of his thoughts. After propelling him twenty years into the past, she had brought him back, breathless, to the present. At first he had imagined he was seeing Aïda, but there was no way this girl could be Aïda, for she was certainly not much over twenty. He had not had enough time to examine her features, but her overall appearance sufficed: the shape of her face, her figure, her spirit, the expressive look of her eyes. . . . Yes, he had never seen anyone with eyes like this, except for Aïda. Could she be Aïda's sister? That was the next person he thought of: Budur. This time he recalled her name. He immediately remembered how fond she had been of him long ago. But it was highly unlikely—if it truly was Budur—that she would know him. The important fact was that her image had awakened his heart and restored to it, at least for the time being, the full rich life it had once enjoyed. He felt agitated and, though he listened to the speaker for a few minutes, spent the rest of the time staring at the girl's head. Inundated by a wave of memories, he patiently savored all the assorted feelings that collided and wrestled with each other inside his psyche.

"I'll follow her to find out who she really is," he told himself. "There's no particular reason for doing it, but a bored man should be a good walker. I long for anything capable of wiping away the accumulation of rust from my spirit."

With this design in mind, he waited for his opportunity. Was the lecture long or short? He had no idea. When it ended, he confided his plan to Riyad, said goodbye, and set off after the girl, carefully pursuing her graceful step and slim figure. He could not compare the gaits of the two women, for he no longer remembered Aïda's clearly. He thought the girl's build was the same. Aïda's hair had been cut in a boyish bob, but this girl's hair was long and braided. Still, the black color was no doubt identical. Because of the crowd of people from the lecture, he was not able to scrutinize her face at the streetcar stop. She boarded number 15 for al-Ataba and squeezed into the women's section. Climbing aboard after her, he wondered whether she was on her way to al-Abbasiya or if his suppositions were merely confused dreams. Aïda had never ridden a streetcar in her entire life. She had two automobiles at her beck and call. But this poor girl . . . He felt as disconsolate as he had on first hearing the story of Shaddad Bey's bankruptcy and suicide.

The streetcar emptied out most of its load at al-Ataba. He picked a spot on the pavement near her and observed the long slender neck of that former era as she watched for the connecting streetcar. He noticed that her complexion was wheat-colored, verging on white . . . not the bronze of the vanished image. For the first time since he had begun his pursuit, he felt regretful. It seemed he had followed her to see the other woman. The streetcar for al-Abbasiya pulled up, and she prepared to board it. Finding the women's compartment full, she got into the second-class car. He did not hesitate but followed right behind her. When she sat down, he took the seat beside her. The places on both sides filled up and then the area in the middle was occupied by standing passengers. Although he derived immense satisfaction from his success in obtaining a seat next to hers, he was sorry to see her sit among the teeming masses of the second class, perhaps because of the contrast between the two images—the former immortal one and this present one beside him. His shoulder brushed gently against hers whenever the streetcar moved suddenly, especially when it started or jerked to a stop. He gazed at her at every opportunity, examining her as best he could. The coal-black eyes, the eyebrows meeting in the center, the regular and charming nose, the beautiful face. . . . It was just as if he were looking at Aïda. Was that really true? No, there was the contrast between their complexions, and a smidgeon of difference here and there. He could not say whether it was more of this or less of that. Even though the discrepancies were slight, they seemed as significant to him as the one degree that separates the temperature of a healthy person from an invalid's. All the same he was in the presence of the closest possible likeness to Aïda. He imagined that he could remember his former sweetheart more clearly than ever by the light of this lovely face. The girl's body was possibly just like Aïda's, about which he had wondered so often. Perhaps he was seeing it now. This one was svelte and slender. The girl's chest was only modestly developed, as was the rest of her body, which bore no relationship to Atiya's soft and full one to which he made love. Had his taste deteriorated over the years? Had his former love been merely a rebellion against his latent instincts? In any case he felt a happy, dreamy love that made his heart tipsy with inebriating memories. The occasional contact with her shoulder heightened his intoxication and his penetration into the private world of his thoughts. He had never touched Aïda, always considering her beyond his grasp. Yet this young woman walked through the markets and sat demurely among the crowds in the second-class section. He felt very sad. The contrast between the two women, although trifling, appeared critical. It exasperated him, disappointed his hopes, and decreed that his old love would remain a riddle forever.

Calling out, "Tickets and passes," the conductor appeared. The girl opened her handbag and took out her season pass to have it ready for the conductor. Looking stealthily at the pass, Kamal discovered that the girl's name was Budur Abd al-Hamid Shaddad and that she was a student in the Arts Faculty of the University.

"There's no longer any doubt. My heart is beating faster than it should. If only I could filch her pass . . . to preserve the closest likeness to Aïda. Oh, if only this were possible. . . . '36-year-old schoolteacher robs Arts Faculty student'? What a temptingly sensational headline for the papers! A failed philosopher close to forty! I wonder how old Budur is. She wasn't more than five in 1926, so she's in the twenty-first year of her happy life. Happy? No mansion, no automobile, no servants, no retinue. . . . She was at least fourteen when her family's disaster struck. That's old enough to understand the meaning of a catastrophe and to taste the pain. The poor child must have suffered horribly and felt terrified, experiencing the cruel feeling I'm so familiar with. Pain, although visiting us at different times, unites us now, much as our old but forgotten friendship once did."

When the conductor reached her, Kamal heard Budur say, "Here it is," as she handed the man her pass. The voice struck his ears like a beloved but long-forgotten melody, spreading a great sweetness through him and evoking many memories. It brought back to life a heavenly period of his past, and his senses circled for a long time in the divine realm of ecstasy, where dreams of a bygone era were plainly visible.

"This warm, melodious tune so full of the magic of musical delight ... let me hear your voice. It's not your voice, my unlucky friend from the past. Fortunately, the mistress of that voice still enjoys a life as luxurious as her old one. The sorrows submerging her family have not reached her. But you have descended to us in the second class. Don't you remember your friend whose neck you would cling to while trading kisses with him? How do you live today, my little one? Will you end up like me, teaching in an elementary school?"

The streetcar passed the former site of the mansion, which had been replaced by an enormous new structure. Kamal had seen it a few times before during visits to al-Abbasiya—after his historic break with the area—especially of late when calling at the home of Fuad Jamil al-Hamzawi.

"Al-Abbasiya itself has changed as much as your house, my little one. The mansions and gardens from the time of my love have disappeared to make way for shops, cafés, cinemas, and huge apartment buildings crammed with occupants. Let Ahmad, who is fascinated by observing the class struggle, rejoice, but how can I gloat over the misfortunes of this mansion and its inhabitants when my heart is buried in its rubble? And how can I despise that extraordinary creature, who has never tasted the adversities of life or the crowded living conditions of the people, when the thought of her is a beautiful idea before which my heart falls prostrate?"

The streetcar paused at the stop beyond the Wayliya police station, she got out, and he followed. Standing on the pavement there, he watched her cross the road to Ibn Zaydun Street, which was directly opposite. This narrow street was lined by old houses inhabited by the middle class, and its asphalt surface was covered with dirt, stones, and scattered bits of paper. She entered the third house on the left through a small door adjacent to an ironing establishment. He stood there, gazing at the street and the house in gloomy silence. This was where Madam Saniya, the widow of Shaddad Bey, resided. An apartment like that would not rent for more than three pounds a month. If only Madam Saniya would come out on the balcony, he could catch a glimpse of her and measure the changes that had affected her. No doubt they were significant ones. He had not forgotten the precious sight of her leaving the men's parlor of her former home, arm in arm with her husband, as they headed for the waiting car. She had sauntered forth grandly, wearing her fluffy coat and glancing about in a regal and self-assured fashion. "Man will never suffer from a more lethal enemy than time," he reflected. Aïda had stayed in this apartment during her visit to Cairo. Perhaps she had passed part of an evening on this shabby balcony. She had quite possibly shared a bed with her mother and sister, for they certainly had only one.

"I wish I had learned she was here in time. I wish I had seen her again after our long separation. Now that I am liberated from her tyranny, I need to see her so I can learn the truth about her and thus the truth about myself. But this priceless opportunity has been lost."

42 ❧

Kamal sat with students from the English Department, listening to a lecture by the British professor. It was not the first time he had attended the course, and he assumed it would not be the last. He had encountered little difficulty in obtaining permission to audit the course, which met three nights a week. In fact, the professor had welcomed him on learning that Kamal taught English. It was, of course, a bit odd for him to think of auditing this class only at the end of the academic year, but he had explained he was engaged in research that made it imperative for him to attend these lectures, even though he had missed the previous ones. Through Riyad Qaldas, who was a friend of the Arts Faculty secretary, Kamal had learned that Budur was a student in this department. In his dapper suit and gold-rimmed glasses, with a bushy mustache under his large nose and a few gray hairs at the temples of his huge head, Kamal looked different enough to attract attention, especially when he sat in the company of a few young men and women. Most of them seemed to be wondering about him. They gazed at him in a way that made him so uncomfortable he imagined he could hear what they were thinking about him. He knew better than anyone else the type of comments his appearance inspired. He himself was amazed at the unusual step he had taken without any regard for the effort and discomfort it entailed. What really lay behind it and what was its goal? He did not know precisely, but the moment he had seen a ray of light in his gloomy life, he had raced off recklessly in pursuit of it, driven by the overwhelming forces of despair, passion, and hope. He paid no attention to the obstacles looming on this road, which was threatened on one side by prim tradition and on the other by the proclivity of students for sarcasm. After his long immersion in despair and ennui, he now chased eagerly after this adventure, which he did not doubt would prove exceptionally entertaining and invigorating. It was sufficient excuse that he had developed an interest in time, that he had hope in view, and that he now aspired to be happy. Indeed, his heart, which had previously been as good as dead, pounded with life. He felt the pressure of time, since the academic year was fast approaching its prescribed end.

His efforts had not been in vain, for Budur, like the other students, had noticed him. Perhaps she had participated in the whispered exchanges about him. Her eyes had met his more than once. She had possibly read in them the interest and admiration flaming within him. Who could say? As if this was not enough, they rode home on the same streetcars—Giza and then al-Abbasiya—often sitting near each other. She certainly recognized him, and that was no mean accomplishment for a total stranger to her neighborhood, particularly since he was a schoolteacher who avidly sought to preserve appearances, acting with the propriety and dignity demanded by this profession. As for his goal in all this, he had not troubled himself to identify it. Life pulsed through him after a period of stagnation, and that made him feel enthusiastic. With all the strength his tormented soul could muster, he yearned to become once more that man in whose psyche feelings squirmed, from whose intellect ideas soared, and to whose senses visions were manifest. He longed for this magic to supplant his peevishness, ill health, and perplexity at being confronted by unanswerable riddles. Love was like wine, but its enjoyment was profounder and the hangover less objectionable.

During the previous week, an event had made a considerable impact on his heart. Obliged to supervise athletics at al-Silahdar School, he had been unable to reach the Arts Faculty on time. When he had entered the classroom late, tiptoeing in to avoid making a sound, their eyes had met for a magical, fleeting moment. She had immediately lowered her eyelids rather shyly. It had not been merely a look exchanged between neutral eyes. She probably did feel a bit embarrassed. Would she have looked down so quickly if his previous glances had been in vain? The young woman had become bashful about his attentions. Perhaps she had perceived that his looks were not innocent ones directed her way by accident. That realization by Kamal awakened a mass of memories within him and conjured up many images. He found himself remembering Aïda and dreaming about her, for no apparent reason. Aïda had never lowered her gaze in embarrassment when she was with him. Something else must have reminded him of her ... a little gesture, a look, or that enchanting secret entity we call "spirit."

Another memorable incident had occurred two days before. "See how she's brought you back to life," he reflected. In the past, nothing had been of any significance whatsoever, or importance had been ascribed only to sterile puzzles, like the will in Schopenhauer, the absolute in Hegel, or the *élan vital* in Bergson. Life as a whole was inanimate and unimportant. "See how a glance, a gesture, or a smile can make the earth tremble today?"

This significant encounter had taken place shortly before 5 P.M. as he was cutting through al-Urman Gardens on his way to the Arts Faculty. He had suddenly found himself being observed by Budur and three other girls, who were waiting on a bench until time for class. His eyes had met Budur's as memorably as in the classroom. He had wanted to greet the girls when he drew closer to them, but the path had veered away, as if refusing to participate in this impro-vised romantic plot. When he had gone a short distance beyond them, he had looked back and seen that the other girls were smiling and whispering to Budur, whose head was resting in her hand, as if to hide her face.

What was he to make of this exquisite scene? If Riyad had been there, he would have been able to describe and analyze it perfectly. But Kamal had no need for his friend's professional skills. They were surely whispering to her about him, and she had hidden her face in embarrassment. Was any other explanation possible? In the words of a popular song, "Had his eyes revealed his love?" Perhaps he had unwittingly gone too far and made himself the target of gossip. Where would he be if the whispering graduated into insinuating re-marks voiced by fiendish male students?

He had seriously considered ending his visits to the Arts Faculty, but that evening he found her sitting next to him on a streetcar bound for al-Abbasiya. The only time this had happened before had been the very first night. He waited for her to look his way so he could greet her, no matter what that led to, but when he felt the waiting had lasted a bit too long, he turned to glance at her himself. Affecting surprise at seeing her seated beside him, he whispered politely, "Good evening."

He had no memory of Aïda ever employing any feminine wiles, but Budur glanced at him as if she too was astonished and then whispered, "Good evening."

Two colleagues had exchanged greetings. There was nothing ob-jectionable about this. He had not been so bold with her sister, but Aïda had been his senior. He had been the young innocent.

"I believe you're from al-Abbasiya?"

"Yes."

"She's not going to take an active role in this conversation," he reflected.

"Unfortunately I missed most of the lectures, since I started to attend so late."

"Yes."

"I hope that in the future I can make up what I missed."

Her only response was a smile. "Let me hear your voice some more," he begged silently. "It's the one bygone melody that time has not altered."

"What do you plan to do once you have your degree? Study at the Teacher Training Institute?"

Displaying some enthusiasm about the conversation for the first time, she answered, "I won't have to go on for further training since the Ministry of Education needs teachers—in view of wartime conditions and the expansion of the school system."

He had craved a single tune but had been granted an entire song.

"So you're going to be a teacher!"

"Yes. Why not?"

"It's a hard profession. Ask me about it."

"I've heard that you teach."

"Yes. Oh! I forgot to introduce myself: Kamal Ahmad Abd al-Jawad."

"I'm honored."

Smiling, he observed, "But I haven't had the honor yet."

"Budur Abd al-Hamid Shaddad."

"The honor's all mine, miss." Then he added, as if astonished by something, "Abd al-Hamid Shaddad! From al-Abbasiya? Are you the sister of Husayn Shaddad?"

Her eyes gleamed with interest as she replied, "Yes."

Kamal laughed as if amazed at the odd coincidence and exclaimed, "Merciful heavens! He was my dearest friend. We spent an extremely happy time together. My Lord—are you the little sister who used to play in the garden?"

She cast an inquiring look at him. It was absurd to think that she would remember him. "Back then you were as wild about me as I was about your sister."

"Of course, I don't recollect any of that."

"Naturally. This story goes back to 1923 and continues to 1926, the year Husayn left for Europe. What is he doing now?"

"He's in the South of France, in the area to which the French government retreated following the German occupation."

"How is he? I haven't had any news or letters from him for a long time."

"He's fine. . . ." Her tone indicated that she did not wish to pursue this subject any further.

As the streetcar passed the site of her former mansion, Kamal wondered whether it had been a mistake to mention his friendship with her brother. Would that not limit his freedom to continue what he had begun? When they reached the stop beyond the Wayliya police station, she said goodbye and left the streetcar. He stayed put, as if oblivious to his own existence. Throughout the ride he had examined her at every opportunity in hopes of detecting the secret quality that had once enchanted him. But he had not discovered it, however close he might have been on several occasions.

She seemed charming, meek, and within his grasp. He now felt a mysterious disappointment and a sorrow that had no discernible causes. If he should wish to marry this girl, no serious obstacles would bar his way. In fact, she seemed responsive and receptive, in spite of or because of the appreciable age difference between them. Experience had taught him that his looks would not prevent him from marrying if he chose to. If he married Budur, he would willy-nilly become a member of Aïda's family. But what substance was there to this ludicrous dream? And what was Aïda to him now? The truth was that he no longer wanted Aïda. But he still wished to learn her secret, which might at least convince him that the best years of his life had not been wasted. He was conscious of the desire, which he had frequently experienced during his life, to look again at his diary and at the candy box presented to him at Aïda's wedding reception. Then his breast filled with so much longing that he wondered whether a man with a thorough understanding of the biological, societal, and psychological components of human affection could still fall in love. But did a chemist's knowledge of poisons prevent him from succumbing to them—like any other victim? Why was his breast so agitated by emotions? Despite the disappointment he had experienced, despite the vast difference between then and now, despite the fact that he did not know whether he belonged to the past or to the present—all these considerations notwithstanding—his breast churned and his heart pounded.

43 ❧

Here at the tea garden, boughs and verdant branches formed the roof, and a duck could be seen swimming in an emerald pool with a grotto behind it. Employees of *The New Man* magazine had the day off, and Sawsan Hammad looked stunning in a lightweight blue dress that revealed her brown arms. Discreetly and cautiously, she had begun using cosmetics. The two had been colleagues for a year, and as they sat across from each other a smile of mutual understanding lit up their faces. On the table between them stood a water carafe and two ice-cream dishes containing only a milky residue colored pink by strawberries.

"She's dearer to me than anything else in the world," he thought. "I owe her all my happiness. All my hopes are pinned on her. We are devoted partners. We have never openly agreed to be in love, but I have no doubt that we are. Our cooperation is perfectly harmonious. We began as comrades in the struggle for freedom, working together like one person—each of us a candidate for incarceration. Whenever I praise her beauty, she stares at me in protest, frowns, and reprimands me—as if love were beneath us. Then I smile and return to the work at hand. One day I told her, 'I love you! I love you! Do whatever you want about it.' She replied, 'Life's an extremely serious matter, but you wish to treat it as a joke.' I said, 'Like you, I think that capitalism is in its death throes, that it has served its purpose, that the working class has a duty to exert its will to guide the process of development—since the fruit will not pluck itself—and that we have an obligation to create a new consciousness. But after all that, or before it, I love you.' Her frown was at least partly feigned as she remarked, 'You keep subjecting me to talk I dislike.' As there was no one else in the office, I felt courageous enough to swoop down on her cheek to plant a kiss there. She glared at me sternly and busied herself with completing the eighth chapter of a book we were translating together on family structure in the Soviet Union."

"If June is this hot, what will the weather be like in July and August, my dear?"

"It seems that Alexandria wasn't created for people like us."

Laughing, he replied, "But Alexandria is no longer a summer resort. Before the war it was, but today rumors of a German invasion have left it deserted."

"Professor Adli Karim reports that most of its inhabitants have fled and that its streets are filled with cats roaming about freely."

"That's what it's like. Soon Rommel will enter it with his troops." Then after a short silence he added, "At Suez, he'll join forces with the Japanese armies, which will have completed their march through Asia. Then the Fascism of the Stone Age will return."

Sawsan responded rather emotionally, "Russia will never be defeated. Mankind's hopes are still secure behind the Ural Mountains."

"Yes, but the Germans are at the gates of Alexandria."

She inquired with a snort, "Why do the Egyptians love the Germans?"

"Out of hatred for the English. It won't be long before we loathe the Germans. The king seems a captive of the British today, but he will break free from them to receive Rommel. Then those two leaders will drink a toast to the interment of our fledgling democracy. Ridiculously enough, the masses of farm laborers expect that Rommel will distribute land to them."

"We have many enemies. Outside of Egypt the Germans and inside it the Muslim Brethren and the reactionaries, who hardly differ from each other."

"If my brother Abd al-Muni'm heard you, he'd be incensed by your words. He considers the Brethren's message a progressive one that is far superior to materialist forms of socialism."

"There may be a socialist aspect to religion, but it's a utopian socialism comparable to doctrines advanced by Thomas More, Louis Blanc, and Saint-Simon. Religion searches in man's conscience for a remedy to human ills, while the solution lies in the development of society. Paying no attention to social classes, it looks instead at the individuals comprising them. Naturally, it has no concept of scientific socialism. Besides all this, the teachings of religion are based on a legendary metaphysics in which angels play an important part. We should not seek solutions to our present-day problems in the distant past. Tell your brother this."

Ahmad laughed with obvious delight and said, "My brother is an educated man and a clever lawyer. I'm amazed that people like him are strongly attracted to the Brethren."

She replied scornfully, "The Brethren have conducted an appalling campaign of misinformation. When conversing with educated people, they present religion in contemporary garb. With uneducated folk, they talk about heaven and hell. They gain adherents in the name of socialism, nationalism, and democracy."

"My darling never tires of talking about her beliefs," Ahmad reflected. "Did I say 'my darling'? Yes, since I stole a kiss from her, I've made a point of calling her that. She protested with words and gestures but eventually started pretending not to notice—as if she had given up hope of reforming me. When I told her I yearned to hear words of love from her mouth, which speaks of nothing but socialism, she scolded me contemptuously: 'This is the traditional, bourgeois view of women, isn't it?' I told her apprehensively, 'My respect for you is beyond words, and I admit that I've been your pupil in the noblest achievements of my life. But I also love you, and there's nothing wrong with that.' I sensed that her anger evaporated then but observed that she did not abandon her vexed look. As I approached with the secret design of kissing her, she somehow guessed my intent. She put a hand on my chest to push me away, but I managed to kiss her cheek. Since what she was trying to avoid did occur, even though she could have taken more serious measures to prevent it, I assumed that she had consented. Although preoccupied by politics, she's an extraordinary individual with a beautiful mind and a beautiful body. When I invited her for an excursion to the tea garden, she said, 'Only if we take the book with us so we can continue translating it.' I replied, 'No, the idea is to relax and chat. If you decline, I'll renounce socialism altogether.' Perhaps what upsets me most about myself is that—steeped as I am in the conventions of Sugar Street—I still occasionally look at women with a traditional bourgeois eye. During hours of lethargic backsliding, I fancy that socialism in the progressive woman is simply another captivating characteristic comparable to playing the piano or to presenting a fine appearance. But it must also be admitted that the year I have worked with Sawsan has changed me a great deal, cleansing me to a commendable degree of the bourgeois attitudes implanted in me."

"It's distressing that our comrades are being arrested in droves."

"Yes, my darling. Imprisonment becomes fashionable in times of war and in periods of terrible repression—although the law sees nothing wrong with standing up for your cause, if you do not combine that with a call to violence." Then Ahmad laughed and continued: "We'll be arrested sooner or later, unless . . ."

While she stared at him curiously, he concluded, "Unless marriage makes us settle down."

Shrugging her shoulders scornfully, she replied, "What makes you think that I'll agree to marry a fraud like you?"

"Fraud?"

She thought a little and then with genuine interest observed, "Unlike me, you're not from the working class. We both struggle against a single enemy, but you have not had my experience with it. I've endured poverty for a long time, and its hateful effects have touched my family. One of my sisters attempted to fight back, but it defeated her and she died. You . . . you're not . . . you're not from the working class!"

He answered calmly, "Neither was Engels."

Her brief laugh brought her feminine side to the fore, and she asked, "What shall I call you? Prince Ahmadov? It's not that I doubt your dedication to the cause, but you still retain deeply embedded bourgeois traits. It seems to me that you're delighted at times to be a member of the Shawkat family."

He replied a bit stridently, "You're wrong and unfair about that. I'm not to blame for my inheritance. I'm no more responsible for my 'wealth' than you are for your poverty. I am referring to the meager income that has supported our lives of indolence. No one should be blamed for a bourgeois background. One is faulted only for backsliding inertia out of keeping with the spirit of our age."

Smiling, she said, "Don't get annoyed. We're both scientific curiosities. Let's not ask where we began. What we're responsible for is our convictions and our actions. I apologize to you, Engels. But tell me: Are you prepared to keep on delivering talks to workers, regardless of the consequences?"

He answered proudly, "As of yesterday, I had given five talks. I've drafted two important manifestos and distributed tens of handbills. I owe the government more than two years in prison."

"I owe them many more years than that!"

He deftly stretched out his hand to place it affectionately and appreciatively on her soft brown one. Yes, he loved her, but his efforts for the cause were not motivated by this love. Did she not seem at times to doubt his sincerity? Was she teasing him or did she feel apprehensive about the bourgeois characteristics she suspected he still harbored? His belief in the cause was as firm as his love for her. He could not sacrifice either.

"What is happiness if not the discovery of a person who truly understands you and whom you truly understand?" he asked himself. "Particularly one from whom you're not separated by artifice of any kind. I worship her when she says, 'I've endured poverty for a long time.' This candid statement elevates her above all the other members of her sex and makes her seem part of me. But we are reckless lovers, and prison lies in wait for us. We could marry and elude these difficulties, contenting ourselves with the pursuit of happiness. But such an existence would lack spirit. How strongly I've felt at times that the cause is a curse cast upon us by an irrevocable decree. . . . Part of my blood and my spirit, it makes me feel responsible for all mankind."

"I love you."

"What's the pretext for saying this?"

"It's true with or without a pretext."

"You talk about the struggle, but your heart is singing of contentment."

"Separating those two things would be as silly as separating the two of us."

"Doesn't love imply contentment, stability, and an aversion to prison?"

"Haven't you heard about the Prophet, whose struggle for the cause by night and day did not prevent him from marrying nine times?"

Snapping her fingers, she exclaimed, "You've borrowed your brother's mouth! What prophet are you referring to?"

Laughing, he answered, "The Muslims' Prophet!"

"Let me tell you about Karl Marx, who devoted himself to writing *Das Kapital* while his wife and children were exposed to hunger and humiliation."

"At any rate, he was married."

"The pool's water could be liquid emeralds," he mused. "This gentle breeze comes to us without any authorization from June. The duck is swimming around with its bill cocked to pluck bits of bread from the water. You're very happy, and your infuriating sweetheart is even more delightful than the rest of the natural world. I think she's blushing. Perhaps she has set aside politics for the time being and begun to think about. . . ."

"What I was hoping, my dear comrade, was that we would have a chance for a sweet conversation in this garden."

"Sweeter than our talk so far?"

"I mean a discussion of our love."

"Our love?"

"Yes, and you know it too."

There was a long silence. Then, lowering her eyes, she asked, "What do you want?"

"Tell me that we want the same thing."

As if merely trying to humor him, she answered, "Yes. But what is it?"

"Let's stop beating around the bush."

She appeared to be reflecting. Although his wait was short, he found it extremely bitter. Then she said, "Since everything is so clear, why do you torment me?"

Sighing with profound relief, he replied, "How glorious my love is!"

The ensuing silence resembled a musical interlude between two songs. Then she said, "One thing is important to me."

"Yes?"

"My honor."

Shocked by the very suggestion, he protested, "Your honor and mine are identical."

She said resentfully, "You are well acquainted with the conventions of your people. You'll hear a lot of talk about family and breeding. . . ."

"Meaningless words. . . . Do you think I'm a child?"

She hesitated a little before saying, "There's only one thing threatening us and that's the bourgeois mentality."

With a forcefulness reminiscent of his brother Abd al-Muni'm's, he responded, "I have nothing to do with that!"

"Do you comprehend your statement's serious implications, both personal and social, for the basic relationship between a man and a woman?"

"I understand them perfectly."

"You'll need a new dictionary for old terms like 'love,' 'marriage,' 'jealousy,' 'faithfulness,' and 'the past.' "

"Yes!"

This interrogation might imply something or it might not. He had often brooded about these ideas, but the situation demanded extraordinary courage. Both his inherited and acquired mentalities were on trial in this frightening inquisition. He imagined that he had caught her drift, but perhaps she was merely testing him. Even if she was serious, he would not retreat. Although gripped by pain as jealousy pulsed through him, he would not back down.

"I consent to your conditions. But let me tell you frankly that I was hoping to win an affectionate woman, not merely an analytical mind."

As her eyes followed the swimming duck, she asked, "To tell you that she loves you and will marry you?"

"Yes!"

She laughed and inquired, "Do you think I'd discuss the details if I had not agreed in principle?"

He squeezed her hand gently, and she added, "You know it all. You just want to hear it."

"I'll never grow tired of hearing it."

"It concerns the reputation of our entire family. If nothing else, he's as much your son as he is mine. But you're free to your own opinions."

As Khadija spoke, her eyes glanced swiftly and anxiously from face to face, from her husband, Ibrahim, who was sitting on her right, to her son Ahmad in the opposite corner of the sitting room, not omitting Yasin, Kamal, and Abd al-Muni'm on the way.

Imitating his mother, Ahmad said playfully, "Pay attention, everyone. The family's reputation is at stake, and I'm your son, if nothing else."

She complained bitterly, "What is this ordeal, son? You won't listen to anyone, not even your father. You refuse advice, even when it's for your own good. You're always right, and everyone else is wrong. When you stopped praying, we said, 'May our Lord guide him.' You refused to go to Law School like your brother, and we said, 'The future's in God's hands.' You said, 'I'm going to be a journalist.' We replied, 'Be a cart driver if you want.'"

He replied jovially, "And now I want to get married. . . ."

"Get married. We're all delighted. But marriage has certain conditions. . . ."

"Who sets these conditions?"

"A sound mind."

"My mind has chosen for me."

"Hasn't time shown you yet that you can't rely only on your own intellect?"

"Not at all. Asking advice from other people is possible in everything but marriage, which is exactly like food."

"Food! You don't just marry a girl. You marry her entire family. And consequently, we marry along with you."

Ahmad laughed out loud and exclaimed, "All of you! That's too much! Uncle Kamal doesn't want to marry, and Uncle Yasin would like my bride for himself."

Everyone laughed except Khadija. Then before the smile vanished from his face, Yasin commented, "If that would remedy the situation, I am more than ready to make the sacrifice."

Khadija cried out, "Go ahead and laugh! This just encourages him. It would be far better if you'd give him your frank opinions. What do you think of a person who wishes to marry the precious daughter of a printshop employee who works for the girl's own magazine? It's hard for us to bear your working as a journalist. How can you want to marry into the family of a pressman? Don't you have an opinion about this, Mr. Ibrahim?"

Ibrahim Shawkat raised his eyebrows as if he wanted to say something but kept quiet. Khadija continued: "If this disaster takes place, the night of the wedding your home will be jammed with press operators, artisans, cabdrivers, and God knows what else."

Ahmad responded passionately, "Don't talk like that about my family."

"Lord of heaven—do you deny that her relatives are people like this?"

"She's the only one I'm marrying, folks."

Ibrahim Shawkat said in exasperation, "You won't marry just her —may God give you as much trouble as you're causing us."

Encouraged by her husband's protest, Khadija said, "I went to visit their home, as custom dictates. I said, 'I'll go see my son's bride.' I found them living in a cellar on a street inhabited almost entirely by Jews. Her mother's appearance differs in no respect from that of a maid, and the bride herself is at least thirty. Yes, by God! If she had even a hint of beauty, I would excuse him. Why do you want to marry her? He's bewitched. She's cast a spell on him. She works with him at that ill-omened magazine. Perhaps she put something in his coffee or water when he wasn't looking. Go and see her yourselves. You be the judge. I've met my match. I returned from the visit scarcely able to see the road because of my chagrin and sorrow."

"You're making me angry. I won't forgive you for saying such things."

"Sorry!" Then, quoting the title of a wedding song, she continued: " 'Sorry, sovereign beauty!' I'm in the wrong! All my life I've been overly critical of other people, and now our Lord has afflicted me with children who suffer from every known defect. I ask the forgiveness of God Almighty."

"No matter what allegations you make about her family, unlike you they don't make false accusations about other people."

"Tomorrow, after it's too late, when you've heard everything, you'll understand that I was right. May God forgive you for insulting me."

"You're the one who has done an outstanding job of humiliating me."

"She's after your money. If she had not come upon a failure like you, the most she could have hoped for would have been a newspaper vendor."

"She's an editor at the magazine with a salary twice the size of mine."

"So she's a journalist too! God's will be done! What kind of girl works outside the home except an old maid, a hag, or a woman who apes men?"

"God forgive you."

"And may He forgive you, too, for all the suffering you're causing us."

Yasin, who had followed the conversation attentively while twisting his mustache, said at this point, "Listen, sister. There's no reason to squabble. Let's give Ahmad the candid advice he needs, but arguing won't help matters."

Ahmad stood up angrily, saying, "Please excuse me. I'm going to get dressed and go to work."

Once he was out of the room, Yasin went to sit beside his sister and, leaning toward her, said, "Quarreling won't do you any good. We can't rule our children. They think they are better and cleverer than we are. If there's no way to avert the marriage, let him get married. If he's not happy with her, it will be entirely his fault. As you know, I was never able to settle down until I married Zanuba. It's just possible that he has made a wise choice. Besides, we gain understanding from experience not from words." Then he laughed and corrected himself: "Although I haven't been enlightened by either words or experience."

Kamal agreed with Yasin. "My brother's right."

Giving him a reproachful look, Khadija asked, "Is this all you have to say, Kamal? He loves you. If you would talk to him in private . . ."

Kamal answered, "I'll leave when he does and have a word with him. But we've had enough quarreling. He's a free man. He has a right to marry any woman he wants. Can you stop him? Are you planning to break off relations with him?"

Smiling, Yasin said, "The matter's quite simple, sister. He'll get married today and divorced tomorrow. We're Muslims, not Catholics."

Narrowing her small eyes and speaking through half-closed lips, Khadija said, "Of course. What attorney does he need to defend him besides you? Whoever said that the son takes after his maternal uncle was right."

Yasin roared out his mighty laugh and said, "God forgive you. If women were left at the mercy of other females, no girl would ever get married."

Pointing to her husband, she observed, "His mother, God rest her soul, chose me for him herself."

Sighing cheerfully, Ibrahim said, "And I've paid the price . . . may God have mercy on her and pardon her."

Khadija ignored his comment and continued regretfully: "If only she were pretty! He's blind!"

Laughing, Ibrahim remarked, "Like his father!"

She turned toward him angrily and snapped, "You're an ingrate, like all men."

The man replied calmly, "No, we're just patient, and paradise belongs to us."

She shouted at him, "If you ever enter it, that will be thanks to me, because I taught you your religion."

Kamal and Ahmad left Sugar Street together. The uncle was skeptical and undecided about this proposed marriage. He could not fault himself for adherence to foolish traditions or for indifference to the principles of equality and human dignity, but still the hideous social reality, which he could not change, was a fact a person could not ignore. In the past he had been infatuated with Qamar, the daughter of Abu Sari', who sold grilled snacks. Despite her charms, she had almost repulsed him with the disagreeable odor of her body. Kamal admired the young man, envying Ahmad's courage, decisiveness, and other qualities that he himself lacked—particularly belief, diligence, and a will to marry. Ahmad could almost have been awarded to the family in compensation for Kamal's stolid negativism. Why did marriage seem so significant to him while for other people it was a normal part of everyday life like saying "Hello"?

"Where are you going, my boy?"

"To the magazine, Uncle. What about you?"

"*Al-Fikr* magazine to meet Riyad Qaldas. . . . Won't you think a little more before taking this step?"

"What step, Uncle? I'm already married."

"Is that true?"

"It's true. And I'm going to live on the first floor of our house . . . because of the housing crisis."

"How provocative!"

"Yes, but she won't get home until after my mother has gone to bed."

After recovering from the impact of the news, Kamal asked his nephew jovially, "Did you marry in the manner prescribed by God and His Messenger?"

Ahmad laughed too and replied, "Of course. We marry and bury according to the precepts of our former religion, but we live according to the Marxist faith." Then, as they parted, he added, "You'll like her a lot, Uncle. Once you see her, you can judge for yourself. She's a wonderful personality, in every sense of the word."

45 ❧

What appalling indecisiveness. . . . It might just as well have been a chronic disease. Every issue seemed to present a multitude of equivalent sides, making it almost impossible to choose between them. Neither metaphysical questions nor the simple operations of daily life were exempt. Perplexity and hesitation posed an obstacle everywhere. Should he marry or not? He needed to make up his mind but fluctuated so much that he felt dizzy. The normal balance between his spirit, intellect, and senses became disrupted. When the maelstrom finally calmed down, no progress would have been made, and the question—to marry or not—would still lack an answer. Occasionally he felt distressed by his freedom and by his loneliness or resented a life spent in the company of dreary mental phantoms. Then he would yearn for a companion, and the loving family instincts imprisoned inside him would groan for release. He would picture himself a husband, cured of his introspective isolation, his fantasies dissipated . . . but also preoccupied by his children, wholly absorbed in earning a living, and oppressed by all the concerns of everyday life. Then, dreadfully alarmed, he would decide to stay single, no matter how much tormented loneliness he suffered. But indecision would soon rear its head again as he started to wonder about marriage once more, and so on and so forth. How could he make up his mind?

Budur really was a wonderful girl. The fact that she rode the streetcar today did not detract from her charms, for she had been born and raised in the paradise of those angels who had inflamed his heart in the old days. She was a meteor that had fallen from the sky, a truly outstanding girl, and an educated beauty of good character. She would not be difficult to obtain. If he chose to proceed, she would be a promising bride in every respect. All he had to do was to get on with it.

In addition to these considerations, he had to admit that she occupied a central place in his consciousness. Hers was the last image of life he saw on falling asleep and the first he greeted on waking. During the day, she was rarely far from his thoughts. The moment he saw her, the rusty strings of his heart began to vibrate with poignant songs. His world of lonely and confused suffering had been transformed. Breaths of fresh air had penetrated it, and the water of life flowed through it. If this was not love, what was it? For the last two months he had sought out Ibn Zaydun Street late each afternoon, traversing it slowly and training his eyes on the balcony until they met hers. Then they would exchange a smile, as was only appropriate for two colleagues. That had started as if by chance, but the continuation could only have been deliberate. Whenever he turned up at the appointed hour, he found her seated on the balcony, reading a book or glancing around. He was certain that she was waiting for him. Had she wished to erase this idea from his mind, she would have needed only to avoid the balcony for a few minutes each afternoon. What must she think of his visit, smile, and greeting? But not so fast. . . . Instincts are rarely mistaken. Each of them wished to encounter the other. This realization sent him into transports of joy and left him drunk with delight. He was filled with a sense of life's value. But this happiness was marred by anxiety. How could it help but be, when it had not yet been coupled with a determination to proceed? A current swept him along, and he yielded to it, not knowing where it would carry him or where he would land. A little reflection might have forced him to be more circumspect, but the joy of life sympathetically diverted him. He was intoxicated with gaiety but not free of anxiety.

Riyad had told him, "Get on with it. This is your chance." Ever since starting to wear an engagement ring, Riyad had spoken of marriage as if it was man's original and ultimate objective in life, saying conceitedly that since he was boldly embarking on this unique experience, he would be granted a new and more accurate understanding of life, one that would create opportunities for him to write about children and couples. "Isn't this what life is all about, you high-soaring philosopher?"

Kamal had answered evasively, "Today you've gone over to the other side, and so you're the last person from whom to expect a fair judgment. I'll miss having you as my sincere adviser."

Viewed from another perspective, love seemed to him a dictator, and Egypt's political life had taught him to hate dictatorship with all his heart. At his aunt Jalila's house, he surrendered his body to Atiya but then quickly reclaimed it, as if nothing had happened. This girl, shielded by her modesty, would be satisfied with nothing less than possessing his spirit and his body, forever. Afterward, there would only be one course for him to pursue: the bitter struggle to earn a living to support his wife and children properly—a bizarre destiny transforming an existence rife with exalted concerns into nothing more than a means of "gaining" a living. The Indian sadhu might be a fool or a lunatic but was at least a thousand times wiser than a man up to his ears in making a living.

"Enjoy the love you once yearned for," he advised himself. "Here it is, resuscitated in your heart, but bringing lots of problems with it."

Riyad had asked him, "Is it reasonable for you to love her, to have it in your power to marry her, and then to decline to take her?"

Kamal had replied that he loved her but not marriage.

Riyad had protested, "It's love that consoles us to marriage. Since you're not in love with marriage—as you say—you must not be in love with the girl."

Kamal had insisted, "No, I love her and hate marriage."

Riyad had suggested, "Perhaps you fear the responsibility."

Kamal had said furiously, "I already shoulder far more responsibilities at home and at work than you do."

Riyad had snapped, "Perhaps you're more selfish than I had imagined."

Kamal had inquired sarcastically, "What inspires an individual to marry if not latent or manifest egotism?"

Smiling, Riyad had retorted, "Perhaps you're sick. Go to a psychiatrist. He may be able to cure you."

Kamal had remarked, "It's amusing that my forthcoming article in *al-Fikr* magazine is 'How to Analyze Yourself.' "

Riyad had told him, "I admit that you puzzle me."

Kamal had answered, "I'm the one who is always puzzled."

Once, walking down Ibn Zaydun Street as usual, he had encountered his sweetheart's mother on her way home. He had recognized her at first glance, although he had not seen her for at least seventeen years and she was no longer the lady he had once known. She had withered in a most distressing way, and worry had marked her even before age could. A person would hardly have imagined that this emaciated woman scurrying by was the lady who had sauntered through the garden of the mansion, a paragon of beauty and perfection. Nonetheless the shape of her head had reminded him of Aïda, and the sight of her had affected him deeply. Fortunately, he had already exchanged a smile with Budur before seeing her mother. Otherwise, he would not have been able to. Then, for no particular reason, he had found himself remembering Aisha and the ill-tempered fit she had thrown that morning when searching for her dentures, after forgetting where she had deposited them before going to sleep the previous evening.

Then one day he noticed that, contrary to her usual practice, Budur was standing on the balcony. He perceived that she was preparing for an excursion. He asked himself, "Will she go out alone?" She immediately disappeared from view, and he proceeded on his way, slowly and reflectively. If she really did come out alone, she would be coming to see him. Perhaps this intoxicating victory would wash away the humiliation he had suffered years before. But would Aïda have done this, even if the moon had split apart? When he was halfway down the block, he turned to look back and saw her coming . . . by herself. He imagined that the pounding of his heart was audible to the neighbors and sensed immediately the gravity of the developing situation. One side of his personality strongly advocated flight. Their previous exchanges of smiles had been an innocent sentimental entertainment, but this encounter would be of unparalleled significance, bringing with it new responsibilities and the need to make a decisive choice. If he fled now, he would give himself more time for reflection. But he did not run away. He continued on with deliberate steps, as if drugged, until she caught up with him at the corner of al-Galal Street. As he turned, their eyes met, they smiled, and he said, "Good evening."

"Good evening."

Conscious of the ever mounting dangers, he asked, "Where to?"

"To see a girlfriend. She lives in that direction." She pointed toward Queen Nazli Street.

He replied recklessly, "That's the way I'm going. May I accompany you?"

Hiding a smile, she said, "If you want. . . ."

They walked along side by side. She had not decked herself out in this lovely dress to visit a girlfriend. It was for him, and his heart welcomed her with passion and affection. But how was he to conduct himself? Perhaps she had wearied of his inaction and had ventured out herself to provide a propitious opportunity for him. He would have to avail himself of it out of respect for her or ignore it and lose her forever. It had come down to a word that if spoken would affect the entire course of his life or if withheld would have consequences he would rue for the remainder of his days. Thus, against his better judgment, he found himself put on the spot.

They had gone quite a distance, and she presumably expected something. She seemed ready and responsive—as if she did not belong to the Shaddad family. In fact, she was not a Shaddad at all. The Shaddad family was finished. Its time had passed. "The person walking along with you is just one of many unlucky girls," he reflected.

She turned toward him with a tentative smile and said gently, "It's been nice to see you."

"Thanks."

Then what? . . . She seemed to be waiting for a further step on his part. The end of the street was approaching. He had to make up his mind to commit himself or to say goodbye. She had probably never imagined that they would part without even a hopeful word. The intersection was only a few paces ahead. He was painfully aware of the disappointment she would suffer, but his tongue refused to cooperate. Should he say something, no matter what the consequences? She stopped walking, and her smile, which appeared more deliberate than natural, seemed to say, "It's time for us to part." His confusion reached a climax. Then she held out her hand, and he took it. He said nothing for a terrible moment and then finally murmured, "Goodbye."

She withdrew her hand and turned into a side street. He almost called out after her. For Budur to depart in this manner, spattered with failure and embarrassment, was an unbearable nightmare. "You're a past master of miserable situations," he chided himself. But his tongue was frozen. Why had he been following her for the past two months?

"Is it in good taste to spurn her when she comes to you herself? Is it nice to give her the same dismissive treatment meted out to you by her sister? When you love her? Will she pass a night similar to the one that, though long behind you, still lights up the gloomy past like a burning coal with its smoldering pain?"

He walked on, wondering whether he really wanted to remain a bachelor so he could be a philosopher or whether he was using philosophy as a pretext for staying single.

Riyad told him later that what he had done was incredible and that he would regret it. His inaction really was unbelievable, but did he also regret it?

Riyad asked, "How could breaking off with her have seemed so trivial to you after you had been talking of her as the girl of your dreams?" She was not the girl of his dreams, for that girl would never have come to him.

Finally Riyad told Kamal, "You won't be thirty-six much longer. After that, you won't be fit for marriage." Angered by this remark, Kamal succumbed to despair.

46 ❧

Clad in a wedding gown, Karima came by carriage with her parents
and her brother to Sugar Street, where Ibrahim Shawkat, Khadija,
Kamal, Ahmad, and Ahmad's wife, Sawsan Hammad, were waiting
to receive them. There was nothing to suggest a wedding reception
except the bouquets of roses lining the sitting room. The men's parlor, which opened on the courtyard, was filled with bearded young
men, in the midst of whom sat Shaykh Ali al-Manufi. Although a
year and a half had passed since the death of al-Sayyid Ahmad,
Amina did not attend the reception, promising instead to offer her
congratulations later.

When Khadija had invited her to this low-key wedding, Aisha had
shaken her head in amazement, replying nervously, "I only attend
funerals." Although she was offended by this remark, Khadija had
grown accustomed to observing exemplary restraint with Aisha.

The upper floor at Sugar Street had been furnished for a second
time with a bride's trousseau. Yasin had outfitted his daughter properly and, to finance this expenditure, had sold the last of his holdings,
except for the house in Palace of Desire Alley.

Karima, who looked exceptionally beautiful, resembled—especially
in the warmth of her gaze—her mother, Zanuba, at her prime. The
girl had only reached the legal age of consent during the last week
of October. Khadija, as was only appropriate for the mother of the
groom, seemed happy. Availing herself of a moment alone with Kamal, she leaned toward him to say, "At any rate, she is Yasin's
daughter and, no matter what, a thousand times better than the work-
shop bride."

A small buffet dinner had been set out in the dining room for the
family and another in the courtyard for Abd al-Muni'm's bearded
guests, from whom he differed in no respect, since he too had let his
beard grow. At the time, Khadija had commented, "Religion's lovely,
but what need is there for this beard, which makes you look like
Muhammad al-Ajami, the couscous vendor?"

Members of the family sat in the parlor, except for Abd al-Muni'm, who kept his friends company. After helping his brother welcome them for a time, Ahmad returned to the parlor, where on joining his family he said jovially, "The gentlemen's parlor has reverted a thousand years back into history."

Kamal asked, "What are they discussing?"

"The battle of El Alamein ... loudly enough to make the walls rattle."

"What's their reaction to the British victory?"

"Anger, naturally. They are enemies of the English, the Germans, and the Russians, too. And so they don't spare the bridegroom even on his wedding night."

Seated next to Zanuba, Yasin, who in his finery looked ten years her junior, said, "Let the armies eat each other alive, so long as they don't do it here. It's our Lord's mercy that He has not made Egypt a war zone."

Smiling, Khadija remarked, "You probably want peace so you'll be free to do as you like." Then she cast Zanuba a sly look that made everyone laugh, for it had recently been reported that Yasin had flirted with the new tenant in his building and that, having caught him in the act, or almost, Zanuba had hounded the woman until she had vacated the apartment.

To hide his discomfort, Yasin said, "How can I do as I like when my home is under military rule?"

Zanuba protested resentfully, "You're not embarrassed—not even in front of your daughter?"

Yasin replied plaintively, "I'm innocent and the woman wrongly accused."

"I'm in the wrong? I'm the one who was caught knocking on her door at night and who then excused himself by saying he had lost his way in the dark? Huh? You spend forty years in a building and then can't find your apartment?"

They roared with laughter, but Khadija said ironically, "He often loses his way in the dark."

"And in the daylight as well."

Then Ibrahim Shawkat asked Ridwan, "How are you getting along with Muhammad Effendi Hasan?"

Yasin corrected his brother-in-law: "Muhammad Effendi Scum!"

Ridwan replied furiously, "He's now enjoying my grandfather's fortune, which went to my mother."

Yasin said argumentatively, "It's a considerable inheritance, but whenever Ridwan approaches her for assistance with some small purchase or other, her insolent husband makes problems for the boy and interrogates him about his expenses."

Khadija told Ridwan, "You're her only child. It would be better if she'd let you enjoy her money while she's still alive." Then she added, "And it's time for you to get married, isn't it?"

Ridwan laughed feebly and answered, "When Uncle Kamal does."

"I've given up on your uncle Kamal. There's no need for you to imitate him."

Kamal listened resentfully to these remarks, but did not allow it to show on his face. If she had despaired of him, so had he. In order to acknowledge consciousness of his guilt, he had stopped walking along Ibn Zaydun Street. He would stand near the streetcar stop, where he could watch her on the balcony without being seen. He could no more overcome his desire to see her than he could deny his love for her or ignore his alarmed aversion to the thought of marrying her. Riyad had told him, "You're sick and refuse to recover."

Ahmad Shawkat asked Ridwan in a knowing tone, "Would Muhammad Hasan interrogate you about your expenditures if your Sa'dist Party were in power?"

Ridwan laughed bitterly and answered, "He's not the only one who calls me to account nowadays. But patience . . . it's only a matter of a few more days or weeks."

Sawsan Hammad asked him, "Do you think the days of the Wafd Party are numbered, as its foes suggest?"

"The length of its rule depends entirely on the English. In any case the war won't drag on forever. Then it will be time to settle accounts."

With great earnestness, Sawsan said, "Primary responsibility for the tragedy lies with the people who helped the Fascists stab the English in the back."

Khadija gazed at Sawsan scornfully and disapprovingly, astonished that her daughter-in-law would join the conversation in such a manly fashion. She could not keep from remarking, "We're supposed to be at a wedding party. Let's talk about more suitable things."

To avoid a clash, Sawsan fell silent, while Ahmad and Kamal exchanged a smiling look. Ibrahim Shawkat laughed and remarked, "Their excuse is that our weddings aren't what they used to be . . . May God be compassionate to al-Sayyid Ahmad and provide him with a fine dwelling in paradise."

Yasin said regretfully, "I've been married three times, but I've never had a proper procession with a shivaree."

Zanuba asked acidly, "You blab about yourself and forget your daughter?"

Laughing, Yasin replied, "We'll have the proper festivities the fourth time, God willing."

Zanuba remarked sarcastically, "Postpone that until you've escorted Ridwan to his bride."

Ridwan was annoyed but said nothing. "God's curse on all of you and on marriage too," he thought. "Don't you realize that I'll never marry? I'd like to kill anyone who brings up this damn subject."

After a short silence, Yasin said, "I wish I could stay at the ladies' buffet, to avoid mingling with those bearded fellows, who frighten me."

"If they knew what you've done, they'd stone you," Zanuba taunted him.

Ahmad said scornfully, "Their beards will get in the food. It will be more like a battle than a dinner. Does my uncle Kamal like the Brethren?"

Smiling, Kamal answered, "I like one of them at least."

Turning to the silent bride, Sawsan asked affectionately, "What does Karima think about her husband's beard?"

Karima hid her laughter by ducking her crowned head but said nothing. Zanuba answered for her, "Few young men are as pious as Abd al-Muni'm."

Khadija remarked, "I admire his piety, which is a characteristic of our family, but not his beard."

Laughing, Ibrahim Shawkat said, "I must acknowledge that both my sons—the Believer and the apostate—are crazy."

Yasin roared his mighty laugh and commented, "Insanity is also a characteristic of our family."

Khadija gave him a look of protest. Before she could say anything, he attempted to humor her by adding, "I mean I'm crazy. I think Kamal's crazy too. But if you want, I'm the only crazy one."

"That is the unvarnished truth."

"Does it make sense for a man to condemn himself to bachelorhood so he can have time to read and write?"

"He'll marry sooner or later and be eminently sensible."

Ridwan asked his uncle Kamal, "Why don't you marry, Uncle? I'd like to know at least the basis for your objections so I can defend myself in a similar way if I need to."

Yasin asked, "Are you planning to boycott marriage? I'll never give you permission to do that so long as I live. Just wait until your party is in power again. Then you can have a spectacular political wedding."

But Kamal told his nephew, "If there's nothing to prevent it, you ought to get married at once."

"How handsome this young man is," Kamal mused. "And he has expectations of status and of wealth. If Aïda had seen him when she was young she would have fallen in love with him. If he favored Budur with a glance in passing, she would become wildly infatuated with him." Kamal went around in circles while the whole world advanced. He kept asking himself, "Are you going to get married or not?" Life seemed to offer nothing but gloomy confusion. His opportunity was neither ideal nor worthless. Love was difficult. It was characterized by controversy and suffering. If only she would marry someone else so he could free himself from this confusion and torment.

Then Abd al-Muni'm, preceded by his beard, came to announce, "Please help yourself to the buffet. Our festivities today are limited to the stomach."

At about ten o'clock one Friday morning Kamal was strolling along Fuad I Street, which was crowded with pedestrians. The weather was pleasant, as it normally is for most of November. He was very fond of walking and had grown accustomed to assuaging his emotional isolation by plunging into crowds of people on his day off. He would wander about aimlessly, entertaining himself by observing people and places.

On his way, he had run into more than one of his young pupils, who had greeted him with a salute. He had returned their greetings politely and cheerfully. How many pupils he had! Some had already found employment. Others were at the University. Most of them were in either elementary or secondary school. Fourteen years of service to learning and education was quite a substantial contribution. Kamal's traditional appearance was little altered: neat suit, glistening shoes, fez planted squarely on his head, gold-rimmed spectacles, and bushy mustache. Not even his civil service rank—the sixth—had changed in fourteen years, although there were rumors that the Wafd was thinking about rectifying such inequities. One visible change was the gray spreading through the hair at his temples. He seemed delighted by the salutations of these pupils, who loved and respected him. No other teacher had garnered a comparable popularity, and he had accomplished this in spite of his huge head and nose and the unruly deviltry in vogue among students.

When his meanderings brought him to the intersection of Fuad I and Imad al-Din streets, he suddenly found himself face to face with Budur. His heart pounded as if a siren had gone off inside. The paralyzed stare of his eyes lasted for a few moments, and then he started to smile in an attempt to obviate some of the awkwardness of the situation. But she turned her eyes away, clearly pretending that she did not know him. She did not soften her expression at all as she walked past him. Then, and only then, did he notice that her arm was around a young male companion's. Kamal stopped and followed her with his eyes. Yes, it was Budur, in an elegant black coat. Her escort, who was just as dapper, was probably not yet thirty. Kamal did his best to control himself, but the surprise had given him a jolt. He wondered with interest who the young man might be ... not her brother or her lover, for lovers do not parade their relationship down Fuad I Street, especially not on Friday morning. Could he be? ... Kamal's heart beat apprehensively. Then without any hesitation he started after them. His eyes never left them, and his attention was fixed so keenly on them that he sensed his temperature rising, along with his blood pressure. The pounding of his heart sounded like a death knell. He saw them pause before the display of a store selling suitcases. He slowly drew closer, directing his eyes toward the girl's right hand until he could see the gold ring. He felt scorched by a burning sensation that seemed a symptom of his profound pain.

Four months had passed since the incident on Ibn Zaydun Street. Had this young man been spying on him from the end of the street, just waiting to take his place? There was no cause for astonishment. Four months was a long time, long enough for the world to be turned upside down. Kamal stood in front of a toy store a short distance away, as if examining the toys. She seemed prettier today than ever before ... the spitting image of a bride. But what was the black color that had transformed all her garments? A black coat was nothing unusual. Although that was quite fashionable, why was her dress black too? Was it attributable to style or mourning? Had her mother died? He was not in the habit of reading through the obituaries, and how did it concern him? What really mattered was that Budur's page in the book of his life had been turned. Budur was finished. The anxious question, to marry or not, had a conclusive answer. After all his anxiety and suffering, he should be happy. He had often wished she would marry someone else, so his torment would end. Lo and behold, she had. He should be delighted to be released from his suffering. He imagined that a person being executed might experience the sensations he was feeling then as the gates of life closed in his face and he was expelled beyond its walls.

He saw them turn and move his way, passing by him nonchalantly. He followed them with his gaze and considered trailing after them but changed his mind almost irritably. He loitered by the toy display and gazed at it without seeing anything. Then he looked after them one last time, as if to bid her farewell. She got ever farther away, vanishing at times behind other people only to appear again. He saw one side of her once and then the other. All the strings of his heart were murmuring, "Farewell." The tormented feeling that gripped him was accompanied by mournful melodies, which were no strangers to

him. He was reminded of a comparable situation in the past. This
emotion pulsed through him, carrying with it various associated
memories. It could have been a mysterious tune, evoking the most
sublime pain but at the same time bringing veiled hints of pleasure.
It was a single emotion in which pain met pleasure, just as night and
day encounter each other at dawn. Then she disappeared, perhaps
forever, exactly as her sister had before her.

He found himself wondering who her fiancé was. Kamal had not
been able to scrutinize the young man, although he would have loved
to. He hoped—if the man was in the civil service—that his rank was
inferior to that of a teacher. But what were these childish thoughts?
It was embarrassing. As for the pain, a person as experienced with it
as he was should not worry, since he would know from experience
that its fate—like that of all things—was death. For the first time, he
noticed the toys that were spread before his eyes. The display was
beautiful and well arranged. Included in it were all the kinds of toys
that children adore: trains, cars, cradles, musical instruments, and
dollhouses with gardens. He was so drawn to this sight by the
strange force welling up in his tortured soul that he could not take
his eyes off the shop window. In his childhood, he had not been
allowed to enjoy the paradise of toys. He had grown up harboring
this unsatisfied longing, and now it was too late to gratify it. People
who spoke of the happiness of childhood—what did they know?
Who could declare authoritatively that he had been a happy child?
How foolish this wretched and unexpected desire was—to become a
child again, like that wooden one playing in a beautiful make-believe
garden. . . . The impulse was both absurd and sad. By their very nature children tended to be unbearable creatures. Perhaps it was only
his vocation that had taught him how to communicate with them and
how to guide them. But what would life be like if he returned to his
childhood while retaining his adult mind and memories? He would
play once more in the roof garden but with a heart filled with memories of Aïda. He would go to al-Abbasiya in 1914 and see Aïda
playing in the yard. Yet he would be aware of the treatment he would
receive at her hands in 1924 and thereafter. Speaking to his father
with a lisp, he would disclose that war would break out in 1939 and
that al-Sayyid Ahmad would die following an air raid. What foolish
thoughts these were. . . . All the same, they were better than focusing
on this new disappointment, which he had just encountered on Fuad
I Street. They were better than thinking about Budur, her fiancé, and
Kamal's relationship to her. Perhaps unconsciously he was atoning

for some past error. How and when had that mistake occurred? Whether an act, a word, or a situation, it was the cause of the torment he was suffering. If he came to know himself thoroughly, he could easily separate the cause from the pains it brought. The battle was not over. The capitulation had not yet taken place. Nor should it. Perhaps this was the reason for the infernal vacillation that had left him biting his fingernails while Budur strolled by arm in arm with her fiancé. He would have to think twice about this torment that concealed within it a mysterious delight. Had he not experienced it once before, when he was in the desert at al-Abbasiya, looking at the light from the window of Aïda's bridal chamber? Had his hesitation with Budur been a trick to put himself into a comparable situation so that he could revive the old sensations, reliving their pleasure and their pain? Before lifting a hand to write about God, the spirit, and matter, he ought to know himself, his individual personality, that of Kamal Effendi Ahmad … Kamal Ahmad … no, just plain Kamal. Then he would be able to create himself anew. He should start that night by reviewing his diary in order to examine the past very carefully. It would be a night without sleep, but not his first. His collection of them could be put into a single album under the title "Sleepless Nights." He should never say that his life had been in vain, for he would leave behind some bones future generations could play with. Budur had vanished from his life forever, and this truth was as doleful as a funeral dirge. She had left behind not a single affectionate memory, not an embrace or a kiss, not even a touch or a kind word.

He no longer feared insomnia. In the past he had faced it alone. Today he had countless ways of diverting his mind and heart. He would go to Atiya in her new house on Muhammad Ali Street. They would continue their endless conversation.

Last time he had told her with a diction slurred by drink, "We're perfect for each other."

With resigned irony she had answered, "You're very sweet when you're drunk."

He had continued: "What a happy couple we'll make if we ever get married."

Frowning, she had said, "Don't make fun of me. I've been a lady in every sense of the word."

"Yes. Yes. You're more delectable than ripe fruit."

She had pinched him mischievously, observing, "That's what you say, but if I asked you for an extra twenty piasters, you'd flee."

"What we have goes way beyond money."

Giving him a look of protest, she had remarked, "But I have two children who prefer money to talk about a loving relationship."

His sorrow and intoxication having reached their climax, he had said sarcastically, "I'm thinking of following Madam Jalila's example and repenting. When I become a Sufi, I'll leave you my entire fortune."

Giggling, she had said, "If repentance catches up with you, that will be the end of us."

He had laughed loudly and answered, "If repentance would harm women like you, I'll certainly forget about it."

This was his refuge from insomnia. Realizing that he had tarried by the toy display long enough, he turned and walked away.

48

Khalo, the proprietor of the Star Tavern, asked, "Is it true, my dear, that they're going to close all the bars?"

With confident self-assurance, Yasin replied, "Inconceivable, Khalo! The deputies say all sorts of things when the budget is being debated, and the government complacently promises to investigate the deputies' requests at the earliest opportunity. But this has a way of never arriving."

The members of Yasin's group in the bar on Muhammad Ali Street vied with each other to offer their comments.

The personnel director said, "For as long as anyone can remember they've been promising to throw the British out of Egypt, to open a new university, and to widen al-Khalig Street. Have any of these pledges been kept, Khalo?"

The honorary dean of pensioners observed, "Perhaps the deputy proposing that had drunk some of the lethal wartime liquor and was attempting to get even."

The attorney said, "No matter what, bars on streets visited by foreigners won't be touched. So, Khalo, if the worst happens, just buy into some saloon or other. Like buildings that stand cheek by jowl, dramshop owners support each other."

The head clerk from mortmain trusts remarked, "If the English advanced on the Abdin Palace with their tanks over a trivial question like returning al-Nahhas to power, do you think they'd stand for having the bars closed?"

In addition to Yasin's group, some local merchants were in the room. All the same, the head clerk suggested blending song with drink: "Let's sing 'Prisoner of love.'"

Khalo scurried back to his place behind the counter, and the friends began to sing, "What humiliations the prisoner of love experiences." Inebriation's tune rang out more clearly than any other one, and the grimaces of the merchants showed their disdain for this performance. But the singing did not last long. Yasin was the first to drop out, and the others followed suit, leaving only the head clerk to finish the piece. The ensuing silence was interrupted only by slurping and smacking noises or by the handclap of a patron ordering a drink or a snack.

Then Yasin asked, "Is there some proven way to induce pregnancy?"

The aged civil servant protested, "You keep harping on that question and repeating it. By God, have patience, brother."

The head clerk observed, "There's no cause for alarm, Yasin Effendi. Your daughter's going to get pregnant."

Smiling fatuously, Yasin said, "She's a blooming bride and the belle of Sugar Street. But she's the first girl in our family not to get pregnant during the first year of marriage. That's why her mother is concerned."

"And her father too, it seems."

Laughing, Yasin responded, "When a wife is upset, her husband is too."

"If a man recalled how nasty children are, he'd detest pregnancy."

"So what! People usually get married to have children."

"That's right! If it weren't for children, no one would ever tolerate married life."

Yasin finished his drink and said, "I'm afraid my nephew may hold this opinion."

"Some men want children so they can regain a bit of their lost freedom while their wives are busy with the kids."

Yasin exclaimed, "How absurd! A woman may be nursing one child and rocking another, but she'll still glare at her husband and ask, 'Where were you? Why did you stay out so late?' All the same, even the best minds have been unable to improve on this universal system."

"What's stopping them?"

"Their wives, who don't let them have time to think about this issue. . . ."

"Have no fear, Yasin Effendi. Your daughter's husband can't forget your son's favor in getting him a government job."

"Anything can be forgotten." The alcohol had begun to addle his brain. Laughing, he continued: "Besides, my darling son's out of power right now."

"Oh! This time it seems that the Wafd has settled in for a long stay."

The attorney said grandiloquently, "If things follow their natural course in Egypt, the Wafd will stay in power forever."

"This idea would be more palatable," Yasin replied cheerfully, "if my son had not left the Wafd."

"Don't forget the traffic accident at al-Qassasin. Had the king lost his life, the enemies of the Wafd would have been finished."

"The king's fine."

"But Prince Muhammad Ali has his ceremonial uniform ready, just in case. He's always been sympathetic to the Wafd."

"Whoever is on the throne—no matter what his name is—will be an enemy of the Wafd by virtue of his position, just as surely as whiskey and sweets don't go together."

Laughing drunkenly, Yasin said, "Perhaps you're right. They say that a man even a day older than you is a year wiser, and some of you have reached your dotage while others are almost there."

"God protect you! You're forty-seven!"

"At any rate I'm the youngest."

Swaying back and forth drunkenly but proudly, he snapped his fingers and added, "One's real age shouldn't be measured by years but by the level of intoxication you attain. During the war years, alcoholic beverages have deteriorated in quality and in taste, but the effect is still the same. Waking up the next morning you have a pounding headache, you need pincers to pry open your eyes, and your breath reeks of alcohol when you belch. But I tell you that any side effects of inebriation are trivial compared to its pleasures. Often a brother will ask, 'What of its impact on your health?' Yes, my health isn't what it was. A man of forty-seven today would be no match for one that age back in the old days. This is a sign that everything has become more valuable during the war except age. . . . In these trying times, a man of forty asks experts for prescriptions to fortify him and a bridegroom on his honeymoon is barely strong enough to stay afloat."

"The good old days! The whole world is nostalgic for them."

With the melodies of intoxication reverberating in his voice, Yasin continued: "The good old days—God have mercy on my father! He frequently beat me to keep me from joining the violent demonstrations of the revolution. But a fellow who can't be frightened off by English bombs is not going to be scared away by a scolding. We met at the coffeehouse of Ahmad Abduh, where we planned the demonstrations and the bombings."

"This same old recording! Tell me, Yasin Effendi: Were you as heavy then as you are today?"

"Yes, or even heavier . . . but in the heat of the struggle, I was as energetic as a bee. The day of the great battle, I walked at the head of the demonstration with my brother, who was the first martyr of the nationalist movement. I heard the whine of the bullet as it sailed past my ear and landed in my brother. What a memory! If he had lived, he would have been one of the select group of cabinet ministers who first rose to prominence during the revolution."

"But you're the one who survived!"

"Yes, but it wasn't possible for me to become a cabinet minister with only the elementary certificate. Moreover, in our struggle, we fought expecting death, not high office. Sa'd Zaghlul marched in my brother's funeral procession, and the leader of the students introduced me to him. That's another momentous memory."

"In view of your dedication to the revolutionary cause, how did you find time to raise cain and fall in love?"

"Listen to that, will you! Aren't the soldiers who screw women in the streets here the same ones who routed Rommel? Armed struggle has no distaste for fun. Don't you realize that alcohol is an essential part of heroism? The combatant and the drunkard are brothers, you genius."

"Didn't Sa'd Zaghlul say anything to you at your brother's funeral?"

The attorney answered for Yasin: "Sa'd told him, 'I wish you'd been the martyr and not your brother.'"

They laughed, for they had reached the point of laughing first and asking why later. Yasin joined in the laughter magnanimously and then continued his lecture: "He did not say that, God rest his soul. He was polite, unlike you, and knew how to have a good time. For this reason, he was broad-minded. He was a politician, a freedom fighter, a man of letters, a philosopher, and a jurist. One word from him could mean life or death."

"May God be compassionate to him."

"And to everyone else. All the dead deserve God's mercy, by the very fact that they've lost their lives ... even the prostitute, the pimp, and the mother who sent her son to fetch her boyfriend."

"Would a mother do that?"

"Everything you can imagine and lots that you can't exist in this life."

"Wouldn't she find someone to send besides her son?"

"Who takes better care of a woman than her son? And aren't you all products of sexual intercourse?"

"Legal intercourse."

"A mere formality ... it comes down to the same thing. I've known unfortunate prostitutes whose bed didn't entertain a lover for a week or more. Show me any of your mothers who went that long without a visit from her husband."

"I've never known any people besides the Egyptians to be so interested in discussing their mothers' reputations."

"We're not very polite."

Yasin laughed and replied, "Time has disciplined us too often. When excessive emphasis is placed on something, the opposite occurs. That's why we're rude but generally good-natured. In the end, most of us repent."

"I'm a pensioner, and I haven't repented yet."

"Repentance doesn't follow the civil service structure. Besides, you're not doing anything wrong. You get drunk several hours every night, and there's no harm in that. One day ill health or the doctor —they amount to the same thing—will prevent you from drinking. By nature we're weak. Otherwise we would not have developed a taste for liquor and we would not put up with married life. With the passing days we grow ever weaker, but our desires remain limitless. How absurd: We suffer and then get drunk again. Our hair goes gray, betraying our age, and some insolent oaf accosts you on the street, saying, 'You shouldn't be chasing women now that your hair is white.' Glory to God! 'What difference does it make to you whether I'm young or old and chasing a woman or a donkey?' You may imagine at times that people are conspiring with your wife against you. Add to that, the officer's truncheon and the aggravations of coquetry, for even the serving girl struts flirtatiously through the vegetable market. You find yourself in a quarrelsome world without a friend to your name save the bottle. Then along come mercenary physicians to tell you as bluntly as possible: 'Don't drink!' "

"Even so, do you deny that we love this world with all our hearts?"

"With all our hearts! Even evil has some good in it. Even the English have redeeming qualities. I once knew some of them intimately. I had some English friends during the revolutionary era."

The attorney cried out, "But you were fighting against them! Have you forgotten?"

"Yes . . . yes. There's a time and place for everything. I was once suspected of being a spy, but the leader of the students rushed to my aid in the nick of time to tell the crowd who I really was. Then they cheered me. That was in the mosque of al-Husayn!"

" 'Long live Yasin! Long live Yasin!' But what were you doing in the mosque of al-Husayn?"

"Answer him! This is an extremely important point."

Yasin laughed and replied, "We were at the Friday prayer service. My father used to take us with him to the Friday prayers. Don't you believe it? Ask the people at al-Husayn."

"You prayed to butter up your father?"

"By God . . . don't think ill of us. We're a religious family. Yes, we're dissolute inebriates, but we all plan to repent eventually."

Moaning, the attorney asked, "Shouldn't we sing a bit more?"

Yasin shot back, "Yesterday when I left the bar singing, a police-man stopped me and cried out to warn me: 'Mister!' I asked him, 'Don't I have a right to sing?' He answered, 'Screeching after mid-night is forbidden.' I protested, 'But I'm singing!' He said sharply, 'As far as the law's concerned it's all the same thing.' I asked, 'What about bombs that explode after midnight—shouldn't that be consid-ered screeching?' He answered threateningly, 'It's plain that you want to spend the night at the station.' I backed away, saying, 'No, I'd rather spend the night at home.' How can we be a civilized nation when we're ruled by soldiers? At home you find your wife on the lookout for you, at the ministry there's your boss, and it's said that even in the grave two angels with truncheons will be waiting to examine you."

The attorney suggested again, "Let's have a tidbit of singing to go with our drinks."

The dean of all pensioners cleared his throat and began to chant:

> *My husband took a second wife*
> *When wedding henna still was fresh*
> *Upon my hands. The day he brought*
> *Her home, her presence seared my flesh.*

With savage enthusiasm they took up the refrain. Yasin was laugh-ing so hard that tears came to his eyes.

49

Khadija often felt lonesome. Ibrahim Shawkat tended to stay home all winter long—especially now that he was approaching seventy—but his presence did little to drive away her loneliness. Performing her household chores hardly lessened it either, for they were no longer arduous enough to absorb all of her energy. Although over forty-six, Khadija was still strong and active—and even plumper. Worst of all, her career as a mother had ended before she could assume that of a mother-in-law. It appeared that she would be permanently denied this opportunity, since one of her daughters-in-law was also her niece and the other worked outside the home and thus was visible only on rare occasions.

In a conversation with her husband, who was wrapped up in his cloak, she voiced her buried feelings: "Our sons have been married for more than a year, and we haven't lit any candles for a baby yet."

The man shrugged his shoulders but did not reply. She continued: "Perhaps Abd al-Muni'm and Ahmad consider having children a fad as outmoded as obeying their parents."

The man answered irritably, "Calm down. They're happy, and that should be enough for us."

She asked sharply, "If a bride doesn't get pregnant and have children, what use is she?"

"Perhaps your sons don't share that opinion."

"They disagree with me about everything. All my efforts and hopes have been in vain."

"Are you sad you're not a grandmother?"

She retorted even more acidly, "I'm sad for them, not for me."

"Abd al-Muni'm has taken Karima to the doctor, who said everything would be fine."

"The poor boy spent a lot of money, and he'll have to spend more in the future. Brides—like tomatoes and meat—are expensive today."

When the man's only response was laughter, she added, "As for the other girl, I'm imploring God's assistance with her by way of the saint at Bab al-Mutawalli."

"You'll have to admit that her words are as sweet as honey."

"That's just shrewd cunning. What do you expect from a laborer's daughter?"

"Fear God, my good woman."

"When do you suppose the 'professor' will take her to the doctor?"

"They refuse."

"Naturally. . . . She has a job. How could she find time to become pregnant and have a baby?"

"They're happy together. That can't be doubted."

"There's no way a woman who works can be a good wife. He'll realize that when it's too late."

"He's a man and can handle it."

"No other pair of young men in this district are as big a loss as my sons."

With the crystallization of Abd al-Muni'm's character and orientation, he established himself as a capable civil servant and an energetic member of the Muslim Brethren. Leadership of their branch in al-Gamaliya devolved upon him. Named a legal adviser to the organization, he helped edit its journal and occasionally delivered sermons in sympathetic mosques. He had turned his apartment into a meeting place where the Brethren talked till all hours of the night under the guidance of Shaykh Ali al-Manufi. The young man was extremely zealous and more than prepared to place everything he possessed— his industry, money, and intelligence—at the service of the cause, which he believed wholeheartedly to be, as its founder put it, "a pure revivalist mission, a brotherhood based upon the Prophet's example, a mystic reality, a political organization, an athletic association, a cultural and scientific league, an economic partnership, and a social concept."

Shaykh Ali al-Manufi said, "The teachings and precepts of Islam provide a comprehensive answer to the problems people confront in reference to this world and the next. Those who assume that its doctrines apply only to the spiritual and devotional aspects of life are mistaken. Islam is a creed, a way of worship, a nation and a nationality, a religion, a state, a form of spirituality, a Holy Book, and a sword."

One of the young men present commented, "This is what we believe, but we're slowed down by inertia. Pagan secularism rules us with its laws, traditions, and people."

Shaykh Ali declared, "We must spread the word and gain zealous adherents. After that, it will be time to act on our teachings."

"How long must we wait?"

"We will wait until the war ends. Then the audience will be ready for our message. People will have lost confidence in the political parties. When the right moment comes for the leader to raise the call, the Brethren will revolt, armed with Qur'ans and weapons."

In his deep and forceful voice, Abd al-Muni'm said, "Let us prepare for a prolonged struggle. Our mission is not to Egypt alone but to all Muslims worldwide. It will not be successful until Egypt and all other Islamic nations have accepted these Qur'anic principles in common. We shall not put our weapons away until the Qur'an has become a constitution for all Believers."

Shaykh Ali al-Manufi continued: "I bring you the good news that by the grace of God our message is reaching every area. Each village has a branch today. It is God's message, and God will not forsake those who assist Him."

Meanwhile, on the lower floor of the building, another operation with totally different objectives was in full swing, although there were fewer participants. Ahmad and Sawsan frequently entertained a limited number of friends from different sects and ethnic groups, most of them in journalism.

Aware of the theoretical nature of the discussions being held there, Mr. Adli Karim, who visited them one evening, commented, "It's fine that you are studying Marxism, but remember that the historical determinism it preaches is different from the inevitability of astronomical events and arises only as a consequence of the volition and effort of human beings. Our primary obligation is not to theorize at length but to raise the proletariat's level of awareness about the historic role they are to play in saving themselves and the world as a whole."

Ahmad answered, "For the educated elite we are translating the most valuable books about this philosophy. We are also giving inspirational talks to rebellious laborers. Both of these endeavors are unavoidable necessities."

The publisher said, "A corrupt society will be transformed only by the worker's hand. When the consciousness of the workers has been filled with the new faith and when people in general share a united will, then neither repressive laws nor cannons will stand in our way."

"We all believe that, but winning over the minds of the intelligentsia will bring control over the group from which leaders and rulers are chosen."

Then Ahmad said, "Sir, there's something I would like to mention. I've learned from experience that it's not hard to convince educated

people that religion is a cultural artifact and that the supposed mysteries of the afterlife are a distracting opiate. But it is dangerous to
address such ideas to ordinary people. The most serious charge that
our enemies can employ against us is that our movement is composed
of atheists and infidels."

"Our primary task is to combat the temptation to settle for the
status quo, lethargy, and hopelessness. The destruction of religion
will be possible only after political liberation has been achieved by
revolution. In general, poverty is stronger than belief. It's always
wise for us to speak to people at their level of understanding."

The publisher smiled at Sawsan as he said, "You once believed in
direct action. Has marriage convinced you of the value of theoretical
discussions?"

Although she sensed that he was teasing her and did not mean it,
she replied earnestly, "My husband gives talks to workers in dilapidated and out-of-the-way buildings, and I never tire of handing out
pamphlets."

Ahmad said glumly, "The weak point of our movement is that it
attracts many insincere opportunists. Some work in hopes of a future
reward and others are trying to advance the interests of a political
party."

Mr. Adli Karim shook his large head with evident disdain as he
answered, "I realize this all too well. But I also know that without
seeming to believe in Islam the Umayyad clan inherited political
power over the Islamic world and, nevertheless, spread Islamic rule
through vast stretches of the ancient world, including what is today
Spain. So we have a right to make use of these opportunists if we
also caution them. Remember that time will favor us if we make
every effort and sacrifice we can."

"What about the Brethren, sir? We're beginning to feel that they
are a serious obstacle to our progress."

"I don't deny it, but they're not as dangerous as you think. Don't
you see that they use our language when appealing to the mind and
speak of socialism in Islam? Even reactionaries feel obliged to borrow
our vocabulary. If they pull off a revolution before we do, they will
realize at least some of our objectives. They will not be able to stop
time's progressive motion to the prescribed goal. Besides, the spread
of learning is as liable to banish them as light is to discourage bats."

Khadija observed the manifestations of this strange fervor with an
astonishment mingled with anger and resentment. She finally com-

plained to her husband, "I've never seen homes like Abd al-Muni'm's and Ahmad's. Perhaps, without telling me, they've converted their apartments into coffeehouses. Not an evening passes without the street being crowded with visitors, some bearded and some who probably aren't even Muslims. I've never heard the likes of this."

The man shook his head, remarking, "The time has evidently come for you to hear it."

She snapped back, "Their salaries aren't big enough to pay for all the coffee they serve."

"Have they complained to you about being short of money?"

"What about the neighbors? What will they say when they see these droves of people going in and out?"

"Everyone's free to do what he wants in his own home."

She huffed: "The sound of their interminable discussions is loud enough at times to be heard in the street."

"So let it be heard down on the street or up in the sky."

Khadija sighed profoundly and struck her hands together.

50

At Abd al-Rahim Pasha Isa's villa in Helwan, they were seeing out the last wave of the visitors who had come to say goodbye to him before his departure for the holy places of the Hijaz.

"Pilgrimage is an aspiration I've long nourished. God curse politics, for that's what has kept me from going, year after year. But a man my age must think about preparing for his forthcoming encounter with his Lord."

Ali Mihran, the pasha's deputy, said, "Yes, God curse politics!"

The pasha's feeble eyes looked thoughtfully at Ridwan and Hilmi. He commented, "Say what you like, but it has done me a favor I shall never forget. It has distracted me from my loneliness. An old bachelor like me would seek companionship even in hell."

Raising his eyebrows playfully, Ali Mihran asked, "Haven't we distracted you, Pasha?"

"Of course you have, but a bachelor's day is as long as a winter's night. A man needs a companion. I admit that a woman is an important necessity. I think often of my mother now. A woman is necessary, even for a person who does not desire her."

Thinking about quite different issues, Ridwan suddenly asked the pasha, "Suppose that al-Nahhas Pasha falls from power. Wouldn't you change your mind about leaving then?"

Waving his hand indignantly, the pasha replied, "Let that disgrace stay in power, at least until I get back from my pilgrimage." Then, shaking his head, he added, "We are all to blame, but pilgrimage washes away sins."

Hilmi Izzat laughed and observed, "You're a Believer, Pasha, even if that fact perplexes many people."

"Why? Belief is broad-minded. Only a hypocrite claims to be absolutely pure. It's foolish to suppose that a man commits sins only when belief is dead. Besides, our sins are more like innocent child's play."

Sighing with relief, Ali Mihran said, "What a beautiful statement! Now let me tell you frankly that I've often felt your determination to perform the pilgrimage to be a sinister omen. I've asked myself, 'Do you think this means repentance? Will it put an end to our pleasures?'"

The pasha laughed so hard that the upper half of his body shook. "You're a devil and the son of one. Would all of you really be sad to learn that I have repented?"

Hilmi groaned: "Like a woman whose newborn babe is slain in her arms."

Abd al-Rahim Pasha laughed again and exclaimed, "Shame on you! Bastards! If a man like me were truly to repent, he would have to prevent himself from seeing beautiful eyes and rosy cheeks and dedicate himself instead to visiting the tomb of the Prophet, may God bless him and grant him peace."

Mihran gloated: "In the Hijaz? Do you know what things are like there? I've heard from people who know. It will be out of the frying pan and into the fire for you."

Hilmi Izzat protested, "Perhaps it's just false propaganda like that spread by the English. In all of the Hijaz is there a face like Ridwan's?"

Abd al-Rahim Isa cried out, "Not even in paradise!" Then, as if experiencing a change of heart, he added, "But, you naughty boys, we were discussing repentance."

Ali Mihran said, "Not so fast, Pasha! You told me once about a mystic who repented seventy times. Doesn't this imply that he sinned seventy times?"

"Or a hundred?" Ridwan interjected.

Ali Mihran said, "I'm satisfied with seventy."

The pasha's face beamed with joy as he asked, "Will we live long enough for that?"

"May our Lord grant you a long life, Pasha. Set our minds at ease and tell us it's your first repentance."

"And the last!"

"Vain boasting! If you provoke me, when you return from the pilgrimage I'll meet you with a moon-faced beauty, or several of them, and then we'll see how long your repentance lasts."

Smiling, the pasha said, "The result will be as ugly as your face, you jinx. You're a devil, Mihran—an indispensable devil."

"I praise God for that."

Almost in unison, Ridwan and Hilmi added, "We praise Him too."

The pasha said with proud delight, "You're my favorite companions. What value would life have without affection and friendship? Life is beautiful. Beauty is beautiful. Musical ecstasy is beautiful. Forgiveness is beautiful. You're young and look at the world from a special perspective. Life will teach you a lot. I love you and the world. I'm visiting God's sanctuary to give thanks, to ask forgiveness, and to seek guidance."

Ridwan observed merrily, "How handsome you are! You exude such serenity."

Ali Mihran remarked slyly, "With only a little friction, he'd exude something quite different. Pasha, you truly have been the mentor of an entire generation."

"And you're Satan himself, you son of a crone. My God—if I'm ever called to account, I'll point to you and that will be an adequate excuse."

"Me! Unjustly accused, by God! I'm just an obedient servant."

"No, you're a devil."

"But an indispensable one?"

Laughing, the pasha answered, "Yes, you scoundrel."

"In your busy life I have represented—and still do—a touching melody, a pretty face, and constantly renewed happiness, your perfidious excellency."

The pasha moaned: "The old days! Children, why do we grow old? May your wisdom be exalted and glorified, my Lord. A poet said:

> *My lance was not deflected by a foe's taunts.*
> *Auspicious times for it were dawn and dusk both.*

Wiggling his eyebrows, Mihran said, " 'By a foe's taunts'? No, you should say, 'By Mihran.' "

"You son of a bitch—don't spoil the mood with your nonsense. It's not right to joke around when we're reminiscing about those beautiful days. At times tears are more becoming than a smile, more humane, and more respectful. Listen to this too, by al-A'sha:

> *She rebuffed me, but the*
> *Events she rejected*
> *Were baldness and white hair.*

What do you think of the poet's use of 'events'?"

Imitating a newspaper vendor, Mihran called out, "*Events of the Day*, the *Egyptian, al-Ahram* . . ."

Despairingly the pasha said, "It's not your fault but . . ."

"Yours!"

"Mine? I'm not to blame for your depravity. When we first met, you were so debauched that Satan would have envied you. But I won't allow you to spoil the ambiance created by these memories. Yes, hear this as well:

Just as a stalk is ravished of
Its leaves, so I was stripped of youth.

Pretending to be shocked by the sexual allusion, Mihran asked, "A stalk, Pasha?"

Looking at Ridwan and Hilmi, who were dissolved in laughter, the pasha said, "Your friend is a corpse with no feeling for poetry. But soon he'll reach the age of regrets, when the only beauties he encounters will be referred to in the past tense." Turning toward Mihran, he asked, "What about our friends from the old days, son of a crone—have you forgotten them?"

"Oh! May God preserve them. They were coy paragons of beauty."

"What do you know about Shakir Sulayman?"

"He was a Deputy Minister of the Interior and a pet of the English until prematurely pensioned off during the second or third government of al-Nahhas . . . I don't remember which. I think he has now retired to his estate at Kom Hamada."

"What marvelous days those were! What about Hamid al-Najdi?"

"He's had the worst luck of any of our dear friends. He lost everything and now tours the public lavatories by night."

"He was witty and charming but a gambler and a boisterous fellow. And Ali Ra'fat?"

"Through his 'exertions' he managed to become a member of the boards of directors of various corporations, but it's said that his reputation cost him a chance at a cabinet post."

"Don't believe what people say. Men whose notoriety has extended far beyond our kingdom have been appointed to the cabinet, but as I have often advised you, I think it is more important for us to develop a virtuous character than for others. If you can manage this, you won't need to worry about censure. The Mamluk sultans, recruited from a corps of military slaves, ruled Egypt for generations, and their descendants still enjoy high status and wealth here. What is a Mamluk? Nothing but a man who can be bought. Let me tell you a story of great import."

The pasha was silent for a time, as if collecting his thoughts. Then he said, "When I was the presiding judge of a court, a civil case concerning a contested inheritance was scheduled to be heard by us.

Beforehand, some of the people involved introduced me to a beautiful young man with a face like Ridwan's, a build like Hilmi's, and . . ." He gestured toward Mihran as he continued: "The grace of this dog in his glory. . . . We saw each other for a time without my learning that he had a secret connection to the case. Then the day the case was heard, what did I know but he was representing one of the parties to the dispute. What do you think I did?"

Ridwan murmured, "What a situation!"

"I withdrew from the case, without any hesitation."

Ridwan and Hilmi displayed their admiration, but Mihran protested, "You didn't reward him in any way for his efforts?"

Paying no attention to Mihran's kidding, the pasha said, "But that's not all. Out of contempt for his morals, I ended my relationship with him. Yes, a man without morals is worthless. The English aren't the brightest people. The French and the Italians are smarter. But the English have mastered morality and this has made them masters of the world. That is my reason for spurning superficial, decadent beauty."

Ali Mihran asked merrily, "May I assume that my morals are satisfactory, since you've kept me on?"

Giving him a cautionary wave of the hand, the pasha replied, "There are many different moral qualities. A judge should be upright and just. A cabinet minister should have a sense of duty and a respect for the public welfare. A friend should be loyal and sincere. Without doubt you are a troublemaker and frequently a rogue. But you're honest and faithful."

"I hope I'm blushing."

" 'God does not impose more on a soul than it can bear.' In fact I'm content with the amount of good that's in you. Besides, you're a husband and a father, and those are virtues too. The happiness they bring can be appreciated properly only by people who must put up with silent homes. Even so, a silent residence is one of the torments of old age."

Somewhat disapprovingly, Ridwan observed, "I thought old people loved peace and quiet."

"The notions young people have about old age are erroneous. The ideas old people cherish about youth are vain regrets. Tell me, Ridwan, what do you think about marriage?"

Ridwan's face fell, and he answered, "You already know what I think about it, Pasha."

"There's no hope you'll change your mind?"

"I don't think so."

"Why not?"

Ridwan hesitated a little and then said, "It's an amazing thing. . . . I don't really understand it. But I find women revolting."

The expression of the man's feeble eyes was sad as he commented, "What a pity! Don't you see that Ali Mihran is a husband and a father? Your friend Hilmi advocates marriage. I feel doubly sorry for you, since I also pity myself. I have often been perplexed by what I've read and heard about the beauty of women. Out of respect for the memory of my mother, I've kept my opinion to myself. I loved her dearly, and she died in my arms as my tears fell on her brow and cheeks. I hope ever so much, Ridwan, that you can overcome your problems."

Looking frightened and somber, Ridwan said, "A man can live without a woman."

The pasha replied, "That's not so difficult, and you may be able to ignore the doubts of other people. Yet what about your own questions? You can say you find women disgusting, but why don't other men feel that way? You fall prey to a feeling that's almost like a disease, an incurable one. It leads you to withdraw from the world and is the worst possible companion for your solitude. Then you may be embarrassed to despise women without having any choice about it."

Ali Mihran snorted cynically and complained, "I had promised myself a cheery evening together for our farewell party."

Laughing, Abd al-Rahim Pasha said, "But it's a farewell party for a pilgrim. What do you know about seeing off pilgrims?"

"I'll see you off with prayerful invocations and welcome you back with rosy-cheeked beauties. We'll find out what you do then."

Clapping his hands together, the pasha answered jovially, "I entrust my fate to God Almighty."

51

In front of the Ritz Café at the intersection of Sharif and Qasr al-Nil streets, Kamal found himself face to face with Husayn Shaddad. They both stopped and stared at each other. Then Kamal cried out, "Husayn!"

Husayn exclaimed in turn, "Kamal!"

Laughing with gleeful delight, they shook hands warmly.

"What a happy surprise after such a long time!"

"A very happy surprise! You've changed a lot, Kamal. But not so fast. . . . Perhaps I'm exaggerating. . . . The same build and general appearance. But what's this dignified mustache? These 'classic' spectacles and this walking stick? And this fez that no one else wears anymore? . . ."

"You've changed a great deal too. You're heavier than I would have imagined. Is this the Parisian fashion? Where's the Husayn I once knew?"

"Where's the Paris I once knew? Where are Hitler and Mussolini? Well, let's not worry about it. I was on my way to the Ritz to have some tea. Do you have any objection to joining me?"

"Of course not."

They went into the Ritz and took a table by the window overlooking the street. After Husayn ordered tea and Kamal coffee, they resumed their smiling examination of one another. Husayn had become huge, expanding vertically and horizontally. But what had he done with his life? Had he toured the earth and the heavens as he had once hoped? Despite their friendly expression, his eyes had a coarse look, as if they had undergone a transformation following childhood. A year had passed since Kamal's encounter with Budur on Fuad I Street. During that time he had recovered from his relapse into love, and the Shaddad family had retreated into a forgotten corner of his mind. Now the sight of Husayn awakened Kamal's soul from its slumbers, and, stretching sleepily, the past reappeared to spread its joys and torments before him.

"When did you return from abroad?"

"It's been about a year."

He had made absolutely no attempt to contact Kamal. . . . But why blame Husayn when he himself had forgotten his former friend and written off their friendship?

"If I had known you were back in Egypt, I certainly would have looked you up."

Showing no confusion or embarrassment, Husayn answered quite simply, "When I came back, I found many problems awaiting me. Haven't you heard about us?"

Kamal frowned as he replied briefly and sadly, "Yes, of course . . . from our friend Isma'il Latif."

"My mother tells me he left for Iraq two years ago. . . . As I was saying, I found a lot of problems waiting for me. And then I had to start working. I've had to work night and day."

This was the 1944 edition of Husayn Shaddad, who had once considered work a crime against humanity. Had that past really existed? Perhaps the only clue to its existence was the pounding of Kamal's heart.

"Do you remember the last time we saw each other?"

"Oh! . . ."

The waiter arrived with their tea and coffee before Husayn could complete his response. But he hardly seemed eager to relive those memories.

"Let me remind you. It was in 1926."

"What a fantastic memory!" Then he said absentmindedly, "Seventeen years in Europe!"

"Tell me about your life there."

Shaking his head, which had gray hair only at the temples, Husayn replied, "Leave that for another time. Content yourself now with these headlines: dreamlike years of travel and happiness, love followed by marriage to a Parisian girl from a good family, the war and exodus to the South, my father's bankruptcy, work in my father-in-law's business, a return to Egypt without my wife in preparation for settling here—what more do you want to know?"

"Do you have any children?"

"No."

Husayn seemed reticent. But what remained of their old friendship to make Kamal regret this? All the same, feeling a powerful urge to knock on the doors of the past, he asked, "What about your former philosophy of life?"

Husayn reflected for a time and then, laughing sarcastically, replied, "For years and years my life has been devoted to work. I'm nothing but a businessman."

Where was Husayn Shaddad's spirit, which Kamal had once employed to put himself into contact with the comforting repose of spiritual bliss? It no longer resided in this bulky person. Perhaps it had come to rest in Riyad Qaldas. Kamal did not know the man sitting across from him. The sole tie linking them was an unknowable past, which he would have liked to recapture at that moment in a living image, not in a dead photograph.

"What line of work are you in now?"

"One of my father's friends got me a position in the press censorship office, working from midnight till dawn. Besides that, I translate for some European newspapers."

"When don't you work?"

"Almost never. What makes all the effort less objectionable is my determination to provide my wife with a style of life appropriate to her before I invite her to join me in Egypt. She's from a good family, and when I married her I was considered wealthy." Saying that, he laughed as if to poke fun at himself.

Kamal smiled to encourage Husayn and told himself, "It's lucky I stopped thinking about you a long time ago. Otherwise, I would be weeping now from the depths of my heart."

"And you, Kamal—what are you doing?" Then he added, "I remember that you were wild about culture."

Husayn was certainly to be thanked for this recollection, since Kamal was as dead to him as he was to Kamal. "We die and return to life several times a day," Kamal reflected. "I teach English," he replied.

"A teacher! Yes ... yes. I'm starting to remember now. You wanted to be a writer."

"What aborted hopes!" Kamal exclaimed to himself.

"I publish essays in *al-Fikr* magazine. In the near future I may collect some of them into a book."

Husayn smiled despondently and remarked, "You're lucky. You've seen your youthful dreams come true. I haven't." And he laughed again.

Kamal felt that the sentence "You're lucky" had a strange ring to it. The only thing stranger was the envious tone in which it was spoken. He was envied and considered fortunate. By whom? ... By the leading member of the Shaddad family. All the same, to be polite, Kamal responded, "Your career is more distinguished."

The smiling Husayn said, "I've had no choice. My one hope is to be able to regain some of my former status."

They were silent for a long time as Kamal's eager scrutiny of Husayn triggered images of the past. Finally he found himself asking, "How's your family?"

Husayn replied noncommittally, "Fine."

Kamal hesitated a little and then said, "You had a young sister, whose name I can't recall. What's become of her?"

"Budur! She got married last year."

"God's will be done! Our children are getting married."

"Haven't you married?"

Wondering whether Husayn had forgotten everything, Kamal said, "No."

"Hurry up. Otherwise you'll miss the train."

Laughing, Kamal replied, "It's already miles ahead of me."

"You may end up getting married without actually intending to. Believe me. Marriage wasn't part of my plan, but I've been a husband for more than ten years."

Shrugging his shoulders, Kamal suggested, "Tell me how you find life here after your long stay in France."

"Following the German occupation, life in France was not much fun. Compared to that, life here is easy." Then he added nostalgically, "But Paris—where, where is Paris now?"

"Why didn't you stay in France?"

Husayn answered disapprovingly, "And live entirely at my father-in-law's expense? No. . . . When wartime conditions made it impossible to travel there was an excuse for staying. After that I felt obliged to leave."

Did this smack of the old arrogance? Feeling driven to embark on a painful and dangerous adventure, Kamal asked slyly, "What news do you have of our friend Hasan Salim?"

After staring uneasily at Kamal for a moment, Husayn replied coldly, "None."

"How so?"

Looking out at the street through the window, Husayn said, "We haven't had any contact with him for about two years."

Unable to hide his astonishment, Kamal started to ask, "You mean. . . ?" But he did not finish the question. The shock was too much for him. Had Aïda returned again to al-Abbasiya as a divorcée? He would have to postpone consideration of all this to some other time. He remarked calmly, "His trip to Iran was the last thing Isma'il Latif mentioned."

Husayn said morosely, "My sister spent only a month with him there. Then she returned alone." In a hushed voice he added, "God rest her soul."

"What?" This word escaped from Kamal in a verbal outburst audible at nearby tables.

Husayn looked at him in amazement and said, "You didn't know! She died a year ago."

"Aïda?"

The other man nodded his head, and Kamal felt embarrassed about blurting out her name in such a familiar manner. But his thoughts immediately raced beyond this moment of embarrassment. Words no longer seemed to mean anything. He felt a maelstrom of oblivion whirling around in his head. He was afflicted by astonishment and dismay, not by sorrow and pain. When he could speak again, he exclaimed, "What distressing news! May you have a long life."

Husayn recounted: "She came home from Iran alone and stayed with my mother for a month. Then she married Anwar Bey Zaki, the chief inspector for English-language instruction. But she lived with him for only two months before falling ill. She died in the Coptic Hospital."

How could his head keep up with revelations that came at such breakneck speed? Husayn had said, "Anwar Bey Zaki." He was the chief supervisor of Kamal's own instructional division. Kamal had perhaps met the man several times during his marriage to Aïda. "Oh Lord. . . ." He remembered then that during the past year he had walked in the funeral procession of the supervisor's wife. Had that been Aïda? But how could he have missed seeing Husayn?

"Were you here when she passed away?"

"No. She died before I returned to Egypt."

Shaking his head in amazement, Kamal said, "I was at her funeral but didn't know that the deceased woman was your sister."

"How could that be?"

"I heard at school that the wife of one of the chief inspectors had passed away and that the funeral reception would be in al-Isma'iliya Square the same day. I went with some of my fellow teachers without ever seeing the announcement in the papers. We walked with the other mourners as far as the Sharkas mosque. That was a year ago."

Husayn smiled sadly as he said, "We thank you for taking the trouble."

Had this death occurred in 1926, Kamal would have gone insane or killed himself. Today it seemed like any other piece of news to him. That he should have walked in her funeral procession without knowing it was in her honor was bizarre. At the time, he had still been subject to the bitterness aroused by Budur's marriage and might actually have thought of the deceased when images of Budur and her family passed through his mind. He remembered the day of the funeral. He had offered his condolences to Anwar Bey Zaki and then had taken a seat with the other mourners. When they had called out, "All rise, the coffin's here," he had looked that way, glimpsing a beautiful casket covered in white silk. Some of his colleagues had whispered that she was the inspector's second wife, that they had only recently married, and that she had died of pneumonia. He had paid his final respects to the coffin without knowing he was bidding farewell to his past. A married man over fifty with children . . . how could the angel of that bygone age have consented to this?

"You assumed she was above marriage," Kamal thought. "But she had to accept divorce and then the fate of being a second wife. A long time will pass before the agitation of your breast settles down —not out of grief or pain, but from your shock and astonishment, from the disappearance of the world's splendid dreams, and from the eternal loss of that enchanting past. If there is any reason for regret in all this, it's that you didn't grieve as much as you should have."

"But what changed Hasan Salim?"

Husayn shook his head scornfully and said, "The scoundrel fell in love with an employee at the Belgian legation in Iran. My late sister was outraged at the damage to her honor and demanded a separation."

"In a situation like mine," Kamal mused, "a man's only consolation may be that even Euclid's self-evident axioms are no longer thought quite so self-evident."

"What about her children?"

"With their paternal grandmother."

"And where is Aïda herself?" Kamal wondered. "What surprises has the year brought her? Is it possible that Fahmy, al-Sayyid Ahmad Abd al-Jawad, or Na'ima has made her acquaintance?"

Then Husayn Shaddad rose, saying, "It's time for me to go. Let's see more of you. I usually have supper here at the Ritz."

Kamal stood up too, and murmured as they shook hands, "God willing. . . ."

They parted this way. Kamal sensed that he would never see Husayn again and that neither of them would have anything to gain from a future encounter. As he left the establishment, he told himself, "I'm sad, Aïda, that I didn't mourn enough for you."

52

Late one night the silence of the Shawkats' residence on Sugar Street was broken by a rap on the door. The knocking continued, waking everyone up. The moment a servant opened the door, heavy footsteps invaded the house, pounded through the courtyard and up the stairs, laying siege to all three apartments. Weak with age, his head still clouded by sleep, Ibrahim Shawkat went to the sitting room, where he found an officer surrounded by policemen and detectives.

The astonished man asked in alarm, "God spare us evil, what's happening?"

The commanding officer asked gruffly, "Are you not the father of Ahmad Ibrahim Shawkat and of Abd al-Muni'm Ibrahim Shawkat, who reside in this building?"

As his face lost its color, he replied, "Yes."

"We have orders to search the entire building."

"Why, your honor?"

Paying no attention to him, the officer turned to command his men, "Search the place!"

As the policemen fanned out into the adjoining rooms in response to this directive, Ibrahim Shawkat asked, "Why are you searching my apartment?"

The officer ignored him. At this juncture Khadija was forced out of the bedroom by the detectives who stormed into it. Wrapping a black shawl around herself, she cried out furiously, "Have you no respect for women? Are we thieves, Mr. Police Chief?"

Glaring angrily at his face, she suddenly sensed that she had seen the man before or, to be more precise, the original version of this countenance before time had marched across it. When and where had that been? "Good Lord!" she thought. It was the same man, without any doubt. He had not changed much. What was his name? Not hesitating, she remarked, "Sir, twenty years ago you were an officer in the police station for al-Gamaliya. No, it was thirty years—I don't remember the year exactly."

The officer looked up at her with curious eyes, as Ibrahim Shawkat gazed from one to the other just as inquisitively. Then she continued: "Your name is Hasan Ibrahim. Isn't that right?"

"Do you know me, ma'am?"

She said imploringly, "I'm the daughter of al-Sayyid Ahmad Abd al-Jawad and the sister of Fahmy Ahmad Abd al-Jawad, who was killed by the English during the revolution. Don't you remember him?"

The officer's astonishment was clearly visible in his eyes. Using a civil tone for the first time, he muttered, "May God be most compassionate to him."

She entreated him even more determinedly, "I'm his sister! Do you enjoy abusing my house like this?"

The officer looked away and replied almost apologetically, "We're just following orders, lady."

"But why, Officer? We're good people!"

He answered gently, "Yes, but I can't say as much for your two boys."

Khadija cried out in dismay, "They're the nephews of your old friend!"

Without looking at either of them, the officer responded, "We're acting on orders from the Ministry of the Interior."

"They haven't done anything wrong. They're good boys. I swear it."

The policemen and the detectives returned to the sitting room without having discovered anything. The commanding officer ordered them to leave the apartment and then, turning toward the couple, said, "We've been informed that suspicious gatherings are held in their apartments."

"A lie, your honor!"

"I too hope this is the case. Even so, I have no choice but to arrest them now. They will be held until the inquiry has been concluded. It's possible that they'll be cleared."

In a trembling voice embellished by sobs, Khadija wailed, "Are you really taking them to the station? This defies the imagination! By the lives of your own children, I beg you to set them free."

"I don't have the power to do that. I have clear orders to arrest them. Have a pleasant evening."

The man left the apartment. Heedless of everything she passed, Khadija rushed down the steps after him, trailed by her elderly husband. Karima, who was standing in front of her apartment in a terrified frenzy, saw them and shouted, "They've taken him, Auntie! They took him to prison!"

Khadija cast a stony glance her way and then sped down to the first-floor apartment, where she found Sawsan at the door as well, observing the courtyard with a gloomy face. Glancing in that direction, Khadija saw Abd al-Muni'm and Ahmad surrounded by policemen, who were taking them out of the house. She could not keep herself from screaming her heart out. She started to rush off in pursuit of them, but Sawsan's hand grabbed hold of her. As she turned furiously on her daughter-in-law, Khadija heard the girl say in a sad but tranquil voice, "Calm down. They didn't find anything suspicious. The police won't be able to pin a charge on them. Don't run after them—out of respect for your sons' honor."

Khadija yelled at her, "Your calm is enviable!"

Gently and patiently Sawsan replied, "They'll come home safe and sound. Don't be alarmed."

Her mother-in-law asked sharply, "What makes you so sure?"

"I'm confident of what I say."

Paying no attention to this remark, Khadija looked toward her husband, clapped her hands together, and said, "Loyalty is dead! I tell him they are Fahmy's nephews, and he says, 'We're just following orders.' My Lord, why do they seize good people and leave the rogues alone?"

Sawsan glanced at Ibrahim and said, "They'll search the family home on Palace Walk. I heard a detective tell the commanding officer he knew their grandfather's house on Palace Walk. The deputy suggested that it should be searched too, so they would be in full compliance with their orders and to make sure that the two boys had not hidden subversive tracts there."

Khadija shouted, "I'm going to my mother's. Perhaps Kamal can do something. Oh, my Lord, I'm on fire."

She got her coat and left Sugar Street with quick and agitated steps. It was cold and still quite dark, but roosters were defiantly crowing back and forth at each other. She shot down al-Ghuriya and traversed the Goldsmiths Bazaar on her way to al-Nahhasin. She found a detective at the door of the house and another in the courtyard. She climbed the stairs breathlessly.

The family had awakened uneasily to the ringing of the doorbell. Then Umm Hanafi had come up to say fearfully, "Police!"

Kamal had rushed down to the courtyard. There he found the commanding officer, whom he asked in alarm, "Can I help you?"

The officer inquired, "Do you know Abd al-Muni'm Ibrahim Shawkat and Ahmad Ibrahim Shawkat?"

"I'm their uncle. . . ."

"What do you do?"

"I'm a teacher at al-Silahdar School."

"We have orders to search the house."

"But why? What charges are you bringing against me?"

"We are searching for subversive tracts belonging to the two young men. We think they may have hidden them here."

"Sir, I can assure you that there are no subversive tracts in our house. But you can search all you want."

Kamal noticed that the commanding officer stationed his men on the roof and the staircase and was the only one who actually entered the living quarters. Instead of turning the house upside down in his search, the officer was content to survey the rooms, casting a superficial glance at Kamal's desk and bookcases. Regaining his composure, Kamal felt enough at ease with the officer to ask, "Did you search their home?"

"Naturally." Then, after a brief moment, the man added, "They are currently being detained at the station."

Kamal asked in consternation, "Has anything been proven against them?"

The man replied with unexpected delicacy, "I hope matters won't reach that point. But the inquiry will be conducted by the prosecutor's office."

"I'd like to thank you for your thoughtfulness."

The officer smiled and replied quietly, "Don't forget that I didn't ransack your house."

"Yes, sir. I don't know how to thank you."

Turning toward Kamal, the man asked, "Aren't you the brother of the late Fahmy?"

Kamal's eyes grew wide with astonishment as he asked, "Yes. Did you know him?"

"We were friends, God rest his soul."

Kamal said hopefully, "What a happy coincidence!" Offering the man his hand, he added, "Kamal Ahmad Abd al-Jawad."

The officer shook the proffered hand and said, "Hasan Ibrahim, commanding officer of the Gamaliya station. I started there as a second lieutenant and have rotated back to it as the commanding officer." Shaking his head, he continued: "Our orders were unequivocal. I hope the boys won't be found guilty of anything."

The sound of Khadija's voice carried to them as she wept and then narrated to her mother and Aisha the events of the evening. The officer remarked, "That's their mother. With her amazing memory she recognized me and reminded me of your late brother—but only after a thorough search of the house had already been conducted. See what you can do to put her mind at ease."

They walked down the stairs side by side. As they passed the second floor, Aisha exploded from the door in an obvious rage. Glaring harshly at the officer, she railed at him, "Why do you arrest people's children for no reason at all? Can't you hear their mother weeping?"

Shocked by this attack, the officer glanced quickly at her, before lowering his gaze politely. He replied, "They'll be set free soon, God willing."

After they were some distance beyond the apartment, he asked Kamal, "Your mother?"

Smiling sadly, Kamal replied, "No, my sister! She's only forty-four, but the misfortunes she's suffered have broken her."

The officer turned toward him as if stunned. Kamal felt the man was about to ask something. But after hesitating for a moment, he apparently changed his mind. They shook hands in the courtyard, and before the officer departed, Kamal asked, "Would it be possible for me to visit them in jail?"

"Yes."

"Thank you."

Kamal returned to join his mother and sisters in the sitting room. He said, "I'm going to visit them tomorrow. There's no reason to be afraid. They'll be released once they've been questioned."

Khadija did not seem to be able to stop crying. Aisha shouted hysterically, "Don't weep! That's enough! They'll come back to you. Didn't you hear?"

Khadija moaned: "I don't know. I don't know. My dear boys are in prison!"

Amina's sorrow had evidently struck her dumb. In a reassuring tone Kamal observed, "The officer in charge knows us. He was one of Fahmy's friends and was incredibly restrained when searching our house. He'll certainly treat them kindly."

The mother raised her head inquisitively, and Khadija snarled resentfully, "Hasan Ibrahim! Don't you remember him, Mother? When I told him I was Fahmy's sister, what did he say but 'We're just following orders, lady.' Orders, my eye!"

The mother glanced at Aisha, who gave no sign of recognizing the name. Taking Kamal aside, Amina said with obvious anxiety, "I don't understand anything, son. Why were they arrested?"

After pondering what to say Kamal replied, "The government mistakenly suspects that they have been working against it."

Shaking her head anxiously, she remarked, "Your sister says they arrested Abd al-Muni'm because he's a Muslim Brother. Why are they arresting Muslims?"

"The government thinks they are working against it."

"And Ahmad? She said he's . . . I've forgotten the word, son."

"A Communist? Like the Muslim Brethren, Communists are suspected by the government."

"Communists? What community is this? The Shi'ah community of Ali?"

Hiding his smile, Kamal answered, "The Communists aren't a religious community like the Shi'ah. They're a political party opposed to the government and the English."

Perplexed, she sighed and inquired, "When will they be set free? Look at your poor sister. The government and the English—can't they find some other place to search besides our afflicted house?"

53

The dawn call to prayer was reverberating through the otherwise silent city when the commanding officer of the police station for al-Gamaliya summoned Abd al-Muni'm and Ahmad to his office. Escorted by an armed policeman, they appeared before his desk. After ordering the policeman to leave, the officer examined the young men with interest. Looking at Abd al-Muni'm, he asked, "Your name, age, and profession?"

Abd al-Muni'm replied calmly and resolutely, "Abd al-Muni'm Shawkat, twenty-five, an investigator in the Ministry of Education's Bureau of Investigations."

"How can you, a lawyer, break the laws of the state?"

"I haven't broken any law. We work publicly—writing in the papers and preaching in the mosques. People who spread God's word have nothing to fear."

"Haven't suspicious meetings been held at your house?"

"Certainly not. There have been some ordinary gatherings, when friends assemble to exchange opinions and advice in order to gain a deeper understanding of our religion."

"Is agitation against allied nations a goal of these meetings?"

"Do you refer to Britain, sir? That deceitful enemy? A state that crushes our honor with its tanks cannot be considered an ally."

"You're an educated man. You should have realized that wartime conditions justify certain restrictions."

"I realize that Britain is our principal enemy in the world."

Turning to Ahmad, the officer asked, "You?"

With the suggestion of a smile on his lips, Ahmad replied, "Ahmad Ibrahim Shawkat, twenty-four, an editor with *The New Man* magazine."

"I have alarming reports here about your extremist articles. Besides, it is generally accepted that your magazine has a bad reputation."

"My articles have never exceeded the bounds of a defense of the principles of social justice."

"Are you a Communist?"

"I'm a socialist. Many deputies in parliament support socialism. The law itself does not censure a Communist for his ideas, as long as he does not resort to violent means."

"Should we have waited until the meetings held at your apartment every evening erupted into violence?"

Wondering whether the authorities had unearthed the secret of his tracts and nighttime talks, he replied, "I entertain only close friends in my home. There are never more than four or five visitors a day. Violence has been the furthest thing from our thoughts."

The officer looked from one to the other. After some hesitation he said, "You're educated and cultured . . . and you're both married— aren't you? Fine. Wouldn't it be best if you attended to your personal affairs and kept out of trouble?"

Abd al-Muni'm replied in his forceful voice, "Thank you for your advice, which I shall not follow."

A brief laugh took the officer by surprise and escaped from his lips. Then he admitted, "During the search, I learned that you are grand-sons of the late Ahmad Abd al-Jawad. Your lamented uncle Fahmy was a dear friend of mine. I assume you know that he died in the spring of his life and that those of his comrades who survived now hold some of the most important posts."

Discerning the secret reason for the officer's courtesy, which had baffled him, Ahmad said, "Allow me to ask you, sir, what condition Egypt would be in if my uncle and others like him had not sacrificed their lives."

Shaking his head, the man remarked, "Think long and well about my advice. Abandon this lethal philosophy." As he stood up he added, "You will be our guests in this jail until the inquiry is conducted. I wish you luck."

On leaving the office, they were taken into custody by a corporal and two armed policemen. The entire group descended to the ground floor, turned into a dark and extremely damp hall, and walked along it a short distance until the jailer greeted them with his flashlight, as if to show them the door to the jail. Opening the door, the jailer let the new prisoners in and then directed his light inside to guide them to their mats. The torch provided enough illumination for them to see the high ceiling of the medium-sized room as well as the small, barred window at the top of the exterior wall. The chamber had several guests: two youngsters, who looked like students, and three men with bare feet and a repulsive, battered appearance. The door was immediately closed, leaving them in darkness, but the light and the new arrivals had awakened some of the sleeping prisoners. Ahmad whispered to his brother, "I'm not going to sit down, for fear this dampness will be the death of me. Let's remain standing till morning."

"We'll have to sit down sooner or later. Do you have any idea when we'll get out of this jail?"

Then a voice—clearly belonging to one of the young men—said, "There's no way to avoid sitting down. It's not pleasant, but standing up, day after day, is worse."

"Have you been here a long time?"

"Three days!"

The room was silent again until the voice asked, "Why did they arrest you?"

Abd al-Muni'm replied tersely, "For political reasons, apparently."

The voice said cheerfully, "Political prisoners now form the majority in this cell. Before you honored us with your presence, we were in the minority."

Ahmad asked, "What are you accused of?"

"You speak first, for we have seniority here. Although there's probably no need to ask, since we saw that one of you has the beard of a Muslim Brother."

Smiling in the dark, Ahmad asked, "What about you?"

"We're law students. They say we were distributing subversive pamphlets."

Incensed, Ahmad asked, "Did they catch you red-handed?"

"Yes."

"What was in the pamphlets?"

"A report on the redistribution of Egypt's agricultural resources."

"Newspapers have published comparable material even under martial law."

"There were also a few enthusiastic exhortations."

Ahmad smiled once more in the gloom, feeling for the first time that he was not alone. Then the other voice continued: "We're not afraid of the law so much as of being detained without a trial."

"There are promising signs of change."

"But we'll always be targets, no matter who is in power."

A gruff voice barked rudely, "That's enough talk out of you. Let us get some sleep."

But these words awakened a companion, who yawned and asked, "Is it morning yet?"

The first man responded scornfully, "No, but our friends think they're in a hashish den."

Abd al-Muni'm sighed and whispered so softly that only Ahmad could hear, "Am I cast into this hole merely because I worship God?"

Ahmad whispered merrily in his brother's ear, "What could my offense be then, since I don't?"

After that, no one felt like speaking. Ahmad asked himself why the three older men had been arrested. Had the charges been theft, fighting, drunkenness, or rowdy behavior? Clad in his overcoat, he had often written about "the people" in his beautiful study. Here they were—cursing or snoring in their sleep. For a few seconds by the light of the torch he had seen their wretched sullen faces, including that of the man who was scratching his head and armpits. At this very moment his lice might be advancing resolutely toward Ahmad and his brother.

"You are devoting your life to people like this," he told himself. "Why should the thought of contact with them worry you? The person on whom mankind's hopes for salvation are pinned should stop snoring and awake to his historic role. Let him rear up and rescue the entire world."

Ahmad advised himself, "Without regard to the differences of taste between us, our common human condition has united us in this dark and humid place: the Muslim Brother, the Communist, the drunkard, and the thief. Despite dissimilarities in our luck and success at looking after ourselves, we are all human beings."

He wondered, "Why don't you busy yourself with personal affairs as the officer suggested? I have a beloved wife and plenty of money. The truth is that a man may be happy with his niche as a spouse, an employee, a father, or a son and yet be condemned to suffer various travails or even death by virtue of the fact that he is a man."

Whether Ahmad was sentenced to prison this time or released, the heavy, glowering prison gates would always hover at the horizons of his life. He asked himself again, "What is pushing me down this dazzling and dangerous road unless it is the human being that lurks deep inside of me, the man who is conscious of himself and aware of his common, historic, human condition? What distinguishes a man from all other creatures if not his ability to condemn himself to death by his own free will?"

Ahmad felt dampness coursing through his legs and weakness penetrating his joints. Snores echoed through the room with a regular rhythm. Then, between the bars of the small window, the first feeble rays of delicate light were visible.

54 ❧

Kamal despondently followed the physician out of the bedroom. Catching up with the man in the sitting room and gazing at him with questioning eyes, Kamal heard him say calmly, "I'm sorry to inform you that the paralysis is total."

Feeling miserable, Kamal asked, "Is that serious?"

"Of course! And she's also suffering from pneumonia. I'm prescribing an injection so she can get some rest."

"Isn't there any hope she'll recover?"

The doctor was silent for a time and then replied, "Our lives are in God's hands. For what it's worth, my judgment as a physician is that she has three days at the most."

Kamal received this prediction of death resolutely and escorted the physician to the door of the house before returning to the bedroom. His mother was asleep or so it seemed. The thick blanket revealed only a pale face with lips closed but slightly awry. Aisha, who was standing by the bed, walked toward him, asking, "What's wrong with her, brother? What did the doctor say?"

From her station by the head of the bed, Umm Hanafi observed, "She's not speaking, master. She hasn't said a single word."

Kamal reflected, "Her voice will never be heard again." Then he told his sister, "An attack of high blood pressure combined with a slight cold. The injection will help her rest."

Aisha commented, perhaps to herself, "I'm afraid. If she lies in bed like this for a long time, life in our house will surely be unbearable."

Turning from her to Umm Hanafi, he inquired, "Have you told the others?"

"Yes, master. Mrs. Khadija and Mr. Yasin will be here at once. What's wrong with her, master? This morning she was hale and hearty."

She had been! He could attest to that. As always each morning, he had passed by the sitting room before rushing off to al-Silahdar School. Taking the cup of coffee she had handed him, he had said, "Don't go out today. It's very cold."

Showing him her gentle smile, she had replied, "How can I have a good day if I don't visit your master al-Husayn?"

He had protested, "Do as you like. You're stubborn, Mother."

She had murmured, "Your Lord preserves us." When he was leaving, she had said, "May our Lord make all your days happy ones."

That was the last time he would see her conscious. The news of her illness had reached him at school this noon, and he had returned home, accompanied by the doctor who had just predicted her death. Only three days were left. How many more did he have?

Going over to Aisha, he asked, "When and how did this happen?"

Umm Hanafi answered for her: "We were in the sitting room. She rose and started toward her room to put on her coat prior to going out. She told me, 'When I finish my visit to al-Husayn, I'll call on Khadija.' She went to the bedroom, and the moment she entered I heard something fall. Rushing inside, I found her stretched out on the floor between the bed and the wardrobe. I ran to her, calling for Mrs. Aisha."

Aisha said, "I came as fast as I could and discovered her here. We carried her to the bed, and I started asking her what was the matter. But she didn't respond. She didn't say anything. When is she going to speak, brother?"

He answered uneasily, "When God wills."

Retreating to the sofa, he sat down and began to look sorrowfully at the pale, silent face. Yes, he should gaze at it for a long time. Soon he would be unable to. This very room would no longer be the same, and the characteristics of the whole house would change as well. There would be no one in the building to call "Mother." He had not imagined that her death would cause his heart such pain. Was he not already well acquainted with death? Of course he was. He was old enough and experienced enough not to be frightened by death, but the sting of an eternal separation was agonizing. Perhaps his heart could be criticized for suffering like a novice's despite all the pain it had experienced. How much she had loved him! How much she had loved all of them! How much she had loved everything in existence!

"But your soul only pays attention to such fine qualities when losing someone," Kamal thought. "At this critical moment your memory is crowded with images of places, times, and events having a profound impact on you. Light overlaps darkness as the blue of early morning blends with the roof garden, the glowing brazier of the coffee hour mingles with religious legends, and the dove's cooing mixes with sweet songs. Heart of an infidel, this was a magnificent love. Tomorrow you may truly declare that death has claimed the person you loved most. Perhaps your eyes will fill with tears until old age reproves you. The tragic vision of life is not free of an infantile Romanticism. It would be far worthier of you to view life courageously as a drama with a happy ending called 'death.' But ask yourself how much longer you will continue wasting your life. Your mother dies after concluding a lifetime of achievements. What have you done?"

He was roused by footsteps as Khadija entered the room in a state of shock. She made straight for the bed, calling to her mother and asking what had happened. His pain was compounded by this scene, and fearing that his sangfroid would desert him, he fled to the sitting room. Yasin, Zanuba, and Ridwan arrived almost immediately. After shaking hands with them, Kamal told them about his mother's condition without going into details. They went into the bedroom, leaving him alone until Yasin emerged to ask, "What did the doctor tell you?"

Kamal answered despondently, "Paralysis and pneumonia. Everything will be over in three days."

Yasin bit his lip and said mournfully, "There is not any power or might save God's." Taking a seat, he muttered, "The poor woman—the whole thing comes so suddenly. Hadn't she complained of feeling poorly of late?"

"Not at all. As you know, she never complained. But she did seem tired at times."

"Shouldn't you have called the doctor earlier?"

"She detested nothing so much as consulting a physician."

Ridwan joined them after a while and told Kamal, "I think she should be moved to the hospital, Uncle."

Shaking his head sadly, Kamal answered, "It wouldn't do any good. The pharmacist will send a nurse he knows to administer the injection."

They fell silent, their concern evident on their faces. At this moment Kamal remembered a matter that courtesy required he should not neglect. So he asked Yasin, "How is Karima?"

"She'll have her baby this week, or that's what the woman physician says."

Kamal murmured, "May our Lord take her by the hand. . . ."

Yasin lamented, "The baby will come into the world while the father is in detention."

The doorbell rang. It was Riyad Qaldas. After greeting his friend, Kamal escorted him to the study. On the way up, Riyad explained, "I asked for you at the school, and the secretary gave me the news. How is your mother?"

"She's paralyzed, and the doctor says it will all be over in three days."

Riyad looked glum and inquired, "Can't anything be done?"

Kamal shook his head disconsolately and remarked, "Perhaps it's lucky that she's unconscious and knows nothing of the destiny awaiting her." When they were seated, he added in an ironic tone, "But who among us knows what destiny awaits us?"

Riyad smiled without replying. Then Kamal continued: "Many think it wise to make of death an occasion for reflection on death, when in truth we ought to use it to reflect on life."

Smiling, Riyad answered, "I think that is better. So let's ask ourselves when anyone dies what we are doing with our lives."

"As for me, I'm not doing anything with my life. This is what I was thinking about."

"But you're only halfway down the road. . . ."

"Perhaps yes, perhaps no," Kamal thought. "Although it's always good for a person to ponder the dreams that tempt him. Mysticism is an evasion of responsibility and so is a passive faith in science. There is no alternative to action, and that requires faith. The issue is how we are to mold for ourselves a belief system that is worthy of life."

He asked, "Do you think I've done my duty to life by sincerely pursuing my vocation as a teacher and by writing my philosophical essays?"

Riyad answered affectionately, "There's no doubt that you have."

"But like any other traitor, I live with a guilty conscience."

"Traitor?"

Sighing, Kamal said, "Let me share with you what my nephew Ahmad told me when I visited him at the jail before his transfer to the prison camp."

"By the way—any new developments concerning them?"

"They've gone with many others to the prison camp at al-Tur in Sinai."

Riyad inquired jovially, "The one who worships God and the one who doesn't?"

"You must worship the government first and foremost if you wish your life to be free of problems."

"In any case, being detained without trial is, I think, a lesser evil than being sentenced to prison."

"That's one way of looking at it. But when will this affliction be removed? When will martial law be lifted? When will the rule of natural law and the constitution be restored? When will the Egyptians be treated like human beings again?"

Riyad started to fiddle with the wedding ring on his left hand. He remarked sadly, "Yes, when! Well, never mind. . . . What did Ahmad say in jail?"

"He told me, 'Life consists of work, marriage, and the duty incumbent upon each person claiming human status. This is not an appropriate occasion to discuss an individual's responsibilities toward his profession or spouse. The duty common to all human beings is perpetual revolution, and that is nothing other than an unceasing effort to further the will of life represented by its progress toward the ideal.' "

After reflecting a little, Riyad said, "A beautiful thought . . . but one open to all kinds of interpretations."

"Yes, and that's why his brother and antagonist, Abd al-Muni'm, accepts it too. I have understood it to be a call to adopt some set of beliefs, regardless of its orientation or goal. So I attribute my misery to the guilty conscience of a traitor. It may seem easy to live in a self-contained world of egotism, but it's difficult to be happy this way if you really are a human being."

In spite of the gloomy nature of the occasion, Riyad's face lit up and he replied, "This is the harbinger of an important upheaval that is about to occur in your life."

Kamal cautioned his friend: "Don't make fun of me. The choice of a faith has still not been resolved. The greatest consolation I have is the fact that the struggle is not over yet. It will be raging even when, like my mother's, my life has only three more days remaining." Sighing, he added, "Do you know what else he said? He told me, 'I believe in life and in people. I feel obliged to advocate their highest ideals as long as I believe them to be true, since shrinking from that would be a cowardly evasion of duty. I also see myself compelled to revolt against ideals I believe to be false, since recoiling from this rebellion would be a form of treason. This is the meaning of perpetual revolution.' "

As he listened, Riyad nodded his head in agreement. Since Kamal was clearly exhausted and tense, his friend said, "I must go now. What would you think about accompanying me to the streetcar stop? Perhaps the walk would help you relax."

They both rose and left the room. Finding Yasin, who had met Riyad a few times, at the entrance to the first-floor apartment, Kamal invited him to join them but asked to be excused for a few minutes to look in at his mother again. On entering her bedroom, he found her still unconscious.

Her eyes red from crying, Khadija was seated on the bed by her mother's feet. The despair that had never left her face since the government had laid hands on her sons was plainly visible. Zanuba, Aisha, and Umm Hanafi sat silently on the sofa. Aisha was smoking a cigarette quickly and anxiously. Meanwhile her eyes scouted the room with nervous agitation.

Kamal asked, "How is she?"

Aisha replied in a loud voice that suggested a worried protest, "She doesn't want to wake up!"

He chanced to turn toward Khadija, and they exchanged a long look of mournful understanding and shared sorrow. Sensing that he might lose control of himself, Kamal darted from the room to rejoin his companions.

They walked slowly down the street and traversed the Goldsmiths Bazaar without saying much of anything. On reaching al-Sanadiqiya, they ran into Shaykh Mutawalli Abd al-Samad, who was hobbling along unsteadily with the help of his cane. He was blind, and his arms trembled as he turned from side to side asking in a loud voice, "Which way to paradise?"

A passerby laughingly suggested, "First turn on your right."

Yasin asked Riyad Qaldas, "Would you believe that this man is almost ten years over a hundred?"

Smiling, Riyad answered, "He's hardly a man now, whatever his age."

Kamal looked fondly at the shaykh, who made him think of his father. He had once considered this man a landmark of the neighborhood—like the ancient fountain building, the mosque of Qala'un, and the vault of Qirmiz Alley. The shaykh still encountered many who were sympathetic to him, but there were always boys to plague him by whistling at him or by following him and imitating his gestures.

The two brothers escorted Riyad to the streetcar stop and waited with him until he boarded. Then they returned to al-Ghuriya. Kamal suddenly stopped and told Yasin, "It's time for you to go to the coffeehouse."

Yasin replied sharply, "Certainly not! I'll stay with you."

Knowing his brother's temperament as well as anyone, Kamal said, "There's absolutely no need of that."

Yasin pushed Kamal along ahead of him, protesting, "She's my mother as much as yours."

All at once Kamal felt fearful for Yasin. It was true that he was brimming with life and as huge as a camel, but how much longer could he endure an existence so dominated by passion's impulses? Kamal's heart filled with sorrow, but his thoughts suddenly flew to the detention camp of al-Tur.

"I believe in life and in people." That was what Ahmad had said. "I feel obliged to advocate their highest ideals as long as I believe them to be true, since shrinking from that would be a cowardly evasion of duty. I also see myself compelled to revolt against ideals I believe to be false, since recoiling from this rebellion would be a form of treason."

Kamal had long wondered what was true and what was false, but perhaps doubt was as much of an evasion of responsibility as mysticism or a passive belief in science.

"Could you be a model teacher, an exemplary husband, and a lifelong revolutionary?" he asked himself.

When they reached al-Sharqawi's store, Yasin stopped and explained, "Karima asked me to get some things she needs for the baby, if you don't mind."

They entered the small shop, and Yasin selected the items his daughter had requested: diapers, a bonnet, and a nightgown. Then Kamal remembered that the black necktie he had worn for a year following his father's death was threadbare and that he would be needing a new one when the mournful day arrived. He told the man, when Yasin was finished, "A black necktie, please."

Each one took his package, and they left the store. The setting of the sun was washing the world with a sepia tint as side by side they walked back to the house.

Acknowledgments

I want to thank Mary Ann Carroll
for being the first reader,
Jacqueline Kennedy Onassis
for her sensitive editing,
Riyad N. Delshad for assistance
with some obscure vocabulary and expressions,
and Sarah and Franya Hutchins
for their patience.
Although others have contributed
to this translation, I am happy
to bear responsibility for it.

—William Maynard Hutchins

About the Author

Naguib Mahfouz was born in Cairo in 1911 and began writing when he was seventeen. A student of philosophy and an avid reader, he has been influenced by many Western writers, including Flaubert, Balzac, Zola, Camus, Tolstoy, Dostoevsky, and, above all, Proust. He has more than thirty novels to his credit, ranging from his earliest historical romances to his most recent experimental novels. In 1988, Mr. Mahfouz was awarded the Nobel Prize for Literature. He lives in the Cairo suburb of Agouza with his wife and two daughters.